THE IBIZA CRONE CLUB

New Beginnings

Josephine O'Brien

Copyright © 2022 Josephine O'Brien

All rights reserved

The characters and events portrayed in this book are fictitious. Any similarity to real persons, living or dead, is coincidental and not intended by the author.

No part of this book may be reproduced, or stored in a retrieval system, or transmitted in any form or by any means, electronic, mechanical, photocopying, recording, or otherwise, without express written permission of the publisher.

ISBN: 9798846131842

Cover design by: Art Painter
Library of Congress Control Number: 2018675309
Printed in the United States of America

*This book is dedicated to writing circles
and reading groups everywhere.*

CONTENTS

Title Page
Copyright
Dedication
Chapter One — 3
Chapter Two — 10
Chapter Three — 14
Chapter Four — 19
Chapter Five — 25
Chapter Six — 31
Chapter Seven — 35
Chapter Eight — 51
Chapter Nine — 63
Chapter Ten — 69
Chapter Eleven — 76
Chapter Twelve — 81
Chapter Thirteen — 86
Chapter Fourteen — 100
Chapter Fifteen — 110
Chapter Sixteen — 122
Chapter Seventeen — 131
Chapter Eighteen — 139
Chapter Nineteen — 143
Chapter Twenty — 149

Chapter Twenty-one	159
Chapter Twenty-two	163
Chapter Twenty-three	171
Chapter Twenty- four	177
Chapter Twenty-five	185
Chapter Twenty-six	191
Chapter Twenty-seven	199
Chapter Twenty-eight	208
Chapter Twenty-nine	215
Chapter Thirty	231
Chapter Thirty-one	239
Chapter Thirty-two	246
Chapter Thirty-three	251
Chapter Thirty-four	264
Chapter Thirty-five	268
Chapter Thirty-six	273
Chapter Thirty-seven	283
Chapter Thirty-eight	289
Afterword	301
Acknowledgement	305
About The Author	307

THE IBIZA CRONE CLUB BOOK 1

CHAPTER ONE

Ryanair's last direct flight of the season was packed. Excited conversation and raucous laughter from the Ibiza-bound crowd drowned the safety announcements. Trying to ignore them, Bláithín turned to watch a rain-sodden Dublin flow beneath her as the plane circled wide over the city. Streetlights were beginning to map out its arteries through the dusk, bidding farewell.

She shared neither her fellow traveler's hilarity nor their enthusiasm. She felt nothing but the same numbness that had been her default position since her boss had dropped the bombshell of her redundancy. Redundancy, after thirty years! Bláithín leant her head against the cold window and sighed. She wasn't fooling herself. This deadening indifference to everything except her work had started long, long before. She dug her nails into her palms and took a deep, shuddering breath. Distraction came in the form of a woman, whose long, trailing, pink sash dubbed her 'Josie - Virgin on the Verge', who swayed past Bláithín's seat topping up her friends' plastic cups from a bottle of 7up. Catching her high heel on the sash, she lurched several paces down the aisle and dropped her bottle. It rolled away, its contents spilling out with every turn. She wailed as she watched it go. "Aw, feck it, girls, that's me bloody vodka gone." She complained her way towards the back of the plane.

Bláithín reached over her head and twisted off the flow of cold air. Leaning down, she rooted in the beige canvas bag between her feet for her new scarf. The burnt orange and ochre paisley design had looked rich and elegant in the shop, but here in this fluorescent and multicoloured crowd, it just looked drab. She folded the soft material into a pillow and wedged it between the curved wall and her head. Before she could even try to relax, she needed to check yet again for the keys and the directions to what would be her new home for the next few months. Opening her bag, she rattled the keys and checked the page tucked into her passport. A short paragraph in her boss's familiar writing gave the address to his apartment and a phone number for a woman named Maite, who looked after it for him. He had assuaged his guilt over the sudden axing of Bláithín's job by offering her his apartment in Ibiza for a 'good' rent. He hadn't been too clear on when he expected to use the apartment again. 'But sure, 'twould do you good to be out of here over ould Christmas and I won't be renting it out again 'til the season starts in May, or it could be April or whenever Easter is next year, but lookit, we won't worry about that now, get Christmas over with and we'll take it from there.' It wasn't the most reassuring of contracts, but the thought of another Christmas spent with her brother and sister-in-law was just too depressing. She twisted in her seat, turning her shoulder to try and cut out the high-pitched, excited babble of the two teenagers next to her. Resting her head against the softness of the scarf, she closed her eyes.

'A cut-price Sodom and Gomorra', Pauline's words rang in her mind banishing sleep. Her sister-in-law had dismissed Ibiza with a wave of her hand and Diarmuid, her brother agreed. He implied Bláithín would be as isolated and lonely as if she were halfway up the Himalayas. In fairness, they *might* miss her, Bláithín supposed. She was Diarmuid's only sibling, though they would probably miss the rent she paid for the apartment at the back of their house even more. Either way, they were adamant it wasn't for her, that she had no experience of 'places like that', and that she was overreacting to everything. All she could counter with was 'I want a change,' and it became her mantra. She was so glad she hadn't shared her plans with them until she had bought her ticket. Desperation had powered her through her own anxiety and their warnings, and here she was, on her way! She sighed and tried to sleep again.

***

"Señora, Señora, ya estamos en Ibiza. Please, Madam, we have landed. These are yours, no?"

Bláithín closed her mouth and opened her eyes. The flight attendant was talking loudly as she tugged a suitcase from the overhead locker followed by a heavy overcoat and put them on the now empty seat next to Bláithín. "Sorry! Yes. Yes, they are. Thanks, I'm ready now." Her mouth was dry, and her cheek stuck to her scarf. Disorientated and groggy, she hurried to follow the last of the passengers disappearing down the air bridge towards baggage reclaim.

As soon as she had her luggage balanced on her trolley, she took out the keys which were attached to a multicoloured, plastic lizard key ring, and the page with the address of the apartment. A glance in the mirrored pillar next to her clearly showed the scarf imprint on her cheek. Her greying, wiry hair, which had been firmly sprayed into place before she'd left in the early morning, misty chill of Kilkenny, was springing out around her head like a mad woman. She shrugged. Maneuvering her trolley with difficulty through the opaque sliding doors, she was straight into the spotlight of expectant gazes. Whoever those people were waiting for, a fifty-five-year-old woman with crazy sleep hair wasn't of much interest, their attention moved on.

Heads turned though, as a six-foot model sashayed past, wearing what Bláithín could only describe as straps. A black one around her breasts and a slightly larger strip circled her hips, black biker boots, a rainbow of colours in her thick, knitted hat, and a black cape. Now, she caught everyone's attention, and who could blame them? Feeling almost invisible Bláithín followed the taxi signs out through the revolving door.

The scent of flowers and a hint of fading heat in the air

enveloped her. The end of October and there were still people in shorts and t-shirts! It wasn't hot, but it certainly wasn't Ireland. She opened her coat, pulled off her scarf, and joined the long queue for the taxis.

"San Antonio? The party capital of Ibiza? You like the discos and the clubbing, yes?" The taxi driver sounded dubious.

"No, no, of course not, it's just … em, I'm sure there's more to San Antonio than that." She wasn't, but she had Googled San Antonio. Filled with shops, restaurants, a marina full of expensive yachts, blue skies, and sunsets to die for. She planned to capture it all with her new camera, a gift to herself from the redundancy payment.

"You stay long?"

"Um, I'm not sure really. A few months anyway."

She tried her mantra out on the taxi driver. "I just want a change."

Despite navigating a roundabout, he turned around to grin at her. "You have come to perfectly the right place."

The sodium lights of the motorway hid any sign of the surrounding countryside and Bláithín's heart sank as it all seemed as modern and normal as the M9 at home, down to the bright yellow circle of a Lidl supermarket.

"You have much friends here, no?"

"Um, no, but I have plans, tons of books to read and I'll be doing lots of photography."

"Ah, you're a photographer!" He was nodding. "You will find Ibiza in winter is most beautiful."

This was hard to credit as they were driving through an increasingly built-up area that could not in any way be described as attractive. In fact, as they turned left and right, the streets became narrower and less well-maintained. Overflowing bins had excess rubbish piled next to them, and most balconies had hanging laundry and bicycles vying for place with plastic chairs and storage boxes.

The driver stopped the car. "Here you are, I can no drive to door. Is only walk from here."

"What? But the Flora Apartments?" Panicked, Bláithín twisted in her seat searching for any sign of life.

"Yes, yes, over there, in that plaza. Twenty-five euros, please. I help with bags. Yes?"

The driver deposited the two large suitcases on the white steps of a building a few meters away while Bláithín searched through her giant canvas bag for her purse. Finding it with a sigh of relief, she paid him.

He pocketed the money and got into the car. "Welcome to Ibiza!" He waved out the window and the green roof light disappeared in seconds down a side street.

The wheels of her trolley rattled like gunfire in the night as she crossed the plaza. She eyed the dark windows. So few lights. Wasn't anyone home? Were they all asleep? A dog barked from a balcony directly above her. She leapt. God Almighty! Her palm pressed her chest instinctively, and she could feel her heart pounding. Stupid bloody dog! She glared up at it, but the very act of looking seemed to send it into a frenzy. It threw itself against the railing, growling and snarling as Bláithín fumbled the front door key into the lock.

The heavy door needed her shoulder against it to push it open into a well-lit courtyard, five floors high and open to the dark sky. It was ringed with palm trees in big urns and huge flowerbeds filled with blood-red geraniums. This was more like it! The struggle to get her suitcases up the four steps and into the courtyard made her think she should probably have left half the books at home. The thud of the closing door shut out the sound of the dog.

She perched on the edge of a wicker chair; one of several pairs dotted around, to get her breath back, and crossed her arms to still their tremble. There was an echoing silence as she looked up the five floors. No TV sounds, no voices, no footsteps. She got to her feet. She needed a cup of tea, a shower, and sleep.

The clear glass lift was bright and spacious, but she was

shaky and tense as she pushed the button for the third floor. This was so far from a normal Thursday night, that it wasn't funny. So far from anything, she'd ever done. Familiar anxiety broke prickles of sweat on her forehead and she began to hyperventilate. She took a deep breath, time to start her anti-anxiety routine of counting things in fives. A gentle bump and the hiss of the doors opening ended her list.

Bláithín pushed her bags out and stepped after them into the corridor. There was a long line of apartment doors on one side and a shoulder-high wall on the other looking down to the foyer. The lift closed, cutting off its illumination. Little wall lights threw soft rectangles of light across the wood-effect flooring, and the light from the lobby gave a background glow as she dragged her cases down to 309, checking it again on the lizard ring. In the dim light, she needed her glasses to get the key into the lock. Of course, the damn things were somewhere at the bottom of her bag. She hadn't yet given in to wearing them around her neck, that was just so... so... well, she just wasn't ready to be her mother yet. Glasses on, the lock turned easily, and the door swung open into pitch black, not a chink of light. She slapped the wall on both sides of the door for a switch, her breath beginning to catch in her chest again. One slap found the switch and the room was revealed in all its starkness.

A last effort got her cases in. She closed her eyes, leant her back against the door, and pushed it closed. The apartment smelled odd. Old coffee, floral air freshener, musty, and... just plain strange. She opened her eyes to the glare and took stock. Black and white floor tiles continued through two open doors. Shiny, brown chairs, square and heavy, flanked a matching brown table. Behind them, a breakfast bar and kitchen units were of the same high gloss brown. Two windows of closed metal blinds, a red sofa, and a TV on the wall, and that was it. The chill of the long-closed, empty apartment made her shiver. Tugging her scarf from her bag, she wrapped it around her shoulders and crossed into the bedroom. Same cheap brown furniture but at least there was bedding on the shelves of the built-in wardrobe and the bedside lamp worked.

Without enthusiasm, she checked out a second identical bedroom, and the bathroom, which was small, clean, and functional. Back in the kitchen, she unpacked the four boxes of Irish tea she had squashed into her suitcase next to a packet of chocolate biscuits. She rinsed the kettle and filled it from the tap. Not sure if the tap water was safe to drink or not, she decided one cup would hardly kill her. The fridge, unplugged and empty, reminded her she had planned on stocking up at the shop that Andy told her was just around the corner. He'd also said that Maite, who did such a great job looking after his apartment, worked there. He had made Bláithín promise to go and introduce herself. "Just so as you'll have a friendly face in the neighbourhood."

Sitting at the breakfast bar with her black tea, she picked chocolate-coated shreds of tinfoil off the chocolate biscuit that had melted and hardened during its journey. A framed map of Ibiza hung on the wall in front of her. The light was too strong. All she could see was her own reflection. She saw a grey ghost. A grey, exhausted, joint-aching ghost, stirring undrinkable tea on the first day of her new life.

She started to cry.

CHAPTER TWO

Anger fueled Cassandra's throw. The mobile phone arced across the room bounced on the sofa, then clattered onto the tiles.

"Bloody Hell! What am I supposed to do now?" Her question hung unanswered in the empty room. In a few short words, her job here in Ibiza had just been cancelled. With a crystal-clear connection, Leonie's dramatic sigh in London had practically warmed Cassandra's ear. "It's the boring money men, Cassandra darling. They said it's become too expensive to bring the whole crew to Ibiza. The photo shoot's been changed to Croatia." Her now ex-boss hadn't given Cassandra any time to react as she airily continued, "But Sweetheart, they said the villa is paid up for another month or so, and it's yours to enjoy in return for the trouble you've already gone to. Just chill and have a stupendous party or two. Have fun, and we'll catch up when I'm back. Ciao."

Cassandra paced the room. Her high-heeled boots on the terracotta tile provided a soundtrack to her anger. She fumed; it was easy for Leonie, running so many successful ventures in London, that cancelling Cassandra's job probably didn't even register. Of course, no one in their circle knew how badly Cassandra needed this job, or how she'd struggled since her divorce from Pierce two years earlier. Naturally, she hadn't told Leonie she'd made damn all headway renewing old contacts in Ibiza. In her eagerness to get away from London, her failed marriage, and her failing business, she had rather oversold her role in Ibiza life and her fabulous connections here. Even with her normal bullet-plated insouciance catastrophically damaged by the divorce, she'd been so sure she could manage Ibiza.

Less than a month ago, in a dismally damp London, she had blithely waved her beautifully manicured hands as she assured Leonie, "Leave it all to me. I know tons of people with exclusive galleries or fabulous, extravagant villas, all perfect backgrounds for the Fantasy Fetish Clothing shoot." How could she have thought she could manage? It was a long time since she'd lived here. Ibiza wasn't the same. She threw herself down on the enormous, white sofa, pulled off her boots, and threw them across the room. "Shit, shit, shit!"

'Cassandra Melissa stop overreacting, it's unseemly and unhelpful.' Her mother's voice, as always, echoed in her head to make a bad situation worse. Cassandra threw a book after the boots, a satisfying crash. She yanked out the carefully arranged pins holding her casual up-do in place and ran both hands through her thick, expensively honey-blond hair. The tips of her long nails massaged her scalp and she closed her eyes. Where were all the people with whom she'd shared moonlight swims, ecstatic dancing, and cacao ceremonies? Where the hell had everyone gone? Yesterday, she had put that exact question to Gabriella, who was now an impressively elegant woman, running a crystal shop. Not the madcap, flower and feather be-decked child that Cassandra remembered.

Gabriella had shrugged at the question. Counting off options on her fingers, she'd said, "They're either at home with grandchildren, left the island, dead, or have become rich businesspeople, take your pick. There are virtually none of my mother's friends from those days left here. Oh, Alexi and Valentina still run their jewelry stall, but their son brings them, sets everything up, and collects them as soon as they get tired."

Cassandra had been indignant. "Oh, them! They were always way older than us. What about the couple who ran the fabulous Ibiza Dreams bar? Their parties were legendary! There's no way they've calmed down."

"Roberto and Franco? Roberto died eight years ago, and Franco owns a gallery in Prague. Even Mum only visits twice a year. She's running a B & B in Goa and finds Ibiza too damp and cold.'

Cassandra had plastered a confident grin on her face as she kissed Gabriella goodbye, but it had faded as soon as she was outside.

The doors of the glass curtain wall still stood open from Cassandra's morning yoga, her daily routine to embrace the light and welcome the day. A practice best done nude and in the fresh air, as she'd discovered in her early days in Ibiza and had later continued in front of her open bedroom windows in London. Even Pierce's frequent admonitions of, "Cassandra, darling, you know you really are scandalising the woman across the road," had never persuaded her to drop it.

Brilliant points of light sparked in and out of existence on the shimmering, blue bay of Cala Vicent, and the dark green forest, even in October, still shot through with fluorescent new growth, crept down to embrace the beach. Faced with this view, Cassandra's anger faded. Deep, full breaths, drawn in through her nose and slowly blown out through her mouth, calmed her mind and spirit. After a short while, she stood and strolled out onto the terrace. The large, uneven tiles were still warm underfoot. Their once colorful, intricate design rubbed off by what must have been centuries of footfall as the very tiles themselves were worn thin in places. The terrace, spread across the front of the whole house, overlooking a stepped garden down to a beautifully mosaiced, heated pool.

She was in no rush back to London. There were no events waiting to be planned and hadn't been since the embarrassingly public disaster of the wrong names on a fortieth wedding anniversary cake. Her clients, Margot and Stefan, had been pleased with the well-attended, hugely successful party CasandraEvents had put on for them, that is until the caterers had produced the cake. An elaborate confection that wished Margot and Pierce many more years of wedded bliss! Had she really called out his name in her very detailed order, spelled it out carefully, and asked for it to be surrounded by hearts? Unfortunately, she could easily believe she had, consumed as she was at the time by the unbelievable implosion of her life. A rattle from the room behind her as her phone vibrated on the tiles interrupted her thoughts. A spark of hope! A last-minute change? A new assignment? She hurried to pick it up.

One glance at the caller ID killed that thought dead, and she pressed decline. "And you can sod off too. I went to his funeral and that was enough," she muttered tossing the phone onto the couch. Stepping outside again, she tugged off her jeans, reached between her legs, and popped open her silk bodysuit. Dropping the coral body onto the jeans she stood enjoying the air chilling her skin before she ran down the steps and flung herself into the pool. Actually, it was going to be rather nice to be free from location scouting. Discovering old haunts that had once been candle-lit warrens of music and conversation, with sweet-smelling drifts of hash smoke coiling around their low rafters, were now purple and chrome minimalist interiors, staffed by gap year students, was depressing. She floated, looking up into an infinity of blue. Something would turn up. Something would happen. Since she had fled home at eighteen, Ibiza had embraced her, been her safe place, her refuge from a life of tension, arguments and fury caused by her mother's coldness and overbearing need to control. Cassandra closed her eyes and relaxed, she was home, Ibiza wouldn't let her down.

CHAPTER THREE

"Would you like a cup of tea, Mum?" Her daughter's voice came through the open window. Pamela opened her eyes and turned her head. The sky-blue shutters thrown back against the white-washed wall, and overrun by magenta bougainvillea in full flower, never failed to delight her.

"Oh, Susan, that would be lovely. Thank you, darling." She continued to study the bougainvillea from her sun lounger next to the pool. She'd often tried to capture this amazing clash of colour with her water paints, but the results were always frustratingly anemic, insipid, and boring. Now she wondered about trying some permanent magenta, perhaps mixed with a bit of Windsor red and maybe a dot of zinc white? Would that bring out the vibrancy? She shook her head in annoyance. It was more than the darn colours, there was no 'feeling' in her work. Maybe she should try oils, just to see how they worked out. She sighed. How often had this idea occurred to her? Oil paints were too 'serious' painter-y, not worth the mess, the smell, or the commitment. Not really suitable for a pastime. Water paints were better, quick and easy to put away.

Susan's voice broke into her thoughts. "Here we are, Earl Grey's finest teamed up with bizcocho, fresh from the market this morning."

Pamela looked up. "Oh, how nice!"

Susan stood next to her, tray in hand. Smooth-faced, and with cropped blond hair, she looked far younger than her thirty-four years. White shorts and matching crop top enhanced her long, tanned legs and gym-toned body. Pamela smiled. Susan took after her father and was nothing like her short, sturdy mother. Moving her book and glasses from the little wooden table, she made room for the tray with mugs, baby monitor, and cake.

Susan sat on a lounger and lay back with a heartfelt sigh. "Oh, bliss! This is absolutely perfect."

Pamela helped herself to a piece of the rich, yellow cake. "Absolutely!" she echoed. "It's hard to believe it's nearly the end of October. Can you imagine what the weather is like today, back in London or Scotland?"

Susan shuddered. "Cold at any rate, even if it's not damp and grey. Do you know, when I was packing Sophie's witch outfit for school, I realized we'll have been here a year this Saturday?"

"Already? It certainly doesn't feel it." Pamela picked up her mug and added, "Mind you, days do tend to blur here, don't they?"

"I suppose so, but as they are mostly sunny, blue days, I'm not complaining. Though I occasionally pinch myself to check I'm not dreaming. How about you, Mum? Still glad you decided to come?"

Pamela nodded. "Glad I let you persuade me, you mean! But yes, I am glad. It made sense."

"Yes, it did. One hundred percent" Susan glanced sideways at her mother. "Daddy would have approved, I know he would. He never intended you to be on your own in Scotland." She stirred her tea. "Bloody unfair!" She blurted. "He'd been so happy with his retirement adventure there. New home, new life, new people, and places.... you had barely started, it was so... awful ..." She trailed off, staring into space.

Pamela reached across and patted her daughter's hand. "I know dear, I know." Jonathan's catastrophic heart attack two years ago had abruptly ended their forty-year marriage, leaving Pamela adrift in the detritus of his plans. "This really came up at the right time. I truly was glad to sell up and leave."

"And you do have enough space, don't you Mum? For doing all your little paintings and everything? I sometimes worry you think I wanted you here just to help with Sophie and Clark. You don't, do you, Mum? You know I wouldn't have moved here without you."

Susan's face, the same darling, little face that had always waited anxiously to see if Mum liked the birthday present, the Christmas gift, the handmade surprise, looked at her now.

"Oh, sweetheart, of course, I don't think that. Where else would I be? I'm very lucky." She raised her mug in a toast. "To Ibiza life!" Susan reached hers across and clinked it. They sat back in silence as the filters in the pool whooshed into life, adding a musical bubbling of water to the buzzing of bees, drawn out by the heat to forage around the banks of wild lavender along the side of the garden. Pamela's thoughts returned to painting.

Eventually, Susan stood and brushed some crumbs off her top. "Nice as this is, I'd better go. Clark is still asleep, and I imagine you'll get another hour out of him. You won't forget Sophie has piano after school today, will you?"

Pam shook her head. "Of course not. Don't worry, we'll be fine."

Susan started for the house but turned back after a few steps. "Oh Mum, I wanted to check with you, would you mind if we met Gretchen and Peter on Saturday evening, just for an hour?"

"No problem. You know once Sophie and Clark drop off, they're gone for the night, and I do love your documentary channel."

"Mum!" Susan came back and stood next to Pamela. "You know we were going to get cable installed in your place, but you said no!"

"Yes, and I was right. It would be wasted. I prefer music or silence when I'm painting."

"As long as you're sure. Anyway, I'll confirm Saturday with the others, thanks a million, Mum." Susan dropped a kiss on her mother's head and loped off to the house. A short time later, she beeped a farewell as her car passed, in clouds of white dust, down the drive to the gate.

Pamela adored her time with the children while Susan

worked. Grand-parenting was all the intimacy, love, and fun of motherhood without the twenty-four-seven weight of responsibility. For two afternoons a week, Pamela had the children to herself, while Susan joined her husband at work in Ibiza town. Glen's successful, internet-based, graphic design company worked as easily from Ibiza as the U.K.

Pamela turned the monitor up full, always afraid that with her hearing, she'd miss a whimper, or God forbid, fail to catch a cry before it turned into a full-blown tantrum. She thought briefly about going back to the house to reapply sunscreen to spare her face from more wrinkles and brown patches but the heat was too delicious and the sunbed too comfortable, so she closed her eyes and lay back. Susan was right; it was perfect here, not too taxing. Glen dropped Sophie to school in the mornings, and Susan and Pamela occasionally went shopping, wandering the narrow, whitewashed streets in Ibiza town. Susan went to yoga and Spanish classes a few mornings a week, leaving two-year-old Clark with Pamela. She loved her time with this curious, affectionate, and utterly enchanting child. Together, they explored the universe of the patio and the living room, and dealing with a few noxious nappies was a small price to pay.

Pamela always carried her small sketch pad with her. Hidden, no, not hidden, just Susan never noticed it. At some stage when Clark was relaxed, a small, soggily heavy, warm body on her lap watching cartoons or dozing, she sketched ideas, points, plans or wrote words like 'try sky blue with red oxide, convey immensity, diagonal design on water.' Anything that might help her put her feelings and emotions on paper, or even help discover what those feelings were. She shouldn't complain. Ibiza was so beautiful, the light and colours were an artist's delight. Not that she'd seen a lot of it in the year she'd been here, though, Glen worked so hard to get the Spanish side of their operation off the ground, and Susan really needed support to get a good routine going. Pamela was glad to help. It never took her long to stop what she was doing, put away her paints, and join in. Even the weekends were well organized. Sometimes a family trip to a market followed by tapas at a wonderful, vine-covered, rustic restaurant. More often than not, Susan and Glen had friends over for a barbeque and Pamela was free to either join in or work in the studio area she had set up at the end of her living room, letting muted conversation, laughter, shrieking and splashing take the place of her background music.

It was a wonderful, perfect place for a sixty-year-old widow. Her life was perfectly mapped out, how could anyone want anything else? How could she not be happy? She sighed, sat up and hugged her knees, staring into the distance. The monitor crackled into life as Clark started banging the bars of his cot with his bottle. Pamela jumped up. There was a small window between happy and howling with Clark that Pamela didn't want to miss, and she hurried back to the house.

CHAPTER FOUR

Cassandra wrapped her hands around a mug of green tea and stared out at the drizzle that had suddenly wiped the sea from view. Ibiza hadn't let her down, but neither had it produced a magic wand and opened a door into a fabulous, well-paid job. Which was exactly what she needed in order to stay on in this house, to which she'd become so attached. She found living here totally calming. An hour's meditation turned unnoticed into two. A yoga session left her feeling elated and relaxed in a way she had never been before, and she slept, a deep restorative sleep which was undoing the damage of months of insomnia. There was something special about this place that connected her to the universe and also helped to clarify the workings of her own mind.

Of course, the house wasn't perfect, the garden needed quite a bit of maintenance, and some tiles in the terrace had recently started rocking as she walked over them as if they were becoming loose. However, there was always Reuben Ibanez, whose name she'd found on the list of useful numbers for tenants, pinned up in the kitchen. A smile tugged at her mouth as she thought of yesterday. She'd rung that number to report she could barely get the kitchen doors to move, and an hour later, she had opened the door to Brad Pitt. Well, if Brad was a few years older, much taller, more deeply lined, and Spanish. She'd waved him in, admiring the fit of his denim jeans as he passed. Jeans that were obviously distressed and faded from actual wear and tear, not from the addition of another forty pounds on the price tag. He took off his jacket and draped it over the back of a chair. She approved; lean, tanned, muscular arms, a worn navy t-shirt, and graying hair so close-cropped it looked like stubble. She had leant, arms folded, against the kitchen counter and watched him while he sanded down the sticking doors. He was focused and intent on what he was doing, and clearly not interested in small talk. She persisted but his answers were mostly monosyllabic, and he didn't look up from his work. However, when he did answer, his Spanish-accented English in a husky voice was very appealing.

Smoothly and easily, he stretched and squatted while working a thick block of sandpaper in vigorous circles up and down the surrounds of the door. "Do you work in many houses around here?" she'd asked, wondering how many bored housewives she'd be competing with for his attention.

"No."

Cassandra shook her head. Making conversation with this guy was hard work. "So why here?"

"My family has the adjoining farm and we've been looking after this particular property forever." He stretched to the top of the door with the sander. His t-shirt rose with his arms, and Cassandra was very impressed by a glimpse of his tanned, flat, muscled stomach. "So, you're a genuine Ibicenco?" she questioned. At last, he smiled. A crooked grin that had her smiling in immediate response.

"Born and bred." He paused and looked across at her. Cassandra had to ignore an urge to groom his unkempt eyebrows to show off the ice-blue eyes beneath. And wonder of wonders, he was still talking. "Well, via boarding school and university in England and about fifteen years working in Barcelona, but yes, my family likes to boast that our roots go back to the original inhabitants. They've no proof, of course, but that doesn't stop them from being immensely proud of it."

"You're not exactly typically Spanish, though, are you?" She knew she was running her eyes approvingly up and down the attractive length of his body, in a way that could have had him shouting 'sexual harassment if he were so inclined. "I mean, blue eyes, and you're what? Six-four?" She used her best flirty smile.

He was already turning back to the door as he muttered, "Dutch great-grandfather. He continued to work in silence.

Irritation at being ignored made her perversely determined to keep chatting. "What's the problem with the door? They look too new to be in need of repair."

"Nothing wrong, only this one does not like damp weather, but I'll soon sort her out."

"You speak like it's alive," Cassandra laughed.

He didn't smile, just nodded. "If you listen to the land, she'll tell you how she's feeling. Same with old houses. You get to know what they need."

Cassandra looked around the ultramodern kitchen. "This house doesn't seem so old."

"Appearances can be deceptive." He put his tools down. "Come with me." He opened the door leading into the laundry room which ran down the gable end of the house. Cassandra followed him. He stopped in front of a row of deep, wooden cupboards. "The top ones were all panelled but down here…" He squatted and opened a small door.

She knelt next to him and was immediately conscious of his sweat-to-aftershave ratio, which was perfect. Happy with the knowledge that she had splurged the end of her duty-free Coco Mademoiselle shower gel the same morning, she leant close to him, bent her head, and looked in. Reuben pushed aside a bottle of detergent and a shrivelled-up sponge. The rough-cut stonework, stained by the red ochre mud used to bind them, glowed out at her. Stones of assorted sizes and hues somehow fitted together creating a solid, sturdy wall. He reached past her and pressed his palm to the wall.

"Feel it," he instructed. She spread her hand next to his, and the skin on the back of it wrinkled into soft folds. Immediately, she bent her knuckles, so the skin tightened. It was damned unfair how women's hands aged so much faster than men's. The stone was dry and crumbly but somehow warm to her touch. "Wow, that's amazing. Is the whole wall like this?"

"Yes, you can't see it from the outside. It's been plastered and painted, but it's probably thousands of years old. This part of the house matches several Phoenician constructions around the island. It may very well be linked to a nearby shrine." As he spoke, he stood up and dusted off his hands.

"I wonder why they didn't make a feature of it," mused Cassandra, as she crumbled some stone into dust between her fingers.

"They used an architect who thought nothing of old stone or island history, though they actually ended up protecting something that might have disappeared otherwise." He looked down at her and offered his hand to help her up. As she met his eyes, she became acutely aware of her position on her knees in front of him. Far too old to be seen blushing, she ignored his hand, sprang to her feet, and led the way back to the kitchen.

She poured them both a glass of water and he returned to work with a small smile deepening the lines around his mouth. Sitting at the kitchen table, ostensibly engrossed in her phone, Cassandra was acutely aware that Reuben's eyes occasionally strayed from his work towards her, but he made no more conversation. Such pussyfooting around was not her normal style but there was a strange reserve about this guy that put a stop to her usual flirty banter. The deeply graven lines on his face were not laughter lines. When he finished with the doors, she'd watched him run his hands up and down the bare, exposed wood, circling his thumbs against the grain in a way that made her envy it. The sawdust was brushed up and the tools packed away before Cassandra could think of any other jobs he could do.

"Thank you," she said as they walked out of the kitchen.

"A pleasure," he replied with the same small smile. At the front door, he hesitated, cleared his throat, and handed her a card. "That's my mobile number if you need anything."

"Anything?" She smirked, can't keep a good innuendo down.

There was a hint of that crooked grin when he answered, "Only if it's something as exciting as a burst pipe, an airport run, or a lost key."

She was looking at the card as she reached for the door and they both jumped when her hand covered his on the handle. She jerked her hand back as if from a hot iron. "God! Sorry, I didn't mean to..."

He smiled, a proper, starting-in-the-eyes smile, that softened his angular face, but he said nothing, just nodded and left.

Knowing exactly how her mother would dismiss him, Cassandra smiled and looked at the card again. Lost keys wouldn't be hard to organize. Shaking her head, she returned to the present. No distractions. Clear focus was what was needed. She picked up her notebook, making lists always helped.

Gabriella from the crystal shop had helped her mum's old friend as much as she could. She'd given Cassandra introductions to various wedding and event-organizing friends of hers. One in particular, Ibiza Instincts, had caught her interest. They'd been looking for someone to deal with the social media end of their business, and that was definitely one of Cassandra's strengths. She had rung them and arranged to drop in tomorrow. She was absolutely sure she could run with this until she maneuvered her way into the actual event organizing side of their business. She underlined the name and looked up the address. It was just behind the port in Ibiza town.

It was perfect. She could already see herself, elegantly dressed, sitting outside a trendy cafe having morning coffee while watching the ferries dock across in the marina.

She strode into her bedroom, threw open the wardrobe doors, and eyed her choices. She needed to look cool, trendy, assured, competent, fun, lively, yet confident and capable - a big ask from a few items of clothing. Her signature look of tight jeans or trousers over a fitted bodysuit, with an open jacket or shirt, had always worked well, and she wasn't going to change it now.

She held a pair of white denims up to her and looked in

the mirror. Thank God for her legs! Long and thin, her thighs were barely bigger than her calves. They'd been the bane of her life in school, where she was nicknamed Raffy, short for giraffe. But later, when she could carry off the shortest shorts and the tightest jeans with aplomb, she thanked her luck in the genetic draw. Even now, at fifty-four, her legs looked as good as they ever did. Turning away from the mirror, she slid the hangers along the rail. No, not jeans, it must be trousers. She was looking for work, after all.

Her white linen trouser suit caught her eye. Team it up with a dark green velvet body and a matching silk scarf, a great accessory, a.k.a. wrinkle camouflage. Shoes? Undoubtedly, the Casadei stiletto heel, white ankle boots. They shouted confidence, elegance and money, a good combination. Pleased with her choice she returned to her green tea and her notebook. She briefly considered sorting out the piles of laundry waiting by the washing machine. No, a relaxing evening and an early night. After all, tomorrow was another day, and she had an important meeting in Ibiza town.

CHAPTER FIVE

Over the next two weeks, Bláithín tried to bring a bit of life to the apartment. She scrubbed every reachable surface and cupboard in every room and polished all the floors. She'd also lugged the linen, blankets, and towels to the launderette. Then washed and polished all the cutlery, cookware, and crockery. Finally, she bought a large, embroidered tablecloth to cover the blank brown expanse of table and added some fresh flowers for colour and fragrance. She was exhausted, yet the place still didn't look much better.

She surveyed the room and decided that, apart from taking a paintbrush to the whole place, there was no more she could do. She looked at her watch, she had an appointment with Maite, the person who took care of Andy's flat. She was the exuberant and glowingly pregnant daughter-in-law of the corner shop owner and had pleaded with Bláithín to help her with her English. Open-faced and friendly, she'd fired questions at Bláithín with such cheerful curiosity it was impossible to be offended. Her brown eyes pinned Bláithín while she interrogated her. 'Why you here alone? How old you? What you do all day? You have brothers or sisters?' She was equally open about her own situation, with exaggerated faces and hand gestures she told the story of her romance with Pedro, and his mother's reaction to them being seven months pregnant walking up the aisle. They became real friends though, the day Maite asked Bláithín if she was constipated.

"What?"

"I think you are constipated. I see from your face."

Bláithín was dumbfounded. Talk about inappropriate! She shook her head and mumbled no, no, she wasn't. Maite frowned and said it was obvious Bláithín was constipated, and she was going to get something to help, something she had in stock for Andy because Andy often was too. Bláithín was mortified and covered her embarrassment by rooting in her bag for some tissues, her eyes were swollen and red in reaction to ammonia in the cleaner she'd used.

Maite had returned waving a box of Beecham's cold remedy at her and it became clear 'constipado' in Spanish did not, as Maite assumed, translate to 'constipated' in English, merely to 'a cold'. Maite's face had been priceless, when she discovered what she'd been saying, and her gales of laughter as she re-enacted Bláithín's shocked face as she had been interrogated about the state of her bowels made them both laugh so much that Maite's mother-in-law appeared around the door to shush them.

As Maite also cleaned other flats in the Flora Apartments building apart from Andy's, English practice included filling Bláithín in on the Flora apartment gossip. "Is mostly summer people, some German families come and go, and Roberto and Carmen, very old, live on floor five but they leave every summer before Flora apartment is all-night party."

Bláithín had shrugged, but there was a tug of disappointment at the realization she would miss seeing the place come to life. Maite always sent Bláithín home with something extra pressed into her hand or tucked into her shopping. Herb cuttings in yogurt cartons were her specialty and citronella, basil, and chamomile were thriving on Bláithín's window ledge.

Back in the present, she looked at her watch again and grimaced, she really should ring her brother. She had texted him the night she arrived to let them know she was safe and sound but had been putting off an actual phone call since. She sat on the sofa, leaned back, and without the slightest enthusiasm, pressed their number. As usual, she had to run the gauntlet of Pauline first. "Well, tell us, is it all you expected? Does Andy's flat live up to all his ould guff about it?"

There was no way she was going to tell Pauline about the impersonal bleakness of the flat or the empty, echoing apartment building. "Ah, well, there are great, big palm trees and loads of flowers, just in the lobby of the place."

"Trees! In the lobby! You'd never get that here, I can tell you."

Bláithín rolled her eyes. "I know. Tell me, is Diarmuid there at all?"

"He is inside watching the match, I'll get him now, but first I must tell you. You'll never guess who I saw in Tesco's the other day." The glee in Pauline's voice made Bláithín dread what was coming.

"You're right, I wouldn't."

Pauline didn't even hear her; she was still talking. "Frank! Him and his wife, and she was as pregnant as O'Sullivan's cow again! Is that number four or five now?"

"How would I know? It's years since I had anything to do with him, Pauline."

"Ah but sure, wasn't he the man that broke your heart and turned you into a lonely -"

Bláithín couldn't bear another word. "That's nonsense Pauline, we just weren't compatible and that was that. Now can I speak with Diarmuid, please?" She could almost see Pauline's mouth turn down and her eyebrows rise, a particularly annoying mannerism she had when she wanted you to know she was right but was, out of charity towards you, not going to say another word. Pauline harumphed. "Well, if that's all the news you have, I'll call himself for you, goodbye."

Across the miles, Bláithín could hear lanky, quiet Diarmuid scuffing his way up the hall, probably already in his slippers and settled in for the rest of the day.

Diarmuid filled her in on the details of the match, asked her if the weather was nice, told her to mind herself and asked her to stay in touch. She hadn't expected any different; he'd left home for university when she was only fourteen. However, they'd always kept in touch and been fond of each other in a distant, polite kind of way. She wished the Kilkenny Cats luck for the second half of the match and closed her phone.

That call had depressed her. Her wasteland years, that was how she thought of her marriage to Frank. She'd been well aware of the amazement in her workplace when Frank McGrath, that tall, reserved guy from management had asked timid, little Bláithín Roche, of all people, from accounts out on a date.

Even Anne, her regular companion on cinema visits, was surprised. "It's not that you're not lovely and everything." She'd said, "and sure, haven't I told you over and over, those big, grey eyes of yours would look great with makeup. But y'know, you're not exactly the life and soul of the party, are you? I mean, I'm not myself either," she'd added hastily lest she offend Bláithín. "How did you get to know him so well, anyway, that I didn't hear about it?"

"I just kept meeting him in the canteen and he started keeping a seat for me. We didn't even talk much. I was in shock when he asked me out."

The following year of courting had actually been the best part of the whole fiasco. He spent a lot of time away, travelling for the company, which naturally, in her view, had slowed the relationship process. They'd had a very pleasant routine going. She'd enjoyed the novelty of holding his hand as they walked around the town. They went to the cinema, for a walk, or a meal out every week he was in Kilkenny, and as she still lived at home, he'd have a cup of tea with her parents most nights before kissing her goodnight on the step. She'd assumed the slightly awkward kisses would become something better with time. When they were married, it would all be fine.

She was wrong.

His bitter words had been flung like darts. 'Frigid' 'Fucking nun!' 'Like making love to a corpse'. She had them all filed away. Her efforts to please him would smooth things for a while, but she'd hated it, feeling like a trussed turkey in some of the outfits he bought for her. What a failure she'd been. He was a quiet man, not much given to displays of emotion, but she'd enjoyed their chats, their evenings in silence as she read and he did crosswords, or an odd meal out, she hadn't wanted much. But that aspect of their life or rather her inability to enjoy it, or even participate in it as time went on, dominated their lives, making him angry and frustrated, and her silent and anxious.

She shot to her feet and with a determined scowl on her face, rammed the phone into her bag and slammed the door on the way out. It made her feel better.

After half an hour with Maite, helping her with the English module for the week, Bláithín headed out into the fresh air. Today the sky was clear and high, and out of wind or shade, the sun was warm. Despite her exhaustion, Bláithín was determined to go out for a walk every day. She decided it was the only way to get to know a place properly. Though she was discovering that in San Antonio in winter, there wasn't much to get to know. Her favourite walk so far was down through the side streets to the marina. On her way down she counted the open businesses, two fruit and veg shops, a hairdresser's, two cafés, and a hardware store. Honestly, there was more life in a midland's high street on a Monday night! She passed buildings where dark windows invited you to peer in at the shadowy stacks of chairs and tables, where padlocked shutters and metal grilles collected rubbish and leaves. She looked up long lengths of silent, depressing streets without a person in view and tried to ignore them as she headed to Rita's Cantina, the one spot that made her feel she had actually gone somewhere interesting.

Rita's Cantina was a warm hub of conversation and a constantly changing cast of intriguing characters. Clever use of old shutters, dark wood, and chandeliers had somehow created decades of atmosphere between the ochre walls of the ground floor in a brand-new building.

She pulled out the old bentwood chair at a table for one and sat, back to the wall surveying the whole café. A waitress with blond dreadlocks tied up in a scarf, smiled questioningly at her. Bláithín was ready for this. "Cafe con leche por favor."

She was determined not to let embarrassment stop her from trying to say a few words every day.

"Muy bien" smiled the server as she keyed it into her pad.

Bláithín pulled a stack of timetables, leaflets, and maps out of her bag and set them on the small, wooden table. Now that her cleaning frenzy was over, she was ready to make plans. For the first time, she was planning to branch out from San Antonio. She studied a map of the Phoenician graveyard on the back hills of Ibiza town. The biggest necropolis in the world spanning three different civilizations would be fascinating. Maybe tomorrow would be the day she'd finally take some photos worth printing. Her photos so far had been disappointing, uninspired holiday snaps, nothing worth even unpacking the printer for. She moved her papers to make room for her coffee which arrived with a little square of cake on the saucer, then opened a map of Ibiza to plot her way from the bus station to the Necropolis of Puig des Molins. Route marked, timed, and written in her notebook, she folded away her papers and opened her book.

Another long cup of coffee later, she was heading out the door. "See you tomorrow!" called the cheery waiter as she cleared away the cups and money. Bláithín grinned, inordinately pleased she had already been marked down as a regular. Still smiling, she started back up towards the Flora apartments. The hill was more of a struggle than usual today. She stopped to catch her breath and found her head was pounding with every heartbeat. Each heavy step on the way back was an effort and she was quite light-headed by the time she once again sat in the foyer chairs to recover. She resolved to walk faster and longer every day, and tomorrow's visit to Ibiza town would be just the time to start.

CHAPTER SIX

Later, Pamela couldn't remember what exactly had started the tears. It could have been when her elbow caught the shaft of her paintbrush, knocking its glass of water to the ground, or it could have been the realization that her last few brush strokes had irrevocably obliterated all traces of depth and interest from her painting. She'd made such a fuss to get it started, inconveniencing people, and made a fool of herself with her enthusiasm, all for nothing.

At five a.m., she had been alive with excitement, a picture clear in her head. Everything, even down to the placement of the masking glue under the palest of blue washes, with which she would cover the page. Five a.m.! She wanted to leap out of bed, tie her hair up, and start at once. But her living room was directly opposite Clark and Sophie's bedroom, and the bright studio light in her work area would shine straight in on them through the gauze curtains. There was no way she could do that. They'd be awake in seconds. She didn't want to go into the kitchen and start sketching; that would kill the idea. She wanted to just do it, now, this second, in her night dress!

But instead, she lay watching the glowing hands of her clock tick off the slow minutes. She went over every detail in her mind until she heard the first sounds from the main house. Pulling on her dressing gown, she ran across and asked Susan if she would mind foregoing her yoga today. Guilt nudged at Pamela, but she was still buzzing with excitement and anticipation. She explained how important it was to start while everything was so clear in her head.

"Don't worry, Mum, I'll sort it. But will you be okay to do the school pick-up? I must bring my car to the garage."

Pamela was heading straight back out the door, her

head, already in her studio, stopped and looked back. "School pick up? Gosh, I don't know, I really just want to get started, Susan, and see what happens, I need to start before I lose it..." Susan's worried face cut through Pamela's excitement. "Of course, darling. After all, it's only eight now. That gives me six hours, loads of time, really." Making a mental note to set an alarm, she hurried across the courtyard.

Deciding paper weight and size, she pulled her shoulder-length white hair back into a ponytail, not willing to waste the time doing her normal French twist. She planned her brushes while she tugged her painting dress over her clothes. She hummed while she set out her paints, then, choosing a wide, flat brush she began.

***

Two hours later she was still buzzing. The wash had taken beautifully, spread in an even layer across the page pinned to her easel. The first outlines of her background were in place just as she had seen them in her dream. There had been a woman in her nighttime vision. A woman slightly hidden, but central and vital to the work. Pamela had only ever done landscapes, so the inclusion of this woman was challenging, even slightly nerve-wracking. A cup of coffee before continuing seemed like a good idea. She wiped her hands and went into the kitchen. Lost in thoughts about the painting, she stared absently out the window as she trickled water into the kettle.

Susan's voice carried through the open window, cutting off her thoughts.

"Hey, Katerina, it's Susan. Listen, I'm sorry I can't pick you up for yoga today. I know, but my mum's very excited about a painting she wants to do, and she can't mind Clark for me... Ha ha! Yes, she does, every day, but somehow today seems extra important so... Okay. Great, thanks. Yes, I'm sorry too. See you soon, bye."

Pamela put the kettle down. Coffeeless, she returned to the easel and stared at it, an argument racketing in her head. Should she have taken Clark? Was she being selfish, and spoiling two people's plans? On the other hand, Susan missing yoga once wasn't that big a deal, surely, she'd understood the request. It wasn't so strange, was it? Pamela's attention returned to the picture. At five this morning she'd had no doubts at all she could do this, but now she wasn't so sure. The closer she came to committing to the figure, the less sure her strokes became. She prepared the flesh tint as she urged herself on. There! Now the woman who had created this garden of exotic plants and ponds, under a wide expanse of clear sky was peering out at her.

Pamela stood back. No, it didn't work, too flat. She kept going, built up some contrasting shades, tried to catch a face. Put in some stronger foliage. Much later, she stood back again with a sinking heart, leant forward, and dabbed on some white highlights but it was clear her unfinished woman was now too hidden, and Pamela had given herself no way back. Disappointment flooded her.

There was a knock on the door. "Mum! What about picking up Sophie? It's nearly two, and I'm just leaving to bring the car to the garage."

Pamela was aghast; she had never set an alarm. "What? Two, already? Surely not!" She turned to check the clock and sent her water jar and brush smashing to the floor, islands of broken glass surrounded with dirty water.

"You okay, Mum?" Susan stepped into the room.

Pamela hadn't realized she was crying until Susan handed her a tissue. "Mum, don't worry, it's only a jar. And is this the inspired painting?" She stepped in front of the easel. "Wow, it's...."

"No, it's not! It's nothing. It's terrible!" Pamela grabbed the painting from the easel and ripped the page from the pad. She needed another tissue.

"Mum, don't worry, just sit here on the couch. I'll cancel

the garage and make you a cup of tea. Then I'll take Clark with me and do the school pick-up. Honestly, maybe you've been overdoing it? Put your feet up. I'll be back in a second."

Pamela leant her head back and closed her eyes, tears dripped off her chin.

Susan reappeared with tea, hovering anxiously. Pamela blew her nose and sat up. "Darling, I'm so sorry. You've had to cancel yoga and the garage appointment today, because of me. And at this stage, I would never be ready in time to collect Sophie." She held up her paint-splattered arms. "Don't worry about me, I'm fine, honestly. I just got a bit caught up in that painting and it didn't work out."

"Well, I thought it looked jolly good," Susan said.

Pamela knew she could never explain the gap between her vision of the glowing, sensuous woman enveloped by the lustrous beauty of her garden, and the flat, lifeless figure overwhelmed by clumsy foliage that had ended up on her page.

Susan left and Pamela cleared up the broken glass, cleaned her brushes, washed the tops of her paint tubes, tied them tightly, and packed them away. That was enough drama. She felt foolish. She resolved to clean out her cupboards for the rest of the day, then get a good night's sleep, and tomorrow maybe she'd take Sophie for a hike up to the top of Dalt Vila in Ibiza. Have lunch out, make a day of it, and forget this ever happened.

CHAPTER SEVEN

Sophie had been thrilled with the idea of a day out with her grandmother. Pamela hid a smile at the outfit Sophie had chosen. A taffeta Minnie Mouse skirt, a striped t-shirt, and a pink Frozen sweatshirt with a hood and one big pocket across the front, had been teamed up with sequined ballet slippers.

"Sophie, you look beautiful, but you positively cannot wear those shoes walking up the old town." Pamela pointed to her own comfortable, solid walking shoes. "Look at me, not the prettiest shoes, I know, but our feet will be doing all the work, so we must be sensible." A compromise was reached with Sophie's light-up, glitter runners. Pamela pulled on a soft grey, crew neck jumper over her white polo shirt and they were ready to go.

They took their time wandering the narrow white-washed alleys. The sudden steps and corners, twists and turns of the centuries-old hill town were a delight. Even at seven, Sophie still wanted to jump up and off every doorstep they passed. Her hand, warm in Pamela's, swung their arms as they walked.

"Look here, Sophie, feel this." Pamela ran her hand down the side of a large, old wooden door.

"Just imagine the people who put up this exact door, who had their hands in the very same spot that my hand is now, were living in a world of pirates and princesses, and knights on horses!"

Sophie's small hand rubbed the wood. "Did they make the doors so big to let the horses in?"

"My word! That's a good question, Soph. I don't know, but I suppose so. They have a small door here cut out for people." She put her hand on the huge doorknob, its metal covering worn paper-thin by many, many thousands of hands.

"Feel this, Sophie. Isn't it amazing?"

But Sophie had lost interest and was tugging Pamela towards a steep flight of steps. "Can we go up this way, Grandma? It looks brill."

Pamela followed her granddaughter up the little alleyway. Wrought iron balconies at either side of the steps leant out towards each other. Purple and pink bougainvillea with stems as thick as young trees climbed walls and surrounded windows. Two or three shops were still open, and vibrant displays of art, clothes, and souvenirs lined their outside walls.

In a shop where cheap hippie tops and designer shirts shared shelf space with souvenirs and faded postcards, Sophie used her pocket money to buy a sparkly snow globe. Clear liquid filled with glitter surrounded a plaster castle, so wonderfully detailed that open shutters even revealed pretty curtains.

Across from the shop was another flight of steps. "Up this way, Grandma!" Sophie was on the move again. "Let's see what's up here," she suggested, tucking the globe into the big pocket in the front of her sweatshirt and starting off up the steps. They wound up at the museum square, high on the hill. The panoramic view across the alleys of the higgledy-piggledy old town was enchanting.

"Oh, isn't this beautiful, Sophie? The perfect spot for a break."

Pamela opened her backpack and took out two cartons of juice, sandwiches, and a bar of chocolate. They sat on the stone ledge along the end of the museum building and shared out the food. Leaning back against the old brick wall, they looked down, over to the new square apartment buildings and office blocks leading out to the ferry port and beyond, on to green hills speckled with white houses. Yachts and fishing boats trailed white wakes through the calm blue spread of sea right up to the old port

Sandwich in one hand, Sophie took out her globe and

inspected it with great seriousness. Pamela watched with a smile as Sophie studied and ate. Two sandwiches later, Sophie finally said, "Grandma, y'know if I look really hard into this, I think I can see people moving. I wonder if it could be magic?"

Pamela didn't miss a beat. "Gosh! I don't really know, but I expect it's amazing what you could find in such old shops like these!"

Sophie nodded. "Mmm," she said, with a serious frown. "That's what I was thinking."

"Okay," Pamela stood up and stretched. "We'd better start moving. We're meeting your mum in an hour. We'll eat the chocolate on the way down."

The walk back was taken up with Sophie's take on who could be living in the castle. The family members were given names, ages, and jobs. She even decided who was nice and who wasn't. Coming out the main gate heading down the sloping road to the market square, Sophie handed the globe to Pamela. "Here Grandma, who do you see?"

Pamela took the globe in both hands and held it in front of her eyes "Hmmm, I think I can see - what did you say the little girl's name was?"

They started down the cobbled incline. "It's Penny, Grandma. Can you see Penny?" Pamela peered closer, and with her next step, her right foot, in her sensible shoe, simply slid from under her on the stone. Polished smooth in places from centuries of use, some paving stones were as slippery as ice. She went down on her left knee and slid several feet on her shin.

"Grandma!" Sophie screamed. "Are you alright?"

"I'm fine, darling, don't worry, just a slip. Look, I didn't even drop your globe." She held it out to Sophie. Then she focused on trying to get up and away before anyone could make a fuss.

Sophie's eyes were filled with tears. "Can you get up? I'll help you." Her little hands tugged at Pamela's arm, unbalancing her and almost preventing her from getting up.

Pamela reached for the wall and used it to pull herself to her feet. Her leg throbbed, but she managed to smile at Sophie. "That's better. I don't know how I would have managed without you."

Sophie was staring, with tears pouring down her little elfin face, at Pamela's leg.

"Now, I'm right as rain. It was just a slip, Sophie, don't make a fuss." Pamela looked down. Her shin had been grated by the stone, and blood was pooling in her sensible shoe. A woman rushed across the road and gripped Pamela by the elbow. Her Spanish was too fast, but Pamela gathered she was being asked if she was okay. "Bien, bien, gracias," Pamela managed, desperately wanting to get away, but the woman was now shouting for her friends to come and help.

A voice cut across the Spanish woman's calls. "You need that seen to, love, and probably a tetanus injection too." A large middle-aged man in an impeccable suit was talking to her. He had a tiny, white Yorkie on a pink lead which was doing a good job of distracting Sophie. Pamela looked down more closely at her leg. Dozens of pieces of grit were embedded in the mottled bloody mess that was her shin. She appealed to the man, "Do you speak Spanish? Can you please get that woman to stop shouting?"

The man spoke Spanish fluently and obviously conveyed Pamela's wishes, as the woman stopped waving her friends over.

Pamela added, "Please tell her 'Thank you very much, but I'm perfectly fine.'"

He did. The woman kissed Pamela on both cheeks, hugged her, said something, patted the man on the arm, and Sophie on the head and headed back to her friends.

"Thank you so much for dealing with her. I really just want to get away from here."

Pamela pulled Sophie close for a cuddle. "I'm fine Sophie, please stop crying. I'm fine, see, I'm even eating chocolate!" She pulled her piece of chocolate out of her pocket and bit off a tiny bit.

"Oh, that's good. Mummy always says if you can eat, you're not that sick."

"Exactly!" agreed Pamela who was hoping the sugar would help with the shock which was making her tremble.

People were slowing down to look as they passed. Blood still streamed down her leg.

The man patted Pamela's arm. "Well, I told her I was taking you to the emergency room at the hospital, immediately." He ignored Pamela's attempt at a protest. "Which is what I'll do." He pointed down the hill. "My car is right there and there's a hospital around the corner, if you have insurance. If not, the other one is not much further."

Pamela shook her head. "Oh, I have my insurance card in my bag, but I couldn't possibly ask-"

He cut across her. "I'm not busy. I'm just passing time while my partner is shopping. I'll have you there in a few minutes." He'd taken her arm and handed the Yorkie's lead to Sophie while he was speaking.

He opened the passenger door to a gleaming white car. He leant in, pushed the passenger seat right back, and turned the floor mat rubber side up. "Might as well have something we can wash the blood off," he said practically. He helped Pamela in and closed the door. While he walked around to the driver's side and started the car, she took a look at her leg. It made her stomach turn, so she hastily looked back at Sophie who was laughing at the little dog's scrabbling attempts to remain upright against the door in order to look out the window.

Her knight in shining Armani glanced across at her as they paused at a traffic light. "How are you holding up? You're lucky it wasn't a lot worse. Those stones are lethal."

"I know! I didn't trip or anything- my foot just slid and there was nothing I could do. I can't thank you enough, I do so appreciate your help."

"Delighted to help, and as you can see, it wasn't much of a bother. We're here already." He was pulling up in front of the hospital's emergency department. It seemed like an effort to move when he opened the door for her. Gingerly, she got out. "Thank you again, you're very kind." They shook hands, and he winked at Sophie. "Keep an eye on your Gran, love."

Sympathetic hospital staff offered her a wheelchair, while they took her card and filled the forms. Pamela thought it might be a step too far for Sophie, who was looking tearful again without the dog to distract her. "No gracias," she waved it away and leant on the counter instead. Finally, she signed a form and the receptionist handed her a number and pointed in the direction of the waiting room.

Pamela limped into the brightly lit room. One wall was taken up by two closed doors, another by a TV. The remaining walls were lined with chairs and there were a few rows in the middle of the room. Sophie had a death grip on her hand. Pamela looked around for a seat where she wouldn't have to interact with anyone. There were two men sitting facing the TV, which was silently showing a football match. A teenager, in one of the centre rows, with a cast on his leg, was oblivious to the world, flying his thumbs furiously over the keypad of his phone. Over against a wall was a tall, blond, elegant woman, of the sort that made Pamela feel fat and dowdy just by existing. The woman had one long, elegant, trouser-clad leg stretched across two chairs. The purple, swollen ankle at the end of it somewhat spoiled the whole look

"Grandma, I'm hungry." Sophie's pale blue eyes, the one thing she'd inherited from Pamela, filled with tears again.

"Come on, sweetie, we'll sit down and see if there's anything left in my bag." They walked past the blond who was swinging a perilously high-heeled boot in her hand, its partner still defiantly in place.

The woman looked at Pamela's leg and grimaced. "Christ! That looks bloody awful. What happened to you?" Pamela glanced down quickly at Sophie to see if she had noticed the profanity, but thankfully it didn't seem to have registered. "I just slipped, nothing much really," Pamela muttered and ushered Sophie to seats on the opposite wall.

As soon as they were settled, she said, "We must just ring Mummy and change our plans a bit." With a sinking heart, Pamela pressed the numbers. "Hi, darling! Now, there's no problem, we're both fine but there's a little change of rendezvous. Could you pick us up from the PolyClinica in Ibiza town instead of at Mango?"

"No! No, Sophie's fine, it's just that I just slipped and grazed my leg."

"No, not yet. It will be looked at in a minute."

Hearing her mother's voice through the phone, reduced Sophie to tears again. "I want to talk to Mummy!"

Pamela cupped her hand around the phone. "Okay, but we don't want to worry her, so let's be cheerful." She spoke into the phone again. "Susan, Sophie would like a word with you. You'll see it's all fine, really. Here Sophie, tell Mummy about your lovely magic globe."

She handed the phone to Sophie who took a deep breath and wailed, "Oh, Mummy! Mummy, it's awful, poor Grandma. There was blood everywhere, and she couldn't get up from the ground and I had to help her, and a woman was shouting and we had to get into a stranger's car and poor Grandma's leg is terrible. This place smells and I want to go hoooome!"

Pamela listened in horror and snatched the phone back. "It's not that bad - No! I didn't have a little turn! I slipped that's all, I just slipped. No, she didn't need to help me up."

Sophie shouted, "I did! I did! You said you couldn't have gotten up without me! You said it!"

Pamela could hear her own voice beginning to shake, "Look, Susan, I'm sure I'm only going to get a tetanus injection and a bandage, please don't worry. Yes, I know she is, and I'm terribly sorry she's so upset, but... Yes, okay, I'll see you when you get here."

Pamela put away her phone and put her hand over her eyes. In her anxiety to get away from the scene and minimize the drama for Sophie, she'd resolutely ignored the vicious stinging pain down her leg, but it was hard to ignore now. She rubbed away an escaping tear with her sleeve.

"Grandma, when's Mummy coming? I'm hungry." Sophie was tapping her arm. "Grandma, are you asleep? Grandma, do you know your leg is still bleeding?"

"Hey, Twinkletoes, can I see that fabulous globe?" The blond held out her hand.

Sophie stared at her, and then glanced at her grandmother for permission. Pamela nodded, and the little girl crossed the short distance, already talking about the inhabitants of her magical world. 'Thank you,' Pamela mouthed, and the blonde smiled back over Sophie's head.

Pamela used the moment's peace to blow her nose, take a few deep breaths and close her eyes. Pamela's respite didn't last as Sophie forgot about her globe and began to question the woman. "What happened to you?"

The woman pointed to her high-heeled boot. "This, and Ibiza's cobbles."

Sophie ran her finger down the spiked heel. "My Grandma said we had to wear sensible shoes. I'm not sure these are sensible, are they?"

"I certainly hope not!" retorted the woman.

Pamela scoffed. "Ha! Well, seems like we've gone from one extreme to another in our footwear," she stuck out her damaged leg with the beige lace-up. "And we've both ended up here."

The woman laughed, a cheerful guffaw. "Can't bloody win, can we?"

Pamela hobbled over to join them and looked from the boot to the shoe. "Yes, one of life's little jokes alright. Have you been waiting long?"

Sophie noticed stacks of leaflets advertising plastic surgery on a nearby table and became engrossed in making rows of tents with them

The blond replied, "I'm waiting on the results of an x-ray. Luckily, they don't think it's broken, as I just went over on it,

I didn't fall flat or anything awful." She immediately glanced down at Pamela's leg and made a wry face. "Oops, sorry, I gather you had a bit of a circus act?" She tilted her head in Sophie's direction. "I couldn't help overhearing the recital on the phone."

"Swan Lake rather than circus, really," Pamela corrected. "I actually slid, in quite an elegant manner. It's quiet here, isn't it? Hopefully, I'll be seen before my daughter arrives, she'll be so worried." She looked at her watch.

"I imagine you'll be looked at next. Those two," she pointed at the men, "are waiting for x-ray, and as far as I can gather, the kid's just waiting for a lift. There's one very cross Irish woman in with the doctor at the moment and that's it. In fact, that's her coat there." She pointed a slender, silver-ringed finger at a heap of grey tweed on the chair beyond her foot.

Pamela leant forward to check on Sophie, who was now absorbed in using the leaflets to build a box for her globe. Sitting back, she asked, "Why was the woman angry? Seems an odd reaction to being in an emergency room."

"Apparently, she'd been having a really nice time wandering the Phoenician burial grounds next door, then she collapsed and when she came to, she was being stretchered in here. She refused to sign any papers or give info until they let her off the stretcher and stopped. Wait, how did she put it? Oh yes, 'making a show' of her."

"I know how she feels. I wanted to murder a woman shouting for help for me."

"Well, I basked in all the attention I got. A chair, a double brandy, a- oh, here she comes now."

Pamela turned in the direction of her gaze. A woman came out of one of the doors, pressing a swab of cotton wool into the crook of her arm. Large, grey eyes under two swoops of heavy eyebrows stood out in a pale face.

The blonde swung her leg down and patted the chair next to her. "Good Lord! You look terrible! Come sit down. What did the doctor say?"

The woman picked her coat up and sat down heavily. "Probably high blood pressure, but she's taken some bloods just in case. So I have to come back tomorrow for results and another check-up. I'd be fine and at home having a cup of tea now, if they'd only let me alone."

"Oh yes," scoffed the blonde. "You'd have been fine. Lying flat out across the path in the burial grounds. They could have left you there, charged extra, and called you 'Work in Progress'."

There was a heartbeat of silence as the three looked at each other before they broke out laughing. Pamela laughed longer and louder than she had for a long time. The men turned around to stare, but the women were oblivious.

"Oh God, that's some image!" the Irish lady said, shaking her unkempt, frizzy hair.

The blonde leant forward and Pamela could see that perfect makeup was not the whole picture in her elegance - great bone structure and well-cared-for skin played a major part in her glamorous look.

"Please tell me," the blonde asked the still-chuckling Irish woman. "What on Earth is your name? I heard the nurse call you in and I still haven't been able to figure out what she said!"

"Well, the nurse said 'Blah- theen', but my name is actually pronounced ' Blaw, rhymed with flaw and heen' sounds like 'lean', but it's spelled b-l-a fada, that's an accent line," She paused, looked at their expressions, smiled and shrugged. "Anyway it's Bláth for short and it means little flower."

"Oh, you Irish and your unspellable names. I'm still having a tough time with my florist Shov-awn, but it's spelled with a b and an h in the middle! I'm Cassandra by the way."

Pamela joined in, "Yes, for sheer spelling craziness I often thought you couldn't beat Featherstonehaugh being pronounced Fenshaw." She paused, then added, "I'm Pamela and that," she smiled across at the little girl, "is my granddaughter, Sophie."

"Nice to meet you both," said Bláithín. She eyed Pamela's leg. "You've been in the wars."

"Yes, I -" She was interrupted by the surgery door opening and her name being called. "Better get this over with." She slowly got to her feet.

"Why don't we help Sophie to build a huge house with all of these folders while you chat to the doctor?" suggested Cassandra.

"What do you think Soph? I'll only be a minute or two, I'm sure."

Sophie looked up from the floor. "Maybe I'll go with you, Grandma."

Cassandra said, "Sophie, we could show Bláithín your globe. I've heard Irish people are very good at spotting magic," She looked over at Bláithín. "Unless you're just leaving?"

"No, I'm waiting for a taxi. I'd love a look at your globe. Who knows what's in there?" Bláithín agreed.

Sophie was sold. She moved next to Bláithín holding out her globe.

"I'm just in here if you want me." Pamela kissed the top of Sophie's head and limped in after the nurse.

The doctor and nurse were both sympathetic and gentle. The tetanus injection was deep, slow, and uncomfortable. But the pain of getting the grit tweezered out, the shredded skin pulled off and cold antiseptic liquid poured over it was sharp, stabbing, and sickening. However, at least she could hear Sophie chatting outside and thank goodness, even laughing. Cassandra's doing, Pamela guessed. Her wound was coated with a thick paste, covered with layers of gauze, and bandaged from knee to heel, yet by the time she opened the door to return to the waiting room blood was seeping through again.

"Grandma! Are you better now?" Sophie flung herself at her and hugged her tightly.

"Oh yes, sweetheart, all better now," Pamela agreed.

Cassandra put her head to one side and arched an

elegant eyebrow at her, so she added, "Well, I do have to come back tomorrow and have the dressing changed, but I'm fine."

The nurse had followed her out the door and was looking at her clipboard. "Cassandra Collingsworth?" She made it sound like an exotic cocktail.

Cassandra pulled a crutch from behind her chair and slowly put her swollen foot on the floor. She winked at Sophie, waved her empty boot at the room in general, then said, "Wish me luck girls." and disappeared into the surgery.

Bláithín watched her go. "She's great, isn't she? People like that amaze me."

"People like what?" asked Pamela.

"Self-assured, confident, like she knows what's going on and how to deal with it. Oh, she told me about your fall, and…" she nodded towards Sophie, "The Phone Call!"

Pamela grimaced. "Oh God, I know! My poor daughter will be frantic by the time she gets here, and it's all coming on top of yesterday."

"Why? What happened yesterday?"

"I made a ridiculous fuss about wanting to work on a painting, forgot to set an alarm, wasn't ready to pick up Sophie from school, ruined my painting, smashed a jar, then broke down in tears. Now this, Susan will think I'm cracking up." Pamela took a deep breath. "I'm sorry, I don't know why I'm unloading all of this on you."

"Because I asked. Anyway, you just slipped. It happens to hundreds of people every day. It's okay, no big deal, don't worry.

"That's just it. It's painful and a nuisance, but it's so much more because I was responsible for -" she glanced towards Sophie who was putting the folders back on the table, "and now I've dragged her through all of this on top of being crazy yesterday."

"I don't know. I've no children myself, but I imagine your daughter will just be glad you're okay."

"Oh, Susan is an absolute darling! Don't get me -" She

was interrupted by Sophie who had come to sit next to her and was resting her head against her shoulder.

"Grandma, I'm really hungry now. When's Mummy coming? I want to go home."

Bláithín stood up. "I'll go and see if there's a vending machine, get some juice or something?"

A voice carried through from reception.

"Mummy!" shouted Sophie and she ran towards the voice.

"Oh, God." Pamela sighed.

Susan came rushing through with Sophie in her arms. Relief at seeing her mother had reduced Sophie to tears again and she had her arms clung tightly around her mother's neck.

Susan hugged her mother tightly with her free arm. "Mum! Are you alright?"

"Yes, I'm fine sweetheart." Pamela injected as much energy and cheerfulness into her voice as she could muster. "Thanks for coming up for us." She stepped back and patted her daughter's arm.

"What did the doctor say? What caused the fall? Did you tell him how upset you'd been yesterday? Shhh, shhh Sophie, it's okay, Mummy's here now."

"Nothing 'caused' the fall, Susan. I just slipped. I have a prescription for pain killers and I must come back tomorrow to out-patients. Sophie has been an absolute brick."

"Oh, Mum, I'm so glad you're okay. I'm going to get you home and into bed and make sure you have a proper rest. It's been an awful experience for Sophie. I can see she's very upset. The poor darling. I'm going to bring her out to the car and get her settled in her seat and then I'll come back in and help you out, okay?" She held her hand up as she saw Pamela starting to stand up. "Just wait a minute, Mum, please. Let me deal with Sophie first."

Pamela sank back into the seat. "Okay, darling, whatever you like." Susan rushed out and Pamela closed her eyes. There was obviously no point in arguing.

"She'll calm down when she has you both safely home," offered Bláithín.

"Still here, girls?" Cassandra's voice rang from the surgery door. Her foot and calf were tightly bandaged and padded. She limped over to them, leaning heavily on her crutch.

Bláithín answered, "Well, Pamela's daughter has arrived and is sorting Sophie out and will be back in to sort her mother out." She smiled sympathetically at Pamela. "And I'm still waiting for a taxi, so yes. We are still here. How did you get on?"

"Apart from having to come back here tomorrow to make sure it hasn't swollen more, or the bandages aren't too tight, it's all good and I should be fine in a week or two." She looked at the other two women and shook her head. "What a day, eh? At least we're all good to go."

Pamela could barely muster a smile for her. The prospect of the journey home was not appealing.

Susan rushed back in. "Okay, Mum. Let's get you up and into the car. Take it easy. Here, take my arm."

"Thanks, darling. That's great." Pamela took Susan's arm and limped a few paces towards the door then she turned. "Thank you both for your company and support here. It was lovely to meet you."

"Likewise," said Cassandra. "Take care."

"Yes, mind yourself," added Bláithín.

Pamela disappeared through the archway to the exit.

Cassandra exhaled loudly. "Poor woman! What she needs is a stiff G and T, and a good rant about the state of Ibiza's footpaths. What I suspect she's going to get is a cup of tea and a gentle chat about how 'at her age' she's doing too much."

Bláithín nodded, staring into the distance. "God love her, I'd say you're right." Suddenly, her face brightened, and she looked at Cassandra. "What time's your appointment tomorrow?"

"Four twenty. Why?"

"Mine's at four ten. Hang on." Bláithín rushed to the front door just as Susan was closing it. "Pamela!" she called.

Pamela looked back at her. "Yes?"

"What time's your appointment tomorrow?"

"Four-thirty. Why?"

"The three of us are back here at the same time tomorrow. I'm wondering if you'd like to come for coffee with us afterwards?"

Pamela's eyes brimmed, but she smiled, "Yes, I'd like that very much actually. What a good idea."

"Okay, see you tomorrow. Bye."

Bláithín went back in to Cassandra. Her face was flushed bright pink. "Wow! I have never done that before."

"What?"

"Run after a complete stranger and ask them to meet up the next day."

"Fuck me sideways, as my mother used to say. I've run after, pounced upon, and thrown myself at many complete strangers over the years!"

Bláithín laughed. "Well, it's a new one for me. You will join us, won't you?"

"Absolutely, count me in," Cassandra grinned. "It'll be nice to be with people I'm not hustling for work or contacts." She took out her makeup bag, opened a mirror and stroked more red onto her lips, patted some powder onto her cheeks, and freshened her mascara. "I may have a disgusting-looking ankle, but it's only my face he'll be looking at, today anyway!"

"Who?"

"Reuben. He's my neighbour, also my handyman, and I'm contemplating another role for him!" She wiggled her eyebrows suggestively and Bláithín snorted with laughter.

"Well, I knew I couldn't drive home with this." She indicated her ankle, "And he'd told me he did airport runs, so I rang him when I arrived." She smiled. "He said he'd come immediately, and I think he sounded glad to hear from me." She shrugged. "Though it's hard to know, he's a difficult one to read."

The receptionist looked into the room. "Señora Roche, your taxi is here."

"Thank you, I'll be right out." Bláithín smiled at Cassandra, "I hope you're not waiting too long."

"Ibiza is only twenty-eight miles long, wherever he is, it can't take too long."

Bláithín gave a thumbs up and said, "Good luck with your him. See you tomorrow."

"Yeah, hasta mañana."

CHAPTER EIGHT

The next afternoon, Susan dropped her mother at the clinic and glared up at the steep steps to the Sala de Curas. "This is ridiculous. I mean what if you had a broken hip or something? How are you supposed to get up there? I'll park and come back and help you up."

"I'm sure there must be other ways of getting there, dear," replied Pamela. "But honestly, this is fine. The walking stick you found for me is a great help."

"Well, okay, if you're sure. Good luck! Text me to say how you got on and where to pick you up. I'll be in town around six."

"I did say I could get a taxi."

"No, no. It's no problem. Glen will be home. Belén, his new assistant, is wonderfully efficient. So there's no pressure. See you later." Susan blew a kiss out the window and drove off.

Pamela's leg throbbed with each step, and after standing in line for ten minutes to get checked in and be given a number, she was glad to hobble around the corner to a short, crowded corridor lined with chairs, and sit down.

She scanned the faces for the two women from yesterday. There was no sign of them.

A door opened and Cassandra stormed out, at least as much as anyone with a crutch under one arm and an oversized, turquoise, leather shoulder bag over the other, could storm. She was an unmissable vision in high-waisted, skin-tight, candy-striped trousers, with a matching cropped waistcoat over a tight lace top. She made a bee-line for Pamela and sat next to her. "That orthopaedic-shoe-wearing teenager in there told me I should consider more appropriate footwear for my age!"

"Oh, dear, that seems a bit unnecessary. How is your ankle today?"

"Fine, it didn't get any worse overnight, so a few days

resting it and I'll be back to normal. But honestly, one look at my age and I was consigned to the 'laced-up-brogue' section of footwear shops."

"Ha! Me, too, in a general sense." A soft voice joined in as Bláithín appeared from around the corner next to them, holding a piece of paper. Her hair was frizzing into a halo and her grey coat was bundled over her arm. "Tablets for high blood pressure. When I asked how long I was to take them for, he checked my chart and said, 'At your age, I'd say for the rest of your life.' That was it. No questions on lifestyle, diet, stress- just I'm fifty-five and that's it."

Cassandra stood up. "Bloody Hell! Right, I'm going out for a cigarette, though I suppose that's not appropriate either, given my one good foot is clearly in the grave! I'll wait outside for you."

Bláithín put on her coat. "I'll go out with you. I'm too cross to sit down."

"Pamela Roberts?" A nurse called out from an open doorway.

Bláithín jerked her thumb towards the exit, "We'll wait for you outside."

"Good luck!" Called Cassandra, already at the door, putting on her sunglasses.

Leaning against a sun-warmed wall, Cassandra took a deep satisfying drag on her cigarette, then waved it around as she spoke. "Why are we so easily dismissable? I mean, I work as hard as I ever did. I like to party as much. I work hard at looking good -"

"And you do. You look stunning. That outfit is amazing."

Cassandra looked down at the tiny waistcoat and tight trousers. "Thank you. It's my first time wearing it, but I wasn't fishing. It's just annoying that a woman over fifty is generally deemed incapable, uninteresting, and invisible."

"Nature, I guess," Bláithín shrugged. "We're not much use, childbearing days over equals the scrap heap as far as the continuation of the species is considered."

Her last words were almost drowned out by the furious shrieks of a thwarted toddler. They watched in silence as a harassed and exhausted woman deftly maneuvered a carton of juice out of a large carrier bag into the hand of the screaming child while cradling a sleeping baby in the other arm.

Cassandra shuddered. "Rather her than me! I never wanted children. What about you? Any rugrats?"

"No, they never seemed to be an option in my life. Mind you, it's not a fact that bothers me. Hey, that reminds me, for some reason, how did you get on with your handyman yesterday?"

Cassandra studied her cigarette, and her answer was slow in coming. "It was… 'interesting'. First of all, he insisted I go in the back of the Jeep so I could stretch my leg out on the back seat, and he'd bought a blanket in case I was in shock."

Bláithín nodded approvingly. "Very considerate. Top marks so far."

"Despite my firm intentions to charm the pants off him -"

"Literally, I'm guessing?" Bláithín teased.

"Yup, that was the long-term strategy. Well, maybe a week or so down the road. Unfortunately, with low music playing, his deep voice, and the heater on, I fell asleep before we'd even left Ibiza town."

"Nothing at all to do with the double brandy and the painkillers you told me about?"

Cassandra raised her chin in dismissal. "I only woke when we hit the camino up to my place. Second of all, he had brought dinner from his own freezer which he put in the oven, saying he didn't imagine I'd feel like cooking, but I must eat. Then, there was also this pot of organic, homemade liniment his sister had given him for me, with strict instructions on how to apply it, which he did. Gently and deliciously massaging my ankl -"

"Whoo, hold on," Bláithín, pink-cheeked, waved her

hand to stop Cassandra. "I don't need too many details."

"Unfortunately, there aren't any more to give you. He was a complete bloody gentleman." Cassandra wasn't quite ready to share the feelings that Reuben had aroused in her. Not the breath-catching excitement of his strong, calloused hands gently stroking her skin, nor her almost overwhelming desire to moan for more when he stopped. All that was well within normal, but what had shaken her was her sudden, ridiculous conviction that all was right with the world because he was there. She'd fought off a desire to lay bare her life, with all its mistakes, hurts, and disappointments, and have him say he understood. She desperately hadn't wanted him to leave. In fact, she'd invited him to share the dinner he'd brought over. But he'd muttered there was only enough for one, and anyway, she needed her sleep. Then he'd backed out the door, offering to drive her to the appointment today.

This morning, she'd put her reaction down to shock, painkillers, brandy, and hopefully, her libido waking up after a divorce-induced hibernation. Thinking she may have come across as too needy last night, she'd taken extra care getting ready today. Planning to both wow him and be charmingly dismissive when he arrived to take her to the hospital. The candy stripe outfit seemed the perfect choice. However, she hadn't gotten the chance to do either, as it was his vivacious, denim-clad sister, Rosa, who'd arrived instead.

Bláithín interrupted her thoughts.

"Ah, here she comes," she said, looking past Cassandra.

Pamela was walking towards them, a wry smile on her face. "Well, it's official. I'm a crone."

"What?" Cassandra and Bláithín spoke in unison.

"They kindly explained to me that at this stage of my life, falls are a more frequent occurrence due to muscle weakness, balance problems, vision issues, or a thousand other things. It didn't matter to anyone that I just slipped. It was to be expected at 'my age', so that was that."

Bláithín put her hand on the sleeve of Pamela's

navy jacket and patted her. "Well, I think we've all been unequivocally put in crone category today."

Cassandra ground her cigarette out in the flower bed and flicked the butt into a nearby bin. "Fuck it! We're Ibiza Crones, and that's something! I suggest we move this meeting of the crone club to the nearest pub and have a carajillio."

"A what?" Pamela laughed.

"Coffee and brandy mixed. It's divine."

"I could certainly do with one," sighed Bláithín. "Though" she added looking from Cassandra to Pamela to the steps, "I'm not sure which of you two I should offer to help down these steps."

Cassandra laughed, "Babe, with a crutch and a walking stick and our newfound crone status, we should be able to fly down! Hop on Bláithín, I'll give you a spin!" and she stood astride the crutch and waggled it behind her.

Limping and laughing they made their way down towards the café at the end of the road. They passed two dreadlocked teenagers, their clothes, a kaleidoscope of colours and patterns, sitting on a step, belting out rhythms on two old bongos

Cassandra sighed. "Ah, bongos! The eternal background music to life in Ibiza, they turn up everywhere. No gathering is complete without them." With difficulty, she rummaged in her purse and dropped a few coins into the waiting basket. One of the players paused and blew her a kiss. Cassandra smiled and said, "Keep the spirit going, chicos."

The aluminium chairs rattled as they pulled them around a wooden table in the café, but it didn't disturb the only waitress, who was holding a loud, enthusiastic conversation with her friends down at the back. The bartender, polishing glasses, was riveted to the match on the TV high in the far corner.

Pamela picked up the menu. "I'm not sure about the brandy thing. It's only five o'clock. Susan will think I'm an alcoholic as well as everything else!"

Cassandra stared at her. "Lord lurve a duck, girl! As my mother used to say. Are you driving?"

"Um, no."

"Are you babysitting later?"

Pamela shook her head.

"Have you had a thoroughly rotten few days?"

Pamela nodded.

"Have the bloody brandy."

Cassandra looked around the café. The barman was still oblivious to them. She reached her crutch out and rapped it on the counter. The bartender turned his head and was met by a hundred-watt smile from Cassandra. "Tres carajillos, Guapo."

He grinned back. "Immediately, Señora."

"How did you know his name?" Bláithín asked.

"What?" Cassandra frowned, then she guffawed. "It means handsome!"

"Ha. Sure no wonder he looked pleased instead of annoyed at all that rapping on his counter. See now, I'd still be sitting here furious at being ignored but too embarrassed to walk out."

Pamela looked up from texting her location to Susan and concurred. "Me, too."

"Oh, well, as my mother used to say, fuck him if he can't take a joke!"

Pamela put away her phone. "Your mother seems like quite a character. She must have been great fun?"

Cassandra looked at her blankly. "My mother was an uptight, controlling, manipulative bitch, and *that* was on a good day."

"Wow," Pamela said.

"But why on earth do you keep quoting her?" Bláithín questioned.

"That just started as a way to annoy her. I'd say the most outrageous and shocking things I could think of, to her society friends or at school and attribute them to her. She's been dead for yonks, but I guess I just got into the habit." She shrugged. "It's a bit weird, I suppose."

Pamela folded her arms on the table and leant forward. "That's both funny and sad, but surely your father had something to say?"

"I don't know. He died when I was three and my mother removed all trace of him and married again. Anyway," Cassandra waved her hand, "it's all ancient history and just as dry, dusty, and boring. Let's enjoy this."

She'd twisted in her seat to allow the waitress set a glass cup in a silver holder in front of each of them. Two packets of sugar and biscuit lay on each saucer.

Pamela tasted her carajillio and grimaced. "Gosh! That's strong."

"Add some sugar," instructed Cassandra, as she ripped open her own sachet and emptied the entire packet into her glass. She put her elbows on the table, held her coffee in front of her nose, and inhaled. "Ah, perfect." She blew at the steam rising from the cup then she looked from Pamela to Bláithín. "Okay, what brought you guys to Ibiza, then, and who are you here with?"

Pamela stirred sugar into her coffee and answered first. "Well, my husband died rather suddenly, two years ago, and then, shortly afterward my daughter, who's our only child, wanted to move here with her family so it made sense for me to come with her."

Cassandra nodded. "Yup, I can see that."

Bláithín shrugged. "I'm here by chance. I was made redundant from the firm where I'd worked all my life. I still don't know if that was a blessing or a curse. But then, my boss, felt a bit guilty and offered his apartment in San Antonio to me for a while at a low rent. I was sick to here -" she held a hand to her nose, "of my life and wanted a change. But sure, if he'd had a place in Greece, I'd be there." She hesitated, "I'm here on my own too. I was married, but 'twas nothing to talk about." She turned her dark eyes on Cassandra. "What about you?"

"Well, I lived here for years when I was younger, but now, I'm freshly divorced and here alone. I was supposed to be scouting locations and contacts for a fashion shoot that fell through. I'm staying rent-free in a fab villa, but my time there is running out and I really don't want to leave. Are either of you enjoying living in Ibiza? Given that neither of you actually chose it."

Bláithín shrugged. "Well, I'm not here that long, only a few weeks and I suppose I am a bit disappointed. I don't know what I was hoping for. I'm not one for parties and crowds, but San Antonio is so quiet and closed. Also, I wanted to take photos, but I just haven't been able to take anything I like."

"Oh?" said Pamela. "What style of photography do you do?"

"I don't... I'm not a... I haven't ever taken more than a dozen photos, and they weren't any good. It's just something I always thought I'd really enjoy, and now I find I'm useless at it." Bláithín sipped her sugarless coffee.

Pamela shook her head. "I know how you feel. There's often a whole picture, a feeling in my head about what I want to paint, but what I put on paper is nothing like it. It's quite depressing really."

Cassandra turned to Bláithín "Is that how you feel too?"

"Maybe, kind of. I'm not an arty type at all. I'm more numbers, totals, and lists, but I've photographed some amazing sunsets and taken shots in the old town part of San Antonio which still has some gorgeous old streets. Yet the photos are flat and dead and say nothing about what I'm trying to photograph." She waved the subject away with her hand. "Anyway, what about you Cassandra? Are you happy here?"

Cassandra put her cup down and sat back. "Y'know... I think..." She stared out the window, her dark brown eyes unfocused. "I actually think... I never, ever want to leave Ibiza again! Honestly girls!" She looked at them with shining eyes. "I've just realized it. I abso-fucking-lutely never want to live anywhere else!" She drained her cup and banged it back on its saucer with a flourish.

"Can you do that? How will you live?" Bláithín asked.

"Not got the foggiest! I think I got a kind of job yesterday but nowhere near enough to pay the rent. Since I moved here, I've been feeling more and more attached to Ibiza, in general, and that house in particular. I really didn't realize before now what I was going to do!" She waved her crutch in the air for attention. "I'm having a white wine before I go, to celebrate my decision. Anything else for you two?"

"A café con leche for me, please," replied Bláithín, who then frowned and added, "That's quite a big decision, isn't it, Cassandra?"

"No, it isn't. It suddenly seems crystal clear that I don't want to go back to my London life, such as it was, ever again."

"Well, I think you're quite right, assuming you can make it work. And I'll just have a water," said Pamela, who was still only halfway through her brandy.

Cassandra hailed the barman, shouted the order across, and turned back to the others. "What about you, Bláithín? How long do you plan to stay?"

"Well, until after Christmas anyway, I suppose. I'm living off my redundancy money and that won't last. I'll have to go back and as the chances are that I won't actually get another job at my age..." She sighed. "I'll probably end up signing on the dole. Not the most attractive of propositions."

"There it is again," scoffed Cassandra. "The dreaded 'At My Age.'"

Bláithín tilted her head to consider then nodded. "Yes, well what did you call us? A Crone Club, wasn't it?"

Pamela shuddered. "How awful."

"No! Hang on a sec," said Cassandra as she rooted in her bag for her phone. The others glanced at each other with raised eyebrows while Cassandra's denim blue nails clicked across the surface of her mobile. "Yes! Here it is! According to the latest feminist literature, women are reclaiming and rebranding the word 'crone'. It is no longer to mean a miserable, dried-up old woman but rather the wise and powerful aspect of the triple lunar goddess." She looked at them triumphantly.

"Yes, that's a goddess representing the three stages of woman, isn't it?" Mused Pamela, "I've heard of that. Maiden, Mother, and Crone."

"Also known these days as Flirty, Fertile, and Fuck off," Cassandra beamed at them.

Pamela's snort of laughter made her choke on the water she was drinking. A giggling Bláithín patted Pamela's back and handed her a tissue for the water reappearing down her nose.

"Well, that didn't feel very goddess-like," declared Pamela when the laughter had died down.

"And I'm not sure I dispense any wisdom either," said Bláithín. The barman delivered their drinks. His smile was clearly directed at Cassandra, who winked at him as she accepted her wine. She fortified herself with a sip and launched straight back to her point.

"No! You are and you do. Not in a magic wand-waving way, but I bet you helped the younger people at work, didn't you Bláithín?"

"Yes, God bless them, most couldn't figure their way through an itemized shopping bill, not to mind a payroll ledger."

"And you, Pamela, I'm sure you advise your daughter on the ups and downs of child-rearing."

"Of course, because I've been through it all before."

"Exactly my point. Three of my staff left to form their own company because of what I taught them. That's just the way it goes, and we should be proud of it."

Pamela laughed at Cassandra's enthusiasm. "You're saying we should embrace our inner crone?"

"No. Our inner crone goddess! And we're Ibiza Goddesses as well. How can we not feel special?"

"Ibiza or not, it's still 'crone', isn't it?" Sighed Pamela. "I hate getting old. I just hate it. The jowls, the saggy, Japanese crackle-glazed skin on my chest..."

"I definitely don't know what that is, but I do know what you mean," said Bláithín. "And I'll add 'eyesight going'."

"Hair getting thin."

"Hearing going."

"Thread veins, spider veins, and varicose veins."

"Drooping eyelids."

"Stop! Stop!" Cassandra waved her glass at them. "That's all true, but you're looking at it the wrong way. Okay, be honest. If you listed all the problems you had when you were in your teens and twenties, what would you say?"

"Terrible acne," admitted Bláithín.

"Horribly shy."

"Insecure."

"No boobs."

"Too thin."

"Too fat."

"Anxiety."

"Exactly!" said Cassandra. "And I could add, feeling stifled and suffocated, no freedom, no money, no friends." She drained her glass.

They looked at each other in silence.

Cassandra continued, "There you are. We don't have problems just because we're getting older- we have problems because we're human. Every age has problems."

Pamela was nodding in agreement.

Cassandra warmed to her theme. "When you're young, you think there are endless years ahead of you for everything to somehow get better. Then the urgency and distraction of work, family, life, love, or whatever, takes over. But when you're older you realize that one fucking problem is replaced by another and, if you're lucky, how little any of them matter in the grand scheme of things."

The waitress came and cleared away their empty glasses. Pamela looked at her watch. "Gracious! The time! It's nearly six. Susan will be here any minute."

"Ooops!" Bláithín stood and started to pull on her coat. "I

must rush, the bus is at half-past six."

Cassandra slapped the table. "Bugger! I must go and collect some business cards before I meet my lift home."

"Oh, the handsome Reuben again?" Bláithín smirked.

Cassandra's mouth turned down. "If only! No, it's his sister Rosa, she's working in Ibiza town today and offered to pick me up." She raised her arm and scribbled in the air for the bill, then paid for it, waving away their objections. "Next time, we'll share."

On the way out, she waved at the waiter.

"Ciao Guapa!" he called after her as she left the café.

Outside, despite the still-shining sun, dusk was streaking the sky with pink. Cassandra put a hand on each of her new friend's arms. "I'd love to continue our chat about our Crone Club. How about we meet up again? Maybe for a meal some evening?"

Pamela's response was instant. "Oh, sounds like a lovely idea. I really did enjoy the afternoon, but I must check with Susan first in case she has any plans."

Bláithín said, "I'm up for it, and I'm free any evening you want."

Cassandra took out her phone. "How about we say this day next week?" The other two nodded. "Right, give me your numbers and we'll arrange it." She had just added them when a horn sounded from down the road and an arm waved out the window.

Pamela waved back. "That's Susan, I'm off. I look forward to seeing you both soon."

"Yes, indeed! Well, take care of yourselves," said Bláithín.

Cassandra slid her huge sunglasses down from their perch on her head, air-kissed them both, and said, "I'll be in touch. Oh, and girls, don't do too much flying!"

Laughing, the three women went their separate ways.

CHAPTER NINE

Cassandra's hands shook as she twisted the metal cannabis grinder. A strong spliff was definitely called for. She'd been so sure of this outfit when she had put it on this morning. She'd felt like a million dollars in it, and now look at her.

Coffee with her crone club had been fab. She'd still been smiling as she navigated the neatly gridded streets of Ibiza's new town. Even with her crutch, it hadn't taken her long to reach the print shop from the café. She took off her sunglasses and stepped through the open door. A girl's voice, speaking rapid Spanish carried from behind a partition. Cassandra put her glasses on the counter and rooted in her bag for the collection docket. The girl finished her call and stepped around into the shop with a smile on her face.

"Wow!" Cassandra couldn't manage more.

The young girl's candy-striped waistcoat was worn over her bare, brown, smooth skin and the high-waisted trousers were moulded to the contours of a tiny waist and curvaceous hips.

"Ha! What are the chances?" The girl swung back her waist-length, blond hair and said, "Cool outfits, aren't they? Did you get yours in Ibiza?" She didn't wait for an answer as she took the docket from Cassandra's immobile hand.

The smell of coffee reached them. A young man sauntered through the shop carrying two takeaway cups. "Ooh, ladies, an embarrassing F.S.S!" Looking at Cassandra's face, he clarified. "Fashion Snap Situation." He smirked as he disappeared behind the screen.

The girl rolled her eyes and handed Cassandra her cards. "Take no notice of him, he's a prat."

Cassandra took the small packet and left.

She patted her head to pull down her shades and realised

they were still on the counter. She stepped back in to pick them up. The conversation was clear.

"Well, that was a definite 'Bring a Matching Granny to Work' moment!"

"Shut up, Leo. I thought she was very brave."

"Brave is fighting dragons, darling, not parading around in clothes that are positively generations too young for you."

"You're a wanker! Leave her alone, bless her."

It had been the pity in the girl's voice that had undone Cassandra.

She'd held herself together until she got home. She'd met Rosa and chatted brightly the whole way and even invited her in for wine, which mercifully, Rosa had declined. Cassandra tore open her waistcoat before she even closed the front door, and soon the whole damn ensemble lay in a heap on the floor.

Now, lying on the couch, her white bathrobe wrapped around her, Cassandra lit her expertly rolled joint and inhaled deeply. With a large glass of white wine half-finished and her spliff lighting, she didn't have to pretend for anybody, and tears transported mascara down her cheeks.

She stared through the window into the dark evening. A watery moon threw purple shadows across fleeing clouds, and the opened curtains turned the terrace into a moonlit stage.

Emotion warred with logic as she tried to figure out what she felt, and why she felt it. When had she crossed the line from stylish and vivacious to old and daring?

She sat up, finished off the glass, and refilled it from the bottle on the floor next to it. She inhaled again and lay back. Releasing the smoke in a thin trickle, she watched it unfurl as it floated and faded its way across the dim room. She spoke aloud to herself, "Get a grip. This isn't a big deal." She closed her eyes as she answered herself. "Maybe not, but that pile of waste material is going into the recycling tomorrow."

***

For some reason, the voice didn't startle her.

"Daughter, why do you bemoan the inevitable rather than celebrate the reality?"

Cassandra opened her eyes. A figure stood silhouetted against the wide window.

"What the fuck?" She waved her hand in front of her to shoo away the image, then she looked at the spliff burning between her fingers and took another hit. She closed her eyes and held the smoke deep and long. She slowly and deliberately exhaled and opened her eyes.

The figure was still there, in a white full-length dress.

"Who the buggery are you? Are you a ghost? If you are -" Cassandra giggled. "or even if you aren't, I admire your taste. I'm pretty sure that's a Chanel dress!"

"I am Tanit. My name is lost to most. My story forgotten."

The long, white curtains swayed and rustled in the gentle breeze and blurred with the loose folds of the woman's dress.

"Here, in ancient centuries, my temple stood. My children came and tended me. Fed by their devotion, I flourished, but war, false religions, and changing times reduced me. You sought me. Your worship of my world awoke me."

"I did? It did?" Baffled, Cassandra squinted at the woman, trying to bring her into focus.

"Child, you are cast down by trifles."

"Trifles!" Cassandra snorted and took another long drink from her glass. She gestured at the bottle. "I don't know who you are, how you got in, or even if you are actually here, but would you like a drink?

"I need no sustenance other than what you have given me these past few weeks."

Cassandra looked again at her spliff trying to remember who she had bought her stash from.

"You have shared mind, heart and soul with me these past times, and have I not filled you up with peace, hope, and energy?"

"Yes! I've felt wonderful. In fact, you know -" she leant

forward and confided, "- just today I decided I want to stay here forever."

"Yes, child, so I have decreed it. And yet the wailing of your spirit disturbs the ether."

"Wailing of my...?" Cassandra considered for a moment. "Well, yes, I suppose I can see that. You see, I had the most fucking, humiliatingly awful experience," she explained as she drained her glass and waved her hand around to feel for the bottle. "I mean, I bet that teenager isn't in tears tonight because she saw me in the same clothes!"

"They spoke out of fear, why worry?"

"Fear?"

"Yes. The greatest fear of youth is old age. It awaits all, with no escape bar death. Humans belittle and revile that which they fear in order to reduce it to an object of ridicule and thus promote their own superiority. Youth is arrogant and blind and possessed of no understanding."

"But I'm old. I'm an old crone."

"Speak not of crones, nor maidens nor hags- all are one. Every timorous, biddable, new moon virgin grows towards the strength of the mother. In every fecund woman waxes the power and knowledge of my Full Moon daughter."

"I notice we're not talking waning moons here?" Cass brought the joint to her lips again and swore as the paper burnt her fingers. "Isn't that what I am? A useless, waning crone?"

The woman stepped closer. Cassandra frowned. "Hey, your hat -" Cassandra jabbed her finger towards it as she spoke. "Is that a... what the fuck is it? I mean, I love it, I think." She tilted her head to study the woman. "It's got a kind of Jackie Onassis look going on." She sat up straighter on the couch. "You remind me of... remind me of... bugger me backwards, as Mother would say, I can't remember, but you... definitely... remind me... of something." She nodded, very satisfied with her powers of observation, and filled her glass again.

The woman's voice was gentle.

"No, child. It is given to all things to wane, but only my

daughters share the cyclical rhythm at my pace. A full-grown woman is not one who has attained twenty summers nor thirty, but one who has lived the cycles of life, and learned to use the power and knowledge she has gained."

"But I never had children. I'm not a mother."

"The mother figure is not merely about children. You created and nurtured a successful endeavor, did you not? Others nurture students, relationships, even homes."

"I get you." Cassandra nodded knowledgeably. "Kind of an all-purpose person really." She waved a finger, "Not all mothers are all porpoises... all proposals... Fuck it, not the same."

"My Full Moon daughters were always the healers, the helpers, the advisors. Their homes were meeting places in times of trouble. They weren't swayed from naming deeds wrong by a handsome face."

"Like the time I let that fabulous looking fucker whatsis name persuade me to 'borrow' my mother's car. Christ on a bicycle, I'd like to see him try now!"

"- or quietened by bullies. As such they were powerful beyond measure. And so, were slowly silenced by king and church. Called evil, heretic, witch, words to push them into the silent corners of history."

The woman's pale face reflected the moon, now free of its cloaking clouds, and she seemed to light up the room.

"Now, in this chaotic age, I feel my Full Moon Daughters move, no longer content to be hidden. They raise their voice. Bring my acolytes to my temple."

"You mean your Crones?" Cassandra laughed.

"Yes, those of my Full Moon daughters granted the gift of a full lifespan by the god of time, Cronus, might well be called such, but it is a boon, not a curse. Crone comes from Croune, meaning crown. Reach for yours, Cassandra, and claim it." She advanced towards the couch.

Cassandra threw her arm across her eyes. The light was too much, it was almost a heat she could feel on her cheeks.

"I'm sorry could you just -"

She opened her eyes to the glare of the morning sun toasting her as she lay on the couch with a thumping headache and an urgent need to pee.

CHAPTER TEN

An hour later, with paracetamol dulling her headache and half a liter of electrolyte sports drink rehydrating her system, the full impact of her visitor hit home. Of course, that figure had been familiar. It was Tanit, that pervasive Ibiza icon. That face, the crazy hat and hair. Cassandra had seen it so often. Everywhere from doggy hairdressers to brothels used the name and image. Years ago, she had even taken part in wonderful, full moon, goddess-worshipping raves, or as she used to think of them, naked drinking parties on the beach, but this was on a different level altogether. It was clear there were only three options, the pot had been major league strong, she'd had a psychotic episode, or Tanit really had really spoken to her!

Real or not, she remembered the whole exchange. One particular sentence from the completely bewildering but strangely sensible conversation was on repeat in her head. 'Bring my acolytes to my temple'.

What the bloody hell was that supposed to mean?

She wondered how she'd recount her experience to the Crone Club, Was it a humorous, drunken incident, a genuine spiritual experience, or a psychotic episode? She was pondering this when the phone rang.

"Hello, Cassandra. This is Evelyn."

"Fuck!" Cassandra muttered under her breath. She did not want to talk to her step-sister now.

"Oh?"

"I've been trying to talk to you, but you keep declining my calls and you never ring back."

"I'm not sure there's much to say."

"I need to talk to you about dad's house. I know he wasn't much of a stepdad to you, but he truly loved your mother."

"Well, he must have, to have stayed with that battle axe for so long," Cassandra scoffed.

"Ha! But then, she never turned that side of her on him or us. She was never as awful to Debs and me as she was to you." Evelyn sounded apologetic.

"Of course, you guys took the precautions of not being her daughters. Having your own mother have custody of you and being sent to boarding school for good measure. Anyway, she's been dead for eons, so what's all this about? I don't suppose your father left me a fortune in his will?"

"Ha, sorry, no such luck! There was only the house and we're going to sell it now, so we need to clear it out. He had a whole room full of your mother's things locked away. Do you want us to send them to you?"

"Christ no! Bin it, for all I care!" The memory of the tall, suffocating house made her shudder. Cassandra had fought her mother's control there for years before she fled to Ibiza. Her stepfather, a staid, ineffectual man, had barely figured in her life.

"But there are some rather lovely clothes here," Evelyn persisted.

"Please don't bring her back to haunt me. It took me years to get over her constant disapproval and control."

"I know, Cassandra. She was way too strict with you."

"Strict?" Cassandra scoffed. "You mean downright abusive. Christ, do you remember when you and Debs were competing in every gymkhana there was? I had to pretend I was working in the school library so I could slip away to muck out the local stables in return for riding lessons." Cassandra heard her voice rising and took a deep breath through her nose and forced herself to calm down. "Sorry, I don't know where that petty piece of memory came from."

Evelyn laughed. "Of course, I remember. I forged your mother's signature for the permission letter for the stables. Oh, God, I remember you getting caught!"

Cassandra groaned. "Bloody hell, yes. That was the

appalling argument where I threw a book and smashed the stained-glass window. I was a never-ending source of disappointment for my mother."

"I'm sorry if I upset you, Cassandra, we just thought we should check first."

"I appreciate it, but dead or not, that woman can fuck right off!"

"Okay, if you're sure, Cassandra, we'll give it all away. In that case, I'll say goodbye and wish you all the best."

"Thanks for checking, Evelyn, I appreciate it. Bye,"

Cassandra put down her phone and exclaimed, "Bloody Hell! After all these years, my mother's clothes! Will she never stop plaguing me?"

Too unsettled to meditate, Cassandra went for the distraction route. It took two minutes to get her laptop going and to begin a search on Tanit. The information was instant. Dalt Vila, that ancient walled village rising up a steep hill in Ibiza town, had once been the site of a temple to Tanit, and so too had this headland of Cala San Vicent. According to the web, somewhere high in the cliffs overlooking the sea, were the ruins of a temple to Tanit. Thousands of little clay representations of her new friend were found there. Placed there by ancient Phoenician and Ibicencan worshippers.

Phoenician? Wasn't that what Reuben said the back wall of her house was? She was on her knees in front of the cupboard before she could think about it, staring in at the ancient stone. Hesitantly, she stretched her hand out and pressed it to the curiously warm rock. Heartfelt words escaped her lips before she could even think of feeling foolish. "Tanit. Mother."

There was no soft whisper in response, no magic tingling down her arm. She stood up, laughing at herself. Wiping the dust from her hands, she returned to the laptop. She continued to click and scroll. The information was endless. Goddess of fertility, agriculture, rebirth, a moon goddess, most closely associated with women, her temples always situated by fresh water. Her eyes widened and she peered closer to the screen. "Child sacrifice? No fucking way!" She scraped her chair back and was on her feet before she deleted the pages and slammed the laptop closed.

"I'm out of here!" she shouted at the empty house. Ignoring the pain in her bandaged ankle she drove her car far too fast down the rutted and crumbling camino to the main road, swearing as loudly and inventively as she could to keep ridiculous tears at bay. She headed to San Carlos, the nearest village, where she sat in the Death Seat on the pavement corner outside Bar Anita. What did she care if a car careered too sharply around the right-angled bend and blew her away?

By the time her double espresso arrived, she was trying to calm herself, to question what she was feeling, and why. A chair was thumped down beside her; Reuben put his coffee on the table and joined her.

"What's wrong, Cassandra? Why do you look so desolate?"

She barely looked at him. "Desolate! That's the word, that's how I feel."

"But what has happened? I was on my way home, but I passed here and saw your face. Can I help?"

To her annoyance, the hot prickle of tears forced her to grab a napkin from its dispenser and scrub at her eyes with the thin, hard paper.

"I don't know, because I don't know what's wrong, exactly. I felt so unbelievably at home in that house, so... everything's coming right, and happy, and then..." she turned to look at him. "Do you know anything about Tanit?"

Reuben didn't blink at this apparent non-sequitur. "Yes, as it happens, I do. I worked some summers at Es Culleram, her temple on the headland. What do you want to know about our Goddess?

"How can a loving fucking mother, Moon Goddess of fertility, life, and rebirth, demand child sacrifice? Explain that!"

Reuben rubbed his chin which was dark with stubble. "I don't think she did, Cassandra."

"Oh no, you don't get off that easily! Sure, there's no mention of it in the guidebooks or the cute ads for the island, but two seconds on the history sites make it very clear that it is widely accepted that horrors were performed in her name, and I can't bear it, for some reason I truly can't bear it."

Reuben leaned forward. "But a bit longer on science sites would have shown you many experts think the whole situation was misread and indeed, used as a form of ancient fake news."

"Oh?"

He plonked his elbows on the table, held out his hands, and counted on his fingers.

"First of all, there are absolutely and definitively no signs of sacrifice at any of her temples in Ibiza. That's been checked and rechecked by scientists and archaeologists after years of thorough research."

Cassandra took a deep breath and found she could now drink her coffee. She also began to regret that she had left home without looking in a mirror.

A second finger went down. "Second of all, in 2010, a Professor Jeffrey H. Schwartz published an in-depth scientific analysis which concluded that these 'sacrificial' sites in Carthaginian settlements, were, in fact, sites reserved for the cremated remains of stillbirths, miscarriages, neonates, babies, and children up to the age of two or three who died of natural causes and were placed in Tanit's temples to be cared for by her until their rebirth."

Cassandra sighed, "That's a much better scenario."

Reuben held up a hand. "I don't think anyone is saying human sacrifice didn't exist. We know it did, from the earliest times. But it certainly wasn't the wholesale horror that people inferred from the burial sites. Given that seven out of ten children were likely to die in their first year, add in plagues, famines, wars, and the fact infants and babies weren't considered real people and weren't buried in the general graveyard, it's no wonder these sites held so many remains." He smiled and picked up his coffee. "Lecture over. Does that help?"

Impulsively, she reached over and caught his hand. "Oh, you have no idea how much."

He stroked the back of her hand with his thumb, "Do you want to tell me what this was all about?"

"You might decide I'm crazy."

"Take the chance."

"I think I spoke to Tanit the other night. I admit I was smoking quite a strong mix, but nevertheless, I think I did."

Reuben nodded. "Sometimes we need some help to see beyond what's around us, and who knows what an opened mind might see?"

Cassandra narrowed her eyes, "Are you humouring me?"

He shook his head and held a palm up. "No, it's true, I swear."

"So, last night, I thought I had a wonderful conversation with her, and she explained a lot to me. Today, when I'd recovered from an appalling hangover, I was totally buoyed up and hopeful. Then, I Googled her and read that awful stuff. It was like an almighty crash and burn that I couldn't cope with. Thank God you came along when you did. I think I was falling apart. Maybe I'm crazy?"

"'There are more things in Heaven and Earth, Horatio, than are dreamt of in your philosophy.'" He raised his eyebrows at the surprise on her face and added, "Advantages of an English education."

"Well, I had one too and I'd go more for 'Why, sometimes I've believed as many as six impossible things before breakfast!'"

His laughter turned heads at neighbouring tables, "Ah, you can't beat Lewis Carroll!"

Cassandra's grin lit her face, "You know it? I'm genuinely impressed."

They became aware of their entwined hands at the same moment and let go. Reuben sat back. "You no longer look desolate, I'm glad to say."

"I don't feel it either. Thank you. I suppose I overreacted, but you arrived just in time."

"How is your ankle? Should you be driving?"

His question reminded her of their last meeting and how overwrought she'd been and here she was, at it again! Annoyed at herself, she tossed her hair back and sat straighter. "Oh, I'm much better, thank you. In fact, I should be going, I've loads to do, new job and all that."

He tossed some coins on the table and stood. "Me too. See you around, Cassandra Collingsworth."

She didn't want him to go, she wanted to ask him to share a bottle of wine with her and chat about random stuff, to make him laugh, to hold his hand again, but she said, "Cool, see you Reuben." He didn't budge, for a moment they stared at each other. His expression was unreadable, but it seemed like an effort for him to turn away and cross the road to his car.

CHAPTER ELEVEN

Maite scrutinized Bláithín. "How are you? Do you need to go back more to the hospital?"

Bláithín gaped back. She'd just called into the shop to pick up some milk.

"Maite! How on Earth did you know I'd been in hospital?"

"Pedro's cousin, Ángeles works there. She saw your name yesterday and she telled me. Is such pretty and funny name, I telled her spelling when she was here last week."

Bláithín was torn between resenting the blatant lack of privacy and liking the concern and interest being shown for her in her new life. She decided to shrug it off as one of those 'only in Spain' things and smiled at Maite.

"I'm fine, thank you. Nothing to worry about, just a bit of high blood pressure, and it's 'she told me.' Irregular verb, remember?"

Maite rolled her eyes. "Oh yes, told, thank you." She patted her stomach, which seemed to Bláithín to have expanded impossibly in the last few weeks. "You must be careful and rest, like me!"

"How are you?"

"Oh, I'm perfect. This little one has three more weeks. Is exciting, no?"

Bláithín took a bottle of milk from the tall fridge and handed Maite the money for it. "Yes, indeed, very exciting."

***

Buoyed up by her meeting with her friends and the prospect of an evening out with them. Bláithín became more proactive with her photography. She'd carried her camera everywhere with her. It was in her shoulder bag because around her neck would be too pretentious or just plain touristy. But apart from the fact the bag was awkward, heavy, and wanted to slip off her shoulder, the very act of taking the big camera out of it made her feel self-conscious straight away.

The next morning, Bláithín emptied the bag onto the kitchen table to see what on earth was making it so darn full. Sheaves of old shop offers and receipts, mostly out of date, tissues, three biros, a notebook, headache tablets, sunglasses, open chewing gum going soft, a novel, lipstick, and a mirror she could never remember using, a small hair brush, hand sanitizer and a packet of deodorant wipes, and her purse. She looked at the mess and wondered what she really needed. Her hands were already answering for her as they pulled open the drawer in the table and swept everything in. She put her purse, glasses, and keys into a zipped pocket in her jacket. Then she put the camera around her neck and went out.

It was strangely liberating, walking around without a bag. Bláithín had never really been comfortable using one, and certainly never had a collection of them to accessorize outfits. She used a plain leather bag until it fell apart, then bought more or less the same again. Fancy handbags had always felt like the badge of some club that she didn't really belong to.

She focused her photographic wanderings around the old alleys and plazas, not pressuring herself to take perfect photos, but just getting a feel for the camera. After just two days, the camera around her neck became part of her.

Over the weekend, Bláithín even unpacked her printer, thinking maybe she'd have some photos to show her fellow crones on Wednesday. Immediately, every reason under the sun why she shouldn't even dream of doing that filled her mind. Bláithín Roche, you're really getting ahead of yourself here, aren't you? Why would anyone want to look at photos you've taken? Right fool you'd look turning up to dinner with your snaps. Somehow, she didn't allow it to stop her from setting up her printer on one end of the dining table.

When the phone rang on Monday morning, she assumed it was Cassandra with an address for meeting up on

Wednesday, which made the switch from happy anticipation to downright shock and horror all the more brutal.

Pauline's voice was shrill. "Bláithín! God love you! Are you alright? We've booked to come out to you for a week. We'll be arriving on Wednesday."

"Whaat? Pauline! No! No, don't! I'm fine."

Pauline was still talking over her. "Oh! When I told Diarmuid that you'd collapsed and had to be brought to hospital by ambulance, he was beside himself! Said he knew we should never have let you go off there to that place. We can help you pack to come back."

"No! No. No. I just fainted. There's no need to fuss. How on Earth did you know?"

"Oh, Andy told me. He rang your one in the shop to talk about arrangements for the flat when she has her baby. It's due soon, y'know, and she told him that his tenant had been taken to hospital after collapsing! God Almighty, it put the heart across us when he rang!"

"Pauline! Of course, I know about her baby! I see Maite every day and I wasn't taken anywhere by ambulance…"

"Oh, you sound very stressed, and why wouldn't you? What a dose, and you there on your own and all."

"Please, there's no need to come, at all."

"Sure, it's booked now, and we don't ever get away. You know Diarmuid, fishing in Kilkee is as far as he'll go. But when he heard of this emergency there was no stopping him, and didn't Andy tell us it was a two-bedroom flat? So it will be grand."

"Oh, God, Pauline," Bláithín said weakly, words failing her at the awfulness of the prospect. "I won't even be here on Wednesday. I'm meeting friends."

"Friends? That was fast! Are you sure you should be doing that? I mean, you just out of hospital and all."

"For God's sake, Pauline! I was only in there for an hour or two, and back in the clinic the next day for a checkup. It's only high blood pressure, half the world has it and I'm taking tabs, I'm fine."

"We'll see for ourselves when we get there. I'll bring some tea and sausages. I won't keep talking now, this is a very expensive call. I'll let you know what time we'll be coming in. God bless!" Pauline hung up and Bláithín was left glaring at the phone as if it were some
how responsible for this debacle.

Bláithín was filled with a paralyzing apathy by the depressing thought of Diarmuid and Pauline in such interfering, meddlesome proximity that her camera lay untouched for the next few days. Even the text from Cassandra confirming a place and time for their evening out just served to underline how miserable she felt.

***

She barely had their bed made up by the time they arrived on Wednesday morning.

The bell made her jump. She made her way down through what she suddenly saw as her corridor, her lift, and her foyer. She buzzed open the front door and was nose to nose with Pauline who was standing on the top step. Two patches of red flared in her thin, grey face and her eyes were glittering with excitement.

"Bláithín! You poor thing!" Bláithín was pulled into an embrace of overpowering duty-free fragrance. Pauline stood back, holding Bláithín at arm's length and inspecting her as if she were a piece of furniture she wasn't too sure about. "She doesn't look too bad, does she, Diarmuid?"

Bláithín moved aside and Pauline stepped in. Diarmuid followed with two suitcases. He looked tired and slightly stooped. The strong arcs of the family eyebrows were as dark as ever, but his thinning hair had receded so much he looked quite monkish.

Pauline scanned the foyer. "Oh, this is very grand indeed."

Diarmuid patted Bláithín on the arm. "Are you feeling yourself again?" he asked gruffly.

"Yes, I told Pauline I was fine. There was no need for you to come." Even as she said it, she realized how ungracious she sounded and added, "But it's kind of you to have made the journey."

"Well, we only have each other." His voice was soft but the sincerity of it hit her like a brick.

She hugged him. "It's nice to see you, honestly."

All the way up to the apartment, Pauline kept up a running commentary on the quality, colour shape, and size of everything. The palm trees were too big and would surely die in those jars, and the chairs in the foyer let the place down, they were too cheap. At least the lift was big enough, but wouldn't you think they'd put brighter lights in the corridor?

Bláithín opened the door to the apartment and Pauline took it in at a glance. "Oh, God love you! There isn't a bit of comfort in here. Thank God you'll be coming home soon. Sit down Bláithín, I'll make us a cup of tea." Bláithín discovered she didn't have the energy to object. Diarmuid was instructed to put the bags away and Pauline bustled around making herself at home. She wrinkled her nose at the milk. "This is very odd. Can't you get real stuff here?"

Bláithín shrugged. "You get used to it."

Diarmuid was put to cooking the sausages and Bláithín watched as her kitchen was taken over. How would she survive a whole week of this? Thank God, she was going out tonight.

CHAPTER TWELVE

Pamela had hurried down the street and sat into the car before Susan could cause chaos with her double-parking. The children, belted into their seats in the back, were watching cartoons on a tablet. Sophie blew a kiss at Pamela. "Hi Grandma, can I see your new bandage?"

"Eye Gamma, banash?" Clark copied.

Pamela lifted her leg up. The pristine thick covering didn't offer much excitement, so they subsided back to their cartoons.

Pamela smiled as Cassandra raised her crutch in salute as she passed.

"Oh, she seems a bit flashy for you, Mum." Susan's remark seemed uncharacteristically snippy. Pamela looked across at her daughter. Susan's mouth was a tight line and she frowned as she edged her way back into the traffic. The fact the children were watching cartoons in the car was unusual too. Susan was usually a stickler that devices in the car were a last resort for long journeys - definitely not normal for a twenty-minute pick-up.

"Are you okay, Susan? I thought Glen was going to be home and you wouldn't have had to take -" she indicated the children with a glance, "- with you?"

Susan scowled. "Well, he wasn't, yet again! Anyway, did they tell you how long you have to go for daily bandage changing?"

Pamela took the hint and changed the subject.

Later, in the kitchen when the children were asleep and Glen still wasn't home, Pamela tried again. "Sweetheart, what's wrong?"

Susan stared down at the plate in her hand then sighed

and pulled out a chair. "It's Glen."

"Oh no! What's wrong with him? Is he ill?"

"No! Nothing like that. I don't know. At least, I'm not sure. It's just that he's not happy."

Pamela leant back in her chair and exhaled loudly. "Oh Susan, he's probably just stressed. The move can't have been easy for him and let's face it, I know you go in two afternoons a week to do emails and invoices but all the concept, design, delivery, everything is all on him."

"But it's what he loves and it's all he ever wanted to do!"

Pamela knew the truth of this. They had spent many nights around her mahogany dining table, the London traffic a constant grumble outside the big bay window, listening to Glen, alight with enthusiasm expounding on their plans. Striding up and down the room he tried to explain his new software to her uncomprehending ears. It was going to allow them to create amazing websites, they were going to target high-profile businesses, a few years of hard slog and they were going to be top of the game. Susan had watched, eyes shining, nodding in agreement.

Now, though, Susan sounded aggrieved. "I never asked him to work so hard."

"Well, look, darling, are you sure? Has he said anything to you or are you just guessing?"

"I know him, Mum! I know when he's not happy!"

"Wait, Susan! Are you thinking he's not happy with you?"

"Um, I don't know. Maybe?"

"Ah, Susan, that's ridiculous! After nine happy years together, something like this isn't going to happen out of the blue!"

Susan trailed her finger around a knothole in the polished wood of the table. "I'm not sure it did Mum. Not really."

"What? Susan, you must talk to him!" Pamela got up as she was talking and filled the kettle. "Problems can be resolved, and very often you find they're not as bad as you imagined when you actually speak about them. Then there's always couples counseling, if things ever get that bad."

"We've already been there, Mum."

Susan's voice was so low Pamela wasn't sure she'd heard her correctly. "What?"

"We did that three years ago."

Pamela replaced the kettle on the unlit hob and sat down again. She spread her hands. "You never said."

Susan looked away. "Well, you two were stressed to the hilt with selling up and moving to Scotland, and I was sure it was only a flash in the pan, and he'd get over it."

Pamela's hand went to her throat. "Get over it? Do you mean he had an affair?"

"God! No! No, the counseling really helped. We were back on track again and I got pregnant with Clark," she smiled. "How could things not have been perfect then?"

"But what was wrong, Susan? What was the problem?"

Susan got up and lit the hob under the kettle. She took out mugs and milk as she spoke. "Ah, it wasn't anything really. I think it was just work-related stress that he blamed family life for."

"What did the counselor say? I can't believe you went through all that and never told me. That's terrible." Pamela covered her mouth with her hand. "Oh God, Susan! What kind of mother was I that I didn't notice?"

"The kind that was emptying, packing, and selling the house they'd lived in for nearly forty years! And, honestly, Mum, I knew it would be fine. I knew it was something Glen just had to work through and be normal again, and I was right."

The beams from Glen's car turning into the courtyard swung through the kitchen like a searchlight. "He's home! Please don't say anything, Mum. We'll work it out, I'm sure."

Pamela, still reeling from these revelations, hugged her daughter close, and slipped out the side door to her own place.

She was awake most of the night wondering how on earth she had managed to miss this major upset in her daughter's life. True, they'd had been preoccupied with the move to Scotland, and any visit by Susan, Glen, and Sophie had been taken up with sorting out boxes of clothes and books, but even examining it with hindsight, she honestly couldn't say she had seen any traces of stress or strain in her daughter.

Around four-thirty, she took her third cup of tea into her little sitting room, her slippers noiseless on the tiles. She curled up at the end of her sofa and cupped her hands around her mug. Maybe Susan was overreacting? Maybe she just wasn't reading the situation correctly?

She stared out at the dappled moonlight shadows across the gravel and the dark banks of the lavender. A movement caught her eye, and parting clouds revealed Glen sitting on the top step of the pool with his head in his hands. Pamela jumped to her feet, absurdly afraid he'd see her, and closed the door behind her as she headed back to bed.

By morning she'd decided her best course was to give them a bit of space. Living with your mother-in-law or even your mother, when you're rowing can't be easy.

It wasn't difficult to keep a low profile. The next morning, Susan honked the car horn and when Pamela looked out, Susan had Clark loaded in and was ready to go. "Mum, you need to rest that leg. I'll take Clark out with me, and after we collect Sophie, Clark has a play date. Don't worry about anything."

Maybe Susan regretted blurting it all out and was trying to avoid any more conversations? It certainly seemed that way over the next few days as they barely saw each other. Every night there were different people at the house for drinks or dinner. It seemed like a good sign. All marriages were different and maybe this is how they were dealing with it. Susan's lively conversation and laughter carried across to Pamela and made her feel a bit better.

Her leg was healing well, so she drove herself to the

clinic for the next two appointments. At last, on Friday, she was loaded with creams and bandages and told to continue treatment herself, unless she was worried.

By Sunday, when the drive was full of cars and the garden full of children, Pamela took her paints out again. While she was setting them up, her phone pinged with a message from Cassandra confirming the next meeting of the newly formed ´Crone Club`. She smiled as she responded with a thumbs up.

She set up her easel and got lost trying to create a moonlit figure against a wind-rippled pool.

CHAPTER THIRTEEN

A tall, young waiter led the three friends through a long, narrow, dark bar, to a courtyard warmed by a wood-fired pizza oven on one side, and the flickering flames of space heaters at the other. Fairy lights twined their way up the tortured branches of an ancient olive tree and glittering chandeliers hung from beams attaching the outside of the main building to the rough stone wall of the courtyard. The place was full and buzzing with conversation. "Bloody good job I booked a table," Cassandra said as they pulled out their chairs at a small, circular, wooden table under one of the glowing chandeliers. "Prosecco all around?" she suggested, as soon as they were all seated. She smiled up at the waiter whose smile was as bright as hers, lighting up blue eyes that were startling against his dark skin. She didn't wait for her friends to answer before adding, "In fact, bring a bottle!" She looked at their faces. "Oops, sorry, I'm doing it again, organizing everyone! Are you both actually okay with Prosecco to start?"

Bláithín laughed. "After my week, you could make it a bottle each."

Pamela said, "I'm not a drinker, but a bottle of anything sounds good right now."

"Wow! Sounds like we all have a lot to talk about tonight! Yup, a bottle please," Cassandra confirmed to the waiter, who left them with a small bow. "I thought a bottle would be good while I told you about an astounding experience I either had or didn't have -" She laughed at the raised eyebrows and the sideways glance between her friends. "It will all become clear. Plus, there's an amazing idea that it all led to, but I'm getting the feeling we all have stuff to get off our chests?" She adjusted the brightly-coloured cushion behind her, reached forward, pulled the handwritten menu cards from their carved stone holder, and handed them out. "Let's get the ordering out of the way, shall we?"

Pamela and Bláithín both reached for their bags and took out their glasses. They read in silence for a moment.

"How about we go for their tapas tasting menu? We all get to try a bit of everything that way." Cassandra suggested.

"Perfect."

"That's grand with me." They slotted the cards back in place.

The waiter reappeared and made them all smile with an elaborate display of opening the bottle and filling the sparkling, long-stemmed glasses, repeating the pour with a flourish each time the effervescent surge of silver bubbles died back. He took their order, offering information and making suggestions.

As soon as he had taken their order and turned to another table, Cassandra rapped her glass with her knife. "I hereby decree this official meeting of the Ibiza Crone Club open and ready to hear all business."

Bláithín didn't hesitate; leaning forward she launched straight into the events of her week. "I'm going to explode if I don't tell you what my brother and his wife did!"

She filled them in, and Cassandra and Pamela were suitably aghast and indignant on her behalf.

"Does she think we don't have sausages here?" asked Cassandra.

Over a platter of blackened Padrón peppers, Bláithín got furious all over again at the unprofessional invasion of her privacy by Maite's cousin in the hospital, which had led to the whole current debacle. Foregoing their forks, they picked up the small, whole, juicy peppers with their fingers and bit them off their stalks.

Eventually, Bláithín wound down. "By the time I left this evening, they'd already been down to say hello to Maite and were opening a bottle of wine she'd given them. All I could think was thank God I'm going out."

The platter, littered with stalks, was replaced by a large bowl of crumbly meatballs in a sauce that smelled of tomato and garlic, and a basket of warm bread.

Pamela broke off some bread and dipped it in the sauce. Her hair was coming loose and feathering softly around her face. Before she put the bread in her mouth, she looked at Bláithín. "I know it's an awful invasion but think how much you must mean to them for them to make such an effort. By the sound of it, this is quite an uncharacteristic move." She put the bread in her mouth and closed her eyes. "Mmmmm, this is delicious."

Bláithín speared a meatball and shook her head. "No, it's just nosiness and control. Apart from a torturous few hours or so every Christmas for dinner, we haven't spent a whole day together for years on end, and now they're spending a week with me? It's incredible." The meatball almost made it to her mouth, but it stopped midway. "I've never done anything, never been anywhere, and now that I have, they are going to spoil it for me to make sure I return to 'normal life', as they see it." She bit into the food. "Oh God, yes, this is divine."

Cassandra pursed her mouth, and her charcoal-outlined eyes were serious. "I'm not sure. My mother was the mistress of control, and she never put herself out in the slightest, not as your brother has just done. I'm not saying it isn't infuriating, but just that the motive may not be what you think it is."

Bláithín said nothing. She reached for the bottle, wiped off the dripping iced water, and topped up their glasses. "I suppose there has always been a kind of wall between us. After my divorce, Pauline kept wanting me to 'talk it out' and I couldn't. I just couldn't talk to anyone, least of all her. She's not my friend or my sister. Not that I have one, but -"

"So, she kinda is like a sister, really?" Cassandra interrupted.

"No! She isn't, and I didn't ever want her close enough to be knowing all my business and all the crap with Frank."

"How long has she been married to your brother?"

Bláithín was slow answering. "Nearly forty years."

"That's a long time to have someone in the family and not to know them."

"Well, there's no law that says you have to get on with your in-laws," interjected Pamela.

"Exactly!" Bláithín's thick hair bounced with each enthusiastic nod she gave. "And Diarmuid was married and gone before I even left school. I barely saw them for years. They only moved back when our parents died and Diarmuid got the house."

"What?" Cassandra almost shrieked. "They left everything to your brother? What kind of archaic, patriarchal bullshit was - "

Bláithín interrupted. "Ah, God, no, it wasn't like that at all. Bless them, they were forever changing their will to try and do the 'right thing'. Sure, before I got married, I was to get the house because Diarmuid had a good job in Dublin, and I was still living at home. Then I was -" her fingers made quote signs and her eyebrows frowned, "-'happily married and settled' in Frank's house. When Diarmuid lost his job and the house that went with it, they put his name in the will for the house. I'm sure they'd have changed it again after my divorce, but they were killed by a drunk driver while they were out on an evening walk."

"Oh no!" Pamela put one hand over her mouth and the other on Bláithín's arm.

"Bloody awful, Bláithín, I'm sorry," said Cassandra.

"Well, it's eleven years ago now, and honestly, I thanked God I was spared having to explain my marriage break-up to them, as I finally got divorced the following year." A red flush coloured her face and mottled her skin down into the crew neck of her navy t-shirt.

Pamela patted her friend's small, dry-skinned hand and noticed the bitten nails. "Don't worry Bláithín. It's only a week, and maybe it will be a time for you to get to know your brother a bit better. It's often easier to talk when you're out of your normal environment. Then they'll go back, and you'll be free to enjoy the rest of your time here."

Bláithín picked up her glass and downed what was left in it.

"Yes," added Cassandra, "and honestly, I can see as much concern as control in their actions. I mean alright…" she shrugged, "it *would* have been fucking polite of them to ask first, but there you go!"

Pamela laughed, and Bláithín snorted, "I don't think politeness and sensitivity is one of Pauline's strong points, but maybe I overreacted a bit. It is only a week. It's just so easy to fall back into old patterns of behavior, into feeling like the same boring failure as always. For a little while here, I was beginning to feel different."

"You're not a failure!" Pamela and Cassandra spoke as one.

"Well, what would you call it? I'm fifty-five with a failed marriage and no job. I'm living in an apartment in the garden of the house where I grew up, I have no life, and I'm so…" her voice faltered and came back barely more than a whisper, "so lonely."

Cassandra leant over and clinked her glass with Bláithín's. "Not anymore you're not!"

Pamela clinked as well. "No, you're a member of the Ibiza Crone Club now!"

Bláithín's pleasure shone in her eyes, and she whispered, "Thank you."

A waitress appeared and they sat back to allow the empty dishes to be cleared and a small mountain of king prawns in herb butter was put in the middle of the table with finger bowls and a stack of napkins. Bláithín used one to wipe her eyes.

"That's very definitely enough about me," said Bláithín. "What's driving you to drink, Pamela?"

By the time Pamela finished relating her shock at Susan

and Glen's troubles, the prawns were being replaced by spicy calamari. Cassandra dipped her fingers, gold nails today to match her silk shirt, into a finger bowl and dried them on a napkin. "No wonder you were knocked for six. That's bizarre,"

Bláithín frowned as she spoke. "I'm gathering you'd have said you were very close to your daughter?"

"Well, yes, I certainly would have. How could I not have noticed? I feel terrible. But, of course, I'm also worried about what's happening now. What do you two think? I mean you've both been through marriage breakups. How long in advance do you think the signals were there?"

"From the day I got married, to be honest," said Bláithín. "I barely knew what was going on in my own marriage or how to deal with it, let alone give advice on anyone else's."

Cassandra shrugged. "And I didn't know what was going on under my nose until a sweet receptionist from the Romantic Getaway Hotel in Cornwall - a place I'd never been to, I might add - rang to ask if, as valued repeat customers, we'd like to choose a complimentary spa treatment for our upcoming visit!"

"Oh, the shite!" exclaimed Bláithín.

"How awful!"

Cassandra lifted the wine bottle, checked how much was left, divided it between the three of them, and replaced it neck down in the cooler, as she replied.

"It wasn't the fact he was having an affair that freaked me out. We'd both had several of those during our marriage." Blithely ignoring any expression of surprise from her friends, Cassandra continued, "It was what he turned that one into."

Bláithín was wide-eyed. "But didn't the affairs bother either of you? I mean what about... y'know... love?"

Cassandra shrugged. "I don't think love is in my DNA. Neither giving nor receiving it. Something I guess I inherited from my mother."

She waved her hand airily. "Anyway, it's all water and bridges now and a long-winded way of saying 'don't ask me about signals' either. If they'd been smoke signals, I'd have choked on them, long before I copped on to it! But Pamela, it seems to me your biggest shock was discovering they'd been to counseling three years ago and you hadn't noticed, as if that somehow made you a bad mother."

"Not bad, bloody awful!"

"Not at all!" Cassandra waved her hand again. "If Susan had wanted you to know, you'd have known. She didn't, so you didn't. End of story."

Bláithín chased a piece of calamari around the dish with her fork. "I think Cassandra's right, Pamela. Of course, you're going to worry about what's going on with them now, but there's nothing to beat yourself up about, with the carry-on three years ago."

Pamela's raised eyebrows added to the lines on her forehead as she stared in surprise at her friends. "You're not just saying this to make me feel better. Are you?"

"No, not at all. It's obvious Susan deliberately hid it from you, but..." Cassandra paused to grab a skewer of barbequed, paprika chicken as a plate passed her on its way to the centre of the table, accompanied by a large bowl of crunchy roast potato chunks covered in a piquant tomato sauce.

"But what?" prompted Pamela.

"I think there's more going on than Susan has told you. You'll just have to wait until she's ready to talk."

"Hmm, maybe you're right, but what else could it be? I know I can't cross-question her, not about this." Pamela gazed across the table at Cassandra. "Were you always so wise and sensible?"

"Actually, that's a definite no! It's just lately things seem a lot clearer and more connected if you know what I mean?"

"No," said Pamela. "Definitely not!"

"Clear and connected has never been a description of me either," laughed Bláithín, her annoyance and irritation with Diarmuid and Pauline abated by her friend's reactions.

Cassandra scrunched up her paper napkin and dumped

it on the empty plate. "This brings us to my week. But first, the prosecco's gone, what's next? We'll need it for my story!" The silky sleeve of her shirt slid up her arm as she waved for the waiter and her multitude of silver bracelets glimmered in the light.

"He's definitely a model between jobs," muttered Cassandra as their waiter approached. Soft black curls were slicked back from his smooth face and his smile revealed long dimples at either side of his mouth, which simultaneously made him endearingly childlike and devastatingly charming.

Bláithín and Cassandra ordered a half carafe of red wine between them, and Pamela went for a glass of white wine. He took their order and produced a dessert menu. Pushing back a stray curl he said, "May I suggest something the ladies might like to try?"

Before he could elaborate Cassandra pouted up at him suggestively. "Oh, I'm sure I'm up for whatever you suggest!" Her face glowed with mischief.

"Señora might be surprised." His dimples deepened.

Cassandra held his gaze for a second. "Oh no! I don't think this Señora would be surprised in the slightest!"

"And now," he put his hand on his heart and shook his head theatrically, "my suggestion of a tasting tray of desserts for sharing sounds disappointing!"

"No, it sounds lovely," said Bláithín, quite pink-faced at the interaction.

"It will have to do, I suppose," Cassandra sighed, and he walked away still chuckling.

"Cassandra! You're terrible!" Bláithín exclaimed.

"What?" said Cassandra innocently. "He's gorgeous!"

"What about Reuben? I thought you were interested in him."

"Oh honestly, Bláithín! Even if I am interested in Reuben, being interested in one guy never stopped me from flirting with another! It's just a bit of fun. And anyway, that waiter's not interested in me."

"He certainly looked it to me, and why wouldn't he be? You look amazing." Bláithín waved her hand encompassing Cassandra's tight black denim jeans, scoop neck, black teddy, and the fine gold shirt.

"No, I mean he's not interested in any of us beautiful women. Couldn't you tell?"

Bláithín looked puzzled. "Tell what?"

"He's more interested in that rather distinguished gentleman over there than he is in any nubile female in the place. Didn't you think so, Pamela?"

"Well, I did think he was rather, em... well-groomed, shall we say?"

Cassandra laughed. "Well put!"

Bláithín looked amazed. "You mean... He's... Mother of God, I can't believe you both could tell by just looking at him!"

Cassandra stared at Bláithín. "And you didn't? Hmm, you really don't know much about men, do you?"

Bláithín changed the subject. "Okay, it's your turn now, Cassandra. What's your story?"

Cassandra folded her arms on the table and leant forward. "Well, I'd like to tell you that I've been visited by the ancient Mother Goddess of Ibiza. Tanit, the one who wears a rather strange headdress, like a pill box hat on steroids."

Bláithín snorted and Pamela stifled a laugh.

"Stay with me ladies, I shit you not. And I'd like to tell you that she is imparting the wisdom of the ages to me, filling me with peace and energy, and offering to help me with my life. But obviously, I couldn't say anything so crazy. Could I? So, let's just say that I had some seriously strong weed after a shitty encounter with a pre-pubescent child who was wearing the exact same outfit I was." she caught Bláithín's smile, and continued. "Well, okay perhaps she wasn't exactly pre-pubescent, but she wasn't a day over nineteen and that's barely out of nappies! And for some reason I still can't explain, it really upset me. I mean, I don't usually care what people are wearing but there was something freaky about coming face to face with this, something horribly like two ends of a journey, and…" she took a deep breath, "the worst part was that she felt sorry for me! Me? The party queen, event organizer to the stars. I should have punched her!"

The waiter carried an elaborate tray of desserts to their table, smiled charmingly as he slid it into the centre of the table, and waited for their reaction. But engrossed in Cassandra's story, the women barely acknowledged him.

"Anyway, obviously a strong spliff was just what I needed, and the rest either did or did not happen. I'm still undecided."

Pamela scrutinized Cassandra's face "You're not seriously thinking it was real? Are you?"

Cassandra raised her eyebrows and spread her hands. "You see, it turns out where I live is near the site of Tanit's temple… so, I'm not saying it wasn't the weed, but… maybe…?"

Pamela turned to Bláithín. "What do you think?"

"Oh, well, I'm Irish, so, despite anything we may claim to the contrary, believing in fairies and spirits is in our genes."

Cassandra guffawed. "Way to go, Bláth! But it gave me a tremendous idea, which in light of both of your trials and tribulations, is going to blow your socks off! She cut off a piece of warm frangipani tart and bit into it. "Mmmm, divine!"

"Go on!" Pamela and Bláithín spoke together.

Cassandra smirked, "Just taking a dramatic tension moment! Right, as you know, I must be out of my house shortly because I can't afford the rent, and you were with me when I had my epiphany about Ibiza being my home now and forever. Sooo… how about… if you guys move in with me and we share the villa and the rent? I'm telling you this house is beyond special!"

She held up her hand as both Pamela and Bláithín were shaking their heads.

"No, wait, just listen." She sipped her wine before continuing. "Pamela, you just said that you thought Susan and

Glen could do with a bit of space. Well, if you moved to my house, they'd have it. And so would you! There's a large room you could use, just for painting. It's all tile and stone so you can splash paint around as much as you like. Also, it has wonderful light because of a great big window."

Pamela topped up her wine with sparkling water; she had stopped shaking her head. Cassandra took this as a good sign. "Second, you have a car, so you could still do all your organized babysitting and pickups, but you wouldn't be living on top of them the whole time."

Pamela was silent. Cassandra turned to Bláithín. "Your brother and sister-in-law wouldn't have to worry about you being alone anymore. That would get them off your back. There's another room where you could set up a studio and really work on your photos. You have to leave where you are anyway in a few months, so why not now?" She filled her glass from the carafe and looked questioningly at Bláithín who held out her glass. Apart from Cassandra's first taste, the dessert plate was untouched. The mango sorbet was beginning to melt through its honeycomb basket.

Pamela's mouth turned down at the sides while she thought about it. Her head moved slowly from side to side. "I couldn't. It would seem terribly ungrateful to Susan and Glen after all the trouble they've gone to, doing up my apartment, and what if they needed me urgently -"

Cassandra interrupted, "You'd only be twenty minutes away. Just think the next time you wake up with an idea in the middle of the night, you'll be able to spring into action!"

"What would I do?" asked Bláithín. "How could I manage it?"

"Look, you're paying some rent here at the moment anyway, so why not pay it to live in a fabulous house with your friends? Your boss is hardly going to object if you hand back the keys sooner, given that it's all kinda his fault, anyway. And who knows what will turn up in the future?"

Pamela scooped some tiramisu out of its glass jar. "It

does seem appealing, but honestly, wouldn't it seem awful to make the move to Ibiza with them and then strike out on my own?"

"But you'd like to, wouldn't you?" prodded Cassandra, catching the interest in Pamela's voice. "Your daughter wanted to move, and you helped her, that's great, but she's a grown woman with her own family, she really doesn't need you on her doorstep, does she? And you know, as you said, maybe she does need a bit of space. Also..." she held up a finger, "we're not getting any younger and if we can't do something like this now, when can we do it?"

"Do you know how much it would be?" Bláithín broke a piece off the honeycomb basket as she spoke.

Cassandra grinned. "To be honest, I'm not sure, but I know someone who might be able to put in a good word for us. And maybe we can swing winter rates for a while, until next May anyway. That's only six months. Pamela, that would be so easy to sell to Susan, I mean, come on! Twenty minutes away for six months? That's nothing." There was silence. Cassandra leaned towards her friends and spread her palms towards them both. "Look, why don't you both come and spend a night at my place, get a feel for it, see what you think, then decide if it's a good idea or not?"

Bláithín's forehead furrowed as she tried to explain her objections. "We're middle-aged women -"

"That's being kind," muttered Pamela.

Bláithín made a wry face but continued, "- who barely know each other. It all seems a bit mad."

Cassandra waved her index finger from side to side. "It's not mad. Kids answer ads on their phones every day of the week and move in with complete strangers. I may be wrong, but I think the three of us have hit it off in a way that I know I haven't with anyone for..." She paused and her eyes widened. "To be honest, I don't think I can ever remember feeling this comfortable with people, ever. Also, this is Ibiza! Strange and wonderful things happen here."

The three women fell silent. Cassandra sat back, happy that Pamela and Bláithín were obviously thinking about it. The hubbub around them had died down to the clatter of plate clearing and the scrape of chairs as most tables around them were empty by now.

Cassandra gave them a bit more space to think before she leant forward, elbows on the table. "Okay, I'm wrapping up my pitch by saying don't decide until you spend a night in my place. That's all - just one night. Then think about it." She grinned at them, and they both smiled. "It'll be fun. I'll ask Reuben to pick you both up and bring you over. We'll have dinner, a bottle of wine or two and chat. Go on, take a chance." She sat back in her chair, swaying her shoulders, circling her elbows, and humming Abba's 'Take a Chance'.

Her friends dissolved into laughter.

Bláithín sat back in her chair. "Sure, one night isn't committing to anything, is it?"

Pamela nodded. "Yes, and why shouldn't we make new friends and do odd things, at this age?"

"That's the spirit, girls! What about next Tuesday?"

"Oh, that's a bit soon, isn't it? I mean Diarmuid and Pauline will still be here, they're not going till Wednesday."

Cassandra laughed. "Probably all the more reason for you to want to get away for a night! They've barely been here a few hours and you were already desperate to make a break for it! Also, I'm not sure how much longer I have in the house, so I must get the ball rolling. I'll ask Reuben to pick you up and drop you back so neither of you have to worry about driving around the crazy caminos trying to find the place."

Pamela pushed back a loose strand of hair and leant forward. "I do feel a bit as if I'm hiding in my rooms in Susan and Glen's place at the moment." Her eyes sparkled. She looked like a twelve-year-old planning to play hooky. "I think I'd love to come and spend a night." She interrupted Cassandra's cheer to hold up a hand and say, "I'm not promising anything about moving in, but it is tempting."

Bláithín's wide grin announced her decision. "I'm on for the night away. I think you're right, Cassandra. By Tuesday, I'll be driven daft by Pauline, and t'would do them good to see that I've got a life of my own going on here. Anyway, they're not going 'til very late the next night, so I'll have whole the day with them. "

Cassandra clapped her hands like a six-year-old. "Wonderful! A sleepover at my house on Tuesday!" She raised her almost empty glass and said, "To the Ibiza Crone Club!"

Pamela and Bláithín reached out, and three glasses clinked in the middle of the table.

"To the Ibiza Crone Club!" they echoed.

CHAPTER FOURTEEN

Early the next morning Cassandra rang Reuben, her 'contact'. As handyman for the villa, she reasoned, he must know the owners. The grin on her face faded when she got the answering machine. It took three attempts to get the right tone of casual spontaneity in her message asking him to call that evening. The last few times they'd met she'd either been asleep, needy, crying, or crazy. She was going to change that. Her preparations for his visit had already begun. She had coated her air in Argon oil; limp and greasy now, it would be wonderfully smooth and silky after her shower. She was planning to do a facial and a manicure before he arrived. Her tightest white jeans and lacy top were ready on her bed. Beer was in the fridge, and wine, both red and white, was waiting to be opened. She'd show him needy!

But now she was slowing down after a strenuous yoga session. Though the November sun still carried warmth, the pine and sea-scented breeze was fresh enough to cool her flushed and sweaty face. The baggy, grey tracksuit ends and bra top, under a long white vest, were old and comfortable, giving Cassandra maximum freedom of movement. She was lost in the zone, lying in a belly twist. Her yoga mat was a bright orange splash on the terrace. She breathed in deeply and slowly, not thinking about anything in particular, but filled with a wonderful feeling of oneness, an awareness of the balance of life, sharing in its fleeting, precious moments.

Doing a slow reverse twist, she opened her eyes to drink in the beauty surrounding her.

Reuben was standing in the garden at the edge of the terrace.

"Christ-all-buggering-mighty! What are you doing? You

Peeping Tom!"

He held up his hands in self-defense. "Sorry, I was about to slip away. I wasn't going to interrupt."

Cassandra sprang to her feet and pulled at her hair, releasing it from its scraped-up bun. "I could have been naked!"

Reuben rubbed his palm around the back of his neck and across his head, his eyes full of laughter. "Well, uh, I'm not too sure how to respond to that. I got your message and I was coming here anyway to drop off this -" he indicated the gas bottle he was carrying "I thought I'd check in case it was anything urgent you needed."

"I wanted to talk to you, but I'm not ready now. I mean…"

"I can come back later or tomorrow, whatever you like." He rubbed his palm across his head again.

Cassandra watched. Imagining how those soft bristles would feel on her hands. Suddenly aware that she was staring at him, she bent down, grabbed her towel and patted her face and neck.

Reuben squatted down and dug his hand into the soil, lifted a handful, smelled it, and let it trickle back to the ground. "I think this needs me to come by and dig in some loam soon." He stood up as Cassandra approached. He was wearing his work jeans and a soft, sky-blue T-shirt that echoed his eyes. In her bare feet, she was a good head smaller than he. The lines around his eyes deepened as he smiled.

"You've obviously been doing yoga a long time. You're amazingly fluid and supple."

Cassandra flushed. "How long have you been watching me?" she asked sharply, thinking of the downward dog pose she'd held for so long and the suggestive movements of the bridge pose.

"I only arrived as you were finishing the belly twist sequence, honestly!"

Obviously, he did yoga, too. She could easily imagine his long, lean body in a myriad of poses. To distract herself she said, "You might as well come in and talk to me since you're here." She swore under her breath as he followed her into the house. "Bloody arsing hell! This is so not what I wanted." She was hot, sweaty, had no makeup, her hair was flat and greasy, and she was wearing a goddamn tracksuit! Too early in the day mood-enhancing alcohol, she grudgingly filled the kettle. "I'm having green tea. Would you like some?"

"That would be nice, thank you." Reuben pulled out a kitchen chair and straddled it.

Cassandra dragged her eyes away from him, turned and gulped down a glass of cold water, dripping it down her chin and t-shirt. Wiping it away with the back of her hand, she forced herself to be calm and pulled out a chair opposite him.

"... lots of really good yoga groups on the island," Reuben was saying. "Would you think of joining one?"

Cassandra thought a moment. "No, I don't think so. Even though I've always liked group classes, but somehow, here, in this house, it's different. It's hard to explain."

"This house has its own ways, for sure. It must like you. You say your yoga goes well here?"

"Yes, it's weird. Time seems to disappear, and I feel amazing after it."

"Yes, I can see you are glowing-"

Cassandra interrupted, "I'd like to see what you'd look like after two hours of Ashtanga yoga!"

"No, I meant actually glowing, like from the inside, calm and happy." He looked at her intently. "You look wonderful."

"I..." She was going to laugh it off, to bat away his compliment with a joke, but it was so sincere and his gaze so steady, she just said, "Thank you. I feel good." Their gaze held. The kettle click broke loudly into the silence. Cassandra jumped to her feet and made two mugs of tea. She was pleased to see her arms looked toned and brown next to her white top, as she stretched them out to put them on the table.

"Any more chats with Tanit?" Reuben didn't sound mocking, only curious.

"No, but then I haven't been smoking weed either, so I'm not sure if it's chicken or egg. Anyway, I really appreciated your help last week. It was the right info at the right time." Time to change the subject. "Do you practice yoga often?"

He nodded. "A mixture of qigong and yoga. I've been doing it every single day for ten years. It's a vital part of my life now."

"Mine too. I couldn't imagine life without it, though I may be overdoing it recently. As I said, I seem to lose track of time. My sessions here can often go on for hours."

"Yes," he nodded as he replied. "I can keep going for two hours some days."

It was too good a straight line. She waggled her eyebrows suggestively. "I bet you can!"

He looked startled, then grinned his crooked grin which animated his face, and let her see the shade of the young man beneath. He shook his head. "I'm out of practice with polite, or even impolite, discourse."

Cassandra winked. "That's easily remedied, you know."

He was so good looking and yet, feature by feature, it was hard to pinpoint what she found so attractive. His eyes were quite deep-set really, and his nose was possibly too big, however, his mouth... Cassandra found she was staring at it while it smiled back at her, broadly. Flustered, again she became businesslike. "I wanted to talk to you about this house. You must know the owners, or at least how to contact them?"

He stirred his tea, slowly flattening the tea bag against the side, squeezing out the flavor before he took the bag out and put it on the saucer. Finally, he said, "What do you need to know?"

"How much more time is it paid up for, how much does it cost per month, is there a winter reduction, and, oh God!" An awful possibility had just occurred to her. "Is it booked for any time soon?"

Reuben nodded. "Yes, of course, I can make enquiries on your behalf, but what is going on?"

All thoughts of flirting left her. She stared down at the table drawing faces with her finger in the wet rings from her mug while she gathered her thoughts. She desperately wanted to convince him of the utter seriousness of her desire to stay in this house. "I fell in love with Ibiza when I was eighteen, but I've never had a home here. It was always crashing in some friend's house, trailer, yurt, whatever, house sitting, dog sitting. I even lived in the abandoned Festival Club for a year. To be honest, I've never felt at home in a house, ever in my life, until now."

"Ever? What about your childhood home?"

The bitterness of her laugh visibly surprised him. "That was the worst of all. I only ever wanted to escape from there. Even when I married Pierce, we only lived on a boat here, before moving into his flat in London."

"Married?" Those wayward eyebrows rose a fraction.

"Married for twenty-five years, divorced for two, but it had been in terminal decline for years before that. We were just too busy to care."

"Doesn't sound like a match made in heaven." His husky voice was gentle and inquisitive.

She flicked a glance in his direction and was caught by his frank perusal. An Amazonian river of emotion connected brown eyes and blue. Cassandra released the breath she'd been holding in a long shaky whoosh.

"I'm sorry," he said. "I'm overstepping boundaries here."

"No, you're not. It's just..." She closed her eyes briefly. How to explain that despite everything her head was telling her, talking to him made her want to strip away every layer of pretence, every barricade of laddishness until she was as bare and exposed as the wood he sanded? She tried to explain, "We were dating but in the loose, casual Ibiza way of the time. I barely knew him let alone loved him. Turned out Pierce was Australian. His visa was up, and he was in danger of being sent back to Australia. It began as a fun arrangement for a green card and an excuse for the mother of all parties." She hesitated, spelling it out like this, it didn't sound as cool as she'd hoped. But there was no point in stopping now.

"We discovered we worked well together in the party world, we had the same goals, didn't want children, and didn't demand too much of each other. Then the Ibiza ship sank, literally. We came back from a party one night to find the boat we were living on had sprung a leak and taken everything we owned to the bottom of the not-very-clean San Antonio harbor."

She rubbed at the marks on the table. "We moved back to London, I opened an event business, and he opened a publishing house. Our client lists complemented each other. It was business as usual, any affairs we had were discreet and short-lived. We spent a long time thinking we were lucky, modern, and as happy as anyone else we knew. We went way over our best-by date."

Reuben nodded slightly. "Oh," was all he said.

"It was seen as a very successful marriage by our friends!" she said defensively, "We never fought, threw the best parties, and had a great time. Until we didn't."

Reuben stood up, took his mug over to the sink, and rinsed it. Cassandra frowned with a surge of annoyance. Was he snow white? At his age and with his looks, he must have taken out storage space for all his skeletons. "And you? What's your story?" she challenged.

"I'm not proud of my history either," he said as he returned to the table.

Cassandra wasn't too sure she liked his use of the word 'either,' after all she hadn't said she was exactly ashamed of it. She wasn't, just deeply hurt by how it had ended.

He turned the chair and sat, his elbows on the table, clasping his work-worn hands in front of him. "Okay, my turn." He took a deep breath. "I was forty when I came back to Ibiza. I left a good job and an ex-wife in Barcelona."

He caught Cassandra's expression and added, "We got married in university and rapidly grew in different directions.

It was all civilized, amicable, and rather stupid."

"Oh, okay," said Cassandra, wondering if the ex-wife would describe her marriage and divorce in those words.

"I hadn't really planned to come back so soon. But my father was ill, and my brother had no interest in running the farm, which I loved. So, I returned to take it over. There was a girl, Angeles, our neighbour's daughter. She was fourteen years younger than me, and they'd always joked how we'd unite the lands one day." He shrugged. "To be honest, I'd barely noticed her. But when I finally came home for good, she had grown into a charming, clever woman and I enjoyed her company, but I had no connection with her." His gaze flicked back to Cassandra, they looked at each other in silence for a moment. She wondered if he could hear her heart thudding. He looked away and spoke down to his clasped hands. "When it became obvious she had hopes of us being together, I told her honestly that it would never happen, as I had no intention or desire to marry again. Not long after, she rang me one night to say her car was broken and ask if I could pick her up from a beach party."

Reuben stared at the table. "She was quite drunk, still in her bikini, and begging me not to let her parents see her like that. I took her home..." he paused at the look on Cassandra's face. "Christ! I'm not that bad! All I did was put her to bed in the spare room with a pint of water. However, she came into my bed early in the morning and I didn't throw her out. I'm not proud of that, but a month later, she's telling her parents she's pregnant and her father is sitting in my front room. Ibicencan families are tight-knit and traditional. There was only one thing to do. We got married a few weeks later and she moved into our family home. Angeles was happy. She said she had love enough for the two of us, and she was sure that I'd come to love her, too. Our families were delighted, what could be better?" He put his head in his hands.

"Not exactly a match made in heaven, either," Cassandra said gently, though the mention of a wife and child had hit her like a wrecking ball to the stomach. She had folded her arms tightly across it.

He looked up but he didn't meet her eyes. He stared out the window at the other side of the kitchen. "No, it wasn't, and I behaved like a complete bastard. I drank, I cheated. I never really tried to make it work and worst of all, I felt so sorry for myself, I could only see our daughter, Amelia, as the embodiment of all that went wrong."

"Where is Angeles now?" Cassandra had to know.

Reuben twisted his hands together but continued staring past her. "After I... I crashed the car with Amelia in it, Angeles took her and left Ibiza."

Cassandra's voice was barely above a whisper when she spoke. "Christ! Was Amelia hurt?"

"No, she was strapped in. I wasn't speeding, I'd been drinking and just fell asleep. But the possibilities of what could have happened will always haunt me."

"I can imagine, Reuben. That's awful. There's no point in saying otherwise."

"I don't blame Angeles. She'd tried for six years to make things work but that was the last straw. She cut off all contact when she left, and I... I disappeared into an alcoholic haze for several years. So badly, I nearly lost the farm."

He looked at her then, the lines on his face telling her that he was judging himself more harshly than she ever would. "I didn't get to see Amelia again until she was eighteen. By then, she wanted no part of me. Angeles had re-married, and as far as Amelia was concerned, her father was Juan Garcia, a banker in Sevilla."

"How awfully, awfully sad for you all."

"I've come to terms with it now, but realizing how selfish and blind I was, came too late to save any kind of relationship with my only child."

"It's never too late, Reuben. Surely you know that living in Ibiza, there's always hope."

Reuben sighed and finally met her eyes. "And to think, I

came here to drop off a gas bottle!"

"There's something about this house, I'm sure."

"I certainly didn't come here with the intention of unloading all this on you, but when you asked..." he spread his hands, "I couldn't help myself. I wanted you to know." He cleared his throat and stood up. "I'm sorry for regurgitating my sad past all over you."

"Well, I did ask. And you had already gotten mine," she shrugged, "Also for some unfathomable reason!"

"I haven't spoken to anyone, ever, about this. Are you not disgusted by my story, wondering what kind of man could behave like that?"

Cassandra caught her bottom lip in her teeth while she considered the question. "Seems to me," she said, drawing out her words, as she searched for the right phrasing. "that you've hurt yourself most. Angeles and Amelia have moved on and made new lives. It's you that's stuck, still punishing yourself." She reached out and put her hand on his arm, to help underline her point. Heat flooded through her at the contact and her eyes darted to meet his, even as she jerked her arm away. He caught her hand before she finished the movement, and still holding it, he paced around the table and stood looking intently down at her. He gently ran his knuckles down the side of her face. The lightest touch, that somehow shot every nerve ending in her body alive.

"What is it, Cassandra Collingsworth? What is it between us?"

She rested her cheek on his opening palm. "I have no idea, I'm in uncharted waters here."

"Me too. Let's hope we're good sailors, Cassandra."

He bent down and kissed her gently on the mouth. His lips were soft, tender, and undemanding, but they sent a visceral thrill of anticipation shooting straight through her. He straightened and stepped back.

"Wow!" She exhaled.

His whisper was husky. "Wow, indeed."

Cassandra wanted to throw her arms around him, to hold him so tightly it hurt, to let their respective miseries drain down through their bodies, through the floor to be absorbed, soothed, and dissipated by the earth's energies. But watching him pull himself together, watching his normal shutter of reserve close his face, she knew this wasn't the time to follow her normal inclinations, so she merely sat back and looked at him.

He rubbed at the nape of his neck. "I have other calls to make. I should go."

Cassandra nodded.

His voice was gruff. "I'll see what information I can get for you, and I'll let you know."

"Thank you," she whispered. The feel of his hand was still warm on her cheek as she watched him walk out the door and into the dusk.

CHAPTER FIFTEEN

Diarmuid's snores were rattling the walls when Bláithín got home after the night out with her friends. Pauline's higher-pitched wheeze provided an equally loud counterpoint. Bláithín gently closed their door and found the pack of earplugs she'd bought for the flight out. She was going to take her friend's remarks to heart and be more patient with her brother and his wife.

That resolve barely made it through the next morning. Pauline took silence as a personal affront. No observation was too trivial or irrelevant to be voiced. Diarmuid with his crossword book open and biro in hand, dropped an occasional affirmative syllable or two into the monologue which barely broke his concentration but seemed to satisfy Pauline. When Bláithín's coffee pot spluttered to a stop, and she brought an aroma-rich, steaming mug to the table with her toast, Pauline eyed it. "That stuff will do you no good. Twill have your nerves on edge for the day. What's wrong with a good old cup of tea?"

"Nothing at all," said Bláithín, making a mental note to stock up on coffee to help her survive the week ahead.

"Do you know what I found on the internet this morning?" The latest iPhone looked incongruous in the pocket of her sister-in-law's knitted white cardigan. "An article about first babies and how late they are likely to arrive in relation to the mother's age, fancy that! I'm going down to Maite after breakfast to tell her, so she can prepare herself."

"Do you think that's necessary?" Bláithín said, alarmed at the thought of Maite being bombarded with this barrage of useless information.

Pauline paused in the middle of ladling out scrambled eggs and fried tomatoes and looked amazed "Sure, why wouldn't it be? Isn't she scouring everything and anything she can get her hands on? The poor creature."

"Is she?" Bláithín said weakly. Her sister-in-law had only been here a day and she was already prying into people's lives.

Pauline handed laden plates to them. Bláithín sighed. Despite being thin to the point of gaunt, her sparrow-like sister-in-law liked to over-feed anyone sitting at her table. The monologue continued non-stop during breakfast, as Pauline rehearsed everything she was going to say to Maite. She eventually drained her teacup and replaced it emphatically on its saucer. "Right so. I'll leave the wash up to you two, while I pop down to Maite."

She patted her hair into place and folded her cardigan across her thin chest and was gone.

The silence was deafening.

Bláithín put down her cup. "Any plans for today?" she asked brightly.

Diarmuid took off his glasses, fished in his pocket for a cloth, and began polishing. "We'll see what herself wants when she comes back. I'm easy."

Bláithín realized she could not remember the last time she'd been on her own with Diarmuid for any length of time.

Glasses back in place Diarmuid began to clear the table.

"It's nice to have you to myself, Diarmuid. We don't often get the chance. I was just thinking that it must be as long ago as back home before you left for university."

He considered this, and his slow smile took years off him as he replied. "Sitting on the couch watching Wanderley Wagon with you and sharing a packet of Taytos."

The wash-up and the tidying were completed almost unnoticed as they reminisced about programmes and outings, the stray dog that had adopted them, the caravan holiday where it rained so much their caravan slid six feet in the mud. Bláithín was giving the table a final wipe when she was prompted to say, "We never say more than two words to each other at home and I'm living at the end of your garden. Why's that?"

Diarmuid's glasses came off again. "Ah, sure Pauline does the talking for the two of us, and I know she's not the easiest person to take to. We're inclined to keep ourselves to ourselves."

"But that's not fair to you," protested Bláithín.

"Life's not fair to anyone, Bláithín. Don't judge Pauline by her manner. She's a great person, but her way now isn't so great."

"I know. I keep imagining poor Maite below being bewildered by Pauline's pregnancy advice." Bláithín laughed. "Pauline of all people!"

"Ah, it's different here," muttered Diarmuid as he pulled out a chair and sat at the table. "No one knows her, and she can share a bit in the excitement."

Bláithín sat opposite him. "But does she want to share in that particular excitement?" Bláithín was genuinely perplexed. Pauline, whose scathing remarks about unruly, messy, loud children, had eventually stopped all neighbours with children from dropping in to visit.

Diarmuid sighed. "Well, we weren't blessed in that department ourselves and each loss made her close in on herself more -"

"What?" Bláithín's face froze in shock. "I never knew anything about this, Diarmuid. I'm so sorry. Poor Pauline."

"Ah sure, how would you know? You were only young when we got married, and later when all this started happening, we didn't tell anyone. There was nothing anyone could do, and Pauline didn't want anyone's pity, or people being nice to her just because she couldn't carry a baby."

Was there a glint in his eye when he said that? Bláithín quailed because she had just been thinking she would have been way nicer to Pauline if she'd known. "How many Diarmuid?" she asked softly.

"Ah, Bláth, it cost me dearly too." He put on his glasses, then took them off again and rubbed his thumbs around the deep arch of his eyes. "Four, Bláithín. Four we had with us for twenty weeks or more before we lost them."

Bláithín found she was crying. Tears for Pauline, tears for Diarmuid, tears for the pain they'd been hiding all those years, tears for the little lost babies and for herself, though she wasn't sure why.

"But why? Why did it happen?"

Diarmuid spread his hands, "This was more than thirty years ago. No one said more than 'the will of God.'"

"Was that what Pauline thought?"

He snorted. "I called in the local priest after the last one. I'd lost my bright girl. She'd even given up work, the nursing she loved! I could barely get her out of bed. She was a crushed woman looking for a bit of hope or encouragement, an explanation as to why she had four in the Angel Garden in Glasnevin while Rosemary O' Donnell around the corner, who drank the children's allowance and kept her house like a pigsty, had eight running loose and uncared for."

"What did he say?"

"Wasn't she lucky the Lord had singled her out to bear such a cross and she should offer it up for the saints."

Bláithín's face flushed and she slapped her hand on the table. "Bloody hell, what stupidity and arrogance."

"I can tell you the next time he showed his shiny face at our door looking for cake and tea in the parlour, and an envelope for the dues, I caught him by the shoulders, turned him around on the doorstep and told him we weren't wanting to see him again."

"Well done, Diarmuid."

"Yes, well, I know she's a bit of a trial and getting worse, but I think it's because she has a big heart and no one to fill it only myself, and so she prattles away and occupies her day with other people's business."

Bláithín ransacked her memory for hints or clues that she must have missed over the years. She was shocked by her own lack of insight and understanding. She had always written Pauline off as a tiresome, interfering busybody to be avoided, never taking the time to wonder why her clever, kind, gentle brother had married someone like that, because of course, he hadn't. How had he described her? *My bright girl'*. The phrase made Bláithín's heartbreak for them.

Getting to her feet, she flicked on the kettle, and poured the remains of her, now savagely strong coffee into two mugs. Topping them up with boiling water, she splashed in some milk and brought them over to the table. She put her arm around Diarmuid and kissed the bald top of his head. "Thank you for telling me."

He looked around the bare room. "This place must be like some sort of confessional. I've never spoken to a living soul about this before." He looked up at her and nodded, "But it was about time."

"It's not this room. It's Ibiza. As a wise friend of mine says 'This is Ibiza, strange things happen here.'"

***

When Pauline returned, they were laughing at a crossword clue Bláithín had just solved: 'A camping ancestor copper fastens ownership, six letters.' Pauline was completely uninterested as to why the answer was 'patent'. She was eager to give them a blow-by-blow account of how she'd communicated the vital information to Maite, despite Maite's lack of English. Bláithín thought they both did a good job of feigning interest.

They spent the rest of the day sorting out a hired car. Pauline ferreted out the best possible deal, crosschecking everything from reviews sites, surcharges, and fuel return policies to hidden costs, staff efficiency, and car cleanliness, before deciding on one.

Bláithín realized she was surprisingly okay with sharing her exploration of the island with them. That evening, over takeaway pizzas, they planned a route for the next day, starting in the north with the tiny rural village of Santa Inès.

"So romantic sounding," cooed Pauline.

Bláithín didn't have the heart to tell her it translated to plain old Agnes. They agreed to continue across the top of the island and aim for a beach location for lunch.

***

The next morning, Pauline's insistence on a cooked breakfast, and the fact they were sharing one bathroom, meant they didn't leave as early as they had planned. However, everyone was relaxed and, as Pauline said, 'Sure, weren't they on holiday? Now that Bláithín wasn't at death's door like Andy had led them to believe, couldn't they please themselves about everything?'

Bláithín sat in the back seat and read out snippets from the guidebooks as they drove. Everything on Santa Inés focused on the magical almond blossom groves in early spring when the mass of delicate pink and snowy white flowers swathe the valleys and illuminate the nights, but now in November, the rows of almond trees thrust their naked, spindly limbs into the air, reaching up to the stark blue sky as if pleading to be dressed in their finery.

Diarmuid's deliberate and unhurried driving style meant they enjoyed Ibiza's varied landscape at leisure. It also meant they were frequently hooted at and overtaken by drivers who didn't share in their relaxed schedule. Thickly wooded, verdant forests climbed the sides of high hills occasionally giving tantalizing glimpses of some millionaire's mansion nestling expensively off the beaten track. Orange trees, rooted in startlingly russet-red earth, still had their heavy fruit hanging low against their dark green leaves and littering the ground around them, glowing out through the grass like tossed costume jewelry.

"It must be like paradise in spring when the wildflowers are out." Pauline sounded wistful.

"Maybe you'll come back," said Bláithín generously. Diarmuid's eyes smiling back at her in the rear-view mirror felt like a reward.

They planned a lunch break in Cala San Vicent. Bláithín was sure that name rang a bell, but she couldn't place it. They drove down the steep, winding cliff road, with the swooping curve of a small metal barrier the only boundary of safety between them and the flat expanse of turquoise sea way down below. But Cala Vicent was closed, literally not a thing open. A long line of empty, locked bars and restaurants, silent apartment blocks, all homogenously blank with white shuttered windows.

Needing to stretch their legs, they decided to park there anyway and stroll along the white, sandy beach. It was almost deserted, apart from a couple sitting on the sand in the far distance and some children in bright jackets playing chase with the sea. The distance and the breeze evaporated any noise the children may have been making, allowing the screeching gulls and the rolling, throaty splash of small waves slapping at the sand to dominate the air.

"If only we'd bought a picnic," bemoaned Pauline.

Bláithín wasn't listening. She was captivated by the twisted, gnarled bark of an ancient pine tree and she waved the others on. Bent, battered, and distorted by years and weather, the tree caused her the first-ever surge of excitement as she took out her camera. Adjusting the focus, she went closer and closer into the grain, finding a world of conflicting patterns, gradients of shadow that fascinated her. Kneeling on the stony ground, ignoring the pain in her knees, she got right in, close to the roots. She rolled over a large rock to stand on, hooked herself over a branch fractured decades ago, and gave her camera a glimpse deep inside.

She was totally absorbed until Pauline rapping at her leg brought her attention back to the world around her.

"Would you come on? We've walked the length of the place, and we're going to die from hunger if we don't eat soon."

Bláithín's urge to snap at her disappeared as soon as she registered the colour in Pauline's thin cheeks and the sparkle in her eyes. Pauline was enjoying herself. "Right, I'll be with you in a second," was all she said, clambering down from the tree.

***

Maite had told Pauline about the bargains to be had at the San Jordi market, so early on Saturday morning, Pauline was preparing like a general leading an attack. "Now, Bláithín, keep your money zipped in your bag, don't take it out until you've decided to buy. Diarmuid, take your wallet out of your back pocket and put it inside your jacket, it's asking to be stolen where it is." She spoke as if she were leading them to a den of iniquity instead of a car boot sale.

Instead of rolling her eyes as she wanted to, Bláithín said, "Yes, I suppose places like this could attract the odd dodgy character."

Pauline beamed. "Yes. And don't forget to hold any purchases close and be vigilant."

At the market, they drove around and around looking for a parking space. There were none to be had in the two large, dusty car parks. Even the adjacent roads were bumper to bumper with vehicles of every description, from rusty, decrepit, mandala-painted vans with dogs hanging out the window, to high-end Mercedes jeeps. The windows of their car rattled with the thumping bass of a sound system up full as a car passed them. The young driver with his hat on backwards, and an arm full of tattoos gestured out the window, pointing back to his recently vacated parking spot.

"Well, now, just goes to show, doesn't it?" observed Pauline as Diarmuid manoeuvred their car into place.

The sound of bongos floated over the wall as they walked towards the hippodrome. "Apparently that's the quintessential sound of Ibiza," Bláithín informed them.

Pauline rolled her eyes. "I could imagine something more musical!"

Stepping out into the huge arena, they were met by an almost medieval spectacle of colour and noise. Vibrant throws, shawls, scarves, and dresses hanging high on racks and poles fluttered like pennants in the breeze. Crowded paths were lined with stalls, stands, tables, boxes, cars, pagodas, and trucks; even the ground itself was strewn with woven carpets displaying heaps of goods. Random snatches of music mixed with barking dogs and vendors' cries cut through the bass drone of a thousand conversations.

A quick scan showed silks, linen, wool, wood, silver, books, coins, handles, art, buttons, designer clothes, cracked pottery, and racks and racks of second-hand clothes. A mix of incense, coffee, flowers, and frying filled the air. Bláithín was dazed, Diarmuid was charmed, and Pauline was in her element.

As soon as Bláithín realized Pauline was going to look at every item on every stall, she said she'd wander around on her own for a while, and arranged to meet them later, in the café at the entrance. Captivated by the energy, the life, the sense of fun, Bláithín drank it all in. A very elderly lady wearing voluminous tie-die was making slow progress in front of Bláithín. She was pushing a Zimmer frame, with a tapestry sign saying 'I brake for no one.'

There were women buying stacks of underwear for their children and shaking out second-hand sheets to see if they had holes, men weighing up one electric screwdriver against another, but there were also outrageous hats and dresses being tried on. A woman, whose thick blond plaits hung well below her waist, handed her bag to her boyfriend while she casually stripped off to try on a fuchsia pink, vintage slip. Down another path Bláithín watched a full-length fur coat going on over Day-Glo lycra shorts. She grinned at the thought of that in the farmer's market in Kilkenny. Despite not needing anything, Bláithín bought a yellow silk scarf for three Euros and a set of mugs with bright swirls of primary colours outlined in gold for five.

She was on her second cup of coffee when Diarmuid and Pauline appeared. Pauline seemed to have gotten over her idea that it was a perilously dangerous place to be. She spread her purchases out on the large, white table, handed her purse to Diarmuid in full view of everyone, and told him to buy something nice for them at the bar. She had a beautiful, lined leather bag, a set of coasters, a necklace, and, touchingly, a large photo album for Bláithín.

"And all for less than twenty Euros! Sure the bag alone is worth three times that!" Pauline was delighted with herself. "Did you ever see anything like the get-up of the people here? Young ones that don't know what season they have, with half their behind hanging out of their shorts, yet they're wearing boots and a scarf! And what about your man in the silk dress? Did you see him on your wanderings? I was just saying to Diarmuid that woman over there should shave her legs before wearing a dress like that, and didn't she turn around and it was a man with a great big beard on him! I nearly died!"

Pauline looked far from dead. She had colour in her cheeks, and, although the lines parading across the edge of her top lip were so deep, they could have been drawn on with ballpoint, she was actually smiling at all of this. Any bit of which would definitely have had her in teeth-sucking disapproval back in Ireland.

Diarmuid came back with three Sprites and three sugar-dusted pastries balanced on a stack of napkins. "They didn't have a lot there and I didn't think you'd want another coffee," he said, eying the two empty cups.

"No, not with her blood pressure problem," agreed Pauline. Bláithín sometimes forgot that Pauline was a nurse and had genuine knowledge buried beneath her flow of trivia.

"I was just telling Bláithín about your man in the dress. Gas, wasn't it?" She sniffed at the pastry, pronounced it a bit dry but edible, and bit into it.

Bláithín fizzed her Sprite into her glass. "Ibiza is certainly a very interesting place. I'm glad Andy gave me the chance to come here."

"Huh," scoffed Pauline, "it was the least he could do."

"It wasn't his fault the business closed," protested Bláithín.

"No, but it was his fault the way he worked you the last few years. Sure the world and his mother knew you were running the department and doing the work of two people, didn't they, Diarmuid?"

Bláithín shook her head. "Ah, I didn't mind. It wasn't as if I had much else to do."

"That's not the point. You've always been controlled by the men in your life, Bláithín."

Pauline had sugar on her nose which made anything she said hard to take seriously. Bláithín smiled. In her head, she'd actually had very little to do with men all her life, her marriage included.

"Sure, God love you, didn't your father always control you, picking your job for you, driving you there with him day in and day out? What choice did you have? We wanted to get you out, didn't we Diarmuid?" Diarmuid, who was watching Bláithín's reactions, nodded.

Pauline continued, "We wanted you to come to Dublin and have a bit of a life with us, but your father wouldn't have it."

Bláithín broke her pastry into small pieces while she spoke. "Ah, sure he knew how shy I was. Anyway, I didn't mind. I liked the accounts."

"You could have done that in Dublin, but your father never said that to you, did he?"

Bláithín stared into the distance. "No, he didn't. He never mentioned it." Then with a start, her gaze returned to Pauline and Diarmuid. "You wanted me to live with you?" Her dark eyebrows signalled her surprise.

"See? I told you, didn't I, Diarmuid? I knew he'd never said it to her! Then, God love you, you went straight into marriage with that Frank."

"Ah now, that was my choice." Bláithín downed her Sprite. This was a bizarre conversation.

"Was it really, Bláithín?" asked Diarmuid, breaking his pastry into pieces. "Or did you do it to get out of home?"

"And that man controlled every breath you took," added Pauline enthusiastically.

"Did he?"

"Didn't he run the house and never even left you money for the pictures?"

"Well, he was good at bills and money, so…"

"You have a head like a calculator on you and he had you believing you couldn't manage an electricity bill! And the high-handed way he'd turn down invitations for you!"

Bláithín wanted to smile. It was as though they were talking about someone else. This outside view of her life was unrecognizable, and the sugar on Pauline's nose kept catching her attention.

"And another thing -"

Diarmuid interrupted Pauline's flow by reaching across with a napkin and wiping the sugar from her nose.

"Oh, thank goodness!" said Bláithín. "I couldn't look at anything else!"

"Well, I bet you're very glad you're spared that now. It's not the most elegant of noses." Pauline popped the last piece of pastry into her mouth. And just like that, a conversation that would have left Bláithín inarticulate with embarrassment and outrage two months ago, ended in laughter.

CHAPTER SIXTEEN

Pamela brewed a cup of chamomile tea as soon as she got home from her night out. Cassandra's proposal was strangely exciting, but she was also disappointed that her friends hadn't shed much light on the state of her daughter's marriage for her. Both of them had seemed incapable of reading their own marriages, not to mind anyone else's. Her personal experience was no help either. Her forty years with Jonathan had been uneventful, apart from the joy of having Susan.

He'd been a very 'nice' man. That was the word everyone used about him at the funeral. Twelve years older than Pamela, he'd seemed like the epitome of elegance and sophistication when he called into the florist shop where she worked to buy a bouquet for his mother. His casual wear was always neatly pressed slacks, an open-necked shirt, and a cravat. Even her friends had been impressed. Added to this, he owned his own house and picked her up from work in his shiny new Lancia, valeted every second Friday without fail. He'd run his life with an unvarying routine, into which Pamela was slotted nicely. She learned to avoid his silent displeasure, which could continue for days, by making sure everything went like clockwork. But he had been a kind and indulgent father to Susan.

Neither high drama nor excitement had any part in their calm and ordered lives, except once a fortnight in the bedroom. Even now, sitting at her table, drinking tea, Pamela's cheeks reddened at some of the memories. Sex was the only time Jonathan shed his overweening need for a calm and orderly life. Pamela had thoroughly enjoyed his enthusiastic and inventive attentions. She'd even been, on occasion, the instigator of some of the more unorthodox activities, urging him on until they collapsed panting and exhausted. Next morning, there was never any sign or mention of that ardour. They were both showered and neatly turned out for breakfast on the dot of seven-thirty. Was it possible that he was somehow ashamed by the feverish passion of their lovemaking? Still, all in all, she'd been content, and he'd told her he loved her every wedding anniversary until the year he died. How could she judge Susan's marriage?

By the time she was washing up her teacup, she'd decided to tell Susan and Glen about Cassandra's idea as soon as she could. She'd also tell them about the invitation to overnight in the villa on Tuesday, maybe she could gauge what the state of play was by their reactions.

Early Friday, Susan tapped on Pamela's door, with Clark in her arms. "I'm doing the school run this morning, Mum. Glen had to go in early." She sighed heavily. "I also have a hairdresser's appointment. Would you mind taking Clark? By the way, Sophie has just announced that she's got to make a beach collage for a class project. So, I'm thinking if I swing by and pick you two up before collecting Sophie, we could all go to the beach and see what we can find?"

"Of course, I'll take Clark, that's no problem. And an afternoon on the beach sounds like a great idea." Pamela held her arms out for her beaming grandson who was already trying to push the end of his soggy, chewed toast into her mouth. "Yuck, that's disgusting Clark!"

"Skustin," he agreed and threw it away. Pamela laughed, "Let's get you some fresh toast. See you later Susan. Have a nice time."

"Thanks, Mum, I'm on the phone if you need me."

A long walk on a beach while the children were distracted filling bags with sea treasures might be just the place for a heart-to-heart about her proposed move. She spent the morning anxiously rehearsing several different approaches in her head, The Light and Breezy, 'Oh just a thought really, don't know if it will come to anything...' The

Concerned, 'I'm really anxious to get your thoughts…' The Plain Speaking, 'There's something I'm going to try…' She was still mulling it over when Susan came to pick her up. She strapped Clark into his seat and sat in next to Susan. She may as well not have bothered with her anxious rehearsals. Susan announced they were meeting up with Katrina, her yoga partner, and her daughter. There would be no alone time.

Pamela knew she sounded aggrieved. "You never said they were coming, too."

"Didn't I?" Susan was cheerful. "I thought I did. We can go to San Vicente beach near them. It will probably be deserted."

Susan was right about having the place to themselves. When they parked their cars in an empty street outside a closed hotel, there was only one other car in view, a mucky Jeep.

Pamela was so annoyed she didn't even want to go scavenging with her grandchildren. She walked to the edge of the beach with them. The only people in sight were an elderly couple, strolling with careful steps up from the far end, and a couple having a picnic way over by the fishermen's huts.

Pamela helped Susan zip the children into colourful jackets, which made them look like little macaws chasing each other around the beach. Then she pleaded a headache and said she'd go back and sit in the car for a while.

"Are you okay, Mum?"

Pamela wondered if Susan knew how cross she felt. "Oh yes, fine. Don't worry." She stalked back to the car while Susan and Katrina sat on a low wall where they could keep an eye on the children as they chatted.

Pamela looked out at the sea and tried some deep breathing to release her irritation. There was always a peculiar stillness and peace in a parked car. The sea was a soft whisper through the window, and her eyes closed of their own accord.

Colours swirled, swathes of gold twined round white columns, deep rich greens overlaid by fronds of sparkling fuchsia, a woman whose glowing, coffee skin was barely contained in a buttercup yellow bikini smiled while she threaded blood-red hibiscus flowers through her long, ebony hair. Thick ridges of paint and swooping brush marks gave texture and life to the scene. Dripping brush in hand, Pamela stepped back to admire her work, her pleasure in it was a warm glow in her chest. The canvas was at least four feet by five feet. It was glorious! Even the children were shouting their approval, though there was no need for them to be banging on the walls about it.

Banging on the walls? No, they were banging on the car window. Startled awake and losing her dream painting to reality was an almost physical ache, and she spent the journey home trying to ignore the children's chatter, to hold on to the sensation of joy and the memory of the magical image which was being dispersed with every word that dragged her back to reality.

Susan had invited Katrina and Beth for dinner that night, so Pamela left them all to the sorting and washing of their beach collection. She fidgeted about in her studio, looking at her small canvases and polite paintings, disgruntled and frustrated with everything.

***

It was two days before there was a moment when Susan and Glen were at home without visitors. Pamela waited until Glen had been home an hour and the night light was glowing from the children's bedroom, before she tapped on their kitchen door and opened it enough to say, "Hi, you two. Got a minute?"

"Of course, Mum, come in," Susan called.

Pamela stepped into the bright kitchen where Susan was loading the dishwasher. The room was warm and smelled of garlic and tomato sauce.

"Is Glen around?"

"I'm in here." He stepped through from the living room, a sheaf of papers in his hand. "Are you okay?"

"Oh, I'm fine, it's just…" Pamela pulled out a kitchen

chair and sat down. She wondered if this really was a good idea. The others sat as well and looked at her. All she could read on their faces was concern. She took a breath and began. "As you know I met my fellow crones during the week -"

"I hate that word. It's too witchy for me," muttered Susan.

Pamela surprised herself by saying, "I've come to quite like it and what it represents to me. But anyway, the point is, Cassandra was wondering if we - that is Bláithín, the other woman, and myself - would like to move into her villa and share the costs." She straightened in her chair. "And the bottom line is we're going to spend the night there on Tuesday and see what we think." She hadn't meant to present it so quickly and baldly, but it was out there now.

Susan and Glen looked stricken. "It's just one night," Pamela added quickly. "Nothing is agreed to or set in stone. It may not even be possible in the end."

"Oh Mum, don't tell me we're driving you away with our silly arguments?" Susan looked reproachfully at Glen.

Glen rubbed his forehead. "Pamela, I sincerely hope that what's going on hasn't made you feel uncomfortable or unwanted. That's the last thing we -"

"There's nothing going on!" Susan's voice had gone up several notches. "You're just tired, you said it yourself!"

"Yes, I'm tired. Tired of these games." Glen snapped.

Pamela gasped, she scraped her chair back and stood up. "I'm sorry, I shouldn't be here for this. We can talk later."

"No, Pamela, please stay." Glen gestured back to her chair and for the first time, she noticed purple crescents under his eyes and deep worry lines between them.

"Yes, Mum, stay and tell him he's overworking and needs a rest." Susan sounded defensive.

"I can't, I shouldn't. I mean, I don't know anything about this." But she was sinking back onto her chair even as she spoke.

"Thank you," said Glen gently. "Pamela, I think you

should know that we went for counselling three years ag -"

Susan cut him off again, waving her hand dismissively. "Oh, she knows all about that already."

"No, I don't," said Pamela trying to interject.

Susan kept talking over her. "Glen, I told Mum how we went the last time you were stressed and how it all worked out fine," her words were rushed, strung together without a breath. "How we decided to put more effort into our relationship and to have another baby," she made a 'there-you-are' gesture with her hands, and continued, "Then we had little Clark, and he's so perfect, who couldn't be happy with him?" She smiled at Glen and Pamela, not quite meeting the gaze of either.

Pamela looked at Susan with narrowing eyes. What was Sue playing at?

Glen's voice was harsh. "Of course, I'm happy with Clark. I adore both my children as you well know. But there was no 'we' in that decision to get pregnant, was there?" He glared at Susan. "You didn't tell me you'd gone off the pill or that you were pregnant until you were four months along."

Pamela was horrified.

Susan flushed, looked briefly at Pamela, and turned back to Glen, "You just needed time to adjust... to -"

Glen's voice was sharp. "What I needed was for you to listen to me! What I needed was my wife to be my friend and partner and not treating me like a... like a..." he searched for words, "like a second-rate support actor in the play of your life."

Susan scoffed. "That's a bit dramatic Glen, isn't it?"

"Is it? Well, what happened to the Rodriguez account I was pitching for? What new account did Belén land for us? What happened at the town hall meeting?"

"Glen! That's not fair, they're all work things!"

"They're my life! And they were yours too. You were in this from the beginning with me. We planned and saved and worked those first few years, and we did it together!"

"But then we had Sophie, and of course, everything changes. That's just normal."

"Yes, things changed. You stopped being interested in anything I did or anything I had to say. As long as I turned up, and the money turned in, you didn't care what was happening."

Pamela's hands were knotted as tightly as her stomach. This was all so unexpected and horrible. She made to leave but a flash of intuition kept her still, they needed her as a witness - if she was sitting there with them, things couldn't get too nasty, could they?

Glen turned to Pamela. "That was exactly the stage we were at three years ago when I suggested couples counselling. Susan didn't want to go, it took months to persuade her, and even then, she stopped going after three sessions."

"Yes! Because she said I was right. You were stressed and tired."

"That wasn't all she said." Glen sounded weary. "It was all you chose to hear, but yes, she did suggest various things to try, special 'us times', to practice 'active listening.'"

"It worked, didn't it? We were happy again and Clark was proof of it."

"Clark wasn't proof of anything, and you know it, Susan!"

Susan ignored him. "And then Daddy died a few months after Clark's birth, and it was all so horrible." Tears over-filled her eyes and ran down her cheeks. Glen reached behind him and handed her the roll of kitchen paper but offered no other comfort.

It seemed to Pamela that he had the air of someone who'd been through this, many times before. An uncomfortable silence, disturbed only by Susan's sniffles and the hum of the dishwasher, was finally broken by Pamela clearing her throat. "It wouldn't take a psychiatrist to think perhaps, Susan has only been trying to recreate what she saw at home. I mean, her father absolutely never spoke about his work at the bank, and honestly, I never had anything whatsoever to do with it."

Glen's answer was instant. "Yes, but I'm not Jonathan, and I never was. Susan knew that from the start. Don't get me wrong, Jonathan was a very nice man, but there's no getting away from the fact that he was fairly introverted and maybe even a little antisocial."

"That's not a very kind thing to say, Glen!" Susan snapped.

Pamela smiled. She took no offense - Glen was quite right.

Glen turned to Pamela. "But I'm not like that, I wanted to be wholeheartedly involved in my family, but Susan just kept pushing me away."

"Oh God, Glen, you're overstating things as always. We made the move to Ibiza as a family, didn't we? Wasn't that good? And haven't we had the best fun for the last few weeks with all our friends popping in and out?"

"We've had an endless stream of people 'popping in and out' because you invited them! And I know it's to avoid having time alone with me since I told you I was so unhappy." He scrubbed his hands over his face, "Yes, I thought the move to Ibiza was worth a try. I really hoped it would shake things up, make a difference, bring us closer, but it didn't take long for the same old pattern to reappear."

Susan tore another sheet of paper off the kitchen roll and began wiping at some crumbs on the table around her. "I'm really not sure what you mean, Glen. We have a wonderful life."

"I loved you so much, and I wanted the world for our family, but I've been terribly lonely and the only place I've felt valued is at work."

Pamela's heart went into a spiralling nose-dive at his use of the past tense, but Sue seemed oblivious.

"Mum, do you think any of this is fair?"

Pamela gulped at being drawn into this. She spread her

hands. "I thought you were a happy, lucky couple."

"You see, Glen!" Susan sounded as if the whole matter had been resolved but Pamela stopped her with a gesture of her hand.

"But Susan, I know now that I only saw what you wanted me to see."

"I didn't think you'd take Glen's side, Mum."

"I'm not taking sides, and I certainly can't tell either of you what to do, but I do know now is the time for being completely honest with yourselves and with each other."

Glen stared out the window silently, and Susan was on the verge of tears again.

Pamela exhaled noisily and massaged her temples. She was getting no prizes for conflict resolution here. "Look, Susan, I loved your father, you know I did, but looking back I can see we lived two, almost completely separate, tightly controlled lives under the same roof. You don't want that." She stood up to leave.

"I'm sorry, Mum," Susan whispered.

"Oh, darling," Pamela came around the table and embraced her daughter. "There's nothing to apologize to me about. Look, nothing is ever one-sided and even if you don't realize it at the moment, things are rarely just one person's fault." Pamela straightened up and looked at the two of them. "You have to be open and truthful with each other. "

Glen looked down at his hands.

Pamela exhaled noisily. "I am going to go to Cassandra's on Tuesday for the night, but I'll discuss any other decision with you."

Susan gave a little laugh. "Oh, Mum, you won't want to leave us, I'm sure of it."

Pamela kissed the top of Susan's blonde head. "Not leaving you, maybe just a change for a while." She patted Glen gently on the shoulder as she passed him and went out into the chill, damp air. Her head was reeling, and Glen's ominous words echoed in her ears.

CHAPTER SEVENTEEN

Cassandra's mobile pinged and a text from Reuben appeared across the top.

'Free for coffee?'

She matched the terseness of his text.

'Yes.'

'Pick you up in ten.'

'Ok'

It had only been yesterday evening they had disclosed their pasts and shared that seismic shake of a kiss. Cassandra had been searching since then to find her normal laissez-faire attitude towards men. Involved but never too involved, emotional but never too emotional, always fun, often passionate, but with an exit strategy clearly in sight. This had disappeared. She had no explanation for what was happening now.

Even this morning, during her yoga, Reuben was a constant presence, as if she only had to reach out to touch him.

Anyway, she had only ten minutes to get ready. Did she need to change her clothes or not? A glance into the hall mirror said no. Her denims were old and washed to a pale blue softness, they were tight and tapered down her long legs, disappearing into leather boots. The November day was holding on to summer colouring but was wrapped in a chilly wind, so her oversized, white cashmere, polo neck jumper was perfect. Team it up with her mulberry, silk pashmina and she would be ready to go.

She went close to the mirror and bared her teeth. No lipstick smudges on them but there was brown oat bran caught between her bottom teeth. One tooth brushing later, she was sitting on the low wall outside the house. With one foot planted flat, and her knee drawn to her chest, the other leg was extended long and straight down to the ground. If he happened to notice her flexibility, so much the better. Ridiculous, childish scenarios ran through her head. Maybe he was going to screech the Jeep to a halt, jump out, run to her, hold her tight and say he should have stayed yesterday and had wild, abandoned sex all night. Maybe he was going to have his head out the window shouting, "The house is yours!" Or was he regretting whatever it was that had happened between them?

White dust clouds travelling along the top of the huge hedge up the lane to her house heralded his arrival. The butterflies dancing in her stomach put on hob-nailed boots. The dust-covered Jeep had mud splatters up to the handles, Cassandra, thinking of her white cashmere, hoped the inside was in a better state. It pulled a U-turn and stopped in front of her; Reuben leant across and opened the passenger door. Dark glasses hid his eyes, and without their blue softness, his face looked grim, no pleasure apparent at seeing her.

She pulled her own shades down, hiding her disappointment. She looked away and took her time getting off the wall and climbing into the Jeep which was cleaner inside than out.

"Thank you for coming." He was already focused on turning. Black denims, a black t-shirt and the shades gave him the look of a hit-man in a particularly uninspired B-movie, though she had to admit, it was a look he wore well

"No problem." She pointedly took out her phone to check for messages. Anxiety stabbed at her. What was this about?

When she realized he was headed for San Vicent, she glanced across at him. "You know there's nothing open down there, don't you?"

"Thermos," he said and jerked a thumb towards the back of the car. She peered over her shoulder. There was a haversack slumped on the floor, an old, black thermos flask sticking out the top.

Without looking at her, Reuben said, "I wanted some

peace to talk to you."

"You could have called to the house."

He glanced at her; at least his head moved in her direction, all she had was a blue-tinted double image of herself reflected back at her. "I don't trust myself there."

Cassandra nodded; she kind of knew what he meant.

A few minutes later, they were parking in an empty side street facing the beach. Cassandra let herself out of the car and strode off with her hands tucked into the back pockets of her jeans. What the hell was going on?

He caught up with her. His smelled of freshly cut wood and aftershave that made her want to breathe it deep into her lungs. The haversack was on his back, and he had a thick blanket under his arm.

"Over there?" He gestured off to the left, towards a row of fishermen's huts tucked in against the foot of the cliff. She shrugged and they strolled, side by side in silence to the first hut. The offshore breeze was ruffling against gentle blue waves. It covered the sea with small, white peaks, like patted frosting on a cake. As soon as he spread the blanket, Cassandra sat down, leant back against the wall, and folded her arms. Her patience was fading fast with this silent carry-on. "So, what's this about?"

Reuben sat opposite her, poured thick, black coffee into two enamel mugs, and handed one to Cassandra. The smell alone was enough to give a caffeine hit.

"Cream? Sugar? Biscotti?" she mocked.

He rooted in the bag and produced two battered tins. "Creamer and sugar," he offered them to her with a spoon.

"Actually, neither thanks." She smiled at being caught out in her pettiness. He was still rummaging in his bag and produced a battered cake tin. Traces of once bright, embossed flowers twined their way around it. Now, metal shone through their faded colours and the gilt-edge had all but disappeared. However, its functionality was unimpaired, because when he opened it, the smell of buttery shortcake was mouth-watering.

He held the tin out to her.

"Make this yourself?" she scoffed.

"Yes, this morning."

They sipped their coffee in silence. Staring out to sea, Cassandra ate a square of the shortbread while racking her brains for something to say.

Reuben cleared his throat. "Cassandra," he began.

She put down her coffee and focused on him.

"I... I..." He picked up the biscuit tin and offered it to her. "Would you like another?"

She pushed her hair behind her ears and took the tin from his hands and set it aside. "Reuben, this is all both mysterious and impressive, but it's also annoying! You want to talk, and to be honest, I'm quite nervous about what you want to say, so please, get the fuck on with it."

He took off his shades and hooked them into the neck of his t-shirt and his abruptly naked eyes were shocking in their vulnerability. Although he was sitting cross-legged and upright, his hands were in constant motion, his palms rubbing circles on his knees.

"I'm nearly sixty, Cassandra, too old for games. Time is too short and too valuable to spend it dancing around people, trying to guess what they're feeling. All I can say is I've honestly never felt like this before about anyone, and I don't know how to deal with it." His breathing was as erratic as if he'd run a marathon. "I'm falling in love with you, Cassandra, and my life has been upside down since the first time I saw you." He spread his hands, making an offering of his words.

"Oh, since the day you fixed my doors and barely spoke to me?" Cassandra was amazed to hear her voice sounding calm and cool, though the shortbread had just become a solid lump lodged immediately beneath her breastbone, making it difficult to breathe.

"No, since the day you arrived in the villa."

"What?"

"I was in the pump house putting away the cleaning

materials from the pool the evening you arrived, and I saw you do the qi gong routine 'Embrace the moon, caress the wind' up on the terrace. I was blown away by the beauty of it, and that this was how you chose to react to the house. You looked magical and powerful, and I knew there was nothing more I wanted in this whole world than to get to know you. But as you now know, I am not a man who has a good track record in life, so I had no intention of approaching you." He shrugged. "And then you rang me."

Cassandra's eyes searched for escape, for distraction from this altogether too serious moment. This wasn't her - she did fun, flirting, affairs, never something that felt as if it was squeezing the breath out of her and ripping her heart open.

She caught a flash of colour down the beach, bringing a random comment to her lips. "I hope there's someone keeping an eye on the kids there, one of them looks very small." Well, at least she'd said something.

Reuben set the cups and the flask to one side and moved close enough for their knees to touch. He reached across and picked up her hands.

"Cassandra, I'm not asking anything of you now, not even a reply, but I want you to know how I feel." He looked down at their hands, shook his head slightly, and glanced back at her.

She wanted to take his face in her hands. She wanted to see a smile light up those amazing eyes. She also wanted to get the fuck out of there, to tear down the beach scattering those children like multicoloured bowling pins, hurtle through an elderly couple struggling up through the soft sand, leaving chaos and mayhem behind her, so Reuben would see she wasn't someone who could ever give him the answer he wanted.

He lifted her hands to his lips and kissed them. "I have neither the time nor the inclination for a part-time, or a half-hearted relationship. I want to commit one hundred percent to discovering where we can go with this... this... *gift* of what's between us."

Cassandra leant forward across the small gap between them and rested her head on the crook of his shoulder, her forehead against his warm neck. She closed her eyes and inhaled deeply. This felt so good, so peaceful, so secure. If they never had to move again, everything would be perfect. But they did, and to end this moment made her feel like crying. Why hadn't he just wanted to take her to bed and have uncomplicated fun? Because it wasn't bloody uncomplicated, was it? She knew it, and he knew it. But she had never been capable of committing one hundred percent to a person, it wasn't a logical step, people weren't like that. An abyss had opened in front of her. Was she going to run to safety or jump? She breathed him in again, deliciously warm, woody, and citrusy. She never felt so scared in her life.

"I meant what I said, Cassandra. You don't have to say anything. I must go away for a few days, which is why I sprung this on you now. I didn't want you to think that I'd disappeared without a word after yesterday."

Every word was a caress of warm air across her cheek. She forced herself to sit up. "Reuben, I… I'm not the best person for commitment."

"And I am?" He questioned with a smile. "I think I'm suggesting something that neither of us has ever done before, Cassandra."

Even the way he said her name was magic.

"Which is why I don't want you to -" He echoed her own thoughts. "-either jump in unthinkingly or run from it in fear." He packed everything away and stood up. This time she took the hand he offered to help her up.

He didn't let go, but she still didn't say anything. They walked back to the car, nodding a greeting to two women sitting on a wall, children's shoes, buckets bags, and towels spread around them.

"See, you needn't have been worried about those children."

"I wasn't."

He smiled. "I know."

The journey home was as silent as the journey down, but it wasn't an impatient, anxious silence. It was more a 'the world waiting to see what was going to happen' silence. Cassandra still couldn't bring herself to speak. She told herself she was being grown up and responsible, taking her time to think, instead of leaping into this obvious nonsense with him.

As soon as the Jeep stopped outside her villa, Reuben got out and opened the passenger door for her. She swung around to get out and found herself for once, at eye level with him. She paused, "Do you want to come in?"

"No, I need to be going, and I also want you to have time to think and decide." He took off his shades and smiled at her, his heart-stopping crooked grin. "I feel like a teenager. I can't believe I've done this. That I've confessed to falling wondrously and magically in love with you!" He shook his head. "But no, I won't come in, because if I do, I'll start talking about how this is obviously meant to be, fated to happen, an Ibiza miracle, or how it feels so damn right being with you, and I don't want to persuade you into your decision. I want you to come to it yourself."

"Yes, it's just as well you kept all those thoughts to yourself in that case." Cassandra mocked gently, returning his grin. He stepped back to allow her climb out, pushed the door closed behind her, tipped his forehead in salute, and strode back to the driver's side.

Cassandra couldn't believe he was going to walk away like that, after everything he'd said? Surely a kiss at least was in the cards? Though she wasn't sure how she'd react. Would she drag him into bed there and then? Possibly. Felt slightly pressured? Maybe.

From inside the car, he leant across and spoke out the passenger window, "I put in some enquiries about the house, and I hope to have some news for you soon."

Reality nudged its way back in.

"Thank you, Reuben. I'm truly anxious to know what the story is as soon as possible. Oh, and another thing, I need to ask you if you or Rosa would be free to pick up Bláithín from San Antonio and Pamela from near San Lorenc to bring them here on Tuesday evening."

"Of course. Text me their numbers and we'll sort something out. Take care, Cassandra Collingsworth." He replaced his shades, but his smile still transformed his face. She watched him go, her thoughts and emotions a complete, looping mass of contradictions.

CHAPTER EIGHTEEN

Saturday morning's clear sky gradually filled with low, sullen clouds, and by half-past six, rain was spitting, glittering down through the streetlights. Hunched over Google maps, Pauline was directing Diarmuid to the correct road for Thomas Green's British shop. They had already picked up a boot full of groceries in the Mercadona supermarket, where Pauline questioned the sanity of the escalator designer. Completely open on one side to the chill air, its views over the green hills and open countryside curtailed by sodium lights and drizzle. "Twouldn't have cost them much to finish it off properly."

Bláithín stared out through the rain-speckled window. Out along the bay, garish signs appeared through the dark, promising 'All You Can Eat! 'Family Karaoke.' 'Free Shots!' 'Girls!' Faded and ripped, the posters looked incongruous and forlorn, on empty, locked buildings. Padlocks, chains, metal shutters, and papered-over windows clearly stated that this long street, mirroring the winding beach, was not going to come to life again until guaranteed sun brought its customers back.

How dismal. Abruptly her attention returned to the inside of the car, and she sat forward in the back seat, straining against her seatbelt. Surely, she'd misheard Pauline. "You did what?"

"I invited Maite and Pedro to Sunday lunch tomorrow."

"But we hardly know them!"

"And sure, we'll never know them if we don't put in a bit of effort," retorted Pauline.

Bláithín tried again. "Maite's too young, she won't want to be spending her Sunday hanging around with a bunch of pensioners!" This friendly spontaneity was completely alien to her, let alone to her view of her sister-in-law, who after all, was only here for a week.

"Sure, she has no family here, the poor creature! Isn't she from Argentina? They were saving to go back to introduce Pedro to her family when she fell pregnant, so that's the end of those plans for a while."

"Oh." Bláithín was taken aback. If she had been asked, she would have described herself as a caring person. She often donated to charity. She occasionally stood on High Street in Kilkenny, sheltering under the high, grey, limestone arches of the town hall, timidly shaking a collection box for a local homeless shelter. She rarely passed a beggar without emptying her purse of coins, but it was becoming clear to her she was actually oblivious to people and what made them tick.

***

When Bláithín opened the doors to their visitors the next day, she could see why Maite had been swept off her feet by Pedro. His handsome features set in the deeply tanned, weathered face of a professional fisherman were a wonderful combination. A gap-toothed grin added to his charm. He barely had a word of English. But it didn't appear to matter. Over Pauline's beef and vegetable stew, he and Diarmuid, an avid fisherman himself, used big hand gestures, Google translate, and Maite to swap fish stories. The stew was finished down to the last spoon of the intense, rich gravy, but the hit of the meal was Pauline's bread-and -butter pudding which she had made despite Bláithín's protests.

"God almighty, Pauline," Bláithín had complained in the supermarket. "What will they think? Old bread, sugar, and eggs! Can't we get a frozen cheesecake or something?"

Pauline hadn't even answered her, just picked up vanilla essence, cinnamon, and muscatel raisins.

Pedro was amazed they'd taken the trouble to make a version of the traditional Ibicencan Greixonera, which as Maite explained was similar but made with stale pastries and not bread.

Pauline laughed at that. "When bread-and-butter pudding first appeared in Ireland, it was far from pastries we were, day-old or otherwise!" She radiated delight as Pedro asked if he could take the last piece home for his mother to try.

After lunch, Pauline insisted Maite move to the couch and gave her a stool to raise up her swollen ankles. Maite sighed as she sat back; she stroked her enormous stomach lovingly. "I am so happy about this little one, but her timing is too bad."

Bláithín brought over their coffees and sat next to her.

"That you couldn't go to Argentina? Just think, when you do manage it, you'll be able to bring your baby with you."

"Not only that! The administration of here," she waved her hand around at the flat, "asked me to make a… a … a lot of persons…"

"A team?" Bláithín guessed.

"Yes, yes, a team, to do all cleaning and fixing broken things in the whole building, a very great opportunity. I could do most all everything, and I made all the papers to make a company but now…" She trailed off. She had everyone's attention as her hand patted the straining pink smock, so they all saw a bulge like an entire hardboiled egg erupt under her hand and ripple across her stomach to disappear under her ribcage.

"My God! Was that a..? What was it?" Bláithín's face was caught between frowning and smiling.

Pedro knelt by Maite and gave the bump a kiss.

"Probably an elbow or a heel," Pauline told them.

Diarmuid wiped his glasses and said, "That's a shame about your company, Maite. Maybe something will work out yet."

Pauline said, "It's a pity we're not here full-time. Diarmuid's a dab hand at the ould repairs. There's not a thing stays broken in our house for more than ten minutes."

"That would be so great. And too, I need someone to

make lots of beds and do polishing?" With a hopeful smile, Maite turned to Pauline. "Maybe you?"

"Ah now, neither of us have the energy for much of that, at our age." Pauline sounded regretful.

The visit ended with Pedro inviting Diarmuid out on a fishing trip the next time he was back, and Pauline promising to make another bread pudding and drop it down to the shop before she left. As soon as the door shut behind Maite and Pedro, Pauline handed out maps and magazines she had picked up from shops and stands over the last few days. "We must plan for tomorrow, see what's there to do if this rain continues."

"Right, so." Diarmuid agreed and picked up a map.

Bláithín shook her head. Where were shuffling, monosyllabic Diarmuid and short-tempered, busybody Pauline? What was it about Ibiza?

CHAPTER NINETEEN

By Tuesday, the weather had cleared. Brisk winds flicked small clouds across a pale, watery sky. Cassandra kicked the table. "I've moved you three bloody times, and now you look better where you started!" The table was clearly unfazed by the criticism. It was important to Cassandra that Pamela be blown away by the possibilities of working in this spacious, bright room as soon as she was shown it. The workroom she had earmarked for Bláithín was more straightforward, lots of table space, shelving, and connection points for a laptop and printers. While she was confident that her friends would love the house as much as she did, she was aware that she had no information about the actual possibility of them all being allowed to stay there. As if her thoughts conjured him, Reuben's name shone from her phone vibrating on the table. Cassandra paused to get her breathing calm and her voice casual before she answered it.

"Hello."

"Hi Cassandra, I wanted to let you know as soon as possible that I heard from the agency. There's good news and bad. The villa is only paid up until the end of next week, but they are happy to let you continue to rent it at a reduced rate of one thousand five hundred per month as I told them you were family."

Cassandra's gasp of delight had nearly drowned out the end of his sentence, but she heard enough to make her smile. "Family, eh?"

"Not pressuring you Cassandra, just using any leverage I could." His smile was evident in his voice. "The bad news is there is a prospective buyer. They said you must allow him, or his agents access whenever necessary. They will, of course, give you at least twenty-four hours' notice."

She wasn't discouraged in the slightest. "This is Spain, nothing happens quickly here. It could take months. All that matters, for now, is that I have it! I have the house. I don't have to -"

Reuben interrupted her. "Cassandra, I must warn you. They mentioned the buyer has surveyed the property already, so the deal must be quite advanced. You may not get much time there."

Even this didn't dampen her spirits. "Sufficient unto the day etcetera, etcetera! Thank you, Reuben, you continue to be a lifesaver. Now all I need is for my fellow Crones to agree to share the cost with me and-"

"Crones?"

"Yes, we are embracing our age and our lives. We are Fabulous Ibizan Crones!"

"Sounds way more interesting than 'middle-aged ladies,'" Reuben laughed. "Talking of your friends, I'll text them for their addresses, and I'll be in San Lorenc at half five and in San Antonio at six. Return journey on Wednesday afternoon. Is that okay?"

"Perfect, thank you."

His voice softened. "Well, this isn't the time for the conversation we need to have, Cassandra. There will be a place and time for that very soon, I promise."

She couldn't think, she couldn't breathe. How could he do this to her? Oh, for fuck's sake she found she was actually fanning her face with her hand like a Victorian maiden.

"See you soon, Cassandra Collingsworth."

Cassandra cleared her throat and croaked, "Thank you, Reuben." She tried 'See you soon' in a careless sort of non-committal way, slurring it to 'Syasun', which made him laugh and her cringe as they hung up.

She danced around the kitchen like a six-year-old trying on a new fairy costume. The lyrics 'I can stay in the house,' alternating with 'Reuben's falling in love with me' until she stopped dead. "Bloody hell! Am I falling for him?" she asked the kitchen. She banished the thought but couldn't banish her grin as she texted her friends.

***

Clark noticed the vibrating phone first, as it skittered across the table. Pamela snatched it just before his yogurt-covered hands got it. She smiled as she read the message from Cassandra, then she rang Susan. She tucked the phone between her ear and her shoulder so she could wipe Clark's hands while she spoke. "Hi Susan, you'll probably be back, but I just want to give you a heads up that I'm being collected at half-past five."

Susan's voice came back exasperated, "Oh, Mummy. You know I'd prefer to get your friend's address and drop you off, then I could see for myself what kind of place you're going to. I mean, you barely know these people."

Pamela was sharp. "I'm not a child Susan. It will be fine. See you later."

She was sure she was being unreasonable, and that Susan meant well, but honestly, she was sixty-four, this should not be such a big deal! Sophie helped her pack her matching grey, silk pyjamas, and robe. Clark was given the very important task of eating a banana while he held Grandma's hairbrush waiting for just the right time to put it into her bag. Sophie scurried around helping to fill her travelling bag with toiletries. They were excited about her going on an adventure on her own and she had to admit that she was, too.

Susan was home in time to take over the children and to cross-question Reuben when he arrived.

Pamela smiled at the expert way he evaded her questions by being busy. He graciously helped Pamela up into the jeep and looked at his watch. "Time to collect the third crone," he said.

"Oh, don't you just hate that expression?" asked Susan.

"No, I don't," he answered. "Cassandra explained her view of it, and I loved it. Why be an ordinary middle-aged woman when you can be a crone goddess?"

"Hmmm," was all Susan had to add, obviously put out at

not being agreed with.

"Bye darlings, see you tomorrow," Pamela called. Sophie and Clark waved and blew kisses behind her all the way down the drive.

***

Bláithín's mobile had pinged as they made their way back up the hill from Rita's Cantina after a long, late lunch. It was a text full of capital letters and exclamation marks from Cassandra.

> Hi, fellow Crones! Half five for P. today and six for B. AND it WILL be REUBEN picking you up!!! He'll text you soon for your addresses. TAKE note because I want your HONEST opinions of him tonight! Also, tomorrow afternoon for return. X

"Oh, I'm being picked up sooner than I thought- quite soon, in fact! Still, I'll be back tomorrow before you go."

Pauline shook her head. "Not if you have any kind of good night, you won't! Our flight is at ten -"

"Yes, I'll be back in the afternoon."

"Ten in the *morning*, Bláth! We're going via Amsterdam. Amsterdam! Imagine that. Mind you, all we'll be seeing is the airport. It's all arranged. Pedro's cousin is picking us up at eight."

"But I wanted to see you off!"

"Well, you'll just have to say your goodbyes now, won't you?"

"Now Pauline," Diarmuid put his arm around his wife and looked at Bláithín. "We're delighted you have friends inviting you to stay with them, it's more than you ever had at home. I hope you have a lovely night, and we'll look forward to hearing about it."

Bláithín nearly blurted out all that was hanging on tonight, but realizing the questioning that would follow, she restrained herself

They reached the Flora Apartments. "Right," said Pauline. "I must crack on with that bread-and-butter pudding and you better get your overnight case ready. Who's picking you up, anyway?"

"A friend of Cassandra's."

"Oh, is she staying too?"

"No, it's a man, and he's only dropping me to her house." Diarmuid forestalled any more chat by dropping an egg. Bláithín texted Cassandra.

> 'Tell Reuben not to call to the flat- Life is not long enough for him to be interrogated by Pauline. Tell him message me when he's outside and I'll come down.'

She had to smile when she caught her reflection in the narrow mirror. There she was, at her age, packing a case to overnight with friends! Her smile became an open grin, which was okay because her white, even teeth were about the only part of her she didn't wish were different.

She threw one of the enormous T-shirts she slept in, a wash bag with the bare essentials, and clean clothes for tomorrow, into a holdall. At the last moment, she threw in her camera. Even if she hadn't gotten around to printing them out, she really was very pleased with the photos she'd taken last Friday. She might even show them to her friends. This thought, of course, tinged her excitement with anxiety but it didn't stop her.

"Oh, my lift's here!" She called out as soon as her phone lit up with Reuben's message.

Pauline craned her head out the window. "Well, if that's your man, for all his age, I wouldn't trust him as far as I could throw him. What do you think, Diarmuid?"

Diarmuid looked out. "Well, God bless your eyesight, is all I can say if you can see his personality from here, in the dark!"

Pauline wasn't finished. "There's someone else in the car! Do you know what you're getting yourself into at all?"

"That's only Pamela. She's my other friend - she was picked up first. Please don't worry, Pauline. I promise I'll let you know when I'm safely installed in my friend's house." Hearing herself say that made her laugh. "I feel like a ten-year-old!"

Diarmuid hugged her tight, "Be sure to keep in touch, Bláth. We won't go back to the old ways."

She stood, still in his embrace, her voice muffled against his chest. "No Diarmuid, we won't."

Pauline's hug was long and warm. Then she stood back and studied Bláithín. "You're looking better than you have for years, I think this place agrees with you."

"To be honest, Pauline, you're looking better yourself too, even after the week. I think the change was good for us all."

Pauline dabbed at her eyes and opened the door. "Go on now, don't keep himself waiting. He has the look of a man with a temper."

With a pang, Bláithín realized she meant more to these people than she had ever known, or than she'd allowed them to matter to her. "Goodbye so," she said and stepped out into the hall. She had enough time on the way down for anxiety to try and take over, questioning everything she was doing and predicting doom.

But Reuben's smile as he greeted the 'Famous Bláithín' and helped her in with her bag put her at ease. He didn't look at all like a man with a temper, just a man that had lived a hard life. However, Pamela's, "Are you all ready for the school excursion?" made her laugh so much as it exactly summed up her earlier excitement, she didn't give feeling anxious another thought.

CHAPTER TWENTY

The short Ibizan dusk was over by the time Reuben's headlights picked out the turning off the narrow country road.

"Nearly there," he said. They jolted up along a bumpy track. Shortly, they turned a corner into a gravelled courtyard bordered by a low wall. He pulled up in front of a semi-circular flight of steps. Old fashioned lamps, bracketed on both sides of an arched, wooden door, threw yellow pools of light on earthenware pots filled with pink geraniums.

"Have a nice night!" Reuben called as he handed out their cases.

Pamela was reaching for the knocker when the door was thrown open to its full extent, releasing bright light, warm air, and the tantalizing smell of cooking out into the night. Cassandra held her arms wide. "Welcome! Welcome my crone sisters!" She waved at Reuben who was already pulling away. He beeped back at her.

"Come in! I'm so excited you're here." They stepped into a white-walled reception area. An ornately-framed mirror took up one wall; a table with an enormous glass jar of wildflowers was centred on a second. The whole area was floored with highly patterned tiles in muted colours which led through an archway and continued down a corridor the length of the house, with wooden doors on both sides.

"This is gorgeous," said Bláithín.

"Beautiful," agreed Pamela.

"It is rather wonderful, isn't it? But quickly, tell me. What did you think of Reuben?"

Bláithín was first to answer. "Well, after an entire three-quarters of an hour with the man, I'd say he seemed sound enough. A bit quiet, but that's all to the good, isn't it?"

Pamela tilted her head, considering her answer. "Good-looking, in a battered, taller, older Brad Pitt kind of way -"

"That's what I thought too, the first time I saw him!" Cassandra interrupted.

Pamela smiled and continued, "And he's charming, Cassandra. Do I gather there's a budding romance between you two?"

"Oh, God! That's a long story and it needs a drink. First, I'll show you around your home-to-be!" She indicated a small door to their left. "That's a guest bathroom." She walked through the archway, opened the first door and flicked on the light. "This is your bedroom, Pamela, double bed with ensuite. That window looks out onto the side garden."

"Gosh! This is perfect!" Pamela loved the bright abstract prints, yellow muslin curtains, and Moroccan rugs. She put her leather overnight case on the floor.

Cassandra moved on and pushed open the next door. "This is yours, Bláithín. There's no difference, I flipped a coin." It was a mirror image except the curtains and bedding were in soft turquoise.

Bláithín's wide-eyed grin spoke volumes as she dumped her canvas bag on the bed. "Wow! It's gorgeous, and enormous compared to what I have in Andy's."

"The third one here is mine, just because I was here first and it's already completely messy. Okay, that's sleeping done. Here is the living room." She turned to the opposite wall and opened a door. She strode through, into a large, comfortable room. A four-seater, white sofa faced away from them, positioned in front of a folding glass wall, soft, white curtains partially drawn across it. A glass-fronted fire with a long, gleaming, black chimney pipe was tucked in the corner next to a large TV, and pushed against the back wall was a long, polished wooden dining table, and eight chairs.

"Kitchen's in there," Cassandra said. Jerking her thumb to one side, where closed, double doors shared the wall with heavy, wooden shelves stacked with colourful rugs and cushions. She headed towards two doors in the side wall. "Your studios are over here." She mimed a trumpet with her hands and blew a fanfare. Opening the first door, she waved Bláithín in, "Bláithín's-" moving on to the other, she pushed it ajar. "-and Pamela's. Have a look around while I'm opening a bottle in the kitchen."

Pamela found the light switch and fell in love with the room. A wooden table, a chair, a couch and a set of shelves were the only furnishings between her and the enormous night-darkened window. It would be wonderful. With a sigh, she left to check out the room next door. Bláithín was pacing her workroom and turned a shining face to Pamela. "If I could have something along the walls to hang prints on, I could have a great overview to develop a series of even more in-depth photos. What was your room like?"

Pamela laughed and said, "Absolutely perfect." They stepped back into the living room. Pamela trailed her hand along the top of the couch. "It's amazing, isn't it? Just as Cassandra said," she whispered.

Bláithín laughed, "I know! I never expected anything so grand!"

One of the kitchen doors opened, and Cassandra waved glasses at them. "I'm opening a bottle of Cava this time girls, Spain's answer to champagne. Come and get it."

"Hang on a sec." Bláithín took out her phone and quickly typed a message to Diarmuid, telling him she'd arrived, the place was great and wished them a safe journey. She pressed send and dropped her phone back into her pocket. The pistol shot of a popping cork greeted her as she followed into the kitchen.

They sat around the kitchen table and Cassandra filled their flutes and raised her glass. "Ibiza Crone Club together again. Any new business?"

Bláithín took the lead and filled them in on her week with Pauline and Diarmuid. "How heartbreaking for them,"

Pamela said when Bláithín had recounted the story of the miscarriages.

"Bloody lousy!" Cassandra slapped the table for emphasis. "No wonder she went a bit doolally. Jesus, and you never knew a thing?"

Bláithín shook her head.

Pamela folded her elbows on the table. "I'm beginning to understand there's far more hidden and unspoken in families than I ever realized, and just because you live with, or close to someone, you may actually not know them at all."

Bláithín was pleased to have her own recent thoughts echoed "On top of all that, Pauline got totally involved with Maite and Pedro! Not in her usual nosey, judgmental way, but genuinely interested. I mean, she even made them a bread-and-butter pudding before she left!"

Cassandra grimaced. "I'm sure that's an honour, but it sounds disgusting."

Bláithín laughed. "It tastes better than it sounds."

"I must say, it seems to me Pauline's more interested in keeping people at bay and not getting involved with them, in Ireland than she is here," said Cassandra as she removed a steaming quiche from the oven, set it on a rack to cool and sat down again.

Bláithín nodded. It was true, and more for her to think about.

"Wait until you hear about my evening with Susan and Glen," said Pamela, reaching for the bottle.

They were shocked at the depth of the problem Susan had been trying to paper over. "I knew there was more to it." Cassandra shaking her head when Pamela finished the story.

"Yes, it was what you'd said that alerted me to Susan's behaviour. As her mother, I can't help feeling a degree of responsibility."

"Nonsense!" Cassandra was brisk. "There comes a time when an adult has to accept responsibility for their own behaviour, and either not hide behind the excuse of a bad upbringing or decide to overcome it."

Her friends were silent. Watching Cassandra take in her own words. She gave a brittle laugh, "Ah no, not me! I positively and consciously did exactly the opposite of what my mother wanted for me, so I'm okay." She began to take salad ingredients from the fridge and spoke over her shoulder to Pamela. "What do you think will happen?"

"I have no idea. Obviously, I hope they work it out, but they seemed on such different wavelengths, and I don't want to be in the middle. I'll just have to wait and see. Now, tell us about Reuben. What's going on?"

"Jesus H. Christ! I have no idea! Well, I do, but it's so bizarre and ridiculous, I can't deal with it." She stepped back to the table and picked up her glass. "Reuben says he's falling in love with me!" She spread her hands. "There you have it, in its absurdity." She downed her cava.

Bláithín frowned at her. "But what's wrong with that? I gathered you had your own plans for him, so isn't that good?"

"My plan was to have fun, to fuck happily for a while, and then part as friends. I can't... I'm not someone who has ever done 'love'."

Pamela was puzzled. "But your marriage, surely-"

"Oh Christ, that! Look, it wasn't exactly a conventional marriage. A few fun-filled, blurry years in Ibiza to get his visa. Then back in the U.K, where we helped each other start our businesses. We were compatible and broke, continuing to share a flat made sense. It was a no-strings-attached arrangement that suited us both."

"Better than a thousand strings and suiting no one," muttered Bláithín, and Cassandra shot her a grateful glance.

Pamela was still perplexed. "But you sounded so upset when you told us about his affair."

Cassandra took her glass back to the counter with her and stood with her back to them as she began chopping ingredients for the salad. "The thing was, it wasn't a normal fling, it wasn't a passing fancy... and she was pregnant."

"Oh."

"Yes, and the other thing was, he wasn't running for the hills or paying to make it go away. He said... Fuck it all, he said he was lucky he hadn't left it too late to grow up. He said our life had been shallow and meaningless, now that he knew what he had been missing. And then the self-righteous prick invited me to the wedding!"

"Cassandra, come sit down, I think you're going to kill the salad." Bláithín took Cassandra's empty glass back to the table and filled it. Cassandra followed. They all knew the threatening tears had not been caused by the onions.

"We'd been the fun couple, madcap and free. We never pretended to love each other so there were never jealousies or dramas. Pierce always said we were the envy of the 'Bored and the Bitter.' I preferred to call them the 'Cheating and the Cheated.'" Cassandra turned her mouth down. "Sounds quite cruel now." She shrugged and continued, "Anyway... then he changed the goddamn fucking goalposts!"

Pamela drained the bottle into their glasses. "How long had you been together?"

"Twenty-five years! Twenty-five years of wasted time!"

"It wasn't though, not really, was it?" Pamela gazed intently at Cassandra.

"What do you mean? He couldn't get away fast enough."

"But... it seems to me that you supported each other through business developments, through sickness, I assume one or other of you were sick at some stage?"

Cassandra rolled her eyes at some memory and said, "You could say that."

Pamela continued, "As well as having fun and holidays and even talking about your affairs too, I imagine?"

"Yes, poor Pierce always had trouble ending them."

"So, even if you weren't 'in' love, you certainly seemed to have loved each other to a degree that enabled you to have a successful relationship, albeit a very unconventional one, for twenty-five years. Not a lot of people can say that."

"Me, for one," said Bláithín.

Cassandra stared at them in silence, her hands clasped on the table in front of her.

Pamela and Bláithín watched the silence grow and exchanged worried glances.

Bláithín reached out her hand. "Jaysus! Cass. Are you okay?"

Cassandra smiled, a sudden lighting up of her eyes.

Bláithín looked around. "What?"

"You called me Cass! No one has ever done that, apart from Pierce, and only when he was very drunk. I love it! You two are the best thing that's happened to me since… I don't know when, actually."

"What about Reuben falling in love with you? Surely that ranks somewhere!"

"Yes, Pamela, but he doesn't realize…"

"What? About your marriage?"

"No, he knows about that already. What he doesn't know is…." She took a deep breath. "I have never, ever in my life loved anyone, and no one has ever loved me. If he's looking for love, I'm not the person to give it to him."

Pamela exchanged a worried glance with Bláithín and said, "But Cassandra, you're a wonderful person. That can't be true!"

Cassandra got to her feet again. "All the fault of my 'mother issues', as Pierce liked to say! But honestly, thank you both. You're great listeners and you've given me a lot to think about. But enough! Let's enjoy ourselves." She brought a colourful platter over to the table. The quiche tasted every bit as good as it smelled and the green salad, peppered through with fruit and seeds, hadn't suffered from Cassandra's anger-fuelled attention. A bottle of rioja followed the Cava and the conversation flowed. Bursts of laughter, voices rising and falling as topics and opinions were randomly and easily discussed and dispensed with. The sounds dispersed through the slightly open kitchen window and disappeared into the dark night.

When they finally loaded the dishwasher and moved into the living room. Cassandra sat on the floor. The red, oriental rug which covered most of the floor space was thick and soft. She lounged back against a large, red, leather pouffe and watched Pamela and Bláithín settle into either end of the couch. "You two look right at home there!"

Pamela pushed a bright yellow, embroidered cushion in behind her back and stretched out her legs. "I feel it," she sighed.

"Me, too," Bláithín agreed.

"Right, well, the really exciting news of the day is... we can have this house from next week, for... Ta daah... five hundred Euros each!"

"What? That's only what I'm paying Andy for his apartment in San An!"

"My pension would cover that." Pamela nodded.

Cassandra grinned up at her friends. "And I'm still living on savings, but I've started a new job and who knows what will turn up!" She held both hands high over her head and waved them. "Full disclosure girls. I don't know how long we will have the place for. They say they have a buyer lined up, but this is Spain, nothing moves quickly. And if we only have it for a few months, isn't it worth it? And all the more reason to do it straight away!"

"But, next week? That's a bit soon." Pamela looked worried.

"What's to wait for?" Cassandra flung her hand towards the studios. "Those rooms are begging to be used, and wait until you see the garden in daylight, it's magic."

"Oh my God!" Bláithín had her hand at the base of her throat. "I think my blood pressure is going through the roof, I'm so excited and nervous. Of course, I'll have to say it to Andy and let him know. I'm paying him by the month. I should -"

"Should nothing." Cassandra's hand sliced the conversation off. "He made you redundant, and he's making money off you for an apartment that sure as hell would be empty at this time of the year. You owe him nothing!"

"You're right, Cass. I'm going to say yes, right now, before I even stay the night! Am I crazy?"

Cassandra's eyes sparkled as she shook her head and said, "Only in a 'perfect, go with the flow, jump at a chance, trust your instincts Ibiza way'! What about you, Pamela?"

"I'm in. It's hardly going to have much effect on Susan and Glen at the moment, and I'm only a short drive away. The thought of doing a big painting and maybe using oils is making my head reel. I know I should say I'll sleep on it and not take such a step without talking to them. But my goodness, if I can't make a decision about my own life at this age, when will I be able to?"

Cassandra was on her feet. "I knew it! I knew it!" She was dancing in circles. She danced into the kitchen and reappeared with a bottle in her hand. "I'd put this in the fridge earlier for our celebration. I just knew you'd decide to stay!" She held up a bottle of pink champagne.

"Gosh! Cass, I think I've had enough already!" Pamela was smiling broadly, and her face was flushed.

"You can have a small glass for the toast, Bláithín and I will finish the rest." She pulled out three flute glasses, carrying them by their stems to the table.

"Cass, I'm not a big drinker either, maybe don't waste -" The explosive crack of the cork interrupted her. Cassandra's skill at pouring the frothing bubbles into three glasses without spilling a drop elicited a round of applause.

Cassandra lifted her glass. "To the Ibiza Crone Club's new home!" Pamela and Bláithín got to their feet and joined Cassandra in the toast.

Then Bláithín raised her glass and said, "To the craziest, most out-of-character thing I have ever done." They drank.

Cassandra said, "To all the wonderful things we will make happen in the next few months." They drank.

Pamela's flute was next up. "To the feeling of freedom

and possibility." They all sipped again.

"To living an interesting and exciting life."

"To being Crone Goddesses!" They needed to top up their glasses.

CHAPTER TWENTY-ONE

Pamela and Bláithín sank back onto the couch. Cassandra slid open a glass door letting in an eddy of fresh, night air. "I'm going to turn on the outside lights so you can get some idea of the terrace and pool area." Still holding her glass, she disappeared from view. Her voice carried into them. "Fuckation! I knew some-buggering-thing was going wrong here!"

"What's up Cassandra? Are you alright?" Pamela headed for the door.

"I'm fine," came the disembodied voice from the darkness. "There've been some loose tiles here for a while. Now there appears to be a lot, and the place is soaking! I hope to shit it's not a burst pipe. I'll ask Reuben to have a look at it tomorrow. He knows this house inside out."

Pamela joined her outside and inhaled deeply. "Sea air, how lovely."

"Yes, if it weren't for those clouds, you'd see the sea down in Cala Vicent."

"They're only light clouds, I can see some stars over there." Bláithín was standing in the doorway.

"Don't slip coming out, the ground's wet." Cassandra flicked off her sandals and stamped her foot. Water splashed and drops flew, spattering Pamela's beige trousers.

"Watch out, Cassandra! That got me."

"A few drops of water never hurt anyone," Cassandra laughed.

Pamela grinned, bent over, placed her palm in a large puddle, and flicked her fingers at Cassandra who shrieked.

"That's not fair! I got you by accident!"

Pamela couldn't answer for laughing.

"You're like two children," said Bláithín from the

doorway. "Don't wet me if I come out."

"Bring the bottle out with you, Bláithín," called Cassandra.

Bláithín turned back to the room but Cassandra's urgent whisper stopped her. "Turn off the inside lights, Bláithín. Quickly! The switch is on the right by the door." Bláithín hit the switch and stepped out. "What's going on?"

The thinning clouds were illuminated by a sharp white moon. Cassandra and Pamela were standing like statues. "Watch the ground," Cassandra instructed.

Then Bláithín saw it, silver sparks running across the terrace. It was gone in seconds. "What was that?"

"Hang on a second," said Cassandra, her face turned up to the sky as she studied the clouds. "Now!"

The clouds cleared and the moon lit the world like a spotlight. Not soft, gentle, creamy, dreamy moonlight but a forceful, revealing, intense light that shone on the three women and the problem. Water bubbled up in little gushes from between four sunken tiles and flowed in meandering rivulets across the terrace. Reflected moonlight at just the right angle, transformed them into glittering, shimmering trails. Cassandra stepped into the molten silver and when she moved, slim, sparkling footprints like an arcade dance game followed her.

"Oh, that's amazing. I must try my footprints. "Pamela leant against the wall and as quickly as she could, she unlaced her shoes and pulled off her socks. She joined them, Bláithín had already kicked off her loafers.

Walking around the terrace, they made trails of shining footprints. Three faces shining with moonlight and enjoyment. Cassandra began to dance, and her friends joined in.

They danced. Twirling and laughing, they danced. Stamping and tiptoeing, footprints crossing and circling, they wove patterns of silver, all across the terrace.

A flotilla of puffed-up clouds trailed across the sky

cutting off the light.

Pamela's breathless voice came from the far side of the terrace. "Oh my! That was extraordinary."

"Pure magic!" Bláithín gasped.

"Hang on there's another gap coming." Cassandra studied the clouds as relaxed as if she'd been sitting on the couch. She picked up her glass, knelt down, and waited.

The gap came, and in the sharp light, she scooped the glass into the spurting water and stood. Holding the glass up to the light, the liquid was totally transparent. Cassandra lifted the glass to her nose and sniffed. "I don't think it's a burst pipe. This doesn't smell like tap water. It must be spring water!" Tentatively, she sipped. "Oh, girls, taste it, it's wonderful."

Holding it up so they could all see the moon perfectly through it, she offered the glass to Bláithín, who raised it in salute and sipped. She handed the glass to Pamela.

"We must be crazy, who knows what's in this?" said Pamela but still she drank. By now, the entire terrace was shining, and they were standing in a lake of silver.

Cassandra was looking up again. "And... three...two... one... it's gone!" They were plunged into darkness and became conscious of a chill wind. The magic was gone. The terrace now was merely dark and damp. They wiped their feet on the mat and hurried back indoors.

Pamela's white hair had fallen down from its neat bun and was hanging down below her shoulders; her cheeks glowed with unaccustomed colour. "Dancing in the moonlight, at our age, I can't believe it. Absolutely crazy." Her eyes were still sparkling with the fun of it.

Bláithín laughed. "Just as well Pauline and Diarmuid didn't see any of that carry-on, they'd have me certified. Though, I hope that water doesn't have us all dead in our beds by morning, Cassandra. I'll never forgive you if it does."

Pamela was mid-agreement when she was overtaken by an enormous yawn. "Oh, excuse me! I feel so tired. I suppose it's at least half-past eleven by now?"

Cassandra checked her phone. "It's... Bloody hell! It's half-past two!"

"No way! Sure, Reuben dropped us here around half-seven at the latest!" Bláithín shook her head.

Pamela swept an elaborate bow. "It doesn't matter. I think I'm quite tipsy, and I know I'm very tired, so thank you both for a lovely evening and goodnight!" She left the room.

"Oh, good exit!" Cassandra called after Pamela's back. She shook the bottle and topped up her glass. She held the bottle up enquiringly to Bláithín.

"No, thank you. What she said."

Cassandra laughed and emptied the bottle into her own glass. With careful, slow moves, Bláithín followed Pamela out.

Cassandra raised her glass to the empty room. "You have your acolytes."

CHAPTER TWENTY-TWO

Nobody was up early the next morning. Cassandra welcomed mid-morning rather than dawn. She was floating in the pool, a smile on her face when voices from the terrace intruded. Bláithín and Pamela were discussing the problematic tiles.

"Come on in, girls! This pool is heated, it's fantastic!" she shouted.

Bláithín shouted back, "I don't have any togs with me, and I'm not a great swimmer anyway."

"Oh, being in a pool isn't always about swimming! It's about enjoying being in a pool, and you'll notice I'm not exactly dressed for the occasion. Or maybe I am!"

Pamela and Bláithín walked down to the pool, Bláithín flushed crimson when she saw Cassandra's naked body floating, spread-eagled in front of her.

Pamela, neatly dressed in a blue polo shirt with her beige trousers, smiled at Cassandra. "Not a fan of the all-over wax, then?"

"God, no! A trim is quite enough for me." Her thick bush of pubic hair was not as golden as the hair which floated around her head like a halo.

"You coming in, Pamela?"

"No, not today. But definitely when I live here. Oh, my, that sounds good!"

"Yes, it does! Let's put on some coffee and make plans." Cassandra turned over. A few easy strokes took her to the side of the pool where her shoulder and arm muscles made short work of lifting her swiftly out. She strode up the steps to her towel. "Girls, I must warn you I do a lot of my yoga in the nude. That's not a problem, is it?"

Bláithín shuffled awkwardly and avoided looking at

Cassandra. "It's not exactly what I'd be used to in Kilkenny, but sure... this is Ibiza!"

"Exactly!"

They sliced avocados, toasted granary bread, and poached eggs while the coffee was brewing. "Was I really drunk last night?" asked Pam. "I mean, how did it get to be half-past two, so quickly?"

"We were having a good time?" suggested Bláithín.

"To be honest, I've often found time disappears on me here. Once I get lost in yoga or meditation, two hours can go by easily. I think we may have been dancing our silver footsteps a lot longer than we thought."

"I don't care," said Bláithín. "It was wonderful, and I feel terrific this morning, not tired and hung-over like I expected."

"Me too, it was the best sleep I've had for ages." Pamela agreed.

They sat in the bright kitchen making plans. A sparkling, calm sea stretched to the blue horn out one window and an untamed tangle of brilliantly clashing bougainvillea was framed by the other.

Cassandra said, "Why don't you start moving in as soon as you can? You might as well."

"It will take me one or two runs to bring over my paints and things."

"I have next to nothing with me, except my books and printer. Oh, that reminds me, would you like to see some photographs I took? I can finally say I took some I quite like."

"Oh, how wonderful! Well done!"

"Bloody brilliant, show us!"

Bláithín got her camera and pulled open the little screen. "You can see them if you-"

"Show me that a sec." Cassandra held her hand out. "If that's a new model I should be able to hook it..." She was walking to the TV in the living-room as she spoke. "Yup, I can connect this, and this..., and... voila!"

The opening sequence of her camera ran enormously

across the screen. Bláithín sat upright and rigid at the edge of the sofa, her hands kneading each other between her knees. Cassandra, lounging alongside, poked her. "Breathe!" she said and smiled.

The first deep-grained swirl of pine filled the screen. There was no way to be sure what it was. Followed by deeper, darker, closer photos, like spirals from another galaxy. Bláithín had infused sepia tones in the next series in an effort to follow the connected patterns of ancient growth. The final ones were like looking down ancient crumbling canyons. Bláithín moved to turn them off.

"No!" Pamela put out her hand to stop her. "Let them run again. They're incredible."

"Oh my God!" Cassandra leant forward to look into Bláithín's face. "They. Are. Fantastic!"

After the fourth run-through, Bláithín clicked them off. "Ah, that's enough now."

Cassandra clapped her hands. "Bláithín, they are truly amazing. I see fame and fortune beckoning." Pamela was quiet, staring at the blank screen. When she spoke her voice was hesitant, "Bláithín, would you think me terribly interfering if I asked you could I do something to one of your photographs?"

"What? Of course, I'm sure there's tons of room for improvement."

"No! I didn't mean that at all!"

Cassandra took the remote from Bláithín's hand and the photos filled the screen again, "Which one, Pamela?"

"That one! Yes, stop there." She was on her knees in front of the screen. "Obviously these are all brilliant on their own. It's simply that in this one I could see a thin line of metallic gold following this contour." She traced her finger across the screen. "Look! Following this, branching off here and spiraling here and here. A fine, gleaming line, subtly exploring some of the less obvious patterns going on here."

"Wow again," said Cassandra.

Bláithín sat on the couch speechless. Pamela wasn't

finished. She moved the photos on. "And on this one, I'd love to paint some tiny golden people - so tiny you might not see them - but if you did you would see a world of them. Because that's what I think you've done here, you've created a world!"

Cassandra was on her feet. "I love it! And I'll open a gallery and those fabulous motherfuckers will sell like hotcakes!"

Pamela looked up from the screen. "Am I terribly intrusive, Bláithín? I mean these are your visions, I'm -"

"No. No, don't worry. I love your idea and I'd be honoured."

"Right girls, what we need to do is get you two moved in as soon as possible so you can start working! Talking of which, I'm planning on asking Reuben in for coffee when he comes to collect you two. We need help moving your stuff and we need to discuss that with him, don't we?" She batted her eyelashes ridiculously.

Pamela snorted with laughter. "Oh, of course, we do. I'm sure it will take at least a good half an hour to discuss that, wouldn't you say Bláth?"

"Mmmm," said Bláithín who was barely listening, elated at her friends' response to her photos, she was busy planning more.

"That man has never seen me in dressed-to-kill mode and I'm going to rectify that today!"

An hour later, she returned, glowing, smoky-eyed, and sultry in a tight leopard print top tucked smoothly down into skin-tight denims, and high-heeled sandals.

"That'll knock him for six," Pamela said, just as a horn beeped twice.

"What timing," Bláithín laughed.

"Act casual, look normal, and put the coffee on," Cassandra instructed as she headed for the door. Pamela sat down and Bláithín began washing out the coffee pot.

The front door banged, and Cassandra appeared in the kitchen waving her fists and making exaggerated expressions of annoyance. Pamela and Bláithín gaped at her. Then in a bright, brisk voice, she announced, "Reuben couldn't come so his sister Rosa is here instead. She's in the loo but she said she'd love to join us for coffee." She hurried to the table and whispered, "I couldn't see who was in the car. I was so sure it was Reuben I just stood in the doorway beckoning him in, and Rosa got out!"

Pamela put her hand over her mouth to stifle her giggles and Bláithín bent double holding in her laughter while she flapped her hand in Cassandra's direction. "All your dolling up...for his sister!" She was wiping away tears of laughter when Rosa walked in.

Not as tall as her brother and several years younger, she shared the blue eyes of their Dutch ancestry, but the long plait of black, glossy hair was definitely Spanish. Well-worn, well-fitting, olive green cargo trousers and a scoop neck t-shirt showed off a wiry, fit figure.

She took in the scene. "What am I walking into here?" she asked, smiling.

Cassandra tossed her hair back. "Oh, sod it! I thought you were Reuben and..."

"Ah, that explains the war paint at this time of the day!" They all dissolved into laughter.

Cassandra shook her finger. "Rosa, you bloody better not say a word about this to Reuben!"

"I won't. I swear."

"Anyway," Cassandra waved away any embarrassment there might have been. "These are my friends who are going to be living here with me for the next few months, Pamela and Bláithín, this is Rosa Ibanez, Reuben's sister."

Rosa strode over to Pam and shook hands. "Nice to meet you," she said, and then she turned to Bláithín, said, "Hi," and held out her hand.

Bláithín took it. Rosa had long soft hands with short smooth fingernails. Bláithín instantly became conscious of her own bitten, ragged ones and pulled her hand away.

"Hi," she said looking away.

"Bláithín? Is that an Irish name?"

"Yes," Bláithín nodded.

"It means 'little flower'," supplied Cassandra from the other side of the kitchen.

"How lovely! Excuse me, Bláithín, but you have amazing hair. I mean it's genuine ringlet hair."

Bláithín's hands flew to her head. "Oh sure, it badly needs cutting now, it's like a bush."

"Oh no, don't cut it." Rosa reached out and touched Bláithín's hair. She had about half a head on Bláithín and smelled of peppermint toothpaste.

Bláithín was taken aback by this woman's forthrightness and by the fingers gently pulling at her hair.

Rosa rubbed a strand of Bláithín's hair between her fingers, "I have just the oil for this. I'll bring some over to you. It needs to be well massaged in and left for days, no washing." She turned back to Cassandra. "Now, did someone offer me coffee?"

"What do you do, Rosa?" asked Pamela while she was pouring the coffee.

"Oh, like most people in Ibiza, a bit of everything. I studied Fine Art in Majorca but then I went to England and studied clinical and remedial massage. So here I work in an art gallery during the summer, do massage in the winter, and do airport runs and deliveries all year!" She paused to add milk to her coffee, then continued. "When are you two planning on moving in?"

"As soon as possible," said Cassandra. "We just need to get their stuff over."

"And I need to talk to my daughter and her husband first. I mean, I'm definitely coming," Pamela added hastily. "But Susan will be distraught. It might take me some time to persuade her it will be a good thing."

"And do you have to check with anyone?" Rosa asked Bláithín. There it was again that disconcerting directness.

Bláithín just shook her head.

"Hey, maybe Rosa could help you move? I mean, you do things like that Rosa, don't you?"

Bláithín jumped in. "Ah, I still have to pack and at least tell Maite I'm going, she'll miss her English lessons -"

"Are you in San Lorenc or San Antonio?" Rosa interjected. "Because I have clients in San An. that I go to regularly and I could drop you over for an hour every week if you wanted."

"Oh, I couldn't, that would be way too much trouble."

"If I'm going that way it's no trouble to bring you along, and if I'm not, I'll tell you, no problem. In fact, I must go now. I have an appointment in San An. shortly. Does anyone need a hand with bags?"

"No, we've nothing except overnight bags with us," said Pamela, getting to her feet.

Cassandra put her arms around her friends as they followed Rosa out to the car. "What an amazing night last night was. The future is going to be fabulous! See you both as soon as possible, text me."

Rosa was holding the passenger door open as Bláithín approached. She would have preferred to get in the back as she felt unaccountably awkward, but Pamela was checking her bag for her phone and wasn't ready. Bláithín climbed up into the passenger seat.

Rosa kept them entertained with stories of growing up between a traditional farming community and the hedonistic, freedom-loving hippies who became synonymous with Ibiza. However, when Pamela waved goodbye, Rosa turned all her attention to Bláithín sitting beside her and fired questions with the same directness as Maite. Family, age, work, parents, there seemed to be nothing these women wouldn't ask about. But Rosa did it all in such a sincere and interested manner that Bláithín actually found herself talking about Diarmuid and Pauline and how she'd been so blind to the reality of their lives and how she'd cut herself off from them, even though they practically lived on top of each other.

"Yes, it's easy to do that when you are trying to hide how unhappy you are. We build shells around ourselves and think we're safe, but of course Bláithín, it doesn't work and you slowly suffocate yourself." She took a hand from the wheel and reached across to press one warm finger gently on the slope of Bláithín's left breast. "The *real* you, the you that's lost, lonely, and locked up."

Bláithín didn't know if it was the words or the warm finger, but some emotion swelled inside her and if it burst it was going to be unstoppable. Thank God they were at the Flora apartments. "I will be here again tomorrow, and I can collect you for Cassandra's again if you like."

"I don't know. I'll text you. Thanks." Bláithín was already out, bag in hand, shutting the door, not meeting Rosa's eyes

"You don't have my number!" Rosa shouted after her.

"I'll get it from Cassandra," said Bláithín. Nothing in the world would induce her to turn back to face those lovely blue eyes.

CHAPTER TWENTY-THREE

Cassandra had been elated when she waved Pamela and Bláithín off. Life was looking up. Her friends were moving in with her. She didn't have to leave the house. Reuben was falling in love with her, and she very definitely fancied him. She refused to think any further.

Her friends - what a wonderful thought.

Despite being a party animal, she'd been solitary all her life. It hadn't been easy to make friends when her mother made them all so unwelcome. Cassandra had tried over and over, with no success.

"Mummy, this is Angela, she has seven brothers and sisters, imagine!"

"Indeed, and where does your family live Angela?"

"We all live with me gran down by the canal."

Angela didn't even get in the door. Cassandra's mother had closed it in her face and sent Cassandra for a bath. "Use the carbolic. God knows what diseases you've caught."

Ursula De Vere hadn't fared any better when she invited Cassandra to go water skiing. She was dismissed as vulgar and pretentious, and so Ursula picked different friends. Later on in life, Cassandra had been surrounded by acquaintances, friends of convenience, and transient connections.

The more she thought about it as she tidied up the kitchen, she realised that Pierce had been the only constant. A funny kaleidoscope of memories flitted through her head. Pierce up a ladder, covered in paint at three o' clock in the morning when some decorator had 'CassandraEvents' down at the last moment. Snowball fights, celebration drinks when either business had a success, late-night chats about the beginning or the ending of some affair, their helpless laughter when he got stuck in a chicken costume after a fancy dress party. Even occasionally... She sat, pole-axed onto a kitchen chair.

They'd been best friends!

For twenty-five years they'd been each other's best friend. They'd been there for each other, supporting each other until... until Pierce actually found love. It wasn't only that he'd revealed their lives as essentially meaningless and shallow, she'd also been eaten up with jealousy!

Her chat last night with Pamela and Bláithín had totally shaken up and rearranged her perspective. She couldn't be happy for him because that would mean admitting she'd been missing out too! She leaned her elbows on the table and put her head in her hands. He wasn't a horrible shit. He just grew up and found love. When she thought of all the times she'd rung him, ranting at him down the phone. He'd never hung up, never shouted back, just listened until she ran out of steam, until she slammed the phone down on him.

She checked her watch, it was midday, that's eleven in London, coffee time in anyone's language. Before she could think about what she was doing, she video called him.

When he answered the call, his voice was flat and wary. "Cassandra! What a surprise."

"Pierce, I wanted to say hi, and to say..." She trailed off and squinted at the screen. His laptop was not set up in a trendy cafe or office. It appeared to be on a very messy kitchen table, and he was scruffy and unshaven, most un-Pierce-like. "Are you okay, Pierce?"

"Yeah, yeah, all good. I'm at home today. The baby is going through a never sleeping stage and we're both wrecked." He scrubbed his face with his hands and sat back. "What is it, Cassandra?"

"Ah, okay... Well, I want to -" she paused.

Pierce was looking off-camera. "Here she is." Lyndsey appeared. The femme fatal was in an oversized, stained T-shirt, the colour clearly growing out of her hair and her eyes red-rimmed with exhaustion. Pierce smiled up at her as if she were a screen idol come to life. She put a hand on Pierce's shoulder and leaned down to look into the camera. "Please don't, Cassandra. Not another tirade. Leave him be."

Cassandra took a deep breath. "Lyndsey, Pierce, I'm actually ringing to say I'm sorry. I'm sorry for being so monumentally blind and bloody-minded, and I really do wish you both well." She rushed on before she lost her nerve. "I had absolutely no right to behave as I did. I have only just realized we truly were best friends, Pierce, and I didn't behave like one."

Pierce leant forward and peered at the screen. "Wow, that's a change! What's happened to you?"

A thud followed by an ear-splitting howl off-screen made Lyndsey sigh and roll her eyes. "That's her bottle out of the cot again, Pierce. I'll go up" He reached out and stroked her arm. "Okay. I'll come and take over in a second."

She peered over his shoulders and said, "It was kind of you to ring and say that, Cassandra. Thank you."

As Lyndsey closed the door behind her Pierce pulled his chair closer and lowered his voice. "Are you in love, Cassandra? Is that what's happened?"

"I moved back to Ibiza, Pierce, and made some amazing friends. Proper, share-everything-with ones. They are moving in to live with me! Can you believe it?"

"Knowing you, I find it almost impossible. But you look and sound different, Cassandra. And love…?"

"I… I met someone… he seems so into me. I really want it to work Pierce, but as you say, you know me. I'm finding it difficult to allow it to happen."

"Let your mother go, Cassandra. Honestly, you can't let her craziness dominate your whole life. If you've found the right person, grab him." The background crying stepped up in intensity. "I must go Cassandra, but thanks for the call. I'm really happy things are working out for you. Please, ignore your mother and take a chance." The cheeky grin she remembered cut through his fatigue. "I'll be in touch to make sure you do. Bye," Then the screen went blank.

Cassandra stripped off and went down to the pool. She couldn't stop smiling. She floated in the warm water, staring up as feathery drifts of clouds were replaced by swelling banks of grey.

She closed her eyes as she pondered the recent upheavals in her life. Finally making peace with Pierce, new friends moving in to live with her, and admitting that she may be the closest she'd ever come to falling in love. Her eyes opened wide as she suddenly wondered if this was all an end-of-life, tidy-up, say-you're-sorry kind of thing going on? She quickly relaxed when she realised the 'to do' list was even longer. There was a gallery to open, a new job, some bastard trying to buy her precious house, and the rather wonderful Reuben situation to deal with. No, life was far from over.

***

"We've a day off today, Grandma!" Sophie had run out to meet Pamela when Rosa dropped her off. She'd clutched Pamela around the waist with all the might of her seven-year-old arms. "We've been doing baking 'cos Mummy has a cold and doesn't want to go out."

"Oh, dear. Well, let's go in and I can see how she is." Sophie led the way in.

Clark was in his highchair, licking a spoon, his beaming face streaked with icing.

"Be with you in a sec, Mum." Susan's voice came from the back hall, followed shortly by Susan, drying her hands. "I'm dying to hear all about it!"

"First, are you okay? Sophie says you're poorly."

"Oh, it's nothing. I've just got the sniffles. It's the changeable weather recently, I'm sure. So go on, tell me about the house!"

"It's beautiful." Pamela tried not to let her excitement and enthusiasm show in her voice.

"When can we visit, Grandma? Mummy says you're going to stay with your friends for a while, to get some peace and to do some painting 'cos your room here isn't big enough."

Pamela was taken aback. This was a lot of definite information for Sophie to have before Pamela had even discussed anything with Susan. "If I go, of course you can visit." She had a momentary pang, wondering if Cassandra would be keen on Sophie and Clark visiting her beautiful villa. Then she remembered Cassandra's relaxed, easy rapport with Sophie in the hospital and knew it would be okay.

"Will you really have a studio to yourself?" Susan had pushed aside the baking and was chopping vegetables, piling them into a casserole dish.

"Yes, a huge, bright room. It would be amazing to set up in. If I decide to stay there, that is."

Susan waved a knife. "Of course, you'll go! It's a great opportunity. If you don't like it, you can always come back. Hey, do you want to have dinner here with us tonight? This will be ready in about an hour."

Pamela didn't know how to react to this turnabout by Susan, so she just said, "What a lovely idea, thank you. I'll pop over to mine and have a shower first, and then I'll join you." Even by the time she'd finished her shower, she still hadn't fathomed this sea change in her daughter. Susan was positively pushing her out the door to Cassandra's and had obviously told Sophie about it as if it were a fait accompli. She realized it was all to the good really, given that she was intending to go anyway. She could pack tomorrow and go on Friday, there was no need to take everything. The knick-knacks and photos she'd brought from the house in London could stay right here. She neither wanted nor needed them in Cassandra's.

***

Bláithín was in a quandary. She had packed the next day and had a remarkably easy phone call with Andy. "Sure, isn't it great you're making a bit of a life for yourself there? Just drop the ould keys into Maite whenever you leave. Tell me, did Diarmuid and herself have a good time over with you?" And that was that, no cross-questioning. No muttering about lost rent. But now, did she get a taxi to the house, or did she ring Cassandra for Rosa's number? Her instinct said to get a taxi, not to make a fuss, but would Rosa be insulted? After all, she *did* offer. She dithered until she finally rang Cassandra.

"Oh, for goodness' sake, get Rosa. She offered, she'll be far more fun and help than any taxi driver! Look I'll text her, tell her the situation, give her your number, then it's up to her, and you'll be spared all this anguishing! One way or another, I'll see you tomorrow." An hour later Bláithín got a text.

Pick you up at 11. X R.

She stared at her phone. "Now I've done it." she muttered. Done what exactly, she wasn't sure, but there was a definite feeling of having set something in motion.

CHAPTER TWENTY-FOUR

By Friday afternoon, Pamela and Bláithín had both moved in.

Pamela arrived first. "Sue as good as bundled me out the door," she told Cassandra as they made trips in and out with boxes and bags. "I don't know whether I'm more relieved or worried."

"Studio or bedroom?" Cassandra waggled a box at her. "I'd go with relieved, if I were you. You'll still be keeping an eye on them, and at least you know she's not miserably pining at home because you're gone."

"Studio please, they're my new paints. I treated myself yesterday to some oil paints and had to force myself out of the shop before I rang up a small mortgage's worth." Pamela hoisted a suitcase onto the bed. "I wasn't going to come here until Sunday. To give Sue and Glen a few days to get used to the idea, but she came over yesterday morning with boxes offering to help me pack! I couldn't believe it."

"Oh, something's definitely up. What did Glen say?" Cassandra paused on her way to the studio.

Pamela was unfolding her neatly packed clothes and hanging them in the built-in wardrobe. "Strangely enough, I haven't seen him for a few days," she spoke over her shoulder. "Sue also said I didn't have to babysit this week because Glen is doing some overhaul at work, and she wasn't going in. I didn't want to question her, but I'm sure there's something she's not telling me. However, as I'd already decided to come here, it was easier to pretend I was convinced by her arguments."

"Quite right, too. Y'know it will all come out eventually," said Cassandra dropping a suitcase on the bedroom floor. "I think that's the last of it. Welcome home!"

***

Rosa arrived to pick up Bláithín at eleven as promised

and whisked her belongings out of the apartment with cheerful energy. Closing up the apartment didn't cause Bláithín the slightest pang, she locked up and left without a backward glance. Rosa was waiting by the car. Her hair was in two plaits, hanging down the front of a thick, white T-shirt under which she was clearly bra-less. Her denim jeans and jacket were soft and well worn. Bláithín wished she had taken more care dressing this morning or had some alternative to her everyday navy t-shirt and trousers combination. She also wanted to tell Rosa how wonderful she looked. A normal thing for anyone to say, for God's sake. So why were the words running around in her head, being inspected for suitability, instead of being spoken aloud?

Before getting into the car, they called into the corner shop where Maite embraced Bláithín warmly, warning her not to forget her promise to drop by often. Finding out that Rosa was the means of Bláithín doing this, she kissed her too. "But of course, maybe next week…" Maite patted her bulge.

Bláithín hugged her again. "You have my number. Let me know if anything happens before I see you again."

As soon as they were in the car, Rosa launched into conversation as if they were continuing from where they'd left off the day before. "Tell me more about Kilkenny." By the time they parked in front of Cassandra's house, the pair were immersed in discussion about life in rural Ireland as opposed to life in rural Spain and were reluctant to leave it. Bláithín twisted in her seat to rest her back against the passenger door and watch Rosa while they chatted. She became so lost in their conversation; she hadn't realised they had pulled to a stop outside Cassandra's house.

Cassandra's shriek of 'Welcome, Bláithín!' from the front door broke the moment.

There was a second or two of silence while the women looked at each other before Cassandra reached the Jeep and yanked the passenger door open.

"Pamela's here already. Come on, Bláth. Rosa, will you

join us for coffee?"

Rosa hopped out of the jeep. "Thanks, but no. I have an airport pick-up to do." She unloaded Bláithín's bags and cases then blew a kiss at them and drove off.

Cassandra threw her arm around Bláithín's shoulder. "I can't believe we've actually done this."

"Hmm, I'm not sure if it's terrifying or fun," Bláithín replied.

"Can be both y'know," said Cassandra grabbing two black bags and a case. "C'mon girl, move your arse. Let's get things started."

A short while later in the kitchen, Cassandra stood at the end of the table and banged her mug on it. "Attention my fellow Crones! Ground rules are necessary in any house-sharing situation." Notebook in hand, she read off the basics, "Rent payable first of the month, which coincidentally is today. Fifty Euros a week each for basic groceries, any overage to be spent on extras or be deducted as we decide. Utility bills, when they arrive, will be divided in three. A cooking and cleaning rota can go up, if necessary, but I suspect at this hour of our lives we're all capable of looking after things, so I don't expect that to be a problem. Eat together or on our own, when and as it suits. Okay? Everybody happy? Anything I forgot?"

"Sounds perfect," said Pamela.

"Agreed," seconded Bláithín, and they banged their mugs on the table in approval. Cassandra held her hand up. "Full Crone disclosure, I rang Pierce."

"What?"

"My goodness!"

"After our talk the other night, I realized I'd been so unfair to him, and that he hadn't broken any promises to me. All he had done was to find love. So, on the spur of the moment, I rang him and apologized, and I'm delighted I did. Thank you, Crones!"

"Well done you, Cassandra!"

"Holy mother, that took some nerve. He must have been

gobsmacked!"

"He was, rather! Cassandra gave a mock bow and sat down. "More coffee anyone?"

They stayed discussing plans and chatting around the table until interrupted by the doorbell. A smiling Cassandra showed Reuben into the kitchen.

Spanish fashion, he kissed Pamela and Bláithín on both cheeks. "Rosa told me you were moving in today. I thought I'd come over and see if you need help with anything."

"Good timing," said Cassandra, beaming at him. "Put your handyman hat on. We were just wondering about getting something put up along the walls in both studios to hang prints and paintings on. And there also seems to be a problem out on the terrace."

He measured the walls in the studios, making sure he knew just what they each wanted. Cassandra took him out to the terrace. He concurred with her that it wasn't a burst pipe, but he didn't think it needed urgent repair, the bubbling water now being reduced to a bare trickle. "I will keep an eye on it. It might just dry up itself, until the next heavy rain. I will be back tomorrow to start the rails," He glanced at the house and lowered his voice, "And when you have your friends settled in here, you and I will talk."

He smiled that smile she couldn't resist, and she grinned back. "I look forward to it."

***

It was as if they had always lived together. There was no 'easing in, getting to know each other' period.

Pamela threw herself into painting immediately. Not having to stop until she wanted to was a miraculous gift. She frequently became a night-time painter, catching up on sleep during the day with a siesta.

Bláithín took her time. She studied her camera and the limits of her printer. She watched tutorials online and discovered the myriad possibilities of lenses and filters. She downloaded books and made lists. She was in her element. On Wednesday, they were both in Bláithín's studio carefully choosing which one of her photos was the one to be printed on canvas and receive Pamela's gold paint. Loud singing carried into them as Cassandra worked from the office she had set up at the table in the living room. Her Twitter campaign for 'Ibiza Instincts' next season was exceeding her expectations. Reuben had been in and out of the house the past few days putting up the rails. The house had echoed to his low, rumbling voice and Cassandra's laughter.

Pamela grinned across at Bláithín. "She seems very happy, doesn't she?"

"Yes, different somehow, less brittle or something. That whole thing with Pierce has made a difference."

Pamela raised her eyebrows. "And perhaps she's come to a decision about Reuben?"

"I hope so. They can't keep their eyes off each other."

Pamela pointed to a photo. "Oh, I think this is the one, Bláth. If we can just crop that edge, there..."

"Rosa's here, and she's brought pastries! Anyone fancy coffee?" Cassandra shouted from the hall.

"Sounds good," replied Bláithín, saving the chosen picture.

Rosa, already sitting at the kitchen table when they went in, waved a bottle of oil at Bláithín. "As promised," she said. Over coffee, Rosa told them about the various farmer's markets around the island where it was possible to buy produce straight from the farm. "There are also stalls selling oils and herbs to make your own products, like the liniment I sent over with Reuben for your ankle, Cassandra. I'd made it that morning."

"Wow! I hadn't realized you'd made it! It was amazing."

"Now this..." Rosa stood, stroking her palms against each other, shaking off any crumbs of pastry, and picked up the brown bottle of oil. She stood behind Bláithín. "This oil, I made yesterday." She opened the bottle and emptied some onto her palms. "Can you put your head back a little, please?" Bláithín complied, and Rosa explained the properties of the oil, where she got the ingredients ,and answered Cassandra's and Pamela's questions while slowly drawing her oiled fingers through Bláithín's hair. Bláithín sat stiff and red-faced. "It's also important to massage the scalp to stimulate the follicles." Her hands disappeared into Bláithín's mass of hair. Despite herself, Bláithín's eyes closed as Rosa's strong fingers circled her scalp up one side of her head and down the other.

"Oh Lord, that looks so good," sighed Cassandra.

"It would be even better if this person wasn't sitting here as rigid as a plank!" replied Rosa with a laugh. She stepped back rubbing the oil into her hands and arms. "Now don't wash your hair for a few days and when you do, use the oil again." A church organ playing Ode to Joy sounded from her pocket and she clapped her hand to her jeans. "Oops, my alarm. Time to go. Thank you all for the coffee."

Bláithín walked her out to the car. "It was very kind of you to think of the oil, Rosa, Thank you."

"You're welcome. That hair is crying out to be treated properly and be released from decades of being forced into what it's not." She got into the car, then opened the window. "Hey Bláth, tomorrow morning I'm delivering vegetables for my friends who run an organic farm." She shrugged. "I told you I do a bit of everything. Anyway, would you like to come? You could bring your camera, you might find something to interest you."

"I'd love to," Bláithín answered faster than the colour could flood her cheeks.

"Okay, I'll pick you up at nine-thirty. See you."

Cassandra was delighted to hear this plan. "Fantastic! If you can get another series as good as the pine tree ones, our gallery will make money hand over fist!"

***

Bláithín didn't even open her camera case the next day - Rosa's delivery date was changed. Instead, they spent the wild, blustery day walking the sandy tracks through the pine-wooded hills down to the hidden beaches of Ses Salinas. Their conversation continued from yesterday, flowing easily from the general to the particular. Rosa was as open as she was questioning. She told Bláithín about her heartbreak when her partner of fifteen years had left her for an exotic dancer. Bláithín responded with the broad details of her disastrous marriage.

Rosa brought a picnic. "I thought there was no point in wasting the day." Sitting on their jackets, they picnicked in a sheltered grove. Rosa produced a loaf of the hard local bread, cheese, garlic olives, and a long vine branch of small, sweet tomatoes. There was a peculiar, agreeable aroma, sweet and woody in the area, that Rosa, a fount of knowledge of all things Ibizan, said came from a species of the tall, twisted pines around them. Juniperus Phoenicia, also known as Sabine trees. "Those trees produced the wooden beams for Phoenician boats, and even today, still hold up the roofs of ancient fincas all over the island."

Bark poked Bláithín's shoulders as she leant back against one of the crooked trees. Her knees complained at her cross-legged position, but biting into a sweet, tangy tomato, and watching Rosa talk, she had never been happier. Rain began pattering through the spindly pine trees, staining the well-flattened earth with brown spots. The women rushed to gather up the remains of their picnic into a bag. Rosa stood and held her hand out to help Bláithín up. Bláithín took it and they made a run for the car. On the way home, Rosa told Bláithín all about Reuben, his marriages and his descent into alcoholism, as well as his long climb out.

Bláithín sighed. "No wonder he looks so grim. How awful. Do you think he told Cassandra all this?"

"I'm sure of it. I have never seen him so light-hearted in

the last twenty years."

"Love would do that to you," Bláithín nodded, adding in a low voice, "I imagine."

They were pulling into the driveway. Bláithín was slow to get out. "Thank you, Rosa. It was an absolutely wonderful day."

"It was, wasn't it? I enjoyed it too. I do have the deliveries tomorrow, so, nine-thirty again?"

A smiling Bláithín nodded. Rosa leant across from the driver's seat and quickly kissed her on both cheeks. Bláithín got out of the car, a tickle of hair, a brush of soft skin,

CHAPTER TWENTY-FIVE

Pamela had paint in her hair. She'd gone into the studio with a cup of tea in her hand at six-thirty that morning. Her dream painting had resurfaced, even more detailed and exciting than the day she'd dreamt it in the car. In bare feet, her hair in a loose plait, her hands and painting dress splotched with rich colours, she looked at her work, suffused with delight. She didn't want or need to do another thing to it. At last! She'd produced something that made her feel. Something satisfying and real. It didn't matter what anyone thought. She was elated, exhausted, and satisfied.

When she finally realized she was starving and tired, her watch showed two-thirty. Bláithín was still out with Rosa, and she could hear Cassandra talking to Reuben, on the terrace.

She showered and made a sandwich. Scrolling through her phone messages while she ate, she realised she hadn't had a satisfactory conversation with Sue since the day she'd left. As soon as she was finished lunch, she'd pop over for a visit.

***

Susan's flustered reaction to her arrival alarmed Pamela, but she was immediately distracted by Clark who'd run, arms up, to be lifted. He clung to her. He wouldn't even look at her, but still refused to be put down. Maybe it was due to the fact that after being with him almost every day, she'd suddenly disappeared from his life. Sophie showed no such sense of abandonment. To Pam's relief, Sophie was excited to hear about the house and eager for an invitation to see it and meet the nice ladies again.

Susan offered a cup of tea but immediately added, "Mum, would you mind awfully if I just popped out for a while? It's just very handy that you're here when I need to-"

"Of course." Pamela cut her off. "Don't worry, whatever

you need to do, I'm delighted to help."

"That's great, thanks. I'll only be an hour or so." She kissed them all before leaving.

Rain fell half-heartedly from a dull sky, and with Clark being a misery, an indoor activity was definitely called for.

They were finally rolling out the cookie dough, painstakingly measured out by Sophie, while Pamela, with Clark on her lap, unobtrusively helped.

"One for me, one for you, one for Clark. One for me…"

"Don't forget to make some for Mummy and Daddy."

"Oh, well, I don't know," Sophie sighed as she patted the dough into shape. "Daddy is so busy at work now, he sometimes doesn't get to come home at all, and I think Mummy's doing her healthy eating again 'cos she keeps getting take-outs for us, but she doesn't have it herself."

Sophie turned her flour-smudged face to Pamela. "Maybe we can bring some to Daddy at work?"

"What a good idea! I'll talk to your mummy about it."

But Susan had her friend Katrina with her when she arrived back.

Is she ever alone? Pamela wondered as they shared the pizzas that had arrived in colourful, grease-stained, cardboard boxes. Pamela noticed Susan barely nibbled at one thin triangle. Clark insisted that Pamela put him to bed, a long-drawn-out process, as he didn't want her to leave. She held his hand through the bars of the cot and sang Baa Baa Black Sheep over and over and over until, eventually, she was just humming it in a whisper. Finally, his little fist relaxed its grasp on her fingers and flopped back, a pudgy, pink, warm starfish on the teddy bear sheet.

"I'm going to head back now," Pamela said as soon as she was back in the kitchen. Sophie hugged her. "I really want to come and visit, Grandma. When can I?"

"Very soon, darling. I'll check it out when I get back, and I'll give mummy a ring to let her know."

Susan stood in the doorway. "I'll say goodbye here Mum,

it's quite wet. See you soon."

"Oh, for goodness' sake, Sue, walk me to the car. It's only a bit of drizzle." Pamela spoke quickly as they walked across the courtyard. "Sue, what's going on? Sophie told me Glen hasn't been coming home."

"Oh Mum, I can't talk about it now, not with Katrina and Sophie inside."

"But you know you can talk to me any time Sue, don't you? I'm not pressurising you. I just want to know you're alright."

"I know. Don't worry Mum. It will all be fine." But the circles under her eyes told a different story. Having learned Susan would only say what she wanted, Pamela didn't press; she just gave her a tight hug and kissed her goodbye.

***

Cassandra stood in the kitchen in a short, black lace dress. Cut high in the front, it swooped down low on her toned, tanned back. Pamela and Bláithín were amazed.

"Wow, you look amazing! I have never seen you in anything other than trousers or jeans," Bláithín said.

"I know," Cassandra acknowledged. "It's hard to explain, but this feels different. I don't want to do what I always do or wear what I always wear. This... this thing with Reuben - and me, is new, so I splurged on something different to wear."

Her friends understood. This date with Reuben had Cassandra excited and flustered.

He'd suggested it yesterday while putting up batons in Bláithín's studio. "Cassandra, will you come on a date with me?" He'd called out as she passed the door.

She stopped dead. "What?"

"A proper, you get dressed up, I collect you, we go for a meal, we talk, and I bring you home date."

"Cassandra stared blankly at him while a gamut of responses from the sarcastic to the witty whirled through her head. She settled on, "Um... ah, I... yes, okay. I will."

"Tomorrow?"

"Okay, but this feels a bit weird like we're teenagers or something."

"Why should it? I want to spend time with you. You want to spend time with me, it's that simple. I'll pick you up at seven-thirty, Is that okay?"

Cassandra smiled. "Yes, that's good."

With a grin lighting up his face, Reuben had returned to his hammering. Out of his eyesight, Cassandra victory-shimmied into the kitchen.

The restaurant he took her to was tucked way up an unlit mountain path. One painted wooden sign, lit by a hanging lantern pointed the way. The inaccessibility of the venue obviously no bar to the dozens of cars parked in rows in an adjacent field.

Cassandra was sure the food was delicious judging by the happy faces around her, but she barely noticed what she ate. Reuben, sitting opposite her, had her full attention. They laughed and chatted with the ease of people who had known each other for years. And then she found herself telling him about her new awareness of the reality of her relationship with Pierce and about her phone call.

Reuben took her hand. "That was an amazing thing to do. It took a lot of guts. How do you feel?"

"Wonderful. I don't know, it's as though there's a role I don't have to play anymore."

"I understand. I played self-pitying, angry drunk for so long I began to believe it was really me."

People occasionally dropped by the table and shook hands with Reuben. He introduced Cassandra to them all.

"I would have thought you were more hibernating bear than social animal," she observed as Reuben was clapped on the shoulder by a passing man who made a phone call sign at him.

"Business connections, I assure you."

"I thought you said you didn't look after any other

houses."

"I don't, but as I studied horticulture and business in England and worked for a food distributor in Barcelona. I was able to develop my family's olive groves into an independent oil producer. We supply organic restaurants both here and on the mainland."

Cassandra was stunned. "So, you're a businessman?"

"No. I'm a farmer. But I'm a successful one and a sometime handyman." As they strolled back to the car and drove home, he filled her in on his struggle to get his farm back on its feet after he came out of his alcohol haze and how one of his biggest regrets was that his parents hadn't lived to see the success he'd made of the land that had been in the family for countless generations.

He parked the car and walked her to the door.

"Do you want to come in?"

"No, thank you. I'll see you tomorrow. I must hang the railings for Bláithín. It was a wonderful evening as I knew it would be. You are wonderful."

She put her arms around his neck. "Thank you, Reuben." In her heels, she nearly matched his height, so she didn't have far to stretch to press her lips to his. He responded instantly, his arms pulling her tight. Their mouths opened. Gently, her tongue licked his, an act of such intimacy and excitement she thought she'd explode. He broke the kiss, and stepped back, smiling at her. "If that's how your kiss makes me feel, Cassandra Collingsworth, I can only imagine what..." he trailed off shaking his head.

"Are you sure you won't come in? The rooms are very well soundproofed, you don't have to worry about the others."

"No, it's not that. It's that I'm totally sure of what I want here. From this relationship. From us. And I want you to be too."

"Oh, God," groaned Cassandra. "That doesn't mean we can't have sex!"

He pulled her back into his arms. "I don't want 'just' sex

or 'only' sex. I want everything. I want you waking up, I want you happy, sad, tired, all of it. I want an 'us' that's real, an 'us' to face life together. But don't get me wrong," his voice lowering into a husky growl, "I want sex too, lots of it!" He kissed her. This time his tongue did the exploring, making her want to devour him. His hand cupped her breast, and his thumb found her nipple through the lacy dress. Cassandra sagged against him, her groan of desire loud despite their joined mouths. His long, hard erection was obvious as she pressed herself against him.

Breathing hard, Reuben lifted his head from their kiss. He looked intently at her. "Goodnight, my Cassandra."

"You can't…"

"See you tomorrow." He gave her a gentle kiss on the cheek and left an extremely aroused, yet happy, Cassandra at the door.

CHAPTER TWENTY-SIX

Rosa picked up Bláithín for the early morning deliveries in San Antonio. Drifting banks of winter mist coiled around green hills or floated low above valley floors, and a weak sun, trying to reclaim the day, streaked the sky with hazy bands of orange and red. Warming her hands around the cup of takeaway coffee that Rosa had arrived with, Bláithín said she felt as if she were sitting slap-bang in the middle of an impressionist painting.

By the time the first deliveries were finished, the sky was a gleaming translucent blue and sharp sunlight dazzled them through the windscreen. As they were in San Antonio, Bláithín suggested they pop in to see how Maite was.

Maite heaved herself off her chair behind the counter with exclamations of delight when she saw them. She was puffy-faced and exhausted, and in a breathless voice, she explained that the only reason she was still working was because it beat being in the house with her mother-in-law all day. Sitting behind the counter with her feet propped up on a stool, she questioned Bláithín about the house in San Vicent and her new housemates, until she had every possible detail. Despite her exhaustion, she was still tending her plant collection and sent Bláithín away with a small cutting of red rose and vigorously sprouting bamboo shoots.

"Love and prosperity," said Rosa looking at them as they headed back to the car.

"What? They have meaning?"

"All plants do."

"So, let's see, over the weeks Maite's given me... Aloe Vera?"

"Healing."

"Chamomile?"

"Tranquility and vitality."

"Basil?"

"Luck."

"Wow, I never knew. Did she think I needed all of those?"

"Perhaps. Let's hope this -" she raised the bamboo, "brings you more luck with your photos today than yesterday," smiled Rosa.

And it did. Not in the crystal-clear landscape of a beautiful December morning, nor in any of the fabulous fincas and villas they delivered to, but in the whorls and ridges of a dark green cabbage.

Rosa came out from a restaurant delivery to find Bláithín lying on the dusty path with a cabbage a few inches from her camera. She smiled at the sight. "You could put it on the car roof," she suggested.

"I did, but it got too much light. I'm sorry. I'll just be another moment. I want to try... and... get..." Bláithín trailed off, lost in the moment.

Rosa sat on an old stone wall, stretched her legs out in front of her, and lifted her face to the sun. "That's okay, I'm in no hurry."

Eventually, Bláithín stood up and slapped the dust off her clothes. "Thank you, Rosa, I'm not sure how these will work out, but it seemed interesting."

"I'm sure they'll be great." Rosa put her arm around Bláithín and kissed her cheek. Taken by surprise, Bláithín turned toward her. Rosa's face was inches from her own. Her heart stopped. Bláithín was sure of it. Rosa stared at her, and then she very gently kissed her. Bláithín's breath caught, a soft, silky pressure of lips on her lips, a smell of coconut oil, a smooth cheek against her own-

"I think it's time for coffee." Rosa said and opened the Jeep door.

Shocked speechless, Bláithín followed her. Rosa glanced

sideways. "Should I not have done that? I thought there was such a connection between us from the start. Was I wrong?"

"No! No, but... I'm not... I was married... to a man!"

"And were you happy?"

"No! It was awful. But that was all my fault."

"Maybe it wasn't anyone's fault, Bláth. Maybe it simply wasn't right?"

"But I'm confused. You told me about your relationship and how he left you for that dancer."

"*She* left me, Bláithín. It was a girl."

"But... you said Noah broke your heart!"

"Yes, that's a girls name, n.o.a.

"Oh, I thought..."

Bláithín turned in her seat to stare wide-eyed at Rosa who was still talking. "I have known I was gay since I was fifteen though I didn't come out to my parents until a whole lot later."

Bláithín shook her head. "Dear God! I just can't imagine that conversation. How did it go?"

"At that stage, they'd seen what being forced into an unhappy marriage had done to Reuben, so they made it clear that all they wanted was for me to be happy." Rosa glanced at Bláithín again. "Did that kiss upset you?"

Bláth thought for a moment. To her surprise, it hadn't, and reliving it, made her heart race. "No, it didn't," she answered honestly.

"How did it make you feel?"

Bláithín couldn't find words. "Like this." She made a heart shape with her hands over her chest, expanding it and expanding it until her hands flew apart. Rosa picked up Bláithín's hand and kissed the palm. "Good," she said, starting the car. "Maybe that means you're making room for me in there? Now, let's find coffee."

Later that night, Bláithín paced the terrace, leaving damp prints every time she crossed the trickle of water from the broken tiles. She found it hard to figure out what she was feeling. Her mind skated away like mercury from a prodding finger when she tried to think of what it was she wanted from Rosa.

Damp air and a sharp breeze made her pull her heavy coat tight. Tucking it under her, she sat on the top step and rested her arms on her knees. Bright, distant stars were scattered in glorious disarray across the black void, and a crescent moon, not bright enough to throw a shadow, presided over all.

The whole hooha about the gay marriage referendum in Ireland hadn't passed her by. She'd voted in favour, after all, love was love.

"Exactly!"

"Jesus, Mary and Joseph! Who's that?" Bláithín's head whipped around, and she caught a white flicker from the end of the steps. She assumed Cassandra was having a late-night swim. "God Almighty, was I talking aloud that you could hear me down there?" She whispered loudly down towards the pool. The last thing she wanted was Pamela coming out to join in. It was bad enough that Cassandra had heard.

"I heard you."

"You're a mad one, in the pool on a night like this! Still and all, you're probably warmer than I am. Well, *you're* hardly one to be shocked at the way my thoughts are going, but is it possible? Could I really be...? Wouldn't I have known...?"

"Love has many forms, embrace it where you find it."

"But I'm fifty-five. Too old to become someone new. Jaysus! What would Diarmuid and Pauline say?"

"Is it new? Or is it something kept secret, locked and hidden in the depths of your being, because you were afraid?"

"I don't know. Maybe? All I know for sure is Rosa kissed me and I liked it. I more than liked it - I loved it. Well, also that I want to see her every day, and I want to feel her hair, and... oh God..." Heat flooded Bláithín's face as her thoughts ran away with her.

Wind-rustled trees, an occasional disturbed wood

pigeon, and a slight splattering of water from the leak as it trickled down the steps were the only background noises to her chaotic emotions.

Finally, teeth chattering, she said, "What would everyone say? If I…"

"In this matter, the opinions of others have no bearing. You are a Crone! Not answerable to anyone. Don't waste time, as it is becoming ever more precious. Open up, my beloved daughter, open up and feel love, feel life."

"What? Did you call me…?" Bláithín shook her head and stood, stretching her stiff muscles. "God, it doesn't matter, Cass. I'm frozen to the bone. You must be like a prune by now. Anyway, thanks for the chat. See you in the morning." She hurried through the house; a hot shower was calling.

***

Bláithín slept late. Her first thought on waking was Rosa. Her second was, how could she face Cassandra after that conversation last night. However, a text from Maite banished that worry. Pulling on her robe she strode into the kitchen to tell her friends. "Maite's had her baby, a little girl."

"How is she?" asked Pamela. "How was it?"

"I don't know, she didn't say. Not too bad I suppose, as she's going home today. She had it yesterday, shortly after we visited. I'll call over to visit her. What should I bring her?"

"With a first child you can't go wrong with clothes, but I always like to put in something for the mother too. You know, you spend nine months being the cosseted centre of attention, then suddenly the baby is there. You're dead on your feet with twenty-four-hour feeding and a traumatized body, and no one spares you a second look. So, a nice body lotion or a special hand cream, something along those lines would be nice."

Cassandra waved the coffee pot at Bláithín offering her some. "I've never met Maite, but I'm sure you'll bring them here to visit soon, so give her my congratulations."

"Do you need a lift over to see her, Bláth? I'll be going

over to Sue's later," Pamela said.

"Or I can drop you," added Cassandra. " I'm going to Ibiza later to get prices for turning those photos into prints and a canvas for you to work on, Pamela."

"Gosh, you're a fast worker, Cassandra! I haven't done any sketching or planning for that yet."

"Seize the day, my friend. We're crone goddesses. We don't wait, we do!"

"Thanks, but I'm fine for a lift. I was already on to Rosa and she's picking me up." Bláithín left the room before the telltale red, blotching its way up her face could give away her embarrassment.

***

The chill, damp air of yesterday had been chased away by a high blue sky and a warm sun. Rosa and Bláithín were sitting in a church square, drinking coffee under the shade of a huge white parasol.

They'd just left an exhausted but elated Maite. Her mother-in-law had been holding court to a house full of relations, so Maite had gratefully slipped out to talk. She had introduced them to baby Laia, who was a swaddled bundle in her arms. All that was visible were two crescents of dark eyelashes on soft, plump olive cheeks, a tiny snub nose, and a pouting little mouth sucking firmly on a pink soother. Maite had burst into tears at Bláithín's present. A beautifully decorated jar of Indian body oil, designed to promote relaxation and calm, and a tiny, soft, white cotton dress embroidered with orange and pink flowers. Waving away her 'crazy baby tears' Maite had hugged them warmly before they left.

Bláithín sat back in contentment. The walls of the whitewashed church would have been blinding against the sharp, blue sky except for the spreading, dark green foliage of the tall trees dotted around the plaza, stippling the walls and ground with shade. Her phone pinged in her pocket, a quick glance showed a message from Pauline. Bláithín clicked it off and put it away.

The cafés around the square were busy with relaxed groupings, meeting and mingling, solitary newspaper readers, laptop users, couples. Bláithín squinted and shaded her eyes. That couple holding hands across the table and laughing were two women, and so were the pair walking past with their arms around each other. "Look, Rosa." Bláthín tilted her head in their direction.

"Yes?" Laughter lit Rosa's eyes as she shook her head and said, "Are you telling me you're only noticing this now?

Bláithín nodded.

"You really have been blinkered, haven't you? There's no need to hide." She pulled a parcel out of her leather satchel and handed it to Bláithín. "I bought this for you while you were lost in baby clothes."

"Oh, no, you shouldn't have!"

"I should and I did. Do you like it?"

Bláithín pulled out a deep turquoise, mandarin-collared tunic with navy embroidery around the neck and cuffs.

Rosa continued, "It's not that I have anything against your extensive wardrobe of navy t-shirts, but a change is good."

The echo of her own words made Bláithín smile. "It's really gorgeous Rosa, but I don't know if it's me."

"It isn't you until you make you! Try it on later and see how it makes you feel."

Bláth fingered the silky material. "I don't know what to say. I'm overwhelmed."

"Say nothing, my little flower, I want to make you happy."

Bláithín took a deep breath. "Rosa, I don't know how to do this. I realize I want to, that I want to try. But I've never, ever... I mean the physical side of things was never good with me." Her face burned uncomfortably. "I don't know if I could..." Rosa stopped her with a butterfly kiss on the lips. "Bláithín. There's so much more to a relationship. There are so many ways of making each other happy. Sex is only one. One I hope we will enjoy eventually, but for now, I want to be your friend, your best friend, your girlfriend. I want to release you from that tortured persona you've been locked behind." She gently tugged one of Bláithín's curls which was becoming soft, glossy, and long with the oil treatment.

Bláithín was in a haze of delight as they paid for their coffee and walked back to the car side by side. Rosa's fingers brushed hers, they intertwined and stayed that way. Bláithín's eyes shone, and her stomach was sick with happiness and shock.

CHAPTER TWENTY-SEVEN

Cassandra was frozen - the temperature had plummeted with nightfall. Back in England, twelve degrees would barely be considered cool, but here, where it had dropped more than ten degrees in a few hours, it felt bloody Baltic. Of course, it could have been the shock of that damn call she'd received just as she was getting into the car in Ibiza that had frozen her to the bone. She slammed the car door shut and headed for the house.

It wasn't fair! They were all so happy; things really seemed to be working out for them. She dreaded having to tell them. Closing the front door behind her, she made for the kitchen, the only room with a light on. Pamela and Bláithín were sitting in silence. Pamela's head was in her hands, and Bláithín, looking amazing in a silk tunic, was red-eyed and staring at her phone.

"Christ almighty! What's wrong? What's happened? Is it Maite?" Cassandra exclaimed.

Pamela looked up, white-faced, her eyes threatening to spill tears. "Sue just rang. Glen has left her. He's been having an affair with that girl in the office, Belén. Sue's distraught and has asked me to move back straight away."

"Christ, no!" Cassandra flopped onto a chair.

Pamela sighed, "That was what was behind her eagerness to get me out. She suspected what was going on and hoped if Glen knew I was no longer there to support her, he'd feel unable to leave."

"Where is she now?" Cassandra asked.

"At Katrina's house. The kids think they're having a sleepover. I have to leave here. She's my daughter and she needs me. I must go back." Her tears spilled down her pale cheeks.

Cassandra turned to Bláithín. "This is bloody awful, Bláth, but we can't go to pieces-"

"I'm not. Well not about that anyway. Though it is pure shite, Pamela. No, no… what's happened is…" Big, noisy sobs burst from her.

"Fuck, Bláth, what is it?" Cassandra handed her the kitchen roll.

Bláth tore off several sheets and blew her nose. "I was so happy… and a text came in and I ignored it… because Rosa gave me this today." Bláth ran her hands over the tunic.

"Yes," said Cassandra slowly, "and it's absolutely fab on you, but I don't see…?"

Tears won again and Bláithín wailed, "Diarmuid and Pauline are coming back!"

"What?"

"They said they guessed that I wouldn't want to go back for Christmas, so they were going to come here. But then… then they said they'd loved it so much they were thinking of renting out their home in Kilkenny, moving out here, and that I could live with them!" The sentence ended with a wail. Bláithín's chest heaved as she tried to calm down. "I can't! I can't be… after talking to you last night, Cassandra, I was thinking I could. And I told Rosa and… then we held hands today. And I wanted to be… And now if they're here, I couldn't possibly…"

"Wait!" Cassandra held up a hand. "This is making no sense. What talk last night? You and Rosa? Who were you talking to?"

"With you, while you were swimming."

"I wasn't in the pool last night. I never swim at night - it's too energizing for me."

"But you told me I should give love a chance. That I was keeping my true self hidden, and you were right." She blew her nose again and wiped her eyes.

"Bláithín, I did not speak to you last night."

"You did!"

"She didn't," Pamela joined in. "Cassandra went to bed way before you did. I think I may have heard you, but assumed you were with Rosa."

They looked at each other.

"Fuck," said Cassandra. "I have goosebumps." She held out her arm and the golden hairs were prickling up along it.

"Who was it so?" Bláithín looked at her friends.

"I think we know," said Pamela looking pointedly out the window at the night sky.

"Holy Mother of -"

"Just stop right there and you might be right!" Cassandra raised a small smile. "But along those lines, we're all too old to get our periods at the same time, but it seems like we're doing a bloody good job of getting our disasters in tandem!" She sat back and raked her hair back from her face with a loud sigh. "I got a phone call this evening from the rental agency. It seems the sale has gone through, and the buyer is coming here sometime tomorrow with his developers to measure up. They want to start work mid-January, so we have to be out!"

Pamela gasped. "Oh, no! Cassandra, I'm so sorry. I can't believe you both have to leave here, too!"

"No! Jasus, is there no end to it? How did it all happen so quickly?"

"Turns out the owner is an efficient Scandinavian, who already had permits in the bag and was ready to leap into action as soon as the deal was closed. What the bloody hell can we do?"

They sat staring at each other in silence, underscored by swearing from Cassandra, sighs from Pamela, and occasional sobs from Bláithín. The doorbell made them jump. Cassandra got up. "Maybe it's Reuben, come to tell us the developer has bloody crashed his car and isn't coming!"

But it was Rosa who rushed in. "Bláithín! What's wrong? That voice mail, I couldn't understand it. You sounded so distressed."

Scraping her chair back, Bláithín hurried over to Rosa who opened her arms and Bláithín fitted right in. Pamela and Cassandra caught each other's eyes and smiled. Bláth took a calming breath and turned to face her friends. "First thing, girls, allow me to introduce you to… my girlfriend." The deep crimson spreading up her cheeks looked hot enough to cook on.

"I was waiting for that to happen from the day you met." Cassandra was smug.

"Go away! You were not!" Bláithín batted Cassandra's shoulder in passing. "You couldn't have. I didn't it know myself!"

Cassandra gave her a Cheshire Cat smile.

Rosa took off her coat and sat down while Bláth recounted the litany of disasters that had overtaken the household in the last few hours. When she finished, Cassandra added, "And the worst part of it is, there's nothing any of us can do right now, except just sit here and worry."

Rosa got to her feet. "In that case, I know what you all need, and I'm going to do it now." She opened the doors to the living room and looked in. "Does that fire work?"

"I assume so," said Cassandra. "I haven't needed it, but it's set with firewood and matches and stuff, so I guess we're meant to use it. Why?"

"If you can light that and get the room warm, I'll bring in my table and give you all an aromatherapy massage."

"Oh, what a fabulous idea!"

"I'm not sure I could relax enough," said Pamela.

"You will, don't worry." Rosa said with complete assurance, put her coat on again and headed to the car.

The fire lit easily, and Cassandra drew the curtains.

Rosa returned wearing her white work coat. "Now you all go and put on comfortable robes."

"I don't think I'm one for a massage. I've never had one," Bláithín was terrified at the prospect. "I'm happy to watch and keep the fire going."

Cassandra caught Bláithín's arm and propelled her from the room. "Come on, Bláth, give it a go."

By the time they came back, Rosa had dimmed the lighting, scented the air by dotting a dozen candles around, and covered the massage table in a thick, white towelling blanket. She dropped some oil on her hands and slid her palms together. "Who's first?"

"Me," Cassandra answered immediately, shrugging off her robe. Her hair in a loose bun on top of her head, she was naked apart from a pink thong. She lay long, tanned, and toned on the table. Rosa folded a fluffy towel in half and laid it across her buttocks and began moving her hands in gentle, slow, swooping movements up and down the length of Cassandra's back.

"Oh, that's so good!" Cassandra's voice was muffled by the face cradle. She sighed. "What are we going to do, girls? We can't possibly leave here."

It was hypnotic and relaxing watching Rosa work, so it was some time before Pamela, who was curled up in a corner of the couch spoke. "I don't see we have much option. They warned us they wanted us out of the house eventually, this is just way sooner than we expected."

Rosa was skillfully kneading circles into Cassandra's shoulders.

"I know," Cassandra eventually agreed, between murmurs of appreciation for Rosa's work. "But it seems all wrong. There must be something we can do."

Rosa worked on.

"I suppose we must wait and see what their exact plans are and maybe we can object or something?" Bláithín, who could not keep her eyes off Rosa's strong, gentle hands stroking and knuckling their way down Cassandra's legs, dropped her suggestion into the relaxed silence.

Finally, Rosa moved to a head massage and a series of feather strokes down Cassandra's back, then rested her palms on Cassandra's shoulders and said, "Okay, Pamela, you're next."

Cassandra objected, "Nooo, I need it all over again! Rosa, you are a genius. That was magic."

Pamela folded her robe and put it on the couch, and lay face down on the table. Rosa draped the towel across the pale blue briefs, and Pamela reached behind to unhook the matching bra and slip the straps off.

Rosa rummaged in her bag. "I'm changing oils for you, Pamela. A bit more lavender and a hint of chamomile, to relieve stress and promote healthy sleep."

Bláithín was amazed. How were these women so confident in exposing their bodies? Even fabulous Cassandra's skin had moved into soft folds as it was massaged, but Pamela's body was definitely soggy and soft. Varicose veins, cellulite, moles, and blemishes, and there she was displayed and chatting as easily as if she were in a coffee shop! Pamela's body was far worse than her own, it was… lived in, used, had borne a child, held love, hurt, kept her going through death and trauma, and here it was, being pampered like it deserved. Christ! Bláithín sat up. Stretch marks, age spots, wrinkles, were all badges of honour, survivor's medals! Nothing to be ashamed of or hidden. They proclaimed life.

Cassandra, wrapped in her thick, red robe again, was lying flat out on the floor with a cushion under her head, said, "Y'know, maybe there was something in what Bláth was saying. Maybe we can organize objections. I mean there's an ancient, possibly Phoenician wall in this house, right? Surely that's worth preserving?"

Without pausing in her work, Rosa said, "It depends on who is looking to make money. Here in Ibiza, despite its wonderful qualities, money has a louder voice than almost anything else. There have been major archaeological finds bulldozed and built on without consequence."

"Bugger!"

The fire crackled in the silence. Rosa's fingers worked on Pamela's scalp, gently moving the skin and pausing on pressure points. She finished with the feather movements and the resting hands.

"Thank you, Rosa, that was amazing, and to think I thought I wouldn't be able to relax," Pamela said, "I feel as if I'm positively melting." Rosa gently re-tied the bra again and handed Pamela her dove-grey robe.

Pamela sighed contentedly as she sat back into the corner of the couch. "Lucky you, Bláithín, to have a girlfriend with hands like that!"

That remark did not help Bláithín at all. Her anxiety was going through the roof for so many reasons. Rosa was going to see her body for the first time, she was stripping off in front of people, she was going to be massaged, in public! It all seemed insane! And yet, a part of her wanted to see it through, to be the person who could do this. Rosa held her hand out and Bláithín shrugged her robe into a heap on the couch and stood up. At least her black bra was respectable, and the navy briefs were fairly new. Matching lingerie was something she had never thought of, let alone bought.

Cassandra shook her head. "Bláithín, you are officially the whitest person I've ever seen. You're like a fucking alabaster statue!"

"I know!" said Rosa. "Isn't she beautiful?"

But that was the only personal moment in the massage. Rosa covered Bláithín's briefs with the towel and began to chat in a gentle voice about what oils she was using and why, what muscles were tight, and what they were affecting. Meanwhile, Cassandra decreed they were all feeling too relaxed and well to return to their problems. She suggested they should make a nightcap and have a game of Scrabble. "Heads firmly in the sand, girls, for the rest of the night, courtesy of Rosa!"

Bláithín finally slid off the table saying "I can't believe I never had that done before! Well, I suppose I can, really. I'd have been too mortified."

"You and your bloody Irish mortification, Bláth!" Cassandra got to her feet. "Hot chocolate with a soupçon of brandy for everyone?"

Pamela and Cassandra volunteered to make the chocolate and Bláithín helped Rosa put away her equipment.

"How did that make you feel?" Rosa asked, handing the towel to Bláithín to fold.

"Once I got over the embarrassment, it was extraordinary. Wonderful. I loved it. I never thought I could feel so relaxed. Though I couldn't stop thinking it was strange that it was you doing it."

Rosa stepped closer, instantly changing the atmosphere. She looked intensely at Bláithín while trailing her finger, the sharp side of her nail turned to leave a gentle frisson, it moved deep down between the crossed neck of her robe and across the swell of her breast.

"How does this make you feel?"

Almost unable to breathe, Bláithín gasped "Weak, watery."

Rosa bent her head and whispered in Bláithín's ear, her hot breath an erotic caress. "We have a lot to explore, my little flower." She might as well have recited the Kama Sutra in detail to Bláithín, such was her reaction. Cassandra's cheerfully intrusive call to hot chocolate broke the moment.

Pamela won the scrabble with a well-placed 'knottier' which netted her an unbeatable one hundred and seven points. But it was Cassandra who kept them in gales of laughter by having a very definite theme to her words. An innocent P was used in phallus, a DI was roped into dildo. Every word she put down became open to a double meaning and laughter filled the amazing house.

Much later, after the others had gone to bed, Bláithín and Rosa sat on the couch in the light of the fire, leaning into each other. They shared stories of long-ago incidents, moments and memories, the inconsequential, vital building blocks of their lives. Bláithín rested her head on Rosa's shoulder. Was there ever a more perfect resting place? The fire crackled, shooting occasional firework displays of dying embers up the chimney. Their conversation slowed. Listening to the peace, their eyes closed, and their breathing synchronized. At some stage during the night, they straightened out and lay full length on the huge couch. Bláithín spooning into Rosa and holding Rosa's covering arm with her own. Through a chink in the curtain, moonlight, on its prescribed journey, inched across the room and kissed their sleeping faces.

CHAPTER TWENTY-EIGHT

At eight o'clock the next morning someone was leaning on their doorbell. A sleep-tousled, bleary-eyed Cassandra opened the door and glared.

"Good morning. I am Marcus Van Groot, the owner of this property." The speaker's charcoal suit and brilliantly white shirt loomed out of the grey, dreary light of the mid-winter morning, He didn't appear the slightest bit apologetic for the unsocial hour. She stared at him blankly, he glanced at the sheaf of papers in his hand and added, "I understand you have been notified to the effect that I have acquired this property, and as such you are now my tenants, albeit very temporary ones."

Bláithín and Rosa, woken from their comfortable couch sleep, appeared behind Cassandra.

"What's going on?" Bláithín hugged her robe around her. "It's freezing and it's very, very early."

Van Groot didn't even glance at her as he continued to address Cassandra. "I also understand you were notified of today's visit. I am a busy man and like to start early. We won't be long; the architects need to do some final measuring." He indicated three men waiting next to a long black car.

Cassandra stepped aside and waved him in. He marched through the hall, immediately followed by his men. They moved through the house and out to the terrace with clipboards, measuring tapes, and large rolls of plans, ignoring the women completely.

"This is awful," hissed Pamela, appearing in her bedroom doorway, hopping around while pulling on her slipper socks.

Cassandra nodded. "He's certainly some pompous prick, alright. I'm going to show him the leak, maybe that will make him think twice." She stomped into the living room where he was standing in the doorway looking at the plans with one of the men. "Mr. Van Groot, perhaps you should take a look at this." She led them out to the terrace. Four sunken tiles and a trickle of water didn't look as threatening as she had hoped.

"As we'll be levelling the house and terrace to put in the foundations for twelve luxury apartments, a burst pipe is of no consequence." He turned back to his plans.

"You can't demolish this house!" Cassandra was beyond horrified.

He glared. "Oh, I assure you we can. Everything is in place. We were waiting on the permits and licenses which came through yesterday." He patted his clipboard with satisfaction. "We will start work early January and have them ready to sell off the plans by the start of summer. Each apartment will have a rooftop Jacuzzi, so that pool down there will be drained, filled, and spread out to give parking for two cars per apartment. Perhaps you are interested in one for yourself?"

Cassandra was too heartsick to answer.

A bare half-hour later, most of it spent outside measuring the fall of the land, he said they were ready to leave, and he handed her the clipboard and a ballpoint with the terse instruction, "Sign this."

She scowled as her eyes ran down the document and glared at him while she held it out for Bláithín and Pamela to read. It baldly stated that he was the owner of the villa, and she was his tenant only until January the tenth when she was to give vacant possession.

"Are you sure you understand this?" he asked Cassandra.

"Christ-all-buggering-mighty, man! I get it! This whole place belongs to you, not to me. You own every brick, window, and God-dammed roofing tile! Just let me sign the fucking piece of paper!" She scribbled her name and handed it back.

He signed and handed her a copy. Without a handshake or a smile, he left, taking his coterie of suits with him.

While the others saw to breakfast, Cassandra rang Reuben and told him about Van Groot. She paced the courtyard outside the house while she spoke. Her anger made her oblivious to the cold.

"Oh, Cassandra, I'm so sorry. I never thought it would happen so soon. Twelve apartments? If the permits have been issued, there will be no stopping them. That would be worth millions!"

"Can you come over?"

"Not at the moment. I'm stuck here for most of the day, organizing for some dead olive trees to be removed. I was hoping to supply you with a winter's worth of wood. Where's the Crone Club going to go now?"

"Oh, God, this isn't even all that's gone wrong. There's a whole damn list of disasters. Why don't you come over for dinner tonight? I'll fill you in and we can talk battle plans?"

"Nice idea, mi amor. I'll see you later."

**

The women were all in the pool, sitting on the steps, just their heads out in the chill air. Rosa had sage burning in the house to clear out the horrible, negative, greedy, destructive aura of Mr. Van Groot. The pool was safe and welcoming, mugs of coffee steamed next to them on the tiled edge. Cassandra's neon pink tankini sent glowing ripples of colour up through the water and her small brown breasts floated just under the surface as she leant back with her elbows on the step behind. In a sonorous voice, she intoned, "Ibiza Crone Club, mermaid division, meeting now in session. All members present, with the new addition of Rosa Ibanez. "

Bláithín's dark eyebrows rose like wings as she opened her eyes wide and looked at Rosa. "How do you feel being co-opted into a gang of crones?" she asked. Her hair was trailing in the water, its weight pulling it into softening ringlets, curling down to the top of her sensible, black one-piece.

"I can't think of a higher honour, or a more fun thing to be, than in your Ibizan Crone Club. Thank you." She put her palms together and bowed around to them all.

Cassandra laughed and picked up her coffee. "God," she sighed, closing her eyes and inhaling deeply. "There's nothing like the first coffee of the day, even if our world is collapsing!"

"I've been thinking about our problems," Pamela began, "and I hope you don't mind, Bláithín, but I think we should start with you because as I see it, you're the one whose problem is self-imposed."

"God in Heaven! How can you say that? Those two are going to ruin my life."

"Are they, really?" asked Pamela. "Is that why they're coming?"

"No. Of course not, but the result will be the same."

"They might ruin the life of the Bláithín who arrived here six weeks ago, but I don't think they can touch the Crone Goddess who has found love, is living with her friends, and has become a fantastic photographer!"

"Fuck, that was well put, Pamela!" Cassandra exclaimed. "It's not that you've 'changed'" she lifted her arms from the water and her fingers quote-marked, dripping water into her coffee. "You have peeled away the years of other people's expectations, done what you wanted, and maybe with some help..." she glanced at the heavens, "finally become yourself. As Pamela said, a true Crone Goddess!"

"I... I..." Bláithín paused and then looked around at her friends, her face a mask of complete and utter amazement. This was her, in love for the first time in her life. Sitting in a heated pool in Ibiza, holding her girlfriend's hand, surrounded by her friends. This was the Bláithín, Pauline and Diarmuid were travelling so far to spend Christmas with. She was bursting with happiness she stood up, raised her arms, looked up to the sky, and shouted, "I am a Crone Goddess! I love, and I am loved!" She shook her fist. "Do not trifle with me, world!"

The others cheered and clapped wildly.

Bláithín subsided with an embarrassed grin. "Well, maybe I could face Pauline and Diarmuid, if you were with me, Rosa."

"We will face them together, Cariño mio," Rosa said and took Bláithín's face between her hands and kissed her, a long passionate kiss in full view of their friends who whistled and cheered.

Bláithín could have cried with happiness.

"See what I meant?" asked Pamela. "That solution was in your own hands. I'm not saying it wasn't undeniably real and very upsetting, but Cassandra and I both knew the Bláithín we'd come to know could deal with it. You just had to admit this Bláithín existed!"

"Second order of business." Cassandra banged her mug for attention. "Pamela, I was thinking about Susan, wondering if we could get her to come here for a night. We know she hides her real thoughts and feelings from you and manipulates the truth to suit her view of what's going on. But between us all, we might ask the questions that would allow her to open up," she gestured around her, and turned to the house. "I mean, you know this place!"

Bláithín agreed, "That's a great idea, Cassandra. Sure, didn't you say Sophie was begging to come here, Pam?"

Pamela sank farther into the water, just her chin above the surface. "It would be marvellous. It would be good for Sue, and yes, Sophie would be thrilled. I really like that idea, Cassandra. Let Tanit work her magic. I'll ask Sue."

"Tanit?" asked Rosa.

Bláth made an I-don't-know-how-you-are-going-to-take-this face at Rosa and said, "I know it sounds crazy, and you don't want a crazy girlfriend, but both Cassandra and I have had a conversation with a woman who wasn't there! And no offence, Cassandra -"

"None taken" Cassandra inclined her head graciously. "Whatever it is you're about to say." She pushed away from the steps and floated with her eyes closed.

"But I could understand Cassandra having hallucinations, given the amount of marijuana and wine she'd consumed on that particular night... But honestly, me? I've no explanation at all."

"It's not too farfetched, you know," said Rosa, "Her temple is quite near here."

Cassandra spoke without opening her eyes. "And Reuben showed me the absolutely ancient back wall of this house. He says it's from Phoenician times too. So, it's also not too farfetched to think there was some connection right here, in this house."

Rosa smiled at Bláithín. "I have no problem believing this. I'll bring you all to her temple someday to leave an offering."

Bláithín looked at her friends. "See why I love her?"

"You do?" Rosa pounced on this admission.

Bláithín blushed furiously. "Ah, go away, you know I do."

Cassandra waved her hand at Bláithín. "Our Bláth, the last of the great romantics!" Floating did not go well with laughing, and she had to return to sit on the steps. "Seriously though, Rosa that sounds like a great idea, and one I think we should do, sooner rather than later." She looked at her hands. "Aargh! Prune alert. I'm out of here."

Cassandra pointed a finger at Rosa on her way up the steps. "By the way, I might as well warn you, I intend to see a lot more of your brother."

Rosa laughed, "You don't have to tell me! For a serious, uncommunicative block, my brother has been doing a great impression of a cheerful, whistling, happy guy. "

"Has he?" Cassandra's transparent delight made them all smile.

They were all back in the house and dressed before they mentioned Mr. Van Groot and his plans. "I don't know," said Cassandra. "Somehow, I can't get too exercised about it. I'm sure there's some objection we can make. Something we haven't thought of yet. I'll call into the planning office soon."

"I'm happy to help with translating," offered Rosa, "Oh, of course, Reuben will do you, won't he?"

"I certainly hope he will," agreed Cassandra, her eyebrows creating the double entendre. Bláithín spluttered and Pamela smiled and shook her head.

"Speaking of Reuben," continued Cassandra, "I've invited him to dinner tonight to discuss our woes. Rosa, would you like to join us?"

Rosa glanced at Bláithín whose smile was answer enough, and said, "I'd love to, thanks, Cassandra."

"Do you need me to do any shopping or anything for dinner?" Pamela asked. She was at the sink, rinsing the mugs. Her hair was never in its perfect chignon anymore. Now, after the swim, it just fell loose, wavy, shoulder-length, and white, softening her face and emphasizing her blue eyes.

Cassandra tapped her index finger on her lip while she thought. "It's okay, thank you. I've no idea what I'm going to cook, so I'm better off to poke around on my own."

Pamela dried her hands. "Well, if you don't need help, I've got a painting to finish."

"And I," said Rosa, "must go home, I'm still in yesterday's clothes."

"Ooh, walk of shame coming up," hooted Cassandra. "None of us would object if you were to leave a change of clothes or two here, would we? Or am I jumping the gun here, Bláithín?"

Bláithín put her arm around Rosa and didn't even blush. "No, I don't think you are."

CHAPTER TWENTY-NINE

That evening, Reuben and Rosa arrived together. She had obviously filled him in on her relationship with Bláithín.

"Who knew," he said after he kissed Bláithín's cheek, "that the anxious lady I picked up in San Antonio so few weeks ago would be the one to finally pry my sister's heart open!"

Hot colour flooded Bláithín's face, but she managed to smile at him. "Is that what she said I did?"

Rosa's wound her arm around her girlfriend's waist and whispered, "You know you did!"

Cassandra clapped her hands. "Dinner is ready. If you would all be so kind..." She waved her hand ushering them all into the living room where she had set up dinner. Vases of purple bougainvillea and pale blue plumbago dotted points of colour around the room, the fire danced in the stove, and the curtains were drawn. She poured drinks and served a starter of warm flaky pastry filled with spinach, pine nuts, and cream cheese. Lifting her glass, she proposed a toast. "Here's to new relationships and friendships, may they be blessed." They raised their glasses, Pamela, Bláithín, and Rosa with red wine while Cassandra joined Reuben with his cranberry juice.

Of course, the imminent destruction of their beloved house was the first topic of conversation. Like the Crones, Reuben was horrified to think of this beautiful home being bulldozed. They discussed their very limited options, and agreed that, at the moment, far from a great strategic battle plan, all they could do was plead for the council to reconsider their approval. Reuben promised to research any possibility that the back wall of the house was, in fact, connected to a Tanit shrine and Cassandra planned a charm offensive on the planning office. Rosa remained doubtful of their success as she felt money had already changed hands, but also suggested she could get a lawyer friend of hers to draft an appeal letter.

The conversation moved on to their other problems. The women felt no embarrassment or restraint discussing their troubles with Reuben. When he was unguarded and relaxed, he was a most empathetic and intuitive man.

Bláithín recounted her woes. "And now, I'll probably have to spend Christmas in Andy's flat in San Antonio with Diarmuid and Pauline." Bláithín ended her story to him and rolled her eyes at the thought. She sat forward. "God Almighty! I'm just after realizing that Christmas is only about two weeks away!"

"Christ, Christmas shopping would be reaching a frenzy point by now back home," Cassandra shuddered.

"Yes, and it's probably been on the go since October!" added Bláithín.

Cassandra laughed. "Can you imagine shoppers all over Ireland and England being told that the shops were going to shut every day up to Christmas between one and five for a siesta. There'd be mass hysteria!"

"I always quite liked Christmas," Pamela said. "The lights, decorations, fun, especially the magic of children and Santa Claus."

Rosa joined in, "Oh, we have that too, on the island. But it doesn't start until Christmas week, and then shops put up decorations, put out red carpets, and hand out treats to the children, it's all very low-key in comparison to England or Ireland." She held up a finger. "And they still close for siesta."

"Sounds perfect," Bláithín said. "But I'm fairly sure Pauline will be looking for full-on Christmas spirit!"

"Well, here's an idea," Cassandra said, drawing out her words as she thought. "How about if we did Christmas day here? Have abso-fucking-lutely everyone?"

"You mean..."

"Yes, Diarmuid and Pauline, Susan and the kids, even Glen, if Sue wants. Fuck it, ask Maite, her baby, and whatever her husband's name is, ask the bloody mother-in-law if they want to. So, with Reuben and Rosa and us, if everyone came, that would be fifteen. Easy-peasy! What fun it would be! Drinks, food, Santa Claus presents for all, just fun, nothing big, Christmas dinner, cheesy movie - what do you all think?"

"A marvellous idea."

"Fecking brilliant," Bláithín beamed. "What do you think, Rosa?"

"Happy to be where you are."

Cassandra got to her feet. "That's decided. Christmas dinner is to be held here. Okay, let's get dinner served before we start making plans. Hand me your plates." Cassandra took the empty starter plates and disappeared into the kitchen.

Reuben followed. "Can I help?" He took the opportunity to pull her close and bestow a brief but passionate kiss, which she returned enthusiastically.

She smiled up at him. "Best help ever." She handed him a basket of warm garlic bread and pushed him toward the table.

Cassandra carried in a large casserole dish and set it on the table. "Help yourselves, it's vegetable moussaka."

Rosa closed her eyes after the first bite. "Mmmm, this is so delicious, Cassandra. It tastes as if it has been marinating for days, but I know you only made it this afternoon!"

"Thank you, Rosa. A trick that always works, it's-"

"Balsamic vinegar, I'd say," Reuben said. He took another bite. "It really is wonderful."

"Yes, it's balsamic vinegar. How did you know?"

The conversation rambled from cookery tricks, through favourite music, best movie lines to worst food experiences. Which Pamela won, hands down. "The first time Jonathan took me home to meet his mother, I asked for a drink of milk. She was a fearful dragon and when she handed me a glass, I just drank it. Lumpy, curdled, watery, and disgusting as the completely sour milk was, I was too afraid to say anything."

"No! That's totally revolting!" Cassandra made gagging noises.

"God Almighty, how was it you didn't throw up?" Bláithín's face crumpled in disgust.

Eventually, they got back to the logistics of Christmas.

"Maite, Pedro and the baby wouldn't stay the night, but what about Pauline and Diarmuid?" Bláithín asked.

"Yes, I was thinking about that," Cassandra said. "Also, maybe Glen might come for dinner too - that's if Sue wants him at all. What do you think Pamela?"

"Oh, yes, I don't imagine he'll stay long, but I know him and he will unquestionably want to see his children on Christmas day. But where would we put everyone staying the night?"

"If you don't mind, Pamela, we could put Pauline and Diarmuid in your studio. The couch there opens up to a double bed, and I don't imagine you'll be doing much painting over those days anyway."

"No, definitely won't." agreed Pamela. "But will they have enough room?"

"I'm sure they will. I could even put in a little rail for them to hang clothes." She turned to Ruben and smiled. "And when I say 'I', I mean you!"

He tugged an imaginary forelock. "Your wish is my command. I could put in a free-standing one or attach it to-"

Cassandra was on her feet and heading to Pamela's studio. "I'll just check, if I may, Pamela? Though I'm sure there's plenty of room."

"Wait! No!" Pamela shot out of her chair. "Don't go in there, Cassandra!"

It was too late. Cassandra had gone in and turned on the light.

"What the actual fuck?" Cassandra's shocked voice was loud.

"Cassandra, they're nothing, they're just..."

"They are just frigging awesome!"

Everyone was in the studio now. All attention was riveted on a row of four paintings hanging down one wall. The paintings glowed and throbbed with vivid colour.

A line of explicit, erotic paintings.

The cheerful, slightly cartoonish people in them radiated health, fun, and sensuality. In the first, a man wearing nothing but a bowler hat was clearly about to make love to a naked, creamy-skinned, long-haired woman who was squeezing her own breasts in delight. Covering every inch around them were lush flowers and butterflies. Further on, the same man without his hat but with neatly patterned socks held up by suspenders under his knees lay on a bed. The same long-haired woman was kneeling astride him. Her head was thrown back, and musical notes were bursting from her mouth. They were almost obscured by tropical birds in violent, clashing, fabulous colours.

Pamela leant weakly against the wall, feeling sick. She had never intended these paintings for public consumption. They had just consumed her when she discovered the freedom of night painting. The hints, the feelings, the ideas and dreams she'd suppressed in the apartment, had all burst free. This was all her, her vision, and she realised, her history. The history of the unspoken happiness of her marriage. Peculiar as life had been with the ultra-controlling Jonathon, they'd shared unbridled ecstasies in the bedroom. There had been no shame, no embarrassment, no limits. This equality had only existed in the bedroom, but, by God, it had existed, and it had been wonderful.

The sound of applause brought her back to reality. Cassandra caught her up in an embrace, "They are fucking amazing! I can see I'll have to open two galleries!"

Rosa too, embraced her. "These are the most magically intimate portrayal of love I have ever seen."

Bláithín was still looking at them. "They are amazing, Pamela. Dreamlike…, and extremely erotic."

Pamela's head was spinning, she cleared her throat. "Anyway, I think we're all agreed, a rail for clothes would fit in here." She turned off the light, then added, "Don't worry Bláithín; those paintings will *not* be on the wall when Diarmuid and Pauline visit!"

"No," said Cassandra, "They won't. I'll have them at the printers, getting a run of high-quality prints done! Do you think you could do one or two more?"

Pamela smiled; she had forty years of them.

Coffees and herbal teas finished off the night and Rosa and Reuben left after somewhat protracted goodbyes. As they washed up later, Bláithín said, "Pamela, I don't know how you did it, but those paintings are simultaneously exotic and erotic, yet the underlying feeling is of everyday life and love. It's amazing."

"Life is amazing, Bláth. I think that's the answer. Life is amazing!"

***

The next day Pamela rang Susan, who readily agreed to a night in the house. "We might as well do it while we have the chance. To be honest, I'll be glad of a distraction for Sophie, she's constantly questioning me about Glen's whereabouts."

It made sense for them to come straight from Katrina's that day. Pamela wondered if Susan was putting off going back to her own house until she went back with her, a depressing thought on so many levels. Though, if they had to be out of here on the tenth of January, that dream was over anyway.

Rosa arrived to collect Bláithín for another day of deliveries and photography. "If we're all still agreed on Christmas, we might call in and invite Maite while we're out," Bláithín said, checking her camera, and patting her pockets to confirm her glasses and purse were in place.

"Oh yes, let's do this!" Cassandra strolled through the kitchen, from her morning yoga on the terrace, the towel around her neck - the only bit of clothing she had on.

Swollen, rain-promising clouds were speeding across the sky, pushed by a gusting wind, when Susan arrived with the children. Sophie did a double-take when Cassandra suggested a swim.

"I'm not sure Mummy will let us in this weather."

"Oh, she might, if she knows it's a heated pool."

She did.

A short while later, they were all in the pool. Clark's water wings puffed out his arms like a little sumo wrestler as he launched himself face-first from the second step. Cassandra began a game of chase, which involved a lot of splashing and laughing. When it was Susan's turn to chase, she towed Clark around with her, and his huge, baby chuckles of delight made the women pause, just to enjoy listening.

By the time they were all out and showered, night had closed in. The wind had won the battle for the sky, which was now a clear, black void pinpricked with sparkles. Bláithín came back, glowing from her day out, and was immediately put to chopping vegetables with Cassandra, while Pam and Sue fed the children.

"Where did you go today, Bláth?" asked Cassandra, deftly chopping three carrots at the same time.

"Rosa took me to the highest part of the Island. Sa Talaia. It was unbelievable. A hair-raising drive, though. I think I had my eyes closed for half it! But, Mother of God! The view from the top was - and I mean this literally - breathtaking. We were so high up, we could see two different coasts of Ibiza spread out down below."

Cassandra began sizzling the vegetables on a high heat, casually throwing in shakes of spices from different containers and packets. "Oh, you must have taken some amazing photos!"

Bláithín concentrated on her chopping. "Um... I took a series on a small snail shell."

"Ha, was it worth going all the way up there for that?"

"It was worth going up there for lots of reasons," said Bláithín turning to the sink to wash her hands, washing them until the red heat cooled from her cheeks.

While Susan left to put the children to bed, the three friends sat around the kitchen table and poured the wine.

Bláithín said, "We called into Maite today. She seemed a bit down, and she looked exhausted. Her mother-in-law didn't leave us alone for a second, so we held off on mentioning Christmas day to her, as we'll be back in San Antonio again tomorrow."

"Good idea," agreed Cassandra. "Give her the chance to make her own decision, as long as you can get rid of the mother-in-law from hell."

"I know! She told us that woman is making plans for Maite to run the shop full-time now that her cleaning business is scuppered."

"How was the baby, in the middle of all this?" Pamela asked.

"Thriving, I'd say. She has more chins than myself now!"

Susan stepped into the laughter-filled kitchen, "That's a good sign in a new baby. I remember Sophie was like Buddha in a baby grow when she was tiny and look at her now. There's not a pick on her."

Pamela nodded. "Gosh yes, I used to call her cherub cheeks. How did they settle for you, Sue?"

"The pool was such a good idea, they were exhausted. I had no trouble getting Clark to settle in the cot, and Sophie is on a one-more-chapter countdown, though I'd be surprised if she makes it to the end of the page. Her eyes are shutting."

Bláithín was still thinking about her friend. "Maite will have to face her mother-in-law down, or at least get Pedro to step up."

Pamela shook her head, "Sometimes it's hard to stand up for yourself, be forceful, proactive, or confident just after you've had a baby."

"I know," laughed Susan, "I couldn't even decide on a grocery list after Sophie was born." She pulled out a chair and joined them at the table.

Cassandra shuddered. "I can't imagine it!"

A timer pinged, and after a flurry of activity they sat down to an aromatic vegetable curry and jasmine rice.

Susan closed her eyes and inhaled. "Mmmm, this smells lovely, thank you."

Ice cubes rattled as Cassandra poured water from a huge jug into their water glasses and topped up their wine.

"I'm so sorry you have to be out of here next month," Susan said. "Mum was telling me. What a shock, and what an awful man!"

"The Crone Club hasn't given up yet! Hopefully, we'll come up with a plan and come out all guns blazing after Christmas. Speaking of which, did Pamela ask you about spending it here with us?"

"No, no she didn't mention it. Gosh, I don't know. It might be better if we all spent it at home, Mum, don't you think?"

"I'm not sure, but whatever you -"

Cassandra interrupted. "The kids would love it! A Christmas tree in there," she jabbed a thumb at the living room. "Lights around the fireplace and pool, decorations, loads of people, party food, sweets. Wouldn't it be better than them sitting at home looking at you saying, 'Where's daddy?'"

Susan gasped. "Mum! Have you been sharing my private affairs?"

Pamela lost her patience. "Oh, Sue, don't be so precious. My friends have both been through divorces, so, if anything, they are far better equipped to understand what you're going through than I am."

Cassandra carried on as if she had heard none of this, "I mean, if you are planning on having Glen over on Christmas day, he's more than welcome here. And that might be easier all around, don't you think? More people, less pressure cooker?"

"You don't understand!" Susan banged her knife and fork hard on the table. "He left me for another woman!"

Cassandra's smile was wry. "Oh, I understand *that* all too bloody well. But it took me two years to understand what was really going on as opposed to what I thought was going on."

"Well, that's a bit complicated for me, but -"

"Do you love him, Sue?" Bláithín's interjection was gentle and calm.

"What? Of course, we've been together for ten years!"

"That's not a reason to love someone. Does he love you?" Cassandra asked.

"Ah, I'm sure he does, it's just this woman has caught him at a vulnerable time. He's stressed with the move to Ibiza and everything."

"So, everything was fine until the move?"

"Well, yes. Some strain is to be expected..." Susan trailed off as she caught Pamela's eye.

Pamela waited to see what was coming, Sue's version of reality, or reality?

Susan pushed away her empty plate and stood up. "Excuse me a minute, I'm going to get some air. It's quite warm in here."

They watched her go into the living room and out onto the moonlit terrace. "I think reinforcements, may be arriving." Cassandra prayer-palmed her hands and gave a little bow to the sky.

They followed her out; Cassandra grabbed some blankets from the shelves on her way, and the others picked up cushions.

Susan, with her arms tightly crossed, stood at the edge of the terrace, looking down at the silver light catching the tops of little wind-ruffled waves crossing the pool. Cassandra draped a blanket over her shoulders. Then, wrapping her own around her, she sat on the top step hugging her knees.

Pamela handed a cushion to Cassandra as she passed. Cassandra smiled, "Thanks, my arse was feeling cold already."

Pamela and Bláithín put their cushions down on the stone bench and sat.

"What is it really, darling?" asked Pamela.

There was a long silence, then Susan finally spoke. "I'm so afraid, Mum."

Pamela started towards her but sat again when

Cassandra shook her head. Pamela contented herself with asking, "But of what?"

"Of... of what's outside being calm and organized. Of failing, of being alone." Susan's words were gasped out in a rush. "Of not being good enough. Of not being able to cope with everything on my own. He can't leave me! He just can't. What would I do?"

"I don't understand, darling. You fail? Impossible. You were always the best at everything."

"Yes, I was, and it wasn't even difficult. I just worked hard at school. You and daddy so believed in me, and home was so safe and calm, and everything was always just right. Everything went the way it was supposed to."

Cassandra lit a match. Her face flared all hollows and cheekbones in its light. "But life isn't like that outside the womb of home, is it?"

"No! I tried so hard to make things right, to be perfect, not allow problems, to run things properly like you, Mum."

Pamela closed her eyes.

Cassandra's cigarette paper sizzled, and sparks shot into the air as she inhaled deeply. Then she asked, "But Glen didn't want that, did he?"

Susan sank onto the top step next to Cassandra, her head leaning back against the pillar, her eyes searching the skies for her answer. "No! No, he kept trying to change things, 'Throw caution to the winds and go for what you want,' he used to say. And it made me feel sick."

"But the move to Ibiza was brave," Bláithín said.

"Yes, it was," agreed Pamela. "And I always had the impression you were driving that."

"I was because I was sure he was going to leave me. He'd been unhappy for so long. He'd always wanted to travel, and I had to come up with something. But I knew you'd come too, Mum, and life could settle down to normal again."

"What about the counselling back home?" asked Pamela.

"A disaster. I had told him he was stressed, the

counsellor told him the same thing." She paused, took a breath and said, "Well, she did say he was stressed, but... she also said... that we weren't communicating well, and that at the moment, we didn't seem to be sharing life goals. That was nonsense. I tried to make him see it was all nothing. That it would all be fine if he'd only... only..."

"Only pretend." Cassandra's words hung in the air. She exhaled and continued, "You tried to make him see things your way, refusing to accept anything he was feeling to keep your mythical 'perfect life' going. But it seems to me that you were pretending just as much. There can't have been much fun there."

Pamela added, "The same way you tried to make me see things your way when you told me your version of the counselling, and your pregnancy."

When she spoke again, Susan's voice was small. "I just didn't want anyone to know."

Pamela sighed. "Oh, Sue, these last few weeks of endless friends and parties have all been about presenting the face you want to the world and avoiding reality. It must have been exhausting for both of you."

There was a long silence. Small waves slapped against the side of the pool, driven by the gusts of wind that rattled the branches and rustled leaves around their feet. Cassandra's smoke coiled around the terrace.

Bláithín raised her head as she smelled the smoke. "Is that....?" she asked in a strangled voice.

"Yes, it is." Cassandra held the joint out to Bláithín. "Do you want some?"

Bláithín's laughter was loud and infectious. "Of all the things I saw myself doing at this hour of my life, having a girlfriend and being offered a joint wouldn't even have made the list!"

Susan turned open-mouthed to look at Bláithín, "Having a..." Her head whipped around to Pamela, "Mum?"

Pamela could hardly answer for laughing, "No, not me. A

beautiful Spanish woman named Rosa."

My God! What is it with this house?" Susan shook her head.

"Well, Bláithín, you've ticked one of those off the list. Do you want to do the other?"

"No thanks. I've never smoked in my life, and I don't think I want to start now."

"Fair enough." Cassandra pulled the pungent roll-up back but a gentle tap on her arm stopped her, Pamela was taking the joint.

"Mum!"

"Let's see what this is all about."

"Don't inhale too deeply or hold it too long if it's your first." Cassandra advised.

Pamela inhaled, short and smooth, and more or less controlled the exhale, followed by a few small coughs.

She handed it back to Cassandra, who smirked and said, "Well, it may be your first joint, but it certainly isn't your first cigarette."

"Mum?" Susan's voice was a high-pitched squeak.

"Women's Institute, Darling. Most of those women smoked like chimneys. I kept my own packet there."

When the laughter died down, Cassandra returned to the conversation of the night. "Sue, it seems to me you were running yourself ragged trying to make everyone share your vision of your life, even though you knew it was crumbling."

"But I didn't want it to change! I wanted things to be the way they should be."

"Obviously, your 'should be' and Glen's 'should be' became very different," Bláithín said, "I know how easily that can happen."

Susan looked around at the three women; anxiety made her voice sharp. "But what would I do if he left me? How would I live?"

Pamela held up a hand. "Hang on Sue. Whatever problems you have with Glen, he's a wonderful father and he would never let his children suffer. Has he said what he plans to do?"

"I don't know. I wouldn't meet him."

"You could always get a job," suggested Cassandra.

"I never qualified as anything."

Cassandra waved her hand. "These days that's nearly completely irrelevant in a lot of areas. It's what you can do that counts." She held out the end of the joint. "Last one, Pam?"

"No, thank you, I just wanted to try it and I may do so again. It's quite nice, kind of floaty, but I think I prefer a nice glass of Verdejo."

Cassandra finished it off, then rubbed out any lingering red in the earth next to her, and popped the roach into her matchbox. "Sue, as Bláithín asked earlier, do you love him?"

"Of... I... I... don't know. I did at the start. Or rather, I loved the safety and security he offered. I'm not sure. Then I just became afraid when I saw he wasn't happ"y and I became paranoid about making sure everything was perfect, but that seemed to make things worse."

"Oh, Sue," Pamela sighed, "that was because he just wanted you, not a perfect life. Susan, I loved your father, you know I did, but I realize I hid myself to comply with his need for control and order. Imagine if I didn't have dinner ready when he got home from work because I'd gotten lost in painting! Or if I presented his six-thirty gin and tonic with my hair down and paint on my hands!"

Susan smiled. "He'd have been horrified."

"Exactly! Your dad wanted a perfect life, and he loved me because I gave it to him. I didn't particularly want that, but I made a conscious decision, early on, to go along with it for a peaceful life. I'm not sure I'd do it now. In fact, I'm damn sure I wouldn't."

Bláithín broke in, "God Almighty, wouldn't you think that being married is a fairly straightforward situation, two people on the same page wanting the same thing? Everyone's marriage should be more or less the same, but it's nothing of the bloody sort. There are more permutations and possibilities for disaster than a… than a…"

Cassandra finished the sentence for her. "Than a basket full of electric eels loose in a cable factory?"

The others smiled.

Cassandra shrugged and said, "Best I can do at the moment." She stood up. "I'm freezing." She held her hand out to Susan to pull her up. "C'mon, we'll have a nightcap."

"I think I'll hang on out here. You've all given me a lot to think about."

"Okay, then. See you in the morning."

Bláithín stood up too. "Yes, I think I'll turn in as well. Here, Sue, take my cushion and make yourself comfortable - this is an amazing place for clear thinking." She followed Cassandra in.

Pamela waited on to see if Sue had any more she wanted to say.

Briefly, the clink of dishes and water splashing into the sink carried out through the kitchen window, accompanied by a gentle murmur of conversation. Then the lights went out and all was silent.

A little while later, Pamela looked at Susan. Her eyes were closed, and she seemed lost in thought. Deciding to let her think in peace, she dropped a gentle kiss on her daughter's head, and padded on past her to the house and bed.

Susan brushed off something landing on her hair, got to her feet and stepped down towards the pool. She paused and spoke back through the dark to her mother. "I think this is the first time I've admitted, even to myself, that I'm not happy with this marriage."

"Well, leave it! You are young. Don't stay bound to the same path forever because you are afraid to step off."

"But I'd be a single mum. I'd be alone. I don't think I could cope."

"You are surrounded by women who support you. You are strong, yet you waste energy trying to keep a crumbling house going. Let it fall, then build one of your own choosing."

"Could I really? I wonder..." Susan sighed. "Mum, you've all been great, but I need some time to think now. I'll see you in the morning." She pulled the blanket around herself like a shawl and walked down to pace around the pool.

CHAPTER THIRTY

A cranky, howling Clark with a bright red cheek, a drool-soaked t-shirt, and a fist in his mouth meant Susan needed to take the children home before breakfast the next day.

"Teething! And all the stuff I need is at home. The poor pet, I'll get some Calpol into him as soon as possible."

Pamela nodded. "Yes, and an ice loll will help numb the sore gum, maybe get him one for the journey back." She took a deep breath before she said, "Sue, would you like me to come back with you now? I will if you want."

"It's okay, Mum. I had a good think about what everyone said last night. Especially, what you said about being strong enough to build a life of my own choosing."

Pam racked her brains; she didn't remember saying that.

"I'm going to go back on my own and arrange a meeting with Glen. I'll get on to you after that. If I'm not going into work, there's no need to drag you away from your friends, especially now that you have so little time left here."

"I'll be there in a heartbeat if you need me."

"I know, Mum." Susan hugged her mother. "Say thank you to Cassandra and Bláithín for me. I'm sorry to be running away so early, especially after how kind they were last night. I really feel like something's different this morning."

Sophie squeezed Pamela around the waist. "I love this place, Grandma. It feels happy. When can I come back again?"

"Very soon, Sophie, and maybe the next time you can do some painting in my studio with me?"

"Did you hear that, Mum? I must pack an apron next time."

Clark wouldn't even look at Pamela, not to mind kiss her and he shrieked furiously at being strapped into the baby seat.

"Drive safely, and don't let him distract you! He'll be

okay." called Pamela, waving them off. She scurried inside, away from the biting wind. Bláithín was sitting at the kitchen table when Pamela went in. She was on the phone but waved Pamela in, as she made to back out.

"Yes, Pauline, yes. I'm sure.

"No, it won't be any trouble, honestly.

"No, I'm not staying at Andy's anymore.

"Of course, I'll still meet you when you arrive."

Pamela signalled did she want coffee and Bláithín nodded.

"Yes, that's right, Christmas eve and Christmas day.

"Yes, a room of your own.

Pamela raised an eyebrow, Bláithín rolled her eyes and continued, "It will all be great.

Yes, we do have loads to talk about, indeed.

Oh, I must tell you, Maite's had her... Oh, you do? She did? Lovely.

Yes, a box of Roses would be great.

Oh, of course, tea too, perfect.

Okay, sure, I'll be seeing you soon enough anyway.

Yes, bye, bye, bye." She thumbed off her phone.

Pamela handed her a coffee, Bláithín took several gulps and closed her eyes. "Aaah, bliss. I should have had that before I rang Pauline. Anyway, I think they are delighted. I spoke to Diarmuid first, but when herself heard the conversation turn to Christmas, she took over, pronto. But I love the thought of making a nice Christmas for them here." She topped up her coffee.

Cassandra came into the kitchen, yawning. "Have we seen Sue yet this morning? Do we know if we helped or hindered last night?"

Pam carried a stack of toast to the table. "She had to leave early. Clark's molar is cutting through and he's a misery. She said to say thank you to you both, but more importantly, she said she felt different this morning. Even though I only saw her briefly, I thought she seemed different too. More focused, less anxious. She's going to arrange to talk to Glen and let me know how it goes. She did thank me for making a comment about building her own life. Do either of you remember me saying that?"

They both shook their heads. Cassandra spread her arms, "As I said last night, I think we had reinforcements!" Not for the first time, she raised joined palms to the sky. Pouring a coffee for herself, she clinked mugs with the other two. "Another success for the Crone Club!"

Serious list-making for the Christmas party began after breakfast. The menu was quickly decided. Turkey and all that goes with it, plus a vegetarian option, Christmas pudding, and a lemon meringue pie. Bláithín, who was heading to San Antonio shortly, was tasked with ordering all they needed from the British supermarket and with inviting Maite. Cassandra volunteered Reuben to look for a tree, while she and Pamela would go on a decoration and Christmas light hunt. They were also going to pick up the prints of Bláithín's photos and the canvas one, for Pamela to add in her golden detail.

"I can't remember Christmas party planning ever being so much fun." Cassandra rocked her chair back on its back legs. "I'm not sure if I ever enjoyed it, and I must have organized hundreds of the bloody things."

"Me neither," said Bláithín. "I feel so… happy is a small, little word, but I do feel happy, and grateful, for both of you and for all of this -" she opened her arms wide, "-even if it is all going to end shortly."

"Oh, well said, Bláithín. My feelings exactly," said Pamela.

"Good thinking!" said Cassandra, "Come with me. No need for coats, just come outside for a moment."

The sun shone brightly, and the winter air gave a crystalline clarity to everything. A flock of gulls flying high looked impossibly, brilliantly white, and the dark green cypress trees tapering to the sky stood as if they had been dropped in from a movie.

"Now, stand like this and copy me," instructed Cassandra, "Feet, shoulder-width apart, hands hanging loosely by the sides, inhale slowly, spread your arms out to the sides, as widely as you can, now slightly curve them, exhale and bring them around in front of you in a big embrace. It's called Buddha embracing the world. Close your eyes and repeat the movement three times, feel as if you are both giving and receiving this embrace."

Bláithín opened her eyes after the last repetition. "Perfect, Cassandra, it's exactly what I wanted to express, thank you."

They went back into the kitchen. "It feels so good, Cass, so simple," said Pamela.

"Doing six of these is a wonderful way to start the day, hugging the world. Now, girls, get to work!"

Bláithín tucked her shopping list into her pocket, hung the camera around her neck, and hurried out the door in response to Rosa's beep. Pamela and Cassandra left shortly afterwards. The house settled into silence. Some wood pigeons cooed from the surrounding forest, and a fresh surge of water pushed more tiles out of place on the terrace.

***

A worn-out Maite came into the shop to talk to Bláithín and Rosa, closing the door on the sound of crying. She was overjoyed with the Christmas invitation. "Oh, Bláithín, I am so sick up until here," she held her hand to her nose, "of my mother-in-law and her friends. I will so love to come. As early as possible. I can help cook, and if your lovely brother is there, Pedro will be happy." She clapped her hands. "Oh, maybe Pauline can make another of her puddings?"

"I'm sure she could be persuaded." Smiled Bláithín knowing full well how Pauline would puff up with delight at being asked.

Maite looked wretched. Lank-haired and red-eyed, she insisted she was fine, but as she explained, losing her English even more in her exhaustion and frustration. "My bebé is crying to feed all time. Some books, they say I must to not feed until every four hours, or I will be bad mother." She wiped her eyes. "Or they say I must to feed all time or be bad mother."

Bláithín and Rosa looked at each other, there was no experienced help coming from either of them. Bláithín spread her hands. "I'm sorry, I honestly know nothing about any of this. What does your mother-in-law say?"

"I think she say only what make me feel bad." Then she brightened, "But now, I have a Christmas with friends to do. I feel happy." She looked back at the door, the crying was intensifying. "I must to go."

Bláithín put her arm around her young friend. "Maite, all I can say is, do what feels right for you. You're her mother. You decide, not the books."

Maite kissed them both, "See you soon," she said and scurried back to her baby.

Rosa drove them to Thomas Green's English supermarket and checked her messages while Bláithín went in and placed their Christmas order. The Christmas cheer in the shop encouraged her to add Christmas crackers and a big, festive box of biscuits to her order. She paid the deposit and arranged to pick them up on the twenty-third.

"Have we time for lunch or do you need to get back?" Rosa asked as they were driving out of San Antonio.

"Oh, no. I've buckets of time. Where do you suggest?"

"We can pass through Santa Eulalia on our way. It has dozens of lovely places." She smiled across at Bláithín as she changed gears. "Hey, did you get a chance to look at your photographs from yesterday? Were there any you can work with?"

The mention of yesterday brought colour flooding to Bláithín's face.

"Whoo-hoo, look at you," teased Rosa gently. "Anyone would think you'd been making out like a teenager yesterday."

Bláithín shifted in her seat at the memory. "Oh, God,

Rosa, what would have happened if someone had come?"

"There was no one there, Bláithín. And we'd have heard anyone coming from miles away. You loved it, didn't you cariño?"

Bláithín's mind instantly supplied her with snapshots. Warm kisses and a questing tongue. Rosa licking her nipples erect. Rosa's jacket on the ground, a barrier to the scrubby grass pressing into Bláithín's arched back. The blue gaze locked onto her own as Rosa's gentle fingers worked unbelievable magic down inside the front of Bláithín's open jeans.

Bláithín pressed her thighs tightly together. "Oh, Rosa stop."

Rosa smirked as she checked the mirrors, indicated, and switched lanes to follow signs for Santa Eulalia. She glanced at Bláithín. "I know what you're thinking. I thought about it all last night!"

"God, Rosa will you stop?"

"Why? It's exciting even to think about, isn't it? And Bláithín? We've only just started!"

"I'd better double my blood pressure meds so!"

"More likely halve them if you keep releasing tension so explosively!"

"I'm puce!" Bláithín laughed, covering her face with her hands. "Doing it is one thing, talking about it seems a step too far."

Taking pity, Rosa changed the subject, "There's a cinema in Santa Eulalia that shows movies in English. Would you like to go tonight if there is something interesting on?"

"I'd love to. Let's check it out."

They sat at one of the cafés lining the wide paseo leading down to the steel grey sea, and people watched while they ate a toasted sandwich.

"You'd never see the like of this anywhere in the world, I'd say," Bláithín said. She was leaning back in her seat. Rosa's arm stretched along the back, her hand casually resting on Bláithín's shoulder. "I mean, look at that couple over there, they must be eighty, and look at the colours in her dress and the flowers in her hair! And I swear he's wearing a skirt."

Rosa leant forward for a look. "More like very wide flowery trousers, I'd say."

"Oh, yes. I see now. Well, isn't it great? They're here and over there-" She nodded at a group of women leaning in towards each other in enthusiastic conversation on a nearby bench. "They'd give my mother a run for her money in the twinset and perm race, but neither group is looking askance at the other."

"Ibiza is a tolerant, welcoming place. I think it's because we've been invaded by so many different cultures over the centuries, we've developed a wide acceptance of people."

While they waited for their bill, a group took the table next to them. Dreadlocked, tattooed, with dogs and children, they dragged two tables together. The waiter welcomed them warmly by name and brought out the huge paella dish they'd obviously pre-ordered. Bláithín smiled at them as she edged past their chairs, and then laughed aloud when she turned the corner and saw a group of earnest and elegant businessmen at a table in the same restaurant. Their papers and iPads spread across the table with their espressos.

The cinema was showing a new release at seven o'clock. "Perfect timing. I have a pick-up around midnight, so I'll have time to drop you home," Rosa said.

"What if we asked Cassandra and Pamela to come? Make a girl's night of it?"

"Great idea!"

Bláithín put the proposition to her fellow crones as soon as she got home.

Pamela was all for it. "Gracious, I haven't been at the cinema for years. I'd love to go."

"Right," said Bláithín. "The movie is early, so we can have a pizza afterwards and Rosa will drop us back before her pickup."

"I can always take my car if she's going to be caught for

time."

"No, she said it would be fine, and anyway, it's more fun to go together. What about you, Cassandra? Any interest?"

"Normally, I'd go for a girl's night like a flash but today, after Pamela and I did some totally successful Christmas shopping, I bought..." she opened one of the bags piled on the table, "a cucumber facial mask, a deep heat hair treatment with lemon..." she emptied another bag, "and apricot kernel exfoliating scrub, avocado face mask, and last but not least, coconut body lotion. Tomorrow, I have another date with Reuben, and I intend to use this fruit salad to make myself utterly irresistible!"

"You know he finds you that already," Pamela said.

"I know! But a girl's got to keep it up, you know. Fabulous doesn't happen by itself!"

CHAPTER THIRTY-ONE

The sign 'completo' was quite clear. There were no more tickets.

"I'm so sorry. I should have thought we might need to book tickets," Rosa apologized for the third time.

Bláithín slid her arm around Rosa's waist. "Don't worry, let's get them for tomorrow night instead. But not for Cassandra, she can't come then either. She's got a hot date with your brother."

"Good idea," agreed Pamela. "Don't worry, Rosa. It's just so nice to be out with friends. We can still go for something to eat, can't we?"

A pizza, a veggie burger, and a pasta salad later, they relaxed in the casual, friendly atmosphere of a cafeteria off the main street. Pamela recounted the story of their attempt to collect the prints earlier that day. "It was so funny. He just looked at us and said, 'No ready'. Cassandra showed him the docket which clearly said today for collection. He looked at it, and said, 'Yes, but no ready.' Cass asked him when, and he said, 'Tomorrow.' She asked him if he was sure, then he looked at us as if we were the customers from hell and shrugged! The silly thing was, *I* felt I should apologize for being unreasonable!"

Rosa laughed. "It's true, we have a funny relationship with deadlines in this country. I think -oh!" She clapped her hand to her pocket. "Sorry, work phone." She looked at the message. "Oh, chicas, just as well we didn't go to the movies, my client now wants to be picked up earlier."

Bláithín pushed her chair back. " We can settle up here and get a taxi back if you need to rush.," she said, already zipping her glasses and her purse into her pocket.

"Ah, no. I've time to bring you back, then we will look

forward to tomorrow."

On the way home, Bláithín rested her head against the window and looked out, up to the sky. With the absence of streetlights, and the occasional house light obscured by trees, the countryside became shadowy banks of trees and hills layered against black, forested peaks. Moonlight tipped everything with silver. "I swear, there are stars here the likes of which I have never seen before."

"The night sky can be pretty spectacular in Ibiza, for sure," agreed Rosa, glancing at her watch.

Bláithín caught the glance. "Why don't you drop us at the foot of our lane, Rosa? It will save you time, and it's easily bright enough to walk."

Pamela agreed. "Oh yes, I like that idea, I can walk off the pizza."

"Well, if you're both sure, that would be helpful. Thank you."

Rosa pulled in at the end of the camino to the villa, kissed Bláithín, waved at Pamela, and took off quickly.

The friends didn't even need their phone torch to show the way, there was moonlight enough to throw their shadows on the ground.

"She's an extremely nice girl, Bláth. You're very lucky."

"I know! I can barely believe it myself. I wonder why I never knew. I mean, I was married for nine torturous fecking years, and all along I blamed myself. I thought if I could only learn the game properly, things would be fine, and we'd be happy"

"I suppose that's the thing Bláth," said Pamela. Their feet sent up little eddies of chalky dust as they picked their way up the uneven, stony track. "There's no instruction book for life. No one has one, every situation is unique."

"Were you happy, Pam?"

There was a long pause before she answered. "Overall, I'd say yes. To be honest, Jonathon and I didn't have much of a relationship. Susan was our point of contact. But it worked out somehow. Now, I'd like to go back to my younger self and say, 'Assert yourself more.' But I also know I probably wouldn't. I was never good at confrontation."

They slowed their pace as the hill became steeper.

Pamela stopped dead and turned to Bláithín. "Oh, Bláth, do you think Susan's awful need for things to be the way she wants, is my fault?"

"Why should it be yours more than your husband's? Anyway, she sounds more like him than you."

"Ha! That's true. Anyway, I suppose there's no point in looking back, blaming the younger me for things. Or for anyone to do it, in fact. Nearly all of us did the best with what we had, with what we knew at the time. Hindsight is no sight. It's not as if you can say, 'Oh, the next time I'm twenty-five, I must remember to behave differently!'

They were laughing as they finally rounded the corner and crossed the gravel to the house. Bláithín opened the front door. The house was in darkness. Further down the hall, moonlight coming through the living room door lit up a patch of the patterned hall tiles.

"Cassandra must be in bed," whispered Pamela.

Bláithín nodded, and mouthed, 'Cup of tea?'

Pamela gave a thumbs up. But they came to an abrupt halt as they passed the living room door.

A naked Cassandra and Reuben took center stage in the moon's spotlight.

Their clothes lay in crumpled heaps strewn around the room. Cassandra stood with her back against the side of the wooden cabinet. One long, smooth, gleaming leg on tiptoe on the floor, the other wrapped around Reuben's thigh. Her hand held her breast, offering it up to his hungry mouth. Moonlight gleamed on Reuben's tanned, muscled back, rounding down over the pale mounds of his buttocks. He stood, splayed between Cassandra's thighs. He thrust into her with a force that shook the solid shelves. The room crackled with powerful energy. It sparkled with passion, sex, love, lust, and happiness.

For a second, as if hypnotized, the two women stood moonlit witnesses to an ancient ritual.

Cassandra turned her head and opened her eyes, meeting the gaze of her Crone sisters. But those dark eyes also seemed to hold shimmering depths. An ancient soul, a myriad of memories. She saw her acolytes, acknowledged a compact, an offering being made, attended, and witnessed. Glancing wide-eyed at each other, Pamela and Bláithín hastily moved on. In the sharp, bright light of the kitchen, Bláithín muttered, "What was that?"

Pamela shook her head. "I'm honestly not sure what we saw."

They looked at each other for a moment, the tea forgotten as they slipped wordlessly away to their own beds.

Still bathed in moonlight, Cassandra's eyes closed, she cried out. Reuben's head flew back. Baring his teeth, his guttural grunts matched her cries. Cushions and blankets tumbled from the shelves until the lovers collapsed against each other, gasping, sweaty, and exhausted.

***

Pamela was up first the next morning and put on a pot of coffee. While she waited for the percolator to finish its spluttering and gurgling, she stared out at the rain, bouncing off the terrace, and tear-dropping its way down the windows. Bláithín came in, tying her robe. "God, Pamela, what did you make of last..." She paused in the doorway. Her eyebrows almost met her hairline, and her mouth opened wide. "Pamela!" she exclaimed as she came further into the kitchen. "Those clothes! You're not wearing... I mean..."

Pamela laughed and said, "I know exactly what you mean, and I agree. I did a bit of shopping yesterday too. Given the colours I've been using recently in my paintings, I was quite suddenly struck by a loathing for my entire polite, pastel wardrobe." She twirled, showing off the deep indigo, linen, harem pants, with pink flowers climbing up the outside seams and her soft cotton, cream top. "This may have been a bit much, the jury's still out," she said, pulling at the trousers. "But they feel great."

"They're beautiful on you," said Bláithín.

"They look fucking amazing!" Cassandra chimed in from behind her. "I hope this is a sign all your scary, old people's home clothes are going to be phased out?"

Both Pamela and Bláithín looked beyond her to see if Reuben was following but there didn't seem to be any sign of him.

"Step one on that road, definitely," agreed Pamela.

Cassandra, her wet hair turbaned in a towel, looked like the cat that got the canary and the cream. She strolled to the window, stretched her hands over her head, interlocked her fingers, and leant languorously from side to side. She spoke as she moved. "Well, my Crone sisters, without going into too much detail, I will tell you that last night after I was exfoliated and beautified, I thought 'Fuck it, why wait?' You guys weren't going to be back for hours, so I rang Reuben and asked him over." A final stretch, she shook out her hands and turned around to them. "Suffice to say, it was the most intense, most satisfying night of my life. I swear, at one stage, I was so ecstatic, I was seeing visions."

Cassandra became serious, her friends had to strain to hear her when she said, "I... I really called him over to say I wanted to give this relationship my best shot. That despite everything in my past, I felt we might have a real chance."

Bláithín clapped loudly. "I'm delighted, Cassandra." She smirked. "I knew that was going to happen!"

Cassandra shot her a look full of laughter. "Touché."

"How did Reuben react?" Pamela inquired.

Cassandra's smile hinted at a precious memory, "As if I had given him the secret of the universe. It was magic. I never knew... I never knew how things could be. Then one thing led to another and... Well, I've told you as much as I'm going to."

Pamela poured some coffee and handed it to Cassandra. "You do know we all saw each other last night?"

Cassandra looked blank.

"Were you drinking?" asked Bláithín, "or smoking?"

"No, Reuben doesn't drink, and believe me, there was no need for stimulants last night. But what do you mean by 'we saw each other? Reuben was long gone before you guys came home."

Pamela and Bláithín looked at each other. This was Crone business, no judgment, no embarrassment. Bláithín took a deep breath and blurted, "We came back early, Cassandra. The movie was sold out and Rosa had to do her pick up earlier than she thought."

Pamela took over, "We thought you had gone to bed, but passing the living room... we... we both kind of got stopped.... We saw... It was weird..." She trailed off.

Cassandra's eyes narrowed. "As I said, last night was wild. Honestly, at some stages, it was as if I were surrounded by people watching. At others, by people joining in."

"Mother of God! We *certainly* didn't join in!" Bláithín was genuinely horrified by the thought. "It's just that the room was so full of moonlight, and you were... and we..." She threw her hands up. "It all seems hard to explain, even now."

Pamela laughed at that. "Yes, it does, but we were definitely drawn in as if ... I don't know, we were meant to be there, maybe witnesses, or something."

"Or acolytes?" Cassandra suggested in a whisper.

Pamela took a deep breath. "Would you think I was crazy if I said I think that for a moment there were more than the four of us in that room last night?"

"No, not at all," said Cassandra.

Bláithín banged her mug down. "I'm going to say it! You stared at us. You didn't see us, but someone else did. There, I'm officially ready for the loony bin now."

Cassandra sipped her coffee and nodded. "Somebody who embodies love and celebrates sex? Somebody who loves and cares for her daughters? I think we have dealt with her before."

Pamela folded her arms and rubbed them briskly with her hands. "This is giving me the shivers."

Cassandra strode over to her friends and put an arm around each of them. "I have no clear memory of last night. All I know is, I had the most amazing night of my life. I think we were all blessed."

Pamela nodded. "It was truly beautiful, moving and powerful."

"It was magic." Bláithín paused before adding, "Maybe it *was* magic!"

Cassandra raised her mug. "Somehow, I think the Ibiza Crone Club Initiation rite has been completed and we are fully-fledged Full Moon Daughters."

She drank her coffee, then her eyes widened. "I hope to fuck that this doesn't mean sex with Reuben will never be as good again without last night's divine input!"

Pamela smiled. "I imagine a precedent has been set that future performances will match, but perhaps without the spectator's gallery."

CHAPTER THIRTY-TWO

The rain continued for the rest of the day. Wind slanted it into the forested hillsides, washing away the stones, rocks, and earth that made up many of the roads leading to hidden houses. It soaked into the darkening ground, and ran down streets and across beaches, sending brown plumes of dirt and mud out to sea. But in Ibiza town where the crones were Christmas shopping, there were no miserable faces, people strolled through the downpour, chatting and relaxed under enormous colourful umbrellas.

Cassandra pointed out the café that would be their rendezvous later. "Okay, girls, don't go mad. A maximum of five euros, to be spent on each present." She tapped the folder under her arm. "Let's hope there's a young good-looking guy behind the desk in the planning office!" They had filled in the form Rosa's friend had sent, and Cassandra had an appointment to hand it in this morning.

"Fingers crossed." Bláithín waved a hand with the corresponding fingers in the air.

"See you later." Cassandra saluted. Her multi-coloured raincoat glistened in the rain as she strode off. She looked like a rainbow dancing down the street as she zoomed in and out through the crowds.

"Happy shopping, Bláth," Pamela said, checking her bag for her list.

"God, I hate shopping. Twenty minutes tops, that's all I'll have patience for. If I haven't found something for people by then they're getting socks!"

Pamela grinned. "Make mine purple!"

An hour later, Bláithín was pleased with herself. A

bargain bin in a book shop had provided Diarmuid's present, an illustrated guide to fishing in Ibiza. It was in Spanish, but Pedro, Maite and Google would sort that. She had almost bought a discounted shower gel and talc set for Pauline, but at the last moment, she asked herself if Pauline would really like this. If this was a smell she would have chosen, or if she even used these things. She replaced it on the shelf. As if in reward for her thoughtfulness, around the next corner a boutique was having a closing sale, and hanging just inside the door was a soft, felt jacket. A Wedgewood blue swirled with tones of heather-mauve and gentle pink. It had wooden buttons and deep pockets. Bláithín fingered the material. It was so soft and warm, and it would look lovely on Pauline. She followed the price decline marked on its ticket. Ninety euros, to fifty, to twenty.

"Is missing the... the..." the young assistant was speaking to her. Struggling for the word, making gestures with her hands, circling her waist.

"Belt," supplied Bláithín.

"Yes, that's it, belt, and too now, I'm sad to say, a button is hanging down. So, today is ten euros."

Bláithín didn't hesitate, and it was beautifully gift-wrapped in a few minutes. Two doors up, an exquisite, filigreed silver hair clasp caught her attention for Rosa. This was a private gift and necessitated her credit card. But best of all were the presents for Cassandra and Pamela. They were carefully bubble wrapped and gift boxed in her shopping bags.

Rosa was waiting for her at the door of the café. "Isn't it wonderful?" She was smiling like a child at a party. "Some decent rain at last!"

"Easily known you're not Irish," Bláithín commented. She hugged Rosa without a second's thought – it was so easy to do in a country where everybody greeted each other like this anyway, but Rosa caught her hands, pulled her close, and kissed her on the lips before they went into the café. Bláithín only went a tiny bit pink. They found an empty table and

Bláithín deposited her pile of shopping bags on the floor.

Rosa said, "In Ibiza, nobody complains about rain. It makes people happy. People pray it will last long enough to fill cisterns and water the crops. Sometimes, if we're lucky enough and we get a week of it, the Santa Eularia River flows again."

"Jasus, if rain could make people happy, the Irish would be the happiest people in the world."

Pamela waved in at them through the steamed-up window. Her arms were full with the prints and the canvas she had just collected. A bright yellow umbrella sheltered her precious cargo. Once inside the door, she wedged her umbrella between a dozen others in an empty mayonnaise bucket improvising as a drip tray, and joined them at the table. Leaning the well-wrapped parcels against her chair, she leant forward, "The prints are amazing, Bláth, I can't wait to get home and show them to you."

They had nearly finished their coffee by the time Cassandra arrived. She was seething. Calling into the planning office had been a total waste of time. "The guy I was supposed to meet wasn't even there, and the receptionist said that nothing would get looked at before Christmas. I told her that was too late, and she just shrugged!"

" Oh, for feck's sake, that's crazy!" Bláithín cleared her parcels off a chair for Cassandra.

"Awfully disappointing," agreed Pamela. Rosa waved a hand to call the waiter.

One double espresso later, Cassandrawas calmer. "We'll figure something out, girls. I'm sure of it. Anyway, let's get home. I'm dying to see the prints, and Reuben is delivering the Christmas tree."

***

As Pamela had said, the prints were amazing. Bláithín's forehead furrowed with anxiety as she carefully pegged up one or two and stepped back.

She was speechless at the sight of her work in the glossy art print. The whorls, depth, and design of the ancient tree were exactly as she wanted them to be seen.

Rosa threw her arms around Bláithín. "You are amazing! Do you know that?"

"Ah, sure they're only..." She stopped. "No, I'm not going to dismiss them. I think they're great, and I'm delighted with them."

Cassandra tilted her head to get another angle on them. "Great? They're fucking fabulous! Just imagine them beautifully framed - they'll be stunning, and I'm a hundred percent certain we'll sell a ton of them."

Pamela itched to get at the canvas version with her gold paint but knew now was not the time to get lost in painting, especially as Reuben knocked at the patio door. His face peered around the side of the bushy tree in his arms. Just four feet tall, but a perfect triangle, the tree was alive and planted in a pot.

"This will be our Christmas tree for many, many more Christmases," he announced as he carried it into the living room. He made a beeline for Cassandra as if she were the only person there, took her face in his hands, looked down at her, and mouthed, 'I love you.'

Without hesitation she mouthed back, 'I love you, too.'

***

Pamela and Cassandra had diametrically opposing views as to how the tree should be decorated. Cassandra favoured a spiralling line of the multi-coloured globes circling the tree in an elegant line, the gaps filled in with only one or two bows. Pamela wanted an all-over, traditional effect.

Bláithín and Rosa left them to it and sat on the couch rocking with laughter as Pamela and Cassandra did their sneaky best to sabotage each other's designs. Removing, replacing, or hiding decorations behind each other's back. Pamela was bent double with laughter as Cassandra danced around in front of the tree waving her hands, trying to prevent Pamela from putting on any more decorations. Pamela pressed her hands to her side and gasped for breath. "I feel like I'm about seven years old," she said collapsing on the couch.

A truce was called, and the tree was declared decorated.

Rosa put on a playlist she had made, and George Michael's Last Christmas started off a night of festive classics. They were oblivious to the battering winds and sheets of rain sweeping across the island as they danced, laughed, and chatted long into the night.

CHAPTER THIRTY-THREE

By morning, the rain had abated to a dull drizzle from a low grey sky. It was dreary, but their Christmas tree filled the house with its distinctive, festive smell, making Pamela and Bláithín smile at the memories it evoked. They were sharing Christmas reminiscences when Pamela's phone lit up. She grimaced as she looked at the screen. It was a text from Glen asking her to meet him for a chat.

She held the phone up for her friends to read, laughed at their squinting eyes, and read it aloud to them. She sighed, "I better meet him, I suppose. Though I don't have a clue what to say."

Cassandra waved a finger. "I sincerely hope he doesn't want to come back. Sue is making such steps towards independence."

Pamela nodded as she texted her reply. "I know what you mean. Perhaps a quick coffee to find out his plans. Maybe I can help, somehow."

They discussed their plans for the day as they finished breakfast. Bláithín planned to spend the day in her studio reviewing her latest series of photographs, and Cassandra was going scouting for a suitable space to open their gallery.

Bláithín's jaw dropped. "Isn't that a bit premature?"

"Absolutely not! First of all, I'm a hundred percent convinced of the commercial appeal of your work and Pamela's. Secondly, you're far better to snap things up here in Ibiza, in winter or early spring before 'Crazy Price Syndrome' sets in."

"One small point, Cassandra. We have no money," Pamela pointed out.

"I'm merely testing the lie of the land. No one will know

whether I'm fabulously wealthy or not! Anyway, I'm off. See you guys later. Good luck with Glen, Pamela." She waved as she left the kitchen, singing. Only the closing of the front door cut off her enthusiastic rendition of 'Deck the Halls'.

***

Glen looked wretched. Puffy, purple skin under his eyes and the deep new lines on his face shocked Pamela.

"I'm so sorry," he said by way of greeting before he kissed Pamela and hugged her tight. He launched into the subject as soon as they had ordered. "I feel as if I've let you and Jonathan down by doing this. It was the last thing I thought would happen."

They were sitting in the cosy oasis of a coffee shop. The scent of strong coffee and fresh pastries swirled on the warm air. The floor was damp from dripping umbrellas and sodden coats, but the atmosphere was bustling and cheerful. Glen toyed with a biscuit, breaking it into pieces and pushing them around his plate.

"What *did* happen?" Pamela asked softly.

"It's been a struggle for so long with Sue. I was worn down trying to get through to her, trying to find… to find something real. I began to spend more and more time at work. At home, I either had to play happy families or be silent."

Pamela knew exactly what he meant, and her heart went out to him.

Glen rubbed his forehead. "Belén expected nothing from me, she just enjoyed my company and shared my interest in developing the software. I began spending more and more time with her. At first, just talking and being friends, but it became something else." He leant across the table. "I want to assure you, Pamela, that I will never let Sue and the children suffer financially. Belén is totally behind me on this. I'm signing the house over to Sue, so your apartment will always be there for you. Sue told me you had to move out of your wonderful villa. I'm sorry you didn't get more time there, it sounded amazing. Sophie is already packing things for her next visit." His eyes reddened. "It's so goddam hard with the children. That's what's breaking my heart."

Pamela patted his arm across the table. "Don't worry too much about Sophie and Clark, Glen. Children are far more resilient than we give them credit for. Give them a happy, loving life between two parents who adore them, even if they're in separate houses, and life will be still be perfect." She sat back and stirred her coffee. "I'm so glad Sue spoke to you at last."

"Yes, surprisingly, she rang me yesterday and asked to meet. That was what spurred me on to contact you. I'd rather been avoiding that."

Pamela murmured, "I can imagine."

"Sue was so different. She was calm and she really listened to me. She said she was beginning to see things in a new light, that there were more ways and options than she'd realized. I've never seen her like this. Should we be worried?"

"No, Glen, we shouldn't. Sue is on her own path now and needs some space to think. Even I've only been texting her about Clark's teething and Christmas things. Talking about Christmas, did Sue tell you she and the children are spending it in the villa with us?"

"Yes, she was quite buoyed at the prospect."

"Please know that you're very welcome to dinner on the twenty-fifth, if you'd like to come."

"If Sue says it's okay, I'd love to come, thank you. Just to see them for a while, I can't bear the thought of not being with the kids on Christmas day."

"Right," Pamela drained her coffee and stood up. "I must go. There's a new canvas and a pot of gold paint screaming for me. Don't worry too much Glen, things have a strange habit of working out for the best. See you on Christmas day."

He stood and pecked her on the cheek before she left. Passing the window, she glanced in and saw him slumped back in his chair staring at the empty coffee cups.

***

There was no sign of Cassandra for the rest of the day. Pamela and Bláithín spent the time in their studios, only coming out as the rhythms of their work dictated. The next morning, they barely saw Cassandra. She did a brief yoga session, muttered something about having a lot to do, and left the house. Painting the gold line onto Bláithín's photograph consumed Pamela for the day. To her delight, it was springing to life. Out-lining and enhancing the textured, meandering lines of the grain, just as she had imagined it. Meanwhile, in her studio, Bláithín was regretting she hadn't taken more angles of the snail. But the cabbage series, using some of the tools available to her in her printing program, was delighting her. She printed out page after page, each time changing the emphasis slightly. The cabbage's normally un-appreciated texture, pattern and depth leapt into life as she adjusted the focus.

That evening, the gold line finished to her satisfaction, Pamela took a deep breath before she knocked on the door of Bláithín's studio. Asking someone to view her work was a first and it was nerve-wracking, but a newfound confidence allowed her to do it anyway.

Bláithín was thrilled with what Pamela had done. The line was so fine in places it was barely seen. In others, the gold flowed in a sinuous wave, following the centuries-old twists of the bark, with smaller lines curling off in glowing tributaries. It turned her treescape into an abstract design and yet, it also gave a deeper exploration of the tree's life. She threw her arms around Pamela and simply said, "Thank you." Looking back at the painting, she added, "As Cassandra would say, these motherfuckers will sell like hotcakes!"

Pamela was still chuckling at this as they headed into the kitchen and turned on the light. "Where is Cassandra, anyway?"

"I don't know. Apart from a few seconds this morning,

I haven't seen her since yesterday. I assume young love, etcetera." Bláithín opened the fridge. "I'm making scrambled eggs, would you like some?"

"Oh yes, please. I'll pop on some toast. Did she seem a bit off to you, this morning?"

"A bit quiet, I suppose."

"Our Cassandra is not a 'bit quiet' person."

"Surely there can't be anything wrong between herself and Reuben?" Bláithín heaped the eggs onto the toast.

"No, we'd definitely have noticed that," Pamela said, picking up her plate. "I'm going to take this into the studio with me, though. I've just thought of another place the tiniest little curve of gold should go."

They didn't hear Cassandra that night, but in the morning, she was definitely moving about in her room. Eventually, Bláithín knocked. "Are you okay, Cassandra? Can I get you anything?"

"I'm fine, thanks!" Cassandra called back. "Hey, if either of you are going out again, could you finish the food shopping? There are still a few items on the list on the fridge."

"Oh, sure. Right, we will. You do realize Christmas is only a few days away, don't you? Rosa is bringing me to the airport to pick up Diarmuid and Pauline tomorrow."

"That's good, Bláth. I'll talk to you later, okay?"

Bláithín returned to the kitchen to Pamela who'd heard it all. "What on Earth was that about?" she asked, shaking her head.

"Oh, maybe Reuben is in there with her, and they were mid-you-know-what?" suggested Pamela.

"Didn't sound like it," said Bláithín.

Later, in town, it became obvious that Ruben hadn't been doing anything in the room with Cassandra that morning. He shouted their names from across the street, and ran over to them, dodging between cars. "I was just going to ring one of you. Is Cassandra alright? She was supposed to meet me last night, but she cancelled. And she's not answering her phone this morning. What's wrong?"

If his haggard, unshaven appearance was anything to go by, he hadn't slept last night.

Bláithín shook her head, her long curls bouncing in time. "We were wondering about her ourselves, Reuben. You two haven't had a fight or anything?"

"God! No."

"Right!" Pamela said decisively. "We'll make sure she talks to us when we get home."

"Will I come over, or should I not? I can't imagine what could be wrong."

Pamela and Bláithín looked at each other, the initiation night going through their heads. They nodded at the same time. Pamela said, "Absolutely! Come over as soon as you can, and we'll see what we can do to help our chief crone."

A monosyllabic Cassandra joined them for the spicy falafel balls and salad they'd bought in a deli on the way home. She'd smiled, kissed Reuben, admired Pamela's painting, and eaten dinner, but none of it reached her eyes or her heart. Pamela didn't want to wait another minute making small talk. "Okay, Cassandra. What is it? What's wrong?"

"Please tell us, Cass," Bláithín pleaded.

Reuben picked up her hand and kissed it.

Cassandra ran her fingers through her hair and released a sigh that gusted across the table. "I wasn't intending to keep it, really. I thought I could get rid of it, and just forget about it. But I couldn't. I just couldn't, and it's sitting there in my room... waiting. And I'm so afraid it's going to destroy me."

"What in the name of all that's good and holy are you talking about, Cass?"

"Gracious, Cassandra, what's happened?"

"No one will destroy you, Cassandra Collingsworth, not while I'm breathing!"

Cassandra scrubbed angrily at her eyes. Their reactions loosened the tight hold she'd had on herself, and the words poured out. "Two days ago, I was coming home from scouting for galleries, remember?" She didn't wait for a response. "A car followed me up the drive, a girl got out and handed me a bag. An old Ibiza Hippy Market bag and a note from my stepsister, Evelyn." She pulled a folded page from her pocket and opened it. They could see a few, short lines in elegant script. Cassandra read it out, "Hi Cassandra, I don't believe in coincidences. This was the only item the house clearing company left behind. I met your friend, Leonie, in a coffee shop and she gave me your address, and my flat mate got a job in Ibiza, all on the same day! So, I gave her this to give to you. Do what you like with it. Love Evelyn" Cassandra pressed her palm hard to her chest and was hyperventilating by the time she got to the end.

"Okay, but what's in the bag that has you so upset?" Pamela's words were soft, slow, and calming.

"A box I used to keep scraps in when I was small, and an envelope."

"Have you opened it?" Bláithín matched Pamela's tone.

Cassandra's shake of her head sent her hair flying. "No! You don't understand! It can only be from my mother! She hated me and everything I did! It took me so long to be able to ignore her and get on with my life. And now..." she looked around at them all. "I'm so genuinely happy for the first time in my life and I'm afraid she's coming to destroy it."

"Oh, dear, I see." Pamela's calm, soft voice was soothing. "What a dilemma. But Cassandra, we're all here together, now. You're not dealing with her alone."

Bláithín chimed in, "Plus, as you said to me, don't forget you're now a fully-fledged Ibiza Crone Goddess."

"And I love you forever, Cassandra." Reuben's husky declaration in front of everyone was accompanied by his frown of determination over embarrassment.

Cassandra gave a weak smile. "Thank you all. The mere thought of her sent me straight back to being small again, hell-bent on defying her, yet heartbroken that I could never make her happy with me."

Bláithín stood up. "Let's lay that bloody woman to rest

for once and for all! Bring out that damn bag."

"I don't even want to touch it. Will you get it, Bláth?"

Moments later, Bláithín placed the bag in the centre of the table. Its colours now faded to muted tones of pale blue. The writing was still legible, Las Dalias Hippy Market.

"I don't know where she got that bag. I must have left it behind sometime."

"Let's do this!" Bláithín pulled out a square cardboard box. Faded pictures were stuck all over it. Cut-outs of cats drinking milk, puppies in shoes, a baker with a pie, and carol-singing children.

"Oh, I remember these," said Pamela. "I had hundreds. My favourites were the fairy ones."

"There's one of those underneath," Cassandra turned the box over. There, two fairies with glitter on their wings waved a wand over a baby in a crib.

Bláithín traced her finger over it. "Ah, innocent days. I rarely had the glitter ones myself, far too fancy."

Cassandra replaced the box and folded her arms; her hands were tight fists dug into her armpits.

Reuben reached for the lid, checked Cassandra's reaction, and opened it. He took out the envelope. All that was left of its original blue colour were the shape of a few of the scraps that had lain on it for so many years.

"What do you want to do, Cassandra?" he asked. "We can just burn it, you know."

Cassandra nodded. "Yes! And stop her poison in its tracks."

Pamela put up a hand. "Cass, when you think about it, a lot went into getting this letter to you. Maybe we should consider there may be a reason."

Bláithín's intake of breath at this was loud.

"Do you think...?" Cassandra's tone lifted towards the end of this unfinished question.

"I think it's possible," said Pamela.

"In that case, would you mind reading it out, please,

Pamela? I don't think I could touch it." Cassandra unfolded her arms and groped for Reuben's hand, which was instantly in hers.

The rustle of the unfolding page was loud in the stillness of the kitchen.

Pamela began- "My dearest, darling Cassandra"

Cassandra made a strangled sound, but Pamela continued.

> *Today you came home to collect some clothes, bringing an Ibiza tan and your boundless vitality. We argued, of course we did. I couldn't stop myself. You're twenty years old and nothing daunts you, nothing makes you stop to think, least of all me!*
>
> *Oh, my baby, today I realized that if I don't let go of my obsessive need to protect you, I will lose you as surely as I could have lost you in all the daredevil things you longed to do.*
>
> *My darling (I could fill the page with the endearments I never used!), you are so like your father, it terrifies me.*
>
> *I was eighteen when I married him. A racing driver, he was a tornado, sweeping me into his hectic, dangerous world. There was nothing he wouldn't attempt in any sport. Competitive and impetuous, he was always searching for something higher, faster, deeper. From the moment I met him, my heart was in my mouth. But he promised me. He promised me, he'd be safe, and I believed him. Then a shortcut during a cross-country race ended in a crevasse. By the time his body was recovered, I had become catatonic with shock and had to be moved to what my parents called a care facility. I was twenty and you*

> *were two.*
>
> *Sweetheart, when I was eventually released from the hospital and collected you from my parents, it was with one driving, absolute purpose. Keep you safe -."*

Pamela paused and looked up. "That's underlined three times, the words, 'keep you safe' Anyone got a tissue?" Bláithín got the roll of kitchen paper and handed her a sheet. They all took one.

Pamela returned to the letter.

> *I think I married your stepdad because he offered safety and security. His idea of a wild time is buying two newspapers at the weekend. Poor man, still, I think he's happy enough. But keeping you safe was a far harder task than I imagined. You are your father's daughter to the core, and it terrified me. I became obsessive and so strict you began to hate me. I thought I could live with that as long as you were safe. But today nearly broke my heart. My beautiful daughter is alive and healthy, and I'm wasting time."*

Pamela paused to blow her nose, "That was underlined too," she told them and returned to the letter. "Oh, God," her voice cracked, and she had to take several deep breaths before she could continue.

> *"Cassandra! I've decided not to post this letter! I'm going to go to Ibiza! Crazy and impulsive, I know. More like something you'd do! Jeffery won't understand, but he won't stop me either. I'll go and I'll stay until I find you and I'll give you this and hope with all my heart you'll forgive me."*

Pamela's hands shook as she put the letter down. "That's all."

There was silence until Cassandra spoke. "Well, I don't know what the fuck to do with that!" Her voice was harsh. "She ruined my life, and a letter from beyond the grave can't fix that." She jerked upright, stalked to the sink, and poured a glass of water. The glass trembled on its way to her mouth. "I mean, what the bloody hell am I supposed to say? 'Oh, that's fine?' My whole life, I knew I was unlovable because my mother had made it crystal clear."

"Until now," Pamela interjected softly.

"Yes," Cassandra sighed, "until now."

"But what happened?" wondered Bláithín, "Why didn't she post it? All those years...?"

"Is there a date?" Cassandra asked Pamela.

Pamela picked up the letter again. "September, the fourteenth, nineteen eighty."

Cassandra covered her face with her hands and her voice was muffled, "That's the day before she died. She had a brain haemorrhage the next day and died that night. She was only thirty-eight."

No one could speak. Bláithín was sobbing; tears ran unchecked down Pamela's cheeks.

Cassandra slammed her palms down hard on the countertop. "Oh, fuck it all! Even now she's breaking my heart."

Reuben went over to Cassandra and stood close. "If she had come to Ibiza the next day if she had found you and given you that letter, would you have understood?"

"Well, things would have made a lot more fucking sense. I can tell you that!"

Reuben put his arm gently around Cassandra's rigid shoulders. "And if she had told you how much she'd always loved you, and if she'd taken you in her arms like this," he turned her into his chest, "and if she had hugged you and kissed your head like this, and told you how sorry she was, how would you have felt?"

Cassandra flung her arms around him and released the heart-rending wail of an abandoned child against his chest.

The sobs continued long after Pamela and Bláithín had slipped from the room. They sat on the sofa in the twinkling colours of the Christmas tree lights. "That poor, poor woman," Pamela whispered.

Bláithín nodded. "And poor Cassandra."

They sat in silence until Cassandra walked in, pulling her jumper off over her head. "I'm going for a swim."

Bláithín made to get up, but Cassandra added, "Alone."

They watched her shed her clothes on the terrace and disappear down the steps to the pool. By the time they'd tidied up in the kitchen and had a cup of tea, Cassandra still hadn't come back. Reuben went out to the terrace. "She's still swimming laps of the pool, he reported when he came back in. "There's nothing we can do but wait for her. She'll come in when she's ready."

They lit the fire and sat staring at the crackling, sparking wood and dancing orange flames. It was a comforting focal point.

"Poor Cass."

"What an awful waste."

"All those years..." Half sentences and sad comments were tossed out as they went over that letter again in their minds.

Finally, Bláithín said, "Pamela, do you think Tanit is helping, outside?"

"She won't abandon her chief crone. Besides, as I said earlier, I don't think those coincidences happened by themselves."

They had put more logs on the fire when a naked Cassandra came in, teeth chattering. Pamela made her hot chocolate with brandy, while Bláithín got her robe. Reuben sat on the floor and rubbed her feet. Cassandra sat back. "I'm so lucky to have you all. I spent my time in the pool half crying for myself, half crying for my poor mother, and half for what we'd missed, what should have been."

"That's three halves, Cass," Pamela pointed out, with a

small smile.

"Fuck it! This is Ibiza," replied Cassandra. The lift in her voice let them all know she was going to be all right.

CHAPTER THIRTY-FOUR

Everyone breakfasted at different times the next morning. Reuben, wearing Cassandra's robe, had filled a tray with coffee, juice, and toast. He'd also dodged out into the steady downpour to pick some fresh flowers for it.

Bláithín turned over in bed when she heard the rain drumming on the roof. Rosa wasn't arriving until much later. They'd been speaking in hushed tones, on the phone, until the small hours. Both in tears at the letter and the sad story surrounding it. "We will learn the lesson, Cariño," said Rosa. "When it happens that one day, there is no tomorrow for one of us, we must know that we made today as wonderful as possible."

Bláithín sobbed her agreement into the pillow.

Pamela had been in the studio since five-thirty. Drawn to paint something to counterbalance the sadness of yesterday, she had filled the centre of her canvas with a bathroom. The edges were irregularly broken up by the lush, fantastical trees, in rainbow colours that bordered the canvas. The figure Pamela was finishing, still with only his bowler hat on, plus a large erection and a smile was rubbing a huge, bright yellow sponge over his wife's back as she sat in a bubble-filled bath, with a glass of wine.

"I'm still shell-shocked and a bit numb," Cassandra told them when everyone finally gathered in the kitchen around lunchtime. "But thanks to all of you," she turned to the window, pressed her palms together in prayer, and bowed, " and you too," she said out the window. "I've realized that my mother died happy and excited, and she was happy and excited because she was coming to find me! To tell me that she loved me! And those are my building block for the future. No looking back and blaming myself for things I couldn't possibly have known."

Pamela and Bláithín looked at each other and smiled, hearing echoes of their own conversation.

"Meanwhile, do you all realize that we have fifteen people coming for Christmas dinner in less than a fucking week! Let's get to it!"

The afternoon was spent plate counting, dish finding, table planning, and task dispensing. Reuben was to bring extra chairs from his house and a folding table to add to the dining table.

"Why not make what we can now, and freeze it? It would save a lot of fuss on the day," suggested Pamela.

"Great idea." Cassandra handed a notepad to Bláithín. "Here, I'll check the cupboard and you write the list. Okay, Pamela, what can we make in advance?"

"Any sauces, mashed veg, stuffing, the cheesecake, they'd all be good to have done."

"Have you got that Bláth?" Cassandra called as she checked the vegetable rack. "We'll need carrots, parsnips, digestive…"

Bláithín was tearing up her list and starting again.

Cassandra looked at Pamela and back to Bláithín. "Bláth, are you okay? You're very fidgety today."

"I'm fine. I'm fine… no, I'm not. I'm scared shitless, as my friend might say." She shot a grin at Cassandra. "I'm scared about introducing Rosa to Diarmuid and Pauline. I was on the verge of deciding that there was no need to tell them, that I'd only be spoiling their Christmas on them, blah, blah, but I called my Crone Goddess to the fore and we're meeting them in an hour in Ibiza airport!"

Pamela rested her hand on Bláithín's shoulder. "Don't worry, Bláth, I'm sure it'll be fine."

Cassandra grinned. "First, tell them that you've become a pole dancer in a nightclub, I guarantee a lesbian will be a relief!"

The friends exploded with laughter, and a short time

later, Bláithín had a spring in her step when she ran out through the rain to Rosa's car.

***

"Dear God!" complained Pauline, scurrying through the rain, holding her handbag over her head. "We might as well have stayed in Ireland, with this weather."

Rosa held the door open for them. "It's not supposed to last long, according to the forecast. It's going to clear today or tomorrow and settle into better weather." Bláithín, wearing her new top to give her courage, hadn't made any announcements at the airport. There were too many people. She just introduced Rosa as her friend.

During the spin to the Flora apartments, Pauline gave them a step-by-step account of their journey via Barcelona. This gave Bláithín way too much time to rehearse what she was going to say. She told herself she was probably going to kill her brother with her news. And of course, Pauline would be terrified that the neighbours would find out. Her stomach was somersaulting with nerves as she walked in the door of Andy's apartment. She closed her eyes, sensing Cassandra, Pamela, and Tanit at her back, and Rosa at her side. She straightened, sliding her arm around Rosa's waist, she said, "Diarmuid, Pauline, I'd like to introduce you properly to my girlfriend, Rosa."

Pauline looked a bit puzzled, "Oh, one of the girls you are living with? But I thought they were called…"

"No, Pauline. I mean she's my girlfriend." She rested her head on Rosa's shoulder and looked squarely at them both.

There was a moment's silence. Pauline cocked her head to one side and said, "Well now, I was wondering what was different about you. I mean, your hair is all long and floosie looking, and that gorgeous top you're wearing is not your normal style at all. But it was something about your manner had me wondering. I thought maybe you'd taken up smoking the strange stuff over here. And all I can say is, whatever it is, it suits you." She gave Bláithín a peck on the cheek.

"Well now," echoed Diarmuid, slightly pink in the cheeks, and not making eye contact with anyone. He coughed and muttered, "I'll put the kettle on, will I?" As he passed Rosa, he gave her an awkward pat on the shoulder and said, "You'll have to get used to strong Irish tea now."

This was enough for Bláithín. She burst into tears and wailed, "I'm so happy."

"Ah, now," said Pauline handing her a tissue from up her sleeve. "I think you have your wires crossed in how you're expressing it!"

The tears were only momentary. Bláithín beamed, her face transformed with happiness. They sat around on the familiar ugly chairs and chatted. Diarmuid mentioned the cost of living in Ireland, and Rosa made Bláithín smile, asking such unheard-of questions as 'How much exactly do you get in your pension?' or 'Do you still have a mortgage to pay off?' The type of question an Irish person wouldn't ask, even under pain of death.

As Bláithín handed her cup down the table for a refill, her gaze shifted beyond Pauline to the map of Ibiza. The reflection of her laughing self, shoulder to shoulder with Rosa, nearly took her breath away.

CHAPTER THIRTY-FIVE

Christmas Eve was a beautiful, alpine-clear day, but the wind was biting and strong. Reuben slid open the door to the living room and manoeuvred his way in with an armful of logs. A blast of cold air rushed in, sweeping out the warm cooking smells, the fragrance of Rosa's potpourri oranges, and flattened the flames in the fire.

Bláithín came out of her studio where she had been wrapping gifts. "Quick! Close the door, before we all freeze."

A shout from the kitchen made them smile. "For fuck's sake! Someone actually bought Brussels' Sprouts? Who even likes these things?"

Bláithín rolled her eyes at Reuben. "I better go confess."

She joined Rosa and Cassandra in the kitchen. "I did. It wouldn't be Christmas dinner for Pauline without them."

Cassandra dangled the net bag from her finger. "They look so innocuous now. Not a whiff from them but boil the little fuckers for ten minutes and you may as well be in the sulphur pits of hell!" She laughed as she tossed them on the table "I may be exaggerating slightly."

"Only slightly," agreed Bláithín. "But after long years of Christmas dinners with Pauline, I have learned a tiny drop of vinegar and a short cooking time helps a lot."

"Christmas is saved!" exclaimed Cassandra.

"Was it in danger?" asked Pamela, coming through the kitchen with her 'unsuitable' paintings in her arms. They were going to be well out of sight in the utility room. The last thing she wanted was for Sue or Sophie to see them.

"Only from all the might of half a dozen brassicas." Bláithín laughed and joined Rosa at a countertop where she was making vegetarian paella for dinner that evening.

Christmas songs in the background, the house was alive with laughter, banter, happiness, and love.

***

That afternoon, Susan and the children arrived, adding another layer of noise, excitement, and Christmas spirit. Sophie and Clark settled down to the important job of writing their names and decorating signs for each of their Christmas socks, and Susan was set to peeling potatoes.

Shortly after, Rosa and Bláithín left to pick up Pauline and Diarmuid. Within an hour, they were ushering them into the kitchen, laden with boxes and bags, all of which had to be deposited on the table before handshaking, and introductions could begin. Diarmuid put down the large, covered platter he was carrying and smiled amiably around. "Well, isn't this grand?"

"Welcome to our house," said Cassandra.

"It's very nice indeed," nodded Pauline. "For all its glamour, it's very homely, not things that go together often."

Cassandra agreed enthusiastically. "That's the nail, hit on the fuc... flipping head, right there, Pauline. Well said."

Bláithín and Pamela didn't even try to hide their grins. Pamela shook hands with them both and introduced Susan, who called the children in to say hello. Reuben arrived carrying extra chairs, and Diarmuid happily offered to help with the trestle table. Sophie and Clark looked on, wide-eyed, as Pauline emptied her bags. She stacked boxes of sweets and biscuits on the table, then pointed to the tray Diarmuid had put down, "Be careful of that," she said to the children, "It's still hot." She looked at the adults and her eyes sparkled, "It's the bread-and-butter pudding for tomorrow, specially requested by Maite!"

Pamela shook her head. "Oh my goodness, you've brought a ton of stuff,"

"Sure, we couldn't have come empty-handed," Pauline answered. "And this..." she opened a large solid cardboard box, "- is the last thing. I don't know how this survived the journey, but it did!" She grunted, lifting out a large, traditional Christmas cake. Santa Claus drove a sleigh across its smooth, white icing, and two snowmen danced around a small green tree. It needed to be whisked out of Clark's reach immediately.

"Oh, That's amazing, Pauline! I haven't had a cake like that for yonks." Cassandra wiped some icing from the lid of the box and licked her finger. "As I suspected – delicious!"

Bláithín was surprised Pauline didn't try to take over in the kitchen. Instead, she followed the children back into the living room to the table where the signs were still being created. Sophie complained Clark had been pestering her so much she was completely 'disconcentrated' and couldn't finish her own sign properly. Pauline winked at her, and drew a big red circle on a page, she asked Clark to help her fill it in. In seconds, he was on her lap, and she helped his pudgy hands do their own drawing.

In the kitchen, Cassandra paused before she pulled the blinds. Looking at the light from the rooms spilling out into the darkness, the terrace was like a well-lit stage in the theatre of the silent countryside. She closed the blinds and the play was over.

The signs were unanimously declared the best ever, and the socks were laid in front of the fire. Clark was back on Pauline's lap, shrieking with laughter as she never seemed to notice he was taking the pencils out of the pencil case as fast as she could put them in. Sophie cuddled back into Pamela's lap. "I thought Clark might be worried about Santa coming down that chimney, so I explained to him, that Santa can squish in and squish out and wriggle around any pipe because he has special Christmas magic. That's right, isn't it, Grandma?"

"Oh, Christmas magic is a very old magic indeed. I think you can be sure Santa will find a way to leave your presents." Pamela hugged Sophie, who didn't stay relaxed long.

Jumping to her feet, she clapped her hands to her cheeks. "Oh, Grandma, we almost forgot! We must leave some carrots for the reindeer, and something for Santa to drink.

I'll ask Mummy." She ran into the kitchen and returned with two carrots. Susan followed, carrying a glass of milk. Sophie arranged them to her satisfaction, then said, "Mummy, will Daddy be here in the morning to see us open our stockings?"

"Erm, I'm not sure he'll get here that early, darling, but he'll be here as soon as he can."

Pamela raised her eyebrows at Susan who shrugged.

Sophie stood up, and her voice trembled as she spoke. "I think he should be here now! He'd love this house."

Pauline looked over from the pencil case game, "Excuse me, Sophie. May I borrow one of your books to read tonight, please? I forgot one of my own."

The question sent Sophie running to her bedroom. "I'll bring in a few and you can pick one!"

Susan sighed. "Thanks, Pauline. She's overexcited and tired, but of course, the problems her father and I are having at the moment are affecting her too."

Pamela didn't even try to hide her pleasure in Sue's new ability to be open. She caught Susan's eye. 'Good on you,' she mouthed and smiled. Susan grinned back as she followed Sophie out of the room, calling to her that it was absolutely and definitely bedtime.

To Pauline's obvious delight, Sophie asked her to read the bedtime story. "You can do it tomorrow, Grandma," Sophie added, keen to share the honour.

With the children settled, the adults gathered in the kitchen for dinner. Rosa served her paella to a round of applause, which she received with a bow, and sat, beaming, next to Bláithín.

Susan produced two bottles of Prosecco, "Mum just might have mentioned that you all like this!"

"And she was a hundred percent right. Thank you, very much," said Cassandra and expertly popped one open.

"Crone Club and friends!" she toasted.

To Bláithín's amazement, it was Pauline who kept the gathering entertained with tales from her early days in nursing. Midnight parties in the wards for patients, when the nurses would share out any build-up of their trove of sweets and cakes given to them by grateful patients. Vases of flowers, regularly being used to douse blankets smoldering from dropped cigarettes. Pauline waved her hand to calm their horrified laughter. "Wait 'til I tell you about our ward sister! She once put a skeleton in a bed in a private room and asked a student nurse if she could help coax the poor creature in room 201 to eat! Well, your one's screech was heard all over the place, we had to tell everyone she'd been stung by a bee!"

Cassandra shrieked with laughter; when she caught her breath she said, "I'd fucking prefer to be in that hospital of yours, rather than any of the super-bug-infested, bureaucrat-laden messes of nowadays!"

"It's like a window to a long past, more humane time," said Pamela.

"Ah well, I have to say there are better medicines available these days, and amazing surgical advances, but the nurses are all overworked, under-supported, and in constant fear of not meeting some target or other, that's usually completely unrelated to the health of their patients. Oh, there was the time…"

Bláithín watched Diarmuid's face full of love and happiness as he watched his 'bright girl' shine.

The eight of them eventually got around to tidying up and soon all was left ready for the next day. Rosa and Reuben took their leave, and bit by bit the house settled into stillness. The stockings, now stretched and bumpy, were filled with surprises and covered with coloured balloons. Reflecting the twinkling fairy lights on the tree, they rustled and bumped off each other, in the slight draft from the fire. Outside the house, another tile slid out of place as a trickle of water gathered force.

CHAPTER THIRTY-SIX

Pamela was woken by a fairy kiss on the cheek. "Santa has come, Grandma! Our stockings are huge!" Sophie's face was white with excitement. Pamela opened her arms, but instead of a hug, one arm was pulled and waggled. "Come on, Grandma, come on!"

Sophie gave a last tug and skipped out of the bedroom. Pamela grabbed her robe and slippers and followed. Susan was sitting on the floor with Clark on her lap, he'd already discovered a packet of chocolate buttons at the top of his stocking and was happily preoccupied with them.

"What time is it, Sue?" Pamela yawned.

"We did really well-it's seven-thirty."

"Oh, that's not too bad at all. What time was it last year? Six?"

"Yes, this is a positive lie-in by comparison."

"Look! Look! Mummy, a writing set with stencils and design stamps! I always wanted...Oh, look!" her voice was getting louder by the minute.

"Mum, perhaps we should shut the door, I don't want to wake the household?" suggested Susan.

"No need, I'll do it," said Pauline stepping into the living room and closing the door behind her. "Can anyone join in to see what Santa brought you?" She waited at the door for an answer.

"Pauline! Quick! Look at this, come here." Sophie waved her in. Pauline in her flowery, flannel pyjamas and plaid dressing gown joined them.

Midway through the stocking-emptying, the light went on in the kitchen and Cassandra called out, "I can't wait to see what Santa stuffed into those stockings, but I'm going to make some special Christmas pancakes first."

Diarmuid arrived and stood next to her. "Can I help?" She set him to cracking eggs.

Clark banged his new car on a book, "Pa'cakes! Pa'cakes!"

Bláithín peeked around the door. "Can I join in too?"

"Yeeeaaaay!" shouted Sophie. "This is the best fun!"

Clark clapped and ate another chocolate. The toys were collected on the couch for everyone's inspection. The first official Christmas gathering of the Crone Club was underway.

***

Around midday, Reuben and Rosa arrived laden with boxes, bags, and bottles. The smell of the slow-roasting turkey was beginning to fill the house. Bláithín apologized to Rosa, "I suppose this is awful for you? I'm sorry."

"My decision, my choice, cariño. I'm not pushing it on anyone. Perhaps, someday you'll make the same choice, but until then..."

"Oh, I'm sharing your nut roast."

"Then you can help me finish preparing it." Rosa put her arm around Bláithín, and steered her to the kitchen. "Will you roll out the pastry, please?"

Bláithín turned her head to answer but was met by a delicious kiss that made her sigh like a Victorian maiden.

Maite, Pedro, and a sleeping Laia arrived to great acclaim and congratulations. Maite had a new lease of life, her colour was better and her eyes were shining. Sophie was enthralled with the tiny baby, and stroking Laia's doll-like fist, she pleaded to hold her but was content with a promise that she could do it when the baby woke up. Returning to her perch on the arm of the couch, she read the instructions for her new board game to Pauline.

Laia's pram was parked in the living room, where she slept peacefully, even though Clark's toy dog barked until it was clapped at, and Clark's soft little hands found it hard to make sufficient noise. So, the dog barked and barked until

Sophie clapped to shut it up, then Clark howled, and touched the dog to start it all off again.

"Laia will never sleep with all that going on, will she?" Susan asked Maite.

"To the noise of his mother," Maite nodded her head in Pedro's direction, "and her friends, this is not a noise!" She rolled up the sleeves of her yellow print dress. "Now, please I can help in the kitchen?"

She was put to chopping the onions Susan was going to fry with sage, for the stuffing. Through their respective language classes, guesswork, and body language they began to chat easily and exchange childbirth stories.

Pedro signalled to Diarmuid to go outside for a stroll with him. "Well, if I'm not needed at the moment, I might as well have a look around," Diarmuid said, picking up his coat.

Cassandra beckoned Pamela and Bláithín into her bedroom. "Before we get on with the day, I want to give you both a small gift. I just had to buy them when I saw them, they're so appropriate."

"Oh, lovely! Give me a sec to pop into my room, I have something for each of you as well." Pamela hurried out.

"Ditto," said Bláithín, and disappeared into her bedroom, emerging with two small, colourful gift bags. Pamela had two beautifully wrapped parcels, and Cassandra handed out two boxes.

The laughter started immediately. They held six identical terracotta busts of Tanit. Cassandra threw her arms around her friend's shoulders. "Great minds, eh?"

Rosa appeared in the doorway, drawn by the peals of laughter. She joined in when she saw the cause, but then said, "I can take you all to Tanit's temple, and you can each leave one, as an offering, just like they used to do in the ancient days. The actual shrine is not open to the public at this time of the year, but we can get close enough to leave your offerings."

"I love that idea, Rosa. One to keep and one to offer. Perfect synchronicity! Let's do it soon."

The doorbell rang and Sophie ran down the hall shouting. "It's Daddy! It's Daddy! I'm sure it's Daddy!" Pamela opened the door. Glen stood there with his arms full of presents. He knelt down, dropped the presents, and bear-hugged Sophie. Susan came out of the living room, Clark shouting in her arms. "Dadadadadada!" he chanted.

Pamela scooped up the presents. "I'll put these under the tree for you, shall I?" Still on his knees, and with Clark in his arm, Glen nodded.

Cassandra came out of her bedroom and into the hall. She waved down at him, and breezily called, "Hi Glen, I'm Cassandra." She indicated her friends as they followed her into the hall. "This is Bláithín, and this is Rosa." Cassandra continued into the kitchen, talking back to Glen, "Welcome to our home. We'll see you in the living room when you're disentangled."

Bláithín and Rosa followed Cassandra. Bláithín wore a long, sky-blue V-neck tunic over black leggings. "The minute I saw that, I knew it would look lovely on you," Rosa murmured, as she ran her hand down Bláithín's back, caressing it through the soft, wool. Bláithín smiled and closed her eyes to enjoy a shiver of delight. They had exchanged their own presents earlier, and Rosa was wearing the silver hair clip at the top of her long, shining plait.

Reuben carried a large tray filled with glasses, prosecco, coffee, and juices into the living room and put it on the table. Cassandra opened the box of biscuits that Pauline had brought. "Sustenance while we give out the presents!" she announced.

Diarmuid and Pedro came in, shaking the rain off their hair. "I can't believe it's started again," said Diarmuid. "It's almost as bad as Ireland."

Outside the glass wall, rain obscured the countryside with a grey veil. Inside, flames danced in the fireplace, the Christmas tree sparkled, and Sophie, in a bright red tutu and with tinsel in her hair, darted around the room handing out the presents. She needed just a little help from Susan to read the names. Cassandra and Reuben presided over drinks; Glen sat at one end of the couch with Clark on his lap while Pauline and Diarmuid relaxed at the other end of it. Bláithín and Rosa sat on the floor, their backs against the couch. Pedro and Maite drew chairs over from the dining table and sat next to the sofa. The noise level rose in the room, with conversations, exclamations, and laughter, but Laia slept blissfully on.

The jacket was a perfect fit for Pauline, and the compliments she got when she tried it on made her glow. Bláithín had fixed the dangling button and had to swear she hadn't spent a fortune on it, that it was pure luck.

"All the better, so," said Pauline. "You can't beat a good bargain."

Sophie finally moved to a game of burying Clark and Glen under all the discarded wrapping. Pedro and Diarmuid were, as Bláithín had imagined, poring over the fishing book. Laia woke, and her little snuffly cries pulled Sophie away from her game. She watched fascinated as Maite breastfed her baby. "Hey Mum!" she shouted, "It's a pity no one told you that you could do that when you had Clark. It's much easier than making bottles."

Susan pretended she hadn't heard.

"I think we're redundant, Susan," said Pamela, gesturing back into the living room.

Pauline was on the floor helping Clark with his game. He screeched with delight every time she tried to fit the wrong piece into a shape. "I can't believe it," agreed Susan. "I've never seen him take to anyone so quickly."

"Well, I'm flabbergasted," Bláithín looked over her shoulder, as she strained the now inoffensive Brussels sprouts. "I'm not," said Diarmuid quietly, as he shook a large tray of roast potatoes to loosen them. "If she could spend all day like that, she'd be happy. She has a great way with children." He slid the potatoes back into the oven.

They all saw the truth of this an hour later when Glen said he had to leave. He'd come into the kitchen, stood next to

Susan and Pamela, and spoken quietly, "I think maybe I should go before dinner. I... I... "

Pamela waited for Susan's reaction. Susan looked up from pouring some frozen peas into a saucepan. "Yes, the closer to bedtime you leave, the worse they'll be."

Glen dug his fingers into his forehead, dragging the skin into furrows as he squeezed his eyebrows together. "This is so awful. I -"

Susan put her hand on his arm. "Why don't you make plans to take them tomorrow, for the day? That will help."

Glen's surprise didn't go unnoticed, and Susan gave a small smile. "The best thing for us, I think, is if we focus on making things right for the children. You know, probably everything else will follow."

Pamela's heart swelled with pride at the steps to independence her daughter had taken.

Sophie glared at her father and stamped her foot. "I don't want you to go! It's Christmas!" Her shouts started Clark crying too. Susan held him out to Glen for a kiss, then whisked him into the kitchen, where he was distracted by a bowl of water and some plastic cups to wash. Glen sat on the floor trying to hold Sophie and make plans for tomorrow, but she wasn't listening. "I don't care, you're spoiling Christmas," she sobbed. Her arms were tight around his neck. She stopped crying when her new writing set, held in Pauline's hand, appeared next to her face. 'Treasure Hunt' was written on the first page in big pink letters, underlined with glitter.

"What?" Sophie looked up.

"Your dad said you were going out together all day tomorrow, and I was thinking that we could plan a treasure hunt for him to follow?"

"You mean, we could decide like he had to find four pink shells and..."

Pauline held her finger to her lips. "We can't discuss it until he's gone, though I suppose finding a shop that sells ice cream could come into it."

Sophie released her hold on Glen. "Yes, and we could- oh no, don't listen Daddy!"

Glen got to his feet. "What a great idea. Please don't make it too difficult for me. What about -"

"No, Daddy, *you* can't decide. It will be a surprise!" She took the writing set. "I'll have to draw lots of maps," She looked at the kitchen. "I hope Clark stays quiet, I'm going to be very busy." She threw her arms around her father a last time. "See you tomorrow." She ran off.

"Thank you, Pauline. That was magic. I'm so grateful." Glen sighed.

"Ah, 'twas nothing. Sure, she'll be busy all night now and happy out."

Glen left, closing the door on the warmth, the fun, and the love that this house exuded. With his head bent against the rain, he trudged to his car.

In the living room, a snow-white tablecloth gleamed down the length of the pushed-together tables. Rosa had sprinkled tiny silver stars and aromatic herbs in circles around candles, glittering in glass containers. And in the heat and steam of the kitchen, people bumped elbows, reached across each other, swapped pots, dropped spoons, laughed, shouted, mixed, boiled, and poured, as they began to pull everything together for dinner.

It was an unequivocal triumph.

***

When the table was littered with the detritus of pulled Christmas crackers, coffee cups were re-filled, and Clark was asleep on the couch while Sophie was engrossed in her map, the adults conversed the length of the table in peace.

"Mum, did you know Maite is trying to start her own business?" Susan said across the table to Pamela.

Pamela shook her head. "No, dear, I didn't."

"A cleaning company and she already has a contract,

quite a big contract, for a block of apartments. Isn't that amazing?"

Bláithín joined in. "Yes, the Flora Apartments, where I was living. You thinking of that again, Maite?"

"Yes, when I was…" she held her arms out in front of her to indicate pregnancy. "My brain didn't want to think. It was big effort. But now, she is here…" she looked misty-eyed, up the table at Laia asleep on Pedro's shoulder, his work-rough hand tenderly stroking the wisps of dark hair on her little head. "Now, I don't want to let it go. My plans are so good, even bank is happy and company who own building, all is already signed. So much official is done already. Now I need to find just right people and I think I can do the job." She turned to Susan, who was sitting next to her, widened her eyes, and raised her brows. "Do you want any work?"

"I… no… well… I suppose I do. But I don't have any experience."

"Ha! Experience, you can get in one day. You have car and energy. And if you can make all home things work, you could do this. Maybe we could work together?"

"What? Cleaning?"

"Think of it as apartment management," chimed in Cassandra. "How many apartments, Maite?"

"Fifty. Is not just cleaning. Is key minding, problem fixing and of course, is Spain, a lot of paperwork." Maite turned to Susan with a big smile. "If your husband is gone, you need something to not go crazy!" She didn't give Susan time to answer, turning to Reuben, Maite switched to Spanish and fired questions at him.

Grinning, he leaned forward to speak down the table to Diarmuid. "Diarmuid, Maite's wondering if she understood properly, that you and Pauline are thinking of moving out to Ibiza, for good?"

Rosa was translating all that was going on for Pedro, who was smiling his gap-toothed grin and nodding enthusiastically.

Pauline sat forward. "We are, alright, and just in the nick of time." She looked around at Cassandra and Pamela. "Bláithín has told us you all have to be out of here soon enough. That's a shame. You all seem to be making such a go of it. But at least, Bláth's room in Andy's will be waiting for her. Isn't that great?"

Bláithín covered her gasp of horror with a cough.

Diarmuid smiled across at her and patted Pauline's hand. "Well, who knows, Pauline? Bláithín may have other plans." He turned to Reuben. "Yes, that's certainly our plan. We're going to rent out the house at home, and Andy's happy to rent his apartment to us."

Maite clapped when Reuben related this to her. "Now, I have my fixer person and he lives in building!"

Diarmuid did a double take, but he was smiling. "Ah, here, steady on a minute. I can do small odds and ends but not big jobs and I don't speak Spanish."

"No, is not problem. Most apartments are rent to peoples that speak English. You just look at problem, and if you can fix, you fix and if no, you tell me and I get who we need."

Diarmuid's eyebrows and nodding head signalled the possibility of this.

Cassandra hooted. "This is a woman after my own heart! What a tornado!"

"What do you think, Pauline?" Pamela asked.

"Well, 'twould get him out from under my feet for a bit of the day." She smiled at him. Years of shared love allowed Diarmuid to understand that she'd be delighted if it made him happy.

Maite turned back to Susan, her hands waving excitedly. "Sue, it would be a good job with contract."

"Maite! I... I don't know... I suppose I could learn as I go? Gosh! Maybe? But realistically, with the children, Sophie's school -"

"All hours is very flexible and of course, is not only us. We will take on girls to help, but we are boss."

Pamela spoke up, "And don't forget, Sue, I did the school

runs and child minding when you were working with Glen, and I can do it if you're working with Maite. Especially as I'll be back in the apartment, and it will be business as usual."

Both Cassandra and Bláithín heard the undercurrent in Pamela's voice. Bláithín raised her hand and said, "And I think you have another babysitter, here next to me!" She jerked her thumb at Pauline.

"Oh, bless us, I don't think they'd want to stay with me," said Pauline, but she was smiling at the thought.

Bláithín continued regardless, "It seemed to me that the children took to you very well. And wouldn't Sue be delighted to be able to leave her children with a fully qualified nurse?"

Sue looked down the table at Pauline. "I would be delighted, absolutely. But I couldn't impose on you."

Maite was listening to Rosa's translation for Pedro and interrupted, "It would be part of work too, Pauline. I think company can pay towards childcare, and maybe some days you take Laia too?"

Pauline's hand was at the base of her throat, and she was swallowing hard. Finally, she said, "I suppose I could go and buy some toys and things, couldn't I, Diarmuid?"

Diarmuid looked at her, his eyes were red. "Yes, my dear, we'll go buy some toys."

Bláithín's eyes were welling too, at the joy and the healing passing between her brother and his wife.

Maite, listening through Rosa to this unfolding, stood and tapped her glass. "To our new business, and to my friends who together we make things possible."

Everyone raised their drinks and Cassandra echoed the toast. "To Maite's business. Hey, what are you going to call it?"

"Oh, I made name last June when I signed papers for next year contract. Is called 'Limpieza de Tanit.'"

"Tanit Cleaning," translated Reuben, smiling at the shocked faces of the Crone Club.

CHAPTER THIRTY-SEVEN

"I always enjoy Saint Stephen's day," said Bláithín the next morning, picking a chocolate from the half-full box on the kitchen counter.

"Do you? When is it?" asked Pamela.

"Today! All the food and treats of Christmas with none of the fuss and pressure."

"Ah, you mean Boxing Day," laughed Pamela. "Yes, I always thought it was one of the best parts of Christmas, too."

Cassandra walked into the kitchen, untying her robe. "Ten minutes of yoga on the terrace, girls?"

Thinking of Diarmuid who might appear any minute, Bláithín asked, "You're not doing it naked today, are you?"

"Ha, no. I don't want to be responsible for your brother's heart attack! I promise I'm respectable." She shrugged off her robe.

Bláithín smiled. Cassandra's tiny shorts and crop top stretched the definition of respectable.

A brisk wind had whisked away the rain clouds of yesterday and replaced them with the high, white, wavering rows of a mackerel sky on a pale blue background. Pamela and Bláithín followed Cassandra's slow, gentle movements, holding poses and breathing according to her instructions. They finished up with the wide arm stretch, Buddha Embracing the world. At each arm closing movement, Cassandra called out, "Gratitude. Love.Peace."

They were finishing breakfast by the time Susan joined them. With her sleep-tousled hair and her pyjamas covered with smiling suns, she barely looked older than Sophie. "Good morning, everyone," she said as she kissed Pamela and beamed at the others. "What an absolutely wonderful day yesterday was. Thank you all!"

Pamela looked closely at Susan. She seemed bright-eyed and light-hearted. "Did you sleep well, Susan?"

"Yes, I did. One of those blissful, deep, ones. I feel a million times better." She filled the kettle.

"So, you weren't lying awake all night, thinking about Maite's business proposal?" joked Bláithín.

"No, not at all. She kind of sold me on it last night. I mean, she has all the official permits and company registration, and everything done, and they're the biggest stumbling blocks. In fact, I was just talking to Pauline and Diarmuid about it. They're very keen. We're going over to talk to Maite today and discuss our business ideas."

Pamela bit her lip to hide her smile at the use of the word 'our'.

Susan glanced down at her phone. "Glen will be collecting the kids soon, so I'd better get them home and ready." She smiled at Bláithín. "Sophie and Clark are inside in bed with Pauline and Diarmuid! They're lovely people, your brother and sister-in-law."

"Yes," Bláithín agreed. "They are."

Pamela finished her tea, stood up and said briskly, "Well, Sue, If I'm moving back, can you take some stuff for me today, please? I seem to have more than I arrived with."

"Oh, Mum, you don't have to rush. Sophie's still on holiday, and I can manage for now."

Pamela was speechless. Not long ago, her daughter had been pleading for her to move back instantly. Susan bent down to take some cereals out of the cupboard. Bláithín and Cassandra smiled at Pamela over her head. 'Well done, Crone Club,' Cassandra mouthed, and Pamela prayer-palmed back.

Bláithín's phone pinged. "Rosa's offering to bring us to Tanit's temple today, while the weather is good."

"Oh, fab!" said Cassandra. "Tell her that's a great idea."

Susan poured out three bowls of cereal. "You see, Mum. You have plenty to do here, anyway. So, it's all working out fine."

"Yes, yes, indeed," was all that Pamela managed. Cassandra made faces at her behind Susan's back. Pamela held her hand over her mouth to hide her laughter.

Bláithín looked up from her phone. "Rosa warns you to wear proper walking shoes, Cassandra!"

"Why would she ever think I wouldn't?" replied Cassandra innocently.

After breakfast, Reuben arrived to drive Diarmuid and Pauline home, and their guests left in a flurry of noise and fuss, car-packing and arrangement-making, kisses, and hugs. Sophie's treasure map was taking up an entire folder, and Clark's barking dog provided constant background noise.

"I think he's going to 'lose' that soon," admitted Susan, then she called across to Diarmuid and Pauline. "See you in Maite's house at two!" They waved out the window as Reuben turned the car in the courtyard.

Susan and the children followed them down the lane and the Crone Club returned to the silent kitchen. Bláithín said, "Wow, who could have seen all that coming? I mean Pauline? Diarmuid?" She spread her hands. "Maite? And Sue, taking such a step, on her own! I mean… it's incredible."

Pamela bowed out the window. "Thank you, Mother, from the bottom of my heart."

Cassandra drained the coffee pot into her cup. "I agree, Pamela. That tapestry at the table last night was woven by very practised hands."

***

They were ready and waiting for Rosa when she arrived, each of them carrying a terracotta figure. Rosa greeted Bláithín with a full-on kiss, and Cassandra wolf-whistled. Bláithín went pink and her eyes shone. "I've felt more like a teenager in the last few weeks than I ever did as an actual teenager!"

Before they got into the car, Rosa said, "As I said, the shrine itself, deep in the cliff is not open to the public at this time of the year, but the way to it is spectacular. And really, just to see the openings into it, on the face of the cliff, is very emotional. And there are still ways to leave an offering."

Cassandra shrugged. "I don't really care about getting in. This is her site. The whole area must be imbued with her spirit. I just want to go as a pilgrim, as her acolyte, as her Full-Moon-Daughter, and leave her a gift." The unaccustomed seriousness in Cassandra's voice affected them all, and without another word, they got into the car.

Rosa drove the steep, winding road that hugged its way up the hillside, high behind the white beach of Cala Vicent. Flanked at both sides by evergreen pine trees, Bláithín closed her eyes whenever a gap between them gave her vertiginous glimpses of the drop into the valley. The road was respectably solid and uniform at first, then slowly disintegrated into a rocky, rugged, uneven trail.

"Thank God, we're in a jeep," Pamela said, just as a wheel dipped into a deep rut and threw her against the door. The gradient got steeper, the turns sharper, and finally, the road resembled a narrow river bed, filled with boulders and shallow crevasses.

Rosa called a halt. "This is as far as I can take the jeep. The rest is by foot. At least the worst of the uphill climb is done." They picked their way carefully up the rest of the incline, along a narrow path of hard earth and loose stones. Ancient, blackened, dead trees shared space with vital new growth and thick, dense vegetation.

"How in the name of fuck, did anyone find their way up here?" Cassandra exclaimed.

Concentric circles of stone marked the start of the steep descent. Two steps took them through the screen of scrub, where they were faced with a breathtaking view, down across the green valley, over Cala Vicent, and far out to where the sea gave small, white frills to distant coves. It lay as it had for thousands of years, a reminder to every traveller of the peace and beauty surrounding them, and the bounty of the Gods.

The trail was downhill now. "Thanks be to Jesus, the

local council got involved here," remarked Bláithín, as she took the descent step by slow step, gripping the guide rope.

Cassandra was striding ahead, climbing up and down off boulders to find footing, she scattered rocks and stones with every footstep. Pamela, with a firm grip on the guide rope, called out, "Slow down! Cassandra, think of your ankle, you could sprain it again, easily."

"I'll be fine!" Cassandra yelled back as she clambered down a steep drop and disappeared from view.

Pamela shook her head. "I can kind of sympathize with her mother."

Cassandra made the cave entrance well before the others. The sight of the three openings in the face of the cliff almost reduced her to tears. The black bars, closing the site for winter, might as well not have existed.

She saw the cavities glowing with the light of a million candles and heard them filled with the sound of a million voices. Voices that pleaded for boons and favours, that chanted prayers for a bountiful harvest, broken voices that begged Tanit's care for dead children. The caves resonated with them all, forever. She smelled the oils, the flowers, the incense, and above all, she felt peace, happiness, gratitude, and love deep in her soul.

Her fellow crones eventually made it down. Their conversation petered out as they approached and stood next to Cassandra. They held hands in silence, then as one, bowed their heads.

Rosa showed them where to scramble, to get to an opening where they could reach in and place their figurines. "Pray for your boon first, then place your gifts. That's the way it's done," she whispered.

"We're not asking for favours, we're just paying homage and giving thanks," Cassandra replied.

"It's always a two-way gesture," explained Rosa "Gods need to show their power by granting favours."

They got the busts safely on a ledge and with the aid of

a long stick, pushed them way farther in, out of view to all except Tanit. Their gifts to her would sit on that shelf, bearing witness to their homage, for another thousand years. It was a quiet journey home. They were lost in the overwhelming emotion of the visit.

Christmas meant parties, which meant Rosa was very busy with taxi runs. So busy, she roped Reuben in to do a few that night. The Crones had a peaceful evening, eating leftovers, drinking wine, and sleeping through a movie.

"It was magic today, wasn't it?" said Cassandra as they headed to bed.

Pamela put her hand on her chest. "I still feel the sense of connection."

"Me too," said Bláithín. "And I'm hoping I can hold onto it. I feel as if the Crone Club has been somewhere enchanted or something."

Cassandra hugged them both into her. "Whatever happens girls, the Crone Club is staying together."

They turned off the lights, and soon the flickering fire was the only movement in the house.

CHAPTER THIRTY-EIGHT

It was just a small tremor at first. Then the house shook, waking the Crones with an inhuman groan. A crack, like a pistol shot, echoed through the house, followed by the thunderous roar of collapsing bricks and timber. It was over by the time they ran from their rooms.

"What the fuck?"

There was nothing unusual to be seen in the dim hall, but the air was filling with dust. Cassandra made for the living room door.

"Be careful, Ca -" Pamela might as well not have spoken. Cassandra had already gone in. The others followed and stood in silent shock.

Pamela's studio had collapsed. Falling outwards, it had taken part of the living room wall with it. Debris filled the terrace. Moonlight glinted on broken glass amid the rubble, and the jagged ends of the remaining roof beams stuck out into the night like lightning-cracked trees.

"Is everyone alright?" Cassandra pulled her friends close. "No incipient heart or panic attacks in the offing?"

Sighing, Pamela rested her head on her friend's shoulder. "I can't believe it. Our house has just fallen down and you're making jokes."

"Who said I was joking?" Cassandra hugged them tighter.

Bláithín's hand was clamped tightly across the lower part of her face. She stared wide-eyed from one side of the devastation to another, slowly shaking her head. It seemed all the more shocking for being in the silent, moonlit hours of a midwinter's night.

Cassandra cocked her head. There was a sound out of place. "Do you hear that?" she asked, stepping further into the room. "Is that running water?"

"Oh, God! Burst pipes as well!" groaned Bláithín.

"I wonder..." Cassandra tip-toed across the room, looked out to the terrace, and gasped. Her voice was a whisper as she spoke. "There's a fucking river pouring down the steps, from under the floor here! It must have washed away the foundations!"

"Thank God I'd moved my paintings out!" said Pamela. "Do you think we should leave, in case more is going to collapse?"

"I suppose it *is* the sensible thing to do," said Bláithín, rubbing her arms in the cold wind blowing around the front room. Her flannel pyjamas flapped around her legs.

"And, yet," murmured Cassandra, "I don't feel any sense of danger. But what am I, a quantity surveyor?"

Pamela looked at her watch. "It's only three am. There's no point in calling emergency services, now. The morning will do. We could go back to my apartment at Sue's, and I can make up the sofa bed for you two."

"It could all collapse at any time. I'd definitely feel safer if we left," said Bláithín moving towards the door.

"Right, grab some clothes and let's go," agreed Cassandra. They closed the door on the devastation.

They barely spoke in the car, just echoed each other's thoughts "I don't believe it!" and "What the fuck!" until they arrived. Pamela turned off her headlights as she drove up the driveway and parked at the top rather than going into the courtyard. They tip-toed into the apartment, their moon shadows going before them. Sitting in the front room, they cradled mugs of very hot tea and whispered.

"Jesus God Almighty," said Bláithín for the hundredth time. "I can't believe it."

"I don't know why I don't feel worried or threatened," said Cassandra. "I mean, the fucking place essentially fell down around us!"

"Imagine if it had been the back that fell instead of the front, we'd be dead," said Pamela.

"I know. But somehow, I don't feel that was ever a possibility," Cassandra shrugged. "I don't know why, but I don't."

Pamela spoke slowly, "I know what you mean. Yes, on the face of it, it seems like we all barely escaped with our lives. But it doesn't feel like it."

"Just making Van Groot's job fucking easier, isn't it? That much of the house gone already!" Cassandra scowled.

"God, imagine if you had been working, Pamela! It doesn't bear thinking about." Bláithín shivered.

"But I wasn't, was I? And all my paintings were safely out of there too!"

Cassandra continued to scowl in the darkness. "I showed Van Groot that leak, and he dismissed it."

"Do you think it had anything to do with the collapse, Cassandra?"

"Well, it would be a bit strange if it didn't. I mean it's the exact area, isn't it?"

Bláithín yawned. "I'm flattened. I think we should try and get a bit of sleep anyway."

Pamela got to her feet. "Yes, and tomorrow will be a long day, sorting this mess out."

They all slept fitfully for a few hours. At eight o'clock, when light was barely smudging the sky, Pamela left a note for Sue explaining the events of the night before they headed back to the villa.

From the car, Bláithín rang Rosa, who was just finishing an early airport run and promised to be right over. Cassandra also made her calls during the drive back to their villa. First, she rang Reuben, telling him about the trickle turned torrent. When he got over his shock and then his subsequent relief that they were all okay, he said he'd call his friend in the town hall and see who they should contact about this. Next on the list was the developer.

Van Groot's secretary was uncomprehending. "You are a tenant, yes?"

"Yes."

"And you have broken Mr. Van Groot's house?"

"No! No, it collapsed. It could have killed us!"

"The house, it just fell down on you?"

"Yes, well, not on us, exactly. Jesus! Will you just tell him Cassandra Collingsworth called and that he's got big problems?" She hung up. "You know, girls, the least he can do is put us up somewhere fancy until the eleventh of January. I mean, we're his legal, paid-up tenants until then, and his house nearly killed us!"

They pulled up in front of their house, which looked serene and unbothered, from the courtyard. Cassandra pushed the front door wide open and wedged it with one of the flowerpots from the top step. "Just in case we have to make a run for it."

"Good thinking," Pamela said and stepped in. There was a fine coat of dust over everything, and the air was chilly. Cassandra opened the living room door.

Daylight conferred an even more surreal quality to the collapse. The Christmas tree was still standing, its decorations sparkling in the emerging sunlight, and twirling in the breeze. The front of Pamela's studio was spread across the terrace. The wall with the fireplace had collapsed too. They crossed the living room to the gaping wound and picked their way over the debris to the terrace.

"Fuuuuck!" Cassandra pointed. What had been a heavy flow earlier was now a wide gushing stream, bubbling up through the foundations, washing a path through the rubble, down the collapsed steps, overflowing the pool with dirty water, plaster and wood before draining away into the pine forest beyond.

"Oh, my God!" Pamela sat on the stone bench on the undamaged side of the terrace. "Our lovely home. This is so sad."

"Jesus, Mary and Joseph," Bláithín gasped. "It's a river that has destroyed it."

"Has it?" Cassandra asked. "Humour me, my fellow Crones. Hold hands!" Pamela stood up again and they all held hands. "Close your eyes." They already had. "Now, what do you feel?"

"Happiness," Pamela was first to answer.

"Peace," Bláithín added.

"Exactly! That's what I feel as well, even a little excitement? Just like last night, I had no sense of fear or danger."

"Cassandra!" Reuben's voice calling her name interrupted her. He strode out to them. "Dios mio!" He stopped to look at the destruction then hugged her tight. "I can't believe how lucky you all were, that water could have brought the whole place down." He looked over at Bláithín. "Rosa's right behind me - she'll be here any minute."

Bláithín went through to the front of the house to meet Rosa and found the courtyard filling up with cars. Two police cars and Mr. Van Groot's car were pulling up next to Rosa's jeep. Bláithín barely acknowledged Van Groot's terse nod as he and his colleagues walked past her and into the house. She waved her hand, indicating for the four policemen to follow Van Groot and she went straight into Rosa's arms. "It's so sad, Rosa, that lovely house. I know it was going to be knocked anyway, but it's still so awful."

"It's unbelievable! I'm just so grateful you all escaped unharmed." She put her hand on Bláithín's cheek. "You can come and live with me if you'd like, mi Amor."

Exhausted, shocked, and distraught by the night, Bláithín reacted to the explosion of happiness that this offer conjured by bursting into tears.

Yet another car drove into the drive and pulled in behind the police car. Two casually dressed men got out, each carrying a briefcase. In Spanish, they identified themselves, and Rosa translated for Bláithín. "These men are from the town hall planning and development department. They're asking if everyone is okay, was anyone hurt."

Bláithín wiped her eyes with her sleeve. "Tell them we're all fine, and they can follow us through."

"I wonder why the police are here. I don't think anyone called them," Bláithín said to Rosa as they headed into the house followed by the planning men.

"I'd say they were notified by the town hall. I'd imagine any collapsed building has implications for public safety."

"I suppose so," agreed Bláithín and led them into the front room.

On the remains of the terrace, Mr. Van Groot and his associates were taking photographs, as were two of the policemen. Two others were talking to Reuben who was translating for Cassandra, standing next to them with her arms folded. Pamela was on her mobile, explaining the situation to Susan. Bláithín and Rosa joined them.

The town hall officials headed straight to where the water began its surging downhill path. They opened their cases and took out instruments which they held in the water as they made copious notes.

Cassandra spoke under her breath. "Those policemen don't look old enough to shave, not to mention carry guns!"

Bláithín nudged her to shut up, but whispered, "I was thinking the same."

Mr. Van Groot crunched across the rubble to Cassandra. "I demand to know what exactly you were doing to cause this."

Cassandra stared at him. "What we were...? It was three o'clock in the morning when this happened! We were fucking asleep!"

Reuben stepped forward. "In fact, Mr. Van Groot, the police are asking me if the ladies want to file a complaint against you."

"What?" Anger flushed Van Groot's face.

"Yes, they say these women, especially at their age," he indicated the three crones, with an unconcealed grin at

Cassandra's expression, "should be able to rely on the safety and security of a properly maintained building. And this -" he waved Cassandra's paper from Van Groot's previous visit, "clearly states that you are the proprietor, and the ladies are your tenants."

"Nonsense! I was here a few days ago and I can assure you the house was in perfect condition."

"Yes," agreed Reuben, "you were, and I've told the police how Ms. Collingsworth pointed out that leak to you and you dismissed it as nothing of consequence."

One of Mr. Van Groot's men moved to put a calming hand on his boss's arm, but it was too late. Van Groot was shouting at the police.

"Always a bad idea in Spain," muttered Rosa into Bláithín's ear.

Mr. Van Groot was shaking a finger at the youngest policeman. "You have no business here! This is a private matter! My insurance will cover it all."

The police stopped taking photographs and stood behind their colleague with their hands on their guns.

Van Groot visibly blanched, put down his finger, and stepped back, but he continued to protest. "This is ridiculous! They must have done something to cause this!"

The officials from the town hall put away their instruments, strode over the rubble, and asked who the owner was.

Mr. Van Groot stepped forward. "I am. It's not a big deal. No one has been hurt and, in any case, this house was scheduled for demolition in a week or so." One of his colleagues translated for him, listened to the town hall man's reply, and said, "They want to see your permits and plans."

"No problem." Van Groot was back on solid ground, his smile was back in place as he held out a thick folder. "Everything is in there. Plans, taxes paid, permits, costings, the lot. The project will be underway in two weeks."

The town hall men looked at the papers, shaking their

heads.

"Oh my God," breathed Rosa.

"What?" asked Bláithín. But Rosa said nothing and just squeezed Bláithín's arm tightly.

Van Groot's colleague, translating what the officials were saying, began stumbling over his words and looking anxiously at Van Groot. "They say, um... obviously some previously unmarked underground river has... broken through its retaining walls, and... em, is flowing at a rate that indicates... significant underground force. There is... there is... no way..." He stopped and stared, wide-eyed from the speaking official to Van Groot and back again.

"What, man? Get on with it!" Mr. Van Groot's face was mottled, and his voice was rising again.

"They say it's impossible to build twelve apartments here." His colleague rushed the sentence, getting it out in a burst.

"Nonsense!" roared Van Groot, holding out his hands for his permits. But the town hall man calmly took the top two and ripped them in half. Van Groot turned purple. His mouth worked, but he was speechless. Still holding the torn licenses, the man continued, and Rosa translated aloud for everyone. "He says it's impossible, in light of these developments, to allow these permits to stand, and he questions the competency of the people who did the initial survey."

Reuben caught Cassandra's hand.

The man continued to talk, the police occasionally nodding agreement and Van Groot's man muttering the occasional word, but Rosa's voice was triumphantly loud. "There will be no permission granted for a development of twelve apartments, in fact, no further building will be permitted here, given the instability of the land due to the underground stream and the potential for future collapse."

The crones looked at each other, the possibilities of this occurred to Cassandra first and she let out a whoop.

Rosa held up a hand and looked across at Van Groot as

she said, "They also said it would be a legal requirement that any potential purchaser be made aware of the situation."

"But I paid one and a half million euros for this place. One and a half!" Van Groot was trembling. "And now, you're telling me it's worthless?"

The happy sound of gushing, rushing water bubbling past them filled the silence as Van Groot registered his loss.

The police spoke to Van Groot's colleague.

"What are they saying?" whispered Bláithín.

"Telling him to warn his boss never again to speak to the police like that or he will find himself in jail. They're also saying they are contemplating bringing charges themselves of criminal negligence if the three ladies here don't want to!"

"Jesus wept, he's having a bad day!" Bláithín suppressed the growing laughter inside her while the police filled in forms, nodded at everyone, and stalked off. The town hall men signed a report and handed it to Van Groot, shook hands with everyone then saw themselves out.

Van Groot stood, papers dangling from his hands, staring at the vigorous stream flowing through his property in disbelief.

Cassandra turned to Pamela and Bláithín. "Crone sisters, I have an idea, are you with me?" There was no hesitation, they stepped to either side of her.

"Mr. Van Groot," Cassandra's smile could have lit a thousand candles. "It seems to me that you are in a bit of a predicament. The police are obviously keen for us to take a case against you for endangering our lives, and equally obviously, the site is now worthless to you. We -" she spread her hands to encompass her friends, "would be willing to buy this site off you for a modest sum."

Reuben joined in. "Mr. Van Groot, as a local farmer, I can tell you categorically that this hillside has no value as arable land. And, as you have just been told, it will never get a permit for a new house. Ms. Collingsworth is in fact, saving you the cost of getting bulldozers up here to finish the demolition. All of which should be reflected in the price. I imagine somewhere in the region of a hundred thousand euros?"

"What? I told you I paid over a million for it! I want at least five hundred thousand."

"But now," interjected Cassandra smoothly, "it's worth absolutely nothing, and you have a potential lawsuit on your hands. Also, if word were to get out that one of your properties collapsed, nearly killing three -" her fingers marked the words, "'elderly women', it would not help the sale of any of your other developments here in-"

Van Groot interrupted her. "You'd have to sign a form saying that I am in no way responsible for this calamity. That each of you waive all rights to any claim against me for personal or material damage arising from this incident. And that at no time in the future can you claim from me or any of my companies, no matter what happens in this bloody place."

"I think we could manage that," agreed Cassandra. Pamela's hand covered her mouth, as she stared wide-eyed at Bláithín.

Van Groot straightened his tie, smoothed his jacket, and turned to his associates, drawing them to one side. He began putting a narrative together he could live with. Words floated across the terrace. "Business mishap, tax write-off, insurance, get it off our books..." He returned to the group who were unable to move or speak while so much held in the balance. "Let's put some of this on paper, shall we?"

The same clipboard that ordered them out of the house by the eleventh of January now offered them ownership for one hundred and fifty thousand euros and a complete absolving of Van Groot of any responsibility whatsoever in perpetuity. The three women signed, he scribbled his name, gave them a copy, and left without a backwards glance. Stunned by the speed of it all, they trooped into the kitchen and sat in silence. The door was closed, shutting off any sign of the destruction beyond.

"So... the Crone Club has its home," Rosa said, shaking

her head. "It's unbelievable!"

Tears welled in Cassandra's eyes. "Finally, a home. A magical, wonderful home of our own."

Reuben wrapped his arm around her and pulled her in for a hug. "I don't want to be a bucket of cold water," he said "but what about the water pouring up through the foundations? What about the damage that's doing?"

"Yes indeed," said Pamela. "That is a consideration, but somehow," her lips turned up as she spoke, "I don't think it will be a problem for long."

Rosa stood up. "Oh, my God! What did you all wish for when you made the offering to Tanit yesterday?"

Cassandra grinned. "I prayed that I could stay in this house."

Bláithín nodded. "Me, too."

Pamela spread her hands. "Me, three. Though, where on Earth are we going to get one hundred and fifty thousand from?"

"Fuck knows, but I don't think Van Groot will be in too much of a rush for it."

Rosa's 'Ode to Joy' sounded. "Oh, God! My deliveries! They are still in the jeep!" She kissed Bláithín thoroughly. "Beloved of Tanit, I will see you later." And she ran out to her car full of herbs waiting for delivery.

Reuben stood. "Practically speaking, we need to get that opening sealed off. You know Ibiza weather at this time of the year - it could rain at any moment. You also need to see about getting the electricity back on, and the debris cleared. I can make a few calls and get a team here as soon as possible."

Cassandra was glowing. "Oh, thank you, Reuben, that would be marvellous."

"Wonderful," said Pamela.

Reuben grinned. "For the Crone Club, it's a pleasure. Meanwhile, I think I have tarpaulins at the farm. I'll get them and we can hang them ourselves if we need to." Reuben kissed Cassandra and made for the door, then he paused. "I can't tell you how happy I am that you saved this house and its ancient wall." His eyes met Cassandra's and they smiled, sharing the memory of their first meeting before he left.

Pamela brushed dust off the table with the palm of her hand. "What on earth have we done? We've committed to buying a falling-down house, at an age when none of us will get a mortgage and we've no income. Why do I feel so unutterably happy?"

"Let's face it," said Cassandra taking three glasses from the cupboard, she wiped the dust off them and uncorked her last bottle of Prosecco. Nobody mentioned the fact it wasn't even lunchtime. "I'm finally at peace about my mother, I'm completely and irrevocably in love, *and* I have found my home!" She began to fill the glasses as she continued, "Pamela, your daughter is finding her own way at last and no longer needs you as a crutch. And you, my dear Crone friend have discovered yourself to be a painter of glorious, joyful, erotic art, which is going to make a fortune!"

She topped up the glasses to the brim. "Bláithín, you have burst out of a closet you didn't even know you were in. Your family have found a new lease of life that doesn't include plaguing you. And you, also my dear Crone friend, are going to be the best-known art photographer in Ibiza, by this time next year."

As the dust settled around them and the stream outside began to bubble a bit less fiercely, the three friends raised their glasses and Cassandra called out,

"To the next chapter of The Ibiza Crone Club!"

AFTERWORD

Thank you for reading The Ibiza Crone Club, I hope you enjoyed it. If you did, it would be wonderful if you could leave a review on one of your favourite platforms or tell me directly on my Amazon author page.

Book Club Questions.

1. Would you recommend this book to someone? Why or why not (or with what caveats)? What kind of reader would most enjoy this book?

2. Did you find the author's writing style easy to read or hard to read? Why? How long did it take you to get into the book?

3. Who was your favorite character? What character did you identify with the most? Were there any characters that you disliked? Why?

4. Did any part of this book strike a particular emotion in you? Which part and what emotion did the book make you feel?

5. How much did you know about this book before picking it up? What surprised you the most about the book?

6. Was there any part of the plot or aspects of the characters that frustrated or upset you? If so, why?

7. How thought-provoking did you find the book? Did the book change your opinion about anything, or did you learn something new from it? If so, what?

8. Did you highlight or bookmark any passages from the book? Did you have a favorite quote or quotes? If so, share which and why?

9. From your point of view, what were the central themes of the book? How well do you think the author did at exploring them?

10. Compare this book to other books you have read by the same author, or other books you have read covering the same or similar themes. How are they the same or different?

11. How would you adapt this book into a movie? Who would you cast in the leading roles?

ACKNOWLEDGEMENT

A huge thank you to all the members of my writing circle whose, enthusiasm, interest and support helped propel The Ibiza Crone Club from tentative idea to fully fledged novel. Also, a big shout out to Shanna Haight Hammerbacher whose kindness and and unflagging support gave me the confidence to go on. She also introduced me th the wonderful Olivia Castetter, an editor who dives fully into a story, and goes way above and beyond. Thank you both.

ABOUT THE AUTHOR

Josephine O'Brien

Josephine is an Irish writer, artist and teacher. She moves between Ireland, Scotland, mainland Spain and Ibiza. She is married, has five children and an increasing brood of grandchildren.

Printed in Great Britain
by Amazon